When A Red Bird Flies

Karen Evancic

Front Porch History

To Dr. Cheri Sears,
May you continue to dare to fly!
With much gratitude...
Karen Evancic
June 24, 2015

While some of the events are loosely based on a real-life collection of stories, this story is a work of fiction. In order to maintain anonymity the names of certain individuals and places, and some of the identifying properties and details, have been changed. Names, characters, businesses, conversations, and many of the events are products of the author's imagination.

I dedicate this book to my vivacious and remarkable grandmother, Lula. Without you, none of this would have been possible; I would not have been possible. You inspire me at every turn, and I can't thank you enough for being who you are. I will always love you too…

The reason birds can fly and
we can't is simply because they
have perfect faith, for to have
faith is to have wings.

J. M. Barrie,
The Little White Bird

Chapter One

Lillie Mae Woodard
Southern Kentucky Sanatorium
Franklin, Kentucky
Tuesday, August 11, 1953

Lillie awoke to whispering. It was a murmur at first, but then the voices slowly became clear.

"A matter of days now, I think." It was the nurse with the husky voice made old before its time by too many cigarettes and not enough fresh air.

"You think it's that long even? Doctor Hunter said it would be just a few hours when he came to see her this morning." This nurse was younger, fresher, and reeked of naivety.

"Who really knows? These things are so hard to predict." A phlegmy cough hit the air, mixing with the stale smell of the forty year old county hospital annex.

"She's definitely in a bad state. God willing, it'll happen fast. Can't hardly stand to look at her." Lillie lay still, afraid to move. She knew this young nurse. She had small hands like a child's and apparently had a weak stomach for the dying.

"Makes my heart ache something fierce," the older nurse said, and followed with another cough that made a heavy hacking sound. Lillie couldn't help but picture the mucus rising and falling in the woman's throat like a never ending teeter-totter, and it almost made her gag.

Lillie shifted slightly on the sheet. Her back ached terribly, and she felt beads of sweat binding her to the crisp white linens, but she was so exhausted that couldn't quite summon the energy it would take to make much of a fuss about it. The afternoon sun was warming the room quickly as it hit the glass windows that ran floor to ceiling. Even with the shades down, the temperature in the room crept hungrily towards ninety. It was the hottest August that Franklin had seen in over a decade, and Lillie felt like she might as well be sitting outside for all the protection the building provided. The wide brick walkways that made up most of the garden in the center courtyard were awash with humidity and steam. It was turning the passageway between the two buildings into a fiery oven.

Lillie knew the nurses were trying their best to keep her cool and comfortable, but today the moisture on her skin felt like it would drown her as it dripped from her pores down to the bottom of her lungs. She felt as though a million tiny ants were feasting on picnic day, with her brittle skin as the appetizer and her dry scalp the main course. Oh the damage she could do to them, she thought, if only she had enough energy to scratch. The wetness just added layers to the unbearable sensation, and all she could manage was a slight shift in position so that she was tilted a bit more onto her right side. From her new spot on the bed and through her clouded and blurry vision, Lillie could almost make out the silhouettes of the two nurses who were whispering about her as if she were deaf, or better yet, already gone.

"Lord, help me," she prayed silently. "Let those women be right. Let today be my day to go home." The only answer she heard to her prayer was the sad, lanky circular fan ticking its way back towards her face. Held together by duct tape alone and also begging for death, the fan provided her three to four seconds of relief before visiting the other side of the room. It wheezed and sighed and said all the things Lillie would have if she could have spoken. Lillie searched for some solace in the repetitive whir and dozed off again, trying hard to push away her discomfort. But the whispering from the other side of the partition brought her back to reality. It was like a bad recurring dream that she couldn't stop. A nightmare she couldn't escape.

"So sad. You know she hasn't had not one visitor in over a month!" the younger voice exclaimed. Something clattered loudly, glass upon glass, and Lillie pictured the nurses carelessly dropping empty syringes and dirty mercury thermometers into large containers of alcohol.

"Dropped at the front door like a bottle of milk on delivery day is what I heard." It was the husky one again, and Lillie could visualize her shaking her head in disapproval.

"Can you even believe it?" The young nurse's voice started to fade as Lillie finally drifted off, lost in her own thoughts.

Lillie remembered the day she had arrived at the hospital slightly differently than the nurses' descriptions, though they weren't terribly far off the mark. She remembered sitting in the passenger seat of her husband's old Terraplane with her back and legs stuck to the mohair-covered seats like there was a layer of honey between them. The eighteen-year-old car knocked as they drove, and its chassis responded to the bumps and rocks on the roads with the creaks and groans of an old barn door. It was early July then, and even riding with the windows open wide wasn't enough to stifle the heat that bound the couple to the rusty seats.

Lillie remembered the drive in vivid detail, but not because of how uncomfortable she was. She wouldn't allow the raspy ramshackle car or the presence of her husband to take away from her last moments out in the world. Her eyes clung to every passing tree, every boysenberry-covered field, every child running carelessly down the dirt paths that led to the small creeks and ponds that dotted the landscape. She took in the young mothers pushing buggies down near Roark's General Store, so caught up with the chaos of toddlers that they barely noticed the dilapidated car pass by. She breathed in the old men sitting on benches outside the hardware store who were likely rehashing the accomplishments or mourning the losses of their sons or grandsons in the great World War. She wondered who they mourned as well, and whether they ever wondered why they had been blessed with so many long years. They were also headed where Lillie was, although at a quite slower pace, and she wondered too if, in their old age, they had ever wished for death. These were to be her last images of the world, and she clung to them warmly as she let her arm fly freely out of the car's window.

Lillie remembered arriving at their destination suddenly feeling defeated and exhausted. She sheepishly exhaled a long sigh, and every last bit of fight she had left her body with a heavy breath. She was no quitter, no one would dare call her that. She was quite the opposite, in fact, and became the definition of persistence every single morning she got out of bed on her weak legs and completely numb feet. When it had gotten really bad with her husband, and the next hit had been harder than the last, she had held her head up high and kept moving. Even when she had lost children; even when she could hardly hold her youngest in her arms for fear of dropping her; even when every movement of her body was so excruciating that she had to give every bit of concentration just to put one foot in front of the other; even then, she hadn't quit. That day she hadn't quit either. She'd just surrendered.

Taking her to the hospital hadn't been her idea, not that it was a bad place. They had been so kind to her during the delivery of her youngest, her only child born in a hospital. It was a nice establishment, built solidly and staffed with the finest medical team in all of Simpson County. It was, actually, the only hospital in a county that was basically 236 square miles of southern Kentucky farmland. Regardless, she would have much rather died in her own bed surrounded by her children, even if it meant she would have to deal with her husband for a bit more time. Like most major decisions in her marriage, it really hadn't been up to her. Her husband was physically a hundred times stronger than Lillie and thirty times emotionally weaker. The moment she'd become a burden and couldn't take care of him any longer, he'd made his decision, and Lillie hadn't bothered to protest. Protests just brought out the beast in her husband like nothing else, and she knew it was a waste of her breath and energy anyway. She had so little of either to spare. Once her husband had made a decision, even God himself couldn't sway him.

Her husband didn't even walk her into the main building to check her in. He pulled off to the side of the road in front of the pristine line of white ash maples and stopped just short of the pathway leading to the double front door. Lillie remembered how she had looked over at the building before her and had taken it all in for the very last time. The original building was full of life and was adorned with the post-Victorian architectural detail that was fashionable in the time it was constructed. The decorative quoined corners gave it a quiet strength, and the gabled roof lines and long rectangular windows projected out just enough to break the flat surface of the front of the building. It was limestone from top to bottom. Sills, dormers, chimneys, and porch, all born of the native St. Genevieve kind from local quarries and built by strong, local, native Kentucky hands.

The hospital was complicated and magnificent and yet simple, but its charm and elegance were always overridden by the annex that had been added on twelve years after the original building had been built. It too was beautifully crafted from strong Kentucky limestone, but sported string courses that ran horizontally and separated the three floors of the long rectangular building. It lay to the east of the main building and hovered over it, blocking the majestic sun as it rose in the morning. It was, no doubt, a handsome structure and strong to boot, but it imposed on its counterpart and dampened its soul.

As Lillie warily eyed the complex, a small breeze blew past and seemingly chuckled at her arrival. Though she couldn't see it herself, Lillie was like the enchanting main building, and her husband was like the tall, brawny, and overbearing annex. He, like the annex, squashed her spirit, blocked her sun, and tore at the essence of her limestone strength. The wind laughed silently at the irony that she would die in a place that resembled the marriage that had brought her there.

Lillie waited for her husband to move from his spot in the driver's seat for what seemed like hours. He sat, stiff as a board, with his eyes staring straight ahead through the dusty windshield. It was like he was boring holes in the old oak tree in front of them that twisted and turned like her grandmother's joints. His jaw was set, his face was proud, and his hands gripped the steering wheel with a tenacity that turned his knuckles white. It was the only sign Lillie had that he felt at all badly. She sat there for some time looking at her husband of twenty-three years, wondering how on earth it had come to this. How he'd come to loathe her so much that he wouldn't even say goodbye. How he'd become so malevolent and hateful that he couldn't even extend her that one last courtesy.

"Well, alright then," he'd said, after several silent minutes had ticked by. "You best get in there 'fore they come out expectin' me to pay 'em." His voice was gruff, without a hint of remorse, and Lillie could smell the familiar scent of coffee on his breath as he spoke.

His words broke Lillie's trance, and she shuddered slightly. *This is it,* she thought. *The end of my road.* She hesitated for only a moment and then she leaned her short body over towards her husband and used the last of her energy to reach up and gently kiss his cheek. His skin felt as cold as ice under her lips, though it was hotter than an oven inside the car cab; but what hurt even more was that he didn't even flinch.

"Goodbye, then," Lillie said as she turned away, grabbing the handle of her small suitcase and swinging open the car door with a weak shove. She stopped short of getting out and turned her head back towards the driver's seat.

"I forgive you, Clay," she said quietly, almost inaudibly. Then she slid her body down the side of the junker, meeting the ground with a silent thump, and painfully pushed the door closed behind her. She set her bag down in the dirt and turned around to face him. If he'd heard what she'd said to him, she couldn't tell. He hadn't moved a muscle. Finally, he lifted one hand off the steering wheel and gestured a wave without looking at her as though he were warding off a pesky fly. Then he hit the gas pedal hard, which spun the tires and released a mound of dirt in his wake. His final goodbye was nothing more than a billowy brown cloud of dust that slowly rose from the road and almost choked her.

He never looked back. Lillie smoothed out her dress and wiped away the freshly laid soot from the worn cotton fabric. She ran her fingers through her short curly hair, gathered what pride she had left, and turned around to face where her marriage had led her. It was a long way to the door, and she feared she'd never make it on her own. As she painfully started down the narrow dirt pathway, each step she took became more excruciating than the last, and she quickly realized that Clay had imparted one last act of cruelty by making her take that walk without any help. When she finally reached the end of the path she took a moment to catch her breath. Then she slowly started climbing the limestone staircase towards the front doorway, alone, carrying her few belongings and a very heavy heart.

Chapter Two

Catherine Otera
Anaheim, California
Easter Day, March 29, 1970

Cornbread. It's as much a part of me as say, my hair or my hazel-gray eyes. It may as well be part of my genes for as much as I ate growing up. It probably soaked right into my cells the same way the small air pockets in the cornbread soaked up the fresh butter we slathered it with. My mom made it differently than how it's made today. It was hearty and full, but drier, too, as it was more meant to fill up your belly than to please your taste buds. It wouldn't so much melt in your mouth as it would simply fall apart before it even got there. I wouldn't use the word sweet to describe it, though, because sweet cornbread meant you had some sugar or honey to spare, and most months both were hoarded like pieces of silver. No, it wasn't much to talk about, that cornbread, but what I can say about it is that it was dependable. When we couldn't count on anything else, we could always count on having cornbread at the table.

It was even there on holidays amongst all the other items that we only saw and ate once or twice a year, if we were lucky. Right beside the big Easter ham and smashed in between the pecan pie and the deviled eggs was my mom's cornbread. On special occasions we dressed it up with not just butter, but local Kentucky honey too. Honey that had been hidden from the summer before. Mom rationed it so we'd have some for the spring and summer, because the bees didn't finish making us more until the end of August, sometimes September. Of course, there were a few months when we couldn't pinch together enough to make a meal, much less stockpile honey for the year. But somehow, some way, when Easter rolled around, mom always surprised us by pulling out a jar she'd hidden in the back of the cupboard. The jar was filled with the liquid gold honey that we called 'a little bit of heaven,' and she would use it to glaze the top of our ham and would drizzle it over the top of our cornbread. That's the cornbread I like to remember from my childhood. The kind dripping with ribbons of sticky sweet honey, not the thick stuff we ate daily and called a staple.

It's Easter today, and my buffet is crowded with holiday dishes like green bean casserole, sautéed celery, and my husband's favorite, a heaping plate of homemade tamales, just like his mother used to make. But this year there is one dish that is new to my typical Easter menu. Shoved precariously between the honey-glazed ham and the roasted asparagus is an oblong pan of southern-style cornbread. It's my mom's recipe, and it's still warm, fresh out of my oven. I dusted it lightly with butter, and drizzled it carefully with honey.

I hadn't intended to make it this year, and in fact, I haven't made it in over thirty years. But as I started to make my husband's family recipe for authentic Mexican sweet corn tomalito, my mom's cornbread kept creeping into my mind. Sweet corn tomalito is like a yellow sweet corn pudding. It's popular in the region of Mexico my husband's parents came from many years ago, and it's made with a lot of the same ingredients as my mom's cornbread. So I pushed aside the corn flour used in the tomalito and pulled out my container of buttermilk, my baking soda, salt, an egg, and, of course, the cornmeal I was going to use in the other recipe. I surprised myself, because I found I didn't need my my mom's recipe card to make it; it was etched in my memory like I'd made a batch just yesterday.

The cornbread reminds me of the place that used to be home to all of us, save my husband, which is probably why I haven't made it in over three decades. I've tried so hard not to think about it over the years. If I'm honest, though, Easter time, even without cornbread, always triggers certain memories for me of where I once called home. Home was Kentucky: a state of gently rolling hills, miles and miles of fertile farm land, and even more fertile farm folks who spent their lives raising big families and harvesting tobacco, along with many other crops of God's bounty. It was where I started my life, in more ways than one, and in many ways, more than once.

As I watched my daughters laughing together through the long wall of windows that graces the back of our new home in southern California, I am reminded that even though I might have been born in Kentucky and raised on cornbread, it doesn't define who I am. Mostly this holiday, for more than just the obvious Christian rebirth reason, reminds me that your life really can begin again. It reminds me that one time, many years ago, spring decided to bring me more than just budding trees and rain showers. One year, just a day after Easter, I had forever been given my daughters and had been granted a rebirth of sorts. It was certainly not the way I expected to become a mother, but they came to me all the same, and I welcomed them with trembling and open arms. Yes, I trembled that day, but not from fear. I trembled from the joy of it. My wait for motherhood was over, and the two precious beings I now watch with pride were finally mine, and I was theirs, and I was forever grateful to the forces in the universe who helped it be so.

So, except on Easter, I don't usually think much about the days I spent so long ago in Kentucky, and I certainly don't talk much about them either, because really, what does it change? I am not silent out of shame, for I have nothing to hide, but I've never felt a need to share much about my past, particularly with my girls. I guess that somehow I felt like I was giving them a fresh clean slate on which to build their lives—that somehow leaving our Kentucky roots in the moist and salty Kentucky dirt would free us all from that kind of life. Mostly though, I think I don't talk about it because I feel so far removed from it all.

I'm not sure why this year has triggered such a need to remember. Perhaps it's because I know that the past can't hurt us now. That my daughters are strong young ladies, not scarred, as far as I can tell, and I know deep down that what I share now isn't going to change the beautiful life I've made for my family. Somehow making the cornbread in my own kitchen today, thousands of miles away from my birth land, well, somehow it shattered my need for silence. All I feel now is a need to remember how I came to where I am. I feel a need to divulge my story and perhaps, more than that even, I feel a need to share it finally with my daughters, who have often asked, and have never been answered.

Like any other story, my story has a beginning and an end, and somewhere along the journey you begin to see how a person can get from one to the other. I don't suppose you can appreciate my ending without understanding my beginning. However, I won't dwell on those early years like most folks, the years they call the formative ones. I had a very large family growing up, and you'd think we'd all have shared the same stories, seeing how we all grew up under the same roof; we all drank the same well water; and we all lived under the same hot and sticky Kentucky sun. Yet, those years formed us all differently, sent us all in a whole lot of different directions in life. So, I'll explain what needs explaining, and tell you what needs telling so you can picture it in your mind, and the rest will be left up to imagination.

As far back as I can remember, I was nothing but a poor sharecropper's daughter on a tobacco farm just outside of Franklin, Kentucky. My pop had been a farmer his whole life and hadn't known anything different. We were up at dawn, in the house by sunset, and ate our suppers by the light of coal oil lamps. We warmed ourselves by a large fireplace, and our newborn babies were warmed not by electrical contraptions like they use today, but by being placed in front of a wood-burning stove. We fit nine people in a three-room house, and not one of us ever found that strange or small. It's just how it was.

If we wanted to iron our clothes or linens for a holiday, we had to heat up the iron on a bed of coals or on the wood-burning stove. There wasn't any electricity in homes until many years down the line, and, of course, people who lived on the farming lands were the last to see it installed anyway. Making supper in the middle of July was always an exercise in composure, and I still can't understand why people use saunas as a means of relaxation. What I wouldn't have given in those days for just one electric fan.

We grew most of our own food in a pretty hearty garden we had behind our house. It was the only things we got from the land that we didn't have to share with the landowners. My family basically ate what we could grow ourselves, and if we couldn't grow it, we'd trade for it. And we were careful. We were careful with absolutely everything. We saved the seeds from our previous crops for the next planting season and poured a little bit of kerosene over our beans to prevent the bugs from getting at them. We dug furrows just before winter to bury our potatoes and cabbage in, then we covered them with hay and let them sit until we wanted to dig them up and eat them. They kept very nicely through the whole winter that way. Mostly though, we canned a lot of our crop. Jams, green beans, beets. Whatever we could preserve, we preserved, because we saw so many cold winter months where the ground gave us nothing and the bosses gave us even less.

We had a small chicken coop that usually gave us plenty of eggs, and sometimes, when a hen got older, we'd have some meat as well. We had two cows, which may not seem like much, but which was more than other folks had. Most of the other sharecroppers had just one on hand, and heaven help them if she dried up or fell ill. We churned our own milk to make our butter, and we made our cows work pretty hard to give us what they could. A family with no cow was a family without cheese, milk, and butter, and quite often was a family with rickets. We parched our coffee beans and then ground them with a coffee mill. You could often tell the state of affairs at my house by the strength of the coffee. Strong coffee meant we were doing alright with a bit to spare. Weak coffee, well, you get the picture.

What we couldn't grow for ourselves, we traded for—meats, flour, sugar. There wasn't really much money that changed hands for goods at the store. We'd ride into town with whatever items my mom was willing to part with, or whatever extra soap she'd made, and we would get what we needed. Eggs were a golden ticket. Mom called it her egg money, and she took really good care of our hens. We didn't own any swine, so any pig product we wanted like pork chops, bacon, ham, and so forth we had to trade or pay for. Same thing with beef. People like to think that farm folks eat steak and potatoes every night. It was more like cornbread or cold biscuits and milk or sugar water with a side of ham or a small serving of beef. I'm still not quite sure why we weren't all anemic.

Television was nonexistent in the 1920s, so we were often outdoors playing and burning off energy. That is, when we weren't doing chores like hauling water in from the well, cleaning the outhouse, or milking the cows. There is always something that needs to be done on a farmstead. We explored a lot too, surveying the little forests and the small creek beds near our house, pretending we were in some far off other country like New York or Maine. We fished in the larger ponds for catfish, and more often than not we'd get lucky. Swimming holes were real and not the stuff of stories, and sometimes they were the only thing that cooled you off the whole of the summer.

We played games on the front porch like Snap until it drove my mom crazy because of all the clapping involved. Another favorite was a game my siblings and I liked to call "In and Out of the Window," which may seem like it needs an explanation but is really just what it sounds like. Mom didn't like that one much either. And cards. We played hours and hours of cards. Slap jack, pinochle, and my pop's favorite, rummy, though he cheated like a criminal and had to bribe us to play with him as we got older. We attended a few neighborhood dances, if you will, meaning some neighbor had cleared out their barn enough to make some room and had pulled out a violin. My grandmother was one of the best banjo players around, and our neighbors would love it on the nights that she showed up to play. Dancing didn't cost a penny, and every now and again even farmers had to let loose. If you were lucky you could catch a radio show with a friend in town, and let me tell you, that's when you'd really see some dancing.

We heated our bathwater on the stove, which was a very tedious task as you might imagine, so like many other families we shared the same water. We took turns as mom saw fit, and I often tried not to anger her too much just so she'd give me a higher place in the line; but I never could figure out how she decided who was the first one in the tub. We did this once a week. I laugh when people complain about the smells from some of the local farms here in California and wonder how their tenants can stand it. I know they can stand it because, most days, your cattle smell better than your siblings. I wore hand-me-down everything, being the youngest, and often wore matching dresses with my sisters, cut from the same flour or chicken feed sack pattern that mom had on hand. Folks could pick out who was whose sibling at the school house because all the girls had matching dresses and the boys had matching knickers. We owned a wagon and would borrow the working mules every now and again to get into town, but to get to the school house we walked. Really, two miles, in the snow, uphill, both ways.

That's my early life in a snapshot. Nothing too surprising if you've ever given thought to what it might be like to live without proper plumbing or electricity, or a vehicle for that matter. Or maybe it is surprising, but that's how I grew up in the 1920s. Farming was hard work—living was harder. However, that wasn't always the case for my family. A little later down the line, as the world changed, my family had the sense to change right along with it. We weren't really the stagnant kind, though to look at us back then you might argue that point. We had so very little, yet most days nobody noticed. My mom and pop just never made a big fuss about it. If they didn't fuss, neither did we, and if the truth be told, except for the family we worked for, which was fairly well off, most folks we knew had it about as bad as we did.

In fact, I can remember the first time I caught a clue that things were slightly less than ideal at my house. I must have been seven or eight at the time, though back then I never kept track of time so that might be up for debate. My mom had made casual friends with my primary school teacher that fall. Mrs. Henrietta Dubois, a transplant from Louisiana, had worked at the schoolhouse called Paradise Primary for many years, and she had a reputation for friendliness with the poorer folks around town. I always thought it was just her deep down southern hospitality. But honestly, up until then, I never realized her being so nice to us meant I was one of the poor kids too. I wasn't sure if she was taking pity on us or just really liked how down-to-earth most of us were. Years later I know it was the latter. Regardless, my mom was attracted to the attention from Mrs. Dubois like a bee to nectar. Yes, my mom, God bless her, invited my teacher over for tea and biscuits, and, of course, some of her cornbread.

I remember my pop being so confused and asking her if she'd lost her mind.

"Folks just don't do that, Mattie. It ain't proper! Any nice thing she do for Catherine now will look like a paid favor." He'd been bright red that day, but not out of fury. It was embarrassment that reddened his cheeks and not anger, and he was simply mortified to bring such a cultured southern woman into his tiny, dusty, and very crowded home.

My mom, quick as she was, just smiled her impish grin and jested back at my pop, saying, "Yes, that's right, Isaac. I'm planning to buy off Catherine's teacher with some weak tea and some day-old biscuits. That ought to get her at least some passing marks this quarter, don't you think?" And when my father started laughing despite himself, she added, "Do you think my homemade jam will cover next quarter too?"

How they laughed about it as my pop finally conceded and said he'd ask his mother to come over to help my mom get ready! I hadn't realized having my teacher over for a snack was such a big to-do until my father had made it so. You should have seen the lengths my mom went to clean up. The buckets of bleach water and all the sweeping she did were beyond what she ever normally undertook. I really knew it was serious when she took my bed sheet and washed it twice and then took the hot iron to it so she could put down a tablecloth that wasn't stained with greasy butter or fatty gravy. She even went so far as to borrow dishes from my grandmother because hers were a little less worn and chipped than my mom's. But the real sign that gave it all away was the spread my mother prepared. Just short of the ham and sweet potatoes, it looked like Christmas dinner in October. I never understood why it was so important to gain my teacher's favor as such, because I knew it really wasn't about my marks in school as my mother had joked. I think it was more about my mother's need to raise her marks in life and to prove she was worthy of such a friendship.

So, the very kindhearted Mrs. Dubois came to our home that early fall afternoon in 1926 and pretended very generously not to notice all the clutter that the three room house held, or all the children it held, or all the years of wear and tear that it showed. Mrs. Dubois was a gracious guest, and as I watched her interact with my mom over buttery biscuits and sugar cookies, I realized her interest in my mom was genuine and that they'd be friends for years to come. She became like the cornbread on our daily table, dependable. That was the first of many visits to our home over the years for Mrs. Dubois, and as it turns out, that friendship my mom forged over my well-ironed bedsheet-turned-tablecloth changed the course of my family's life some few years before I left town.

Those years were hard, and though I didn't realize it at the time, they were mostly about survival. While I don't think on them much anymore, when those days come to mind, I don't think of them as necessarily bad. They were just years in my life, like any others, with ups and downs, good days and not so good days. We were just living. I try to picture them like the honey-covered cornbread rather than the kind that came on our dinner plates nightly. Those days on the farm served their purpose like that cornbread. They made me strong, were mostly dry and hard, but every now and then, they were dressed up with a touch of something special like my mom's home-made butter and that sweet succulent honey.

Chapter Three

Lillie Woodard
Tuesday, August 11, 1953

"Wish we could contact her kin, surely they'd want to see her before she goes." Lillie's nap hadn't lasted long, and she was disturbed to find she was still the topic of conversation amongst her nurses.

"Nelly told me that her husband strictly forbade us to give out any information about her. He dropped her off and then stopped by here a few hours later saying so. I bet her kin don't even know she's here!" This was a new nurse, one she thought she hadn't heard before. She wondered if the whole hospital knew her story by now, given that she'd been there so long.

Lillie only stirred at first, but was quickly fully awakened by the indignant voices. These were new nurses and part of the next shift, and Lillie thought she recognized one of them as the nurse who'd help to bathe her the week before. She was the nurse with the soft hands and gentle touch. She had hummed an easy soothing melody while she cleaned Lillie, and Lillie had been quite fond of her. That seemed like forever ago, in the days when Lillie could still sit up. Lillie lay quietly on her back, staring up at the ceiling while breathing in the rancid air of her hopelessness. In and out, in and out. She supposed she was still alive, then, if she was still breathing.

Her bed was cooler, her coverlet warm, and the room slightly darker as sunset approached.

"She got seven kids, 'ya know... and not one's been here to see their mama." The nurse sniffed as if it were truly the saddest thing she'd ever heard.

"Sad, so sad. She seems like a real nice lady. Except for that man of hers."

Ah, Clay, Lillie thought. *They must be talking about* my *Clay.* She knew why her children and family hadn't come to visit her, and the reason started and ended with her husband Clay. The disgruntled nurse was

15

correct about him, and Lillie knew Clay hadn't told her children where she was. Her four oldest kids were out of the house and easily put off, from Clay's perspective, for he was nothing if not manipulative. She could almost hear the conversations he would spin as if she were a fly on the wall of her home.

"Nah, Mr. Garrett," he'd probably say sweetly, "Lillie's been off the farm to help my sister with her young'ins for a few weeks. She'll be back right soon." Or, "Sorry, Ben, your mama's caught herself a ride to town. She won't be back till much later." Or, "Sorry, Josie, ain't the best time to be stopping by. Lillie's real busy now, 'ya hear?" If Lillie's family had known any bit of the truth, she wouldn't have been lying on the narrow bed all alone with the thin mattress and sticky sheets that were about to drive her into madness. Her neighbors surely suspected, but minding your own business in Franklin was as much one of the Ten Commandments as "Thou Shalt Not Kill," and many folks, though they loved Lillie dearly, thought it best to let Clay take care of his own. Clay, however, had left the care part out of minding his kin, and had just taken. He'd taken time, he'd taken money, he'd even taken life; but he hadn't taken care.

Lillie remembered sitting at her kitchen table some months before when she'd finally admitted to herself and her best friend Josie how little care Clay had taken. Josie had come down to visit from Ohio, and it had been a particularly woeful day when Lillie had been in a good bit of discomfort. Josie cradled Lillie's hands in her own across the tumbledown wooden table, sympathy glistening in her eyes as she stared in despair at her friend's damaged body.

"Lills, I'm... I'm so sorry. If I'd known it was this bad I would have..." Josie could barely finish a sentence because the shock of it was so bad. Lillie looked swollen at best, and bruised and purple at worst, and for Josie it was an unsettling array of colors on a typically neutral canvas.

"What, Jos? You gonna start a one-woman war with a giant? He'd snap you in two like a toothpick and use one half of you to get the gristle out from between his molars." Lillie smiled at her friend of thirty-five years and gently patted her trembling hands. "Besides, this ain't your fight. It's mine, and I think I done finally lost this battle." Lillie sat with a look of quiet complacency on her face, though she knew how bad she probably looked.

"Lillie..." Josie started.

"No, ain't no good now. I should'a done something about it long ago and I didn't. Now I got to live with that, and that ain't nobody's fault but my own. But I tell you what, Josie, that man can scar my flesh and yell as loud as he wants until he gets even God and Jesus to take notice, but the one thing he ain't never gonna do is touch my soul. I got that tucked way down deep." *Down deep inside, indeed*, she'd thought, where his fists couldn't reach and his harsh words couldn't touch. Lillie had protected it as best she could, like it was a vault full of gold and silver.

"Well, Lillie," Josie replied, "yours is maybe one of the only souls I know that's still just as beautiful as the day you were born." She squeezed her friend's hand, realizing finally just how far gone things were, and knowing that, short of a miracle, not much was going to change the trajectory of Lillie's future.

Lillie got up from the kitchen table and wandered slowly over to the stove to put on some water for coffee. She caught sight of her youngest playing in the yard, and it triggered so many memories from her own childhood.

"Josie, you remember when we first met?" she asked softly. Lillie certainly remembered.

Josie laughed loudly. "Are you kidding? Of course I do. What year was that again, though, it's been so long now?"

Lillie smiled as she stoked the small flame in the wood-burning oven. "I right can't remember my name some days, but I remember that year like it was just last Wednesday. It was May of 1916, and the summers were just as long and sticky then as they are now." It was hard for Lillie to believe that it had been three and a half decades, but then time is a funny, fickle thing. Lillie was just seven when her family had settled into the small, wooden-framed home on the south side of the Finn property, and this past year she had just celebrated her forty-fourth birthday.

"You been here so long it's like you was born here instead of in Logan. I can't rightly remember a time without you around, actually. I can't remember, though, why your daddy moved you here. Logan is nothing but twenty-five miles or so northwest of here."

"Well, Logan wasn't very big back then, and I guess my daddy felt like Franklin had better work for growers and he wanted to try his hand at tobacco. Was a risky move, and my mama wasn't too happy about it at first, but Lord bless us, my daddy's good name helped him get on with your daddy's farm right quick." Looking back, Lillie realized it had been a crapshoot just up and moving like that, and sometimes

Lillie couldn't help but think that Lady Fate had more to do with it than she'd been given credit. A sought-after boss with a reputation for paying well, Josie's daddy, Mr. James Finn, was a fifth-generation Kentucky farmer who owned quite a bit of the rich soil that fell inside the boundaries of Simpson County. The Finns grew a multitude of crops, but the cash crop, the one that paid the bills, was tobacco. It was as hard on the farmers as the tobacco was on the soil, and the work of it required many more hands and strong backs than the Finns had in children. Like so many others in the area, James Finn enlisted sharecroppers to get the job done.

Josie burst out in a fit of laughter and Lillie joined her, not really knowing what was so funny, but laughing despite herself.

"What is so funny, Jos?" Lillie finally blurted out.

Josie wiped her eyes and caught her breath and finally said, "I was just thinking about the first time my family saw your family. We kids was watching you all from the upstairs window, and it was like watching a gaggle of ducks wandering down to the pond. Your daddy pulled up with his ox driven cart and one by one you each climbed down and followed the other into the house. How many of you was there back then?"

Lillie laughed. "Eight, I think, including my folks. That's not so many, Josie. I got seven of my own, not counting Clay and me! Most sharecroppers got them large families. It's not like in the big cities where you are in Ohio now, with folks just having three or four kids." Lillie laughed again, though, as she imagined how they had looked to the Finns. "'Ya, I guess we must'a been quite a sight! So glad we didn't scare your daddy off right away with our mess of kids."

Josie got up and imitated a gaggle of ducks, and the two old friends laughed until they wept and their sides hurt.

Lillie grinned as she recalled their silliness, but her mind began to wander away from her conversation with Josie and landed on her early times in Franklin.

The countryside surrounding the town of Franklin was occupied by many sharecropping families like the Garretts, all of them living on the outskirts of the land they worked, but within the boundaries of the farmland that fed their families. It was a system started long before, when the South was rebuilding after the Civil War, and it had survived long into the next century in Kentucky, mostly on tobacco farms, where the work was hard and the needs were many.

18

Tobacco farming was a new commodity for Mr. Garrett, as he had previously grown mostly wheat and corn. It took just three months on the Finn farm to figure out that growing tobacco was a whole lot more work than he had bargained for.

Tobacco was easy enough to grow; its roots took easily to the wholesome, fertile dirt, but the rest of the process of debugging, cutting, and drying, made for long and tedious work. However, he wasn't in it alone; and like with most of his neighbors, making a living required that it be a full-fledged family affair. From his eldest to his youngest, Mr. Garrett quickly instilled the family motto, *Work hard or we'll starve.*

By the end of the first few months, Lillie had perhaps been the only one who hadn't yet grown weary of picking bugs off the plants or helping her mama tend the large garden behind the house that sustained her family throughout the year. Although the days seemed endlessly the same to her brother and sisters, Lillie was seemingly content with whatever plant or grub might be in her line of sight at the time. Every day was the same as the last for the most part, but she was young enough that every leaf and creepy crawler was intriguing to her and held some amount of fascination.

Lillie, unlike her older siblings, tended to remember the long days spent in the sun working in the garden or tobacco fields with the same fondness that a privileged city kid might recall their youth. Instead of art museums and orchestras, she'd had real life lush green landscapes and melodious bird song. Instead of swimming pools and ballroom galas, she'd had tire swings over small ponds and barn dances with self-taught banjo players. In her mind, her childhood had been just as rich, just as cultured, and just as fulfilling as anybody else's, and the truth is she didn't know any different anyway.

"Lord, I don't think there's a stickier, more miserable place in hell as Kentucky in July," Lillie's older sister Vera complained one steamy afternoon. "Or a job more disgustin' than picking these hornworms off'a these leaves." She scrunched up her face and flung a particularly nasty little critter into the collecting basket. "I think this one might'a feasted on a whole acre of tobacco! High as a kite this one is, and fat as a hog!"

"Quit your whinin', girl or I might well send 'ya to find out if there's any place hotter than here," Ernest jested with a big friendly grin. At the precocious age of fifteen, Ernest was the oldest of the Garrett children, and was often a calming voice in an otherwise chaotic household.

"I don't much mind it," said Lillie quietly. "Sun feels kind'a good, makes my feet wanna dance a bit, actually." A smile spread across her seven-year-old face as she turned it upwards to bask a little more in the sun's heavy warm glow. She laughed loudly as she whirled and twirled up and down the row of crops, adding, "And the worms are kind'a cute."

"Oh, Lills, you have always got it so backwards, child!" Vera retorted, and she teasingly tousled Lillie's limp brown hair as Lillie twirled and twirled like a ballerina in a child's jewelry box. "Makes you wanna dance? Ha! Lord, child, it's so hot out here it makes me wanna take a nap!"

"Leave the girl alone," chimed in Evelyn, smirking. "At least Lillie *can* dance! *Your* dancing makes *me* wanna take a nap, Vera!"

"Truer words were never spoken, Eva." Ernest laughed, who welcomed a small bug thrown in his direction by Vera.

Lillie giggled in her infectious way and wrapped herself around Evelyn's long and strong legs. "Ah, Lills, always the ray of sunshine, even as the sun is burning our backs to bacon!"

These were the memories of childhood that pirouetted through Lillie's mind like a blurry dancer across a moonlit stage.

That was the same day that Josie and Lillie's paths first crossed, and it was cataloged as one of the best days of her life. It had been a day like any other day in the middle of the summer, hot, long, and draining, as if some invisible force somewhere had siphoned off all the energy in the house and replaced it with a peevish humor. Lillie's family was, as a whole, very short-tempered that night, each of them so wrapped up in their own hot misery that no one noticed when Lillie slipped away after supper. She was just one less body warming up the small family room or stealing whatever humid breeze might creep by anyway.

She snuck out the back door on nimble bare feet and ambled down the footpath that wandered around by the small creek separating the Finn's farm from the neighboring McNeil's farm. She had no particular place in mind, but she always seemed to gravitate towards the small crick bed because the trickling water soothed her and even seemed to call her name on hot nights like that night. Like an oasis in the middle of a big city street, it calmed the blithe mayhem that was Lillie's home life—pots banging, little ones screeching, mama hollering, little feet scrambling on wooden floorboards—an orchestra of individually beautiful sounds that all added up to very loud bedlam. But down there, by the creek, it was just her and God's tapestry. There, on the water that called her name, she could almost hear the soft rustling of His smooth and glassy voice telling her that life was, indeed, a precious gift.

Josie had found herself with a bit of time to fill that evening and had wandered down her own footpath to the little creek. Josie was little for her seven years, but strong, and had skillfully made her way five branches up one of the numerous old oaks that lined the crick. She watched quietly as the wind pushed around the summer leaves and dirt, and was wondering where they'd end up, when suddenly her eyes landed on Lillie. Lillie was busy hopping from one foot to the other and from one large boulder to another, up and over, steady and balanced. Lillie was concentrating so hard and was so lost in her thoughts that she hadn't noticed the wide-eyed, curly-headed little girl regarding her from up above.

"Hey there!" Josie hollered. Lillie startled so that her balance on one foot turned uncertain. She wavered back and forth slightly, and finally found her footing before she looked up to search for the source of the small voice. Her eyes darted around the creek bed at first, then out to the rolling fields, and eventually rested on Josie high up in the tree.

"Hey there yourself. What'ya doing way up there?" Lillie hollered.

"Well, watchin' you jump around," Josie replied matter of fact with hands on her petite hips. "Wanna come up?"

Lillie shrugged a 'what for' and knitted her eyebrows, but then found her hands quickly discovering the knobs and crooks in the old oak that would lead her up to the tiny blonde-headed girl. She sat herself deftly next to Josie, who had taken no note of Lillie's disheveled appearance or patched-up clothing. "I like your view from up here," offered Lillie as a greeting while she settled in tight next to Josie.

Josie furrowed her brows, looking hard at Lillie and replied, "Well, it's your view too, far as I can see."

Lillie grinned a little and said, "Well, reckon you're right. I'm Lillie, by the way."

Josie's face softened, and she slipped her little hand under Lillie's and said, "Josie, nice to meet 'ya."

They sat there for well over an hour, not saying much, just watching the evening breeze move over and through the tall, green crops. Small words and nonsensical boasting about who and what they were weren't necessary. They just needed a bit of time sitting on an old oaky branch, and a gentle breeze, and their bond cemented effortlessly. That night, just before the social lines of primary school could have a chance to draw a wedge between them, the tenant farmer's daughter Lillie formed an inseparable bond with the landowner's daughter Josie, and it wasn't anything either of them could ever explain.

Chapter Four

Catherine
Franklin, Kentucky
1929

While most people want to know about my childhood on a farm, I'm more excited to talk about what happened after I left Kentucky. That's when I feel like I went from *just* living to *really* living. It didn't happen overnight, but the further I got from Kentucky, the closer I got to finding me. I suppose that's why I never feel a need to look back.

In 1929 I was about eleven going on twenty, and it was just my older sister Lina and me left at home, though she didn't stay for long. We were like two peas in a pod, Lina and I, no farm pun intended. Lina was my closest sister, and in many ways, though she was only six years older, she was also like a mother to me. We, like many other farm families of that time, lost a sibling to sickness when he was very young. He was the child that had been born in between Lina and me. I never knew my older brother. I wasn't born until six months after he died, so I don't feel terribly sad about it except I know it was devastating for my mom and pop.

While I don't obviously remember his death, I do remember feeling like I spent the whole of my childhood with a ghost of a mother. My older siblings would speak about the mom before his death and it was as if they were describing somebody else's mother altogether. I think I got a watered-down tattered version of who my mom had been to my sisters and brothers. Though he didn't mean it, my brother's death robbed me of something, and I knew it too. Every day I knew something was missing with my mom and me, but I couldn't quite tell you what.

It wasn't as though she wasn't loving or respectful. She was. Or generous or warm, because she was that too. She was just distant. Like you could look in her eyes and just keep going. Like you could fall on through because there wasn't anything there to hold you. They were just so hollow. It never made me mad, her being that way, though I suppose I could have let it. It just left me feeling a little bit empty in some places, with an urge to fill up those spaces with something exciting. I tell you this not to speak ill of my mom, but so that it's easier understand why it was so painless for me to leave her. There just never was any sort of bond there. Her ability to form them had been buried ten feet under the cold Kentucky dirt in a tiny cemetery just off the main road before I had ever been born.

Now I'm getting a little bit ahead of myself, I suppose, so let me backtrack a bit. As I said before, Mrs. Dubois had a small hand in changing things for us. She'd been a good friend to my mom over the years, and to tell the truth I think she's a lot of the reason my mom started to come back to life even a little bit after my brother's death. I saw a change in her after the fall that they had met when I was eight; it was subtle, but it was still there. It was a glimpse of the mother I should have had, or could have, if my brother hadn't died. I will be forever grateful to Mrs. Dubois for those small moments when the better version of my mom would show up and smile at us all as if all was right in her world.

Mostly, though, I am grateful for the hand she had in getting us off the farm—and, in some ways, changing my fate. Though I would have sworn on my brother's grave that my pop would be a farmer until he lay in the ground himself, Mrs. Dubois saw another future for him—and for us, I suppose. Her husband, Charlie, worked for the city and had for years, and he needed a trustworthy sidekick of sorts. The job came with the benefit of a tenant home in town for a quicker jog to work when necessary. For a quickly aging man like my pop, whose wife needed more support than the solitude that farm life could offer, it was a deal too good to pass up.

So we moved into town that summer, just off Peach Street, on the other side of the tracks, if you will. The house wasn't much to speak of, but it was bigger than what we'd ever had, with more amenities. My older sisters and brother were all married, and only one remained near Franklin, so there was only four of us that would be living in the new, larger home: my mom, my pop, Lina, and me. When mom first saw it she had said it just needed a little elbow grease and some spit and shine, and then it would fix up real nice. She was right, and we were settled faster than I'd expected we would be. Lina was seventeen then, and felt like she should just stop going to school and find a job in town. But she ended up meeting a boy before she ever found work, and found herself rushing to get married before her belly started to show too much. I think my mom and pop were just fine with her leaving when the time came, and my pop had no objections to her marrying the boy, except that it just hadn't been soon enough. I felt otherwise. I missed my sister desperately, and was soon alone in the new house in town with my parents.

So, in the months following my sister's shotgun wedding, I found myself with a bit too much time on my hands. I still went to school—mom made sure of that—and I still had some chores to do, though nothing like what the farm had required. We had electricity and real running water in town, so things like getting water from the well or making sure the oil lamps were full were no longer on our to do list. I could walk a half mile and find myself at Roark's General Store where I'd use real money from my pop's job to buy things instead of trading eggs. We still didn't have a car, but we didn't need one; everything was so close we just walked.

I wish I could tell you that's when my life started taking a turn for the better. In some ways it did, I suppose; it made things easier, for sure, and more comfortable. But, to be honest, it just all felt so foreign. I felt more alone in those years, all crowded in town with everybody else, than I ever had out on the farm.

My mom didn't make it any easier, either. After Lina left, and with most of my other siblings having moved away, gone into farming, and starting families of their own, she just kind of shut down. Like she decided she was done mothering me, if she ever had at all, and she just sort of let me make my own course. That might sound nice, to be a teenager and be let loose, but the truth is I just wanted my mom to be a mom.

I spent a whole lot of time reading and a lot of time wandering the square with my schoolmates. If you poke around Franklin too long you might well find a few dozen trees with "C was here" carved in them in girlish scrawl. I know every nook and cranny of Franklin, every crack in the sidewalk, every loose board on every porch, and when the best time of the day is to catch Mr. Boycott, the owner of the small ice cream shop, so he'll give you free samples. In a town of over three thousand folks, I bet I could name you two thousand, nine hundred, and ninety-nine just from picking up gossip on the streets in the town square. At fourteen years old I was a fixture there, just like the maple trees that dotted the lawn, only I never felt quite as rooted.

So when an offer came from my aunt Rachel, my mom's sister, who lived up in Hazel Park in Michigan, I didn't so much leap at it as I ran full force towards her car. She'd written my mom some months prior to her visit, bragging about the great schools up near her new home in the fine state of Michigan. Aunt Rachel was a teacher, educated in Bowling Green, and her husband was a city council member in a town near Detroit. Together they claimed to know all the ins and outs of all the best educational opportunities on this side of the country. My aunt's community hadn't been hit quite as hard during the depression as some others had been, and so her family stayed fairly prosperous through those years. Rachel promised me an education and a chance to finish high school, with a possibility for me to go on to a university. She was giving me a chance at a life outside of a farm town like Franklin.

My mom protested at first, and I'd like to say that her concerns were real, but truthfully I think she protested because that's what she thought Rachel would expect. What mother would let their daughter go without some sort of fuss about it? A tired mom, a mom who had lost her ability to parent—in other words, my mom—but for appearance's sake, she at least tried to convince pop it wasn't a good idea. My pop though, he knew better, and he made the argument on my behalf—though again, he didn't have to put up much of a fight. After a few weeks had passed and all the arrangements had been made, I took a bus up to Michigan. I was fifteen at the time, and nervous about leaving the only home place I'd ever known; but as I watched Franklin grow smaller through the back window of the bus, I knew it was the last time I'd ever live there. I was young and convinced I had bigger adventures to sow than the dirty tobacco fields could ever have offered me.

Unfortunately, I soon found that some fortunes are but fool's gold. My aunt Rachel quickly settled me into her new home and all too eagerly showed me the ropes of the household chores. My cousins were all younger than me, and were as abundant in number as they were in energy. I was so overwhelmed, even having come from a big family, and I just couldn't comprehend how my aunt cared for so many children in addition to her job as a teacher. I soon discovered just how Aunt Rachel managed things, as I found myself the 'unofficial' nanny to seven children under twelve years of age. It turned out that Aunt Rachel had difficulty retaining employees as her dear, sweet offspring were often labeled a challenge, a detail which no one had shared with me before I came all that way. After a few weeks of doing nothing but cleaning and watching my cousins, I quickly began wondering about my aunt's intentions. Every time I would inquire about when I might start my schooling I was always met with a silent resistance. I knew something was awry, but I couldn't quite put my finger on what.

"Soon, Catherine. I'll take you soon. Let's just get you settled in first," Aunt Rachel would say. That, or "Next week child, Lord, there's so much needs doing 'round here I just don't see how I'll possibly do it without you!"

I quickly got the sinking feeling that my move up to Michigan had been more about helping my aunt than learning, and I soon found out I was regrettably correct in my assessment. Whenever I would broach the subject again, my aunt would reply, "Now, Catherine, we ought to just be grateful for all we've been given. You could still be back at that shack of yours in that farm town with all that dirt under your fingernails. At least your home here is a nice one, child, and you aren't out running around town by yourself doing Lord knows what!" It was obvious she felt like I owed her something.

I was angry, and I didn't feel grateful the way my aunt suggested I should. I just felt duped and betrayed. I'd been lured so far from home with promises of greatness and educational enlightenment only to find myself bound by the shackles of childcare and household chores at the tender age of fifteen. I hated the way Rachel had preyed on my mom and pop, dangling an educated daughter in front of them like it would be what saved all their souls. It was pitiful. I was given no money for the work I did, just the room and board, and so I had nothing with which to even purchase a bus ticket home. I was literally at the mercy of Aunt Rachel, and I felt not one bit of gratefulness in my bones for my supposedly bettered circumstances. I quickly felt enslaved.

"At least your home here is a nice one, child," my aunt had said so many times that sometimes I just wanted to take her and shake her tall thin frame until she woke up to what a beast she was. That's what kind of person she made me, angry. At least in Franklin I had been respected by my family and was free to be myself. At least in Franklin I hadn't been a prisoner. No, grateful was not quite the word.

I wish I could say things changed with Aunt Rachel over time, that she saw my potential and loved me enough to help me pursue it. But I never did attend a day of high school in the pretty southeastern corner of Michigan. I did, however, find myself tutoring my young cousins and setting the table for dinner every night. I readied Aunt Rachel's children every morning to go to the same schoolhouse I had been promised, and each day that they walked through the schoolhouse doors and I turned to walk back to Aunt Rachel's house, I would seethe just a little bit more. My 'schooling' came in the form of which dinner fork went where in the place setting and what were the proper linens to set for the women's society tea.

I was angry, but I was also determined not to become bitter about my life because of it. I tolerated this treatment by Aunt Rachel with as much poise as I could. Just because I'd been born on a farm didn't mean I was going to give her the satisfaction of seeing me act like a barnyard animal, moaning or squealing like a pig at slaughter. It was something I'd learned from watching my mom when she'd dealt with difficult neighbors and relatives. Breathe in and breathe out and try to remember who you really are. I knew in my heart I would finish schooling someday, and I would take the first avenue out of my aunt's estate as soon as I had the means to do so.

I spent two years like that, mostly in my aunt's house with very short trips out to the store and back, or out to run her an errand or two. I didn't make any friends. I didn't have the means, nor the time, and looking back now I was feeling so down that I didn't have the heart to even try. I just kept biding my time, knowing that some day I would set myself free from what I'd come to think of as my enslavement, and I would leave the great lady of Michigan in my rear view mirror. Not long after I turned seventeen, an opportunity for my freedom literally presented itself on my aunt's doorstep, and I was the one to open the door and let it in.

A man came knocking on my aunt's door in the spring of 1936 to deliver a piece of furniture that my aunt Rachel just had to have in her front room. To me it was an oversized ugly chair with an old lady pattern all over it, but Aunt Rachel just couldn't stop raving about how perfect it was. I knew it was more about the fact that the chair had once graced a bedroom in the governor's mansion than how fantastic the shape of the wingback was, but as I often did, I held my tongue. I let the man in the door and showed him to the front parlor where the ugly chair would go. The man looked to be around thirty or so, which made his empty ring finger a little curious. I was still a girl really, at seventeen, and was completely unimpressed with both the furniture

28

and the man, so I decided I was better off leaving him be and going to find my aunt to let her know her chair had arrived.

That's when he stopped me with a kind and surprisingly soothing voice and said, "Going so soon? I could use a little help with where it ought to be placed."

"It's none of my—never mind. Place it where you like. Front yard is as good a place as any, if you ask me," I'd replied with sass. I was tired, and irritated by the chair, and sincerely thought it would make a better lawn ornament than a good addition to the already overcrowded parlor.

"Not a fan of all chairs, or is it just this one you detest?" the man jested and I could hear his smile in his tone.

I stopped then, mid-step, and turned to really look at him. I have to admit I was slightly taken aback with how handsome he was, and I was certain then that he had at least a decade on me. My quick look at him earlier had perhaps been too hasty, and I felt my eyebrows rise in surprise and my pulse quicken with excitement. No one, not even all the boys down in Franklin who had heatedly tried to get my attention, had ever made my heartbeat speed up like that. There was something different about him and intriguing, and the only thought that kept coming to my mind was how completely dapper he was. He was delivering furniture that was not likely from a store he owned, yet he didn't have the look of just a delivery man. He was extremely well-groomed and almost overdressed for the task he was doing. He definitely had more to his story than what I had first surmised, and perhaps warranted a second chance.

He stood staring at me as I stared at him, and I realized I hadn't answered him. I didn't know what to say; it was like all my irritation and my sarcasm had run out the front door that he'd left hanging wide open. He finally broke the tension and said, "I have many more coming into the store every day. Perhaps you and your ma could come down some time and have another look around?"

My ma? Oh, Lord help me if that were the case. My irritation found me again quickly. "Ah, she's not my ma. This is my aunt's house. I just look after the children and the dirty linens," I said, trying to keep the annoyance out of my voice and failing miserably.

"Do you ever get a night off?" He was forward and bold, and so sure of himself, and he ignited something in me so fast that I did what I do best when I feel threatened: I lit my fire of feistiness.

"Well, I'm not her employee! I can take off whenever I'd like," I spat back with my eyebrows furrowed. That wasn't entirely true, but he didn't need to know it. I wasn't sure if I felt as gutsy as I sounded, but my reaction seemed to be out of my hands. I wasn't good at hiding who I was, which is why perhaps I fought so with my aunt Rachel. For all the years she'd spent trying to tame my inner fire, all she'd ended up doing was stoking it. I was learning fast that I didn't like anyone else in charge of my destiny.

"Besides," I continued, as my sharpness began dripping from my words and spilling all over his well-polished shoes, "typically a man introduces himself before asking a gal on an outing." I extending my hand to the poor bloke, who didn't know quite what to make of me, and said, "I'm Catherine, by the way." He looked at me with a curious playful grin, and then accepted my handshake as he made a loud clicking sound out the side of his mouth.

"Well then, Miss Catherine, I'm Jackson Edens. Nice to meet you. What are you doing tomorrow night? There's a big dance downtown. A bunch of us are going, I mean, my friends and I. If you'd like to join me, I'd like to accompany you."

"You always so forward, Mr. Edens?" I swallowed my surprise and tried to hide my excitement.

"Jack, actually, and not on most days. You always so spirited, Miss Catherine?" He raised his eyebrows in amusement.

"Just Catherine, please, and you have no idea." And so began my very first romance.

Chapter Five

Lillie
Tuesday, August 11, 1953

Lillie's delusions came and went as she lay alone with her pain. They haunted her dreams and disturbed her few waking moments. The toxin buildup was overtaking her brain, and Lillie knew and implored daily that the nurses' murmurs were right. Her inner clock ticked down and illness gnawed at her lucidity, giving her only brief moments of reflection, small windows through which to revisit her life. Her children flashed in succession in her mind like the shuffling of cards. They were imperfect and frightened. They were goodhearted and beautiful. They were her life's work, and in the end she felt as if she'd failed them. She cried silent tears into her stubby eyelashes as she wondered how the younger ones would fare under Clay's command, and she promised God unbelievable things if her older girls would stay off his radar.

Clay. What was her life like before him? Had she been happy then? Her neurons were firing slowly, and her sluggish memory wandered back to the week she'd met him. She was sure she'd had some sort of premonition about him before their paths had actually crossed. But when was that again? The memory flooded forward to Lillie's consciousness, and Josie again entered the picture in her mind's eye.

It was February of 1929, and Lillie had just finished up her work at the sewing shop where she'd worked with Josie's mother, Mary, for a quite a few years by that time. Lillie closed the door of the shop and turned the key in the old latch, wiggling it just a little to get it to work. It had always been a persnickety lock. Her fingertips were sore and her hands were swollen and stiff as she slipped the small silver key into her pocket. She opened and closed her fists several times, trying to relieve the pain, but found her body only mildly agreeable to her wishes. While she continued to try to free her hands from her day's work, she sighed heavily and looked up towards the clouds that hung low over the courthouse.

The sky was the deepest of purples, surrounded by mesmerizing shades of yellow, red, and orange. She stood for just a moment taking in the beauty of the early evening, and then her eyes came to rest on the shop before her. A slender wooden door was squeezed between two large picture windows. Windows that Lillie loved because of all the light they let in, but also despised because of the lack of privacy they offered. She often felt a little bit like the knickknacks that were on display at Erma's gift shop a few doors down—ceramic vases, porcelain kittens, silver jewelry boxes, all candy for the shopper's eye—only Lillie didn't care much for being ogled like a piece of merchandise by those passing by. She didn't care much for the limelight.

"Never you mind them, Lillie," Mary would always say. "Most of them are just looking at their own reflections in the glass anyhow. They're deciding if they need more rouge, or could use a haircut. Just pretending to see us sitting here working, but the truth is that most people can't look past their own noses to really see anybody else anyhow."

Over the years Lillie found much truth in Mary's observation, and it wasn't something that bothered her because most days she liked to pretend she was just another red brick along the back wall. She was sturdy and strong, and holding up the shop with no one but Mary to notice.

Mary's shop took up the left side of the old building, and as Lillie surveyed the architecture her eyes came to rest on the sign just above the door. Finn & Finn it read, in simple block lettering. Lillie had to chuckle a bit to herself, because the truth was there wasn't a second Finn in the shop, only Mary Finn and herself—and since Mary hadn't been feeling well lately, it was mostly just Lillie, who was, in reality, not a Finn at all.

It was an impregnable building, built by local masons long ago, and made to withstand torrential winds. Detailed gray stonework covered the entire storefront and married seamlessly with the red brick siding. Eight long, rectangular windows elevated the building's presence three floors high, and the windows were set in two groups of four with a large wide space defining the two separate shops below. Mary's shop was on one side and Mr. Duncan's shoe store was on the other—all of a patron's dressing needs on one tiny corner. Each window was beautifully flanked north and south by detailed stone lintels and sills, and Lillie often wondered how long it had taken to shape each delicate and hardy piece of rock. Capped with a flat roof and white decorative parapet, the building commanded the attention of the little square like Mayor Runn at a monthly town hall meeting. It was certainly something special, especially to Lillie.

"Hands hurting again?" said a loud, bubbly voice behind Lillie as she stood there looking at the building. Her spine jolted with surprise. Lillie turned around to see a very familiar face.

"Geez, Jos, you scared the fright out of me! What are you doing in town? Groceries?" Lillie looked at her quizzically.

"Nah, I actually came to see you, but looks like you're heading out a bit earlier than usual, eh? Hot date with that boy from the mill, Miss Lills?" Josie teased her friend as she raised and lowered her perfect eyebrows in quick succession, suggesting that a romance was brewing.

Lillie laughed, and responded, "Nah, not tonight. My fingers are aching cause I been pickin' up your mama's part. And, Lord, there must be a storm a comin' 'cause my pains are a fright worse than usual. Anyhow, mama's got some sewing she wants me to do for her on top 'a that. My day never ends, 'ya know." Lillie's smile faded quickly. Her face was awash with exhaustion, the dark creases under her eyes stealing from her usual chipper demeanor.

"It only took twelve years of working with my mama to make you old, huh?" Josie teased as she needled her friend gently in the ribs with her knobby elbow.

"Watch it," Lillie teased, "or I'll be beating you with my cane soon." Lillie jested tiredly, and she felt the creakiness in the small joints of her fists as she pretended to hit her friend with an imaginary walking stick. She wasn't sure how much time she had before the arthritis set in permanently, but she mostly enjoyed her work and was delighted to be employed off the farm, so she tried hard not to complain about her discomfort.

Josie laughed her hearty laugh and spouted, "A cane? At twenty years of age, eh? I think you can at least make it to thirty before needing one of those, dear girl!"

Lillie chuckled at her response and tossed her short arm around her friend's high waist as they started to stroll down the street. "Don't suppose you'd give an old girl a lift home, would 'ya?"

"Not any old girl, but since it's you I'll consider it. I need to stop in and see mama anyway, and I suppose you'll do for company on the way." Josie grinned and feigned pain as Lillie pinched her side in retaliation.

"Ah, Jos, you don't even know how lucky you are to have me," Lillie jibed jokingly.

Josie draped her arm around her friend's back and squeezed Lillie's shoulder. "I'm not certain of much, Lillie Mae Garrett, but that, old girl, I am sure of!"

Lillie and Josie climbed into the newly purchased Ford Model A pickup truck that was as green as an army boot and headed south on Main Street towards the Finn farm. Josie rattled on about her day, her sweet young husband, and their plans to take in a picture show that weekend. Lillie tried to listen with the interest she always did, but found herself distracted. She listened to her friend talk and added the appropriate "hmmm" and "uh-uh" when they was called for, but she let her mind wander a bit. As Josie drove, Lillie watched her like she was seeing her for the first time. Time had straightened Josie's blonde curls and darkened the shade a bit, and her once-petite frame had grown onto a long and lean pair of legs. She was still warm and unassuming, and for all her long years of education and time out of farm life, Josie really hadn't changed too much. Lillie's mind wandered back to what it was like when they had first met, she and Josie, and how she'd come to be where she was today.

While sharecropping relationships were always a tad delicate for the adults, it was pretty unpretentious from the start for Lillie and Josie. Neither girl seemed to notice any difference between them. It was as if they'd both been born into the same family. Lillie could still picture herself and Josie as young girls as if she were watching a movie at the Roxy theater in town. They had been inseparable, and most of Lillie's childhood memories included Josie in some form or fashion. They would slip away together after finishing school and their chores, to explore the farmlands and bits of woods surrounding their homes. More often than not they found themselves in the fields just behind the tobacco barn. If it wasn't curing time, the girls would sometimes pry open one of the hinged cladding boards meant for ventilating and drying the crop, and sneak on into the barn. They'd climb up and over, in and out, weaving through the labyrinth of tier poles and cross beams with the zeal of a sleuth, pretending there was a puzzle to be solved, a maze to be conquered, or a new game to be invented.

As Josie drove and chatted on, a tape played back in Lillie's mind of one such typical afternoon some three decades past, and she could almost smell of the remnants of the old tobacco crop that had hung in the rugged old barn the month before.

"Hey, Lills, I'm the biggest meanest spider you ever did see!" Josie spat out in a whisper and in between giggles. "And I just caught you in my web. Just look how big my tentacles are!"

"Ha! Spiders don't have tentacles," Lillie offered back, "but they do have fangs!"

Josie scrunched up her small nose until it resembled a small grape and said, "Ya, just like Mr. McNeil!"

Lillie responded by imitating old Mr. McNeil, the farmer who owned land adjacent to the Finns' farm and didn't particularly find the children's antics amusing. "When I catch you, Josie Finn," Lillie said with on hand on her hip and the other one wagging a condescending finger at her, "I'm a'gonna squish 'ya with the back 'a my heel!"

"That's if you can catch me!" Josie whispered loudly and then took off fast, going over and under, in and out of the makeshift web, her tiny body as nimble as a wisp. They wiggled into the barn and squeezed between the posts and cross beams meant for hanging the tobacco sticks, all the while making sure to be as quiet as they could. The grand wooden structure with its gabled roof and sturdy support was a fine playground in a place where playgrounds were not to be found, but playing in the tobacco barn could cost them a good walloping with something almost as bad as a tobacco-hanging lathe. Farmer's daughter or not, Josie would get it as much as Lillie if they got caught, but the girls thought the fun of it was well worth the risk: and so the game of cat and mouse, or spider and squasher, could go on for hours.

Over time Lillie became a fixture at Josie's dinner table, where the butter biscuits, honey-sweetened tea, and roasted pork loin made the difference between the two families quite obvious to any outlier peeking in. The sharecropper's daughter's presence at the Finn's table would probably raise a few eyebrows down on the square. The Finns didn't much care what other folks thought, though, and if the Finns as a whole weren't the stereotypical class-conscious landowners, then Josie's mother Mary Finn certainly wasn't the typical matriarch.

Mary had learned the craft of sewing from her mother and grandmother, and was a rare case of a farmer's wife who had a marketable skill outside of gardening and milking cows. Even more rare was that her husband James not only supported it but encouraged it. The Finns owned a small custom clothier shop in the heart of town and serviced families of all kinds for miles around. No one hemmed, mended, or tailored quite like Mary, and she was the most sought-after seamstress in the greater part of Simpson county. The local paper had even featured her in the business section one Sunday and had raved about her 'magical hands.' For her neighbors or friends who couldn't afford her shop services, Mary would darn or fix for free, accepting only small tokens of appreciation like a winter squash or fresh-picked berries. She treated a third-generation hand-me-down dress that needing patching like she handled the county judge's finest garments. It was all the same to her, so she had understood perfectly when Josie and Lillie had taken up such a close friendship, and hadn't balked a bit. The apple, indeed, hadn't fallen far from the tree.

For every two or three stories that Lillie could recall about Josie, she probably had at least one or two that included Mary. Lillie's relationship with Mary was one that Lillie's mother had encouraged her to seek out; and in the end Mary had perhaps mothered Lillie more over the years than her own mother had. Lillie well remembered the day that her mama had suggested she go see Mary, and her memory played it out like it had just happened yesterday. Lillie could almost smell the late summer air.

"Mama, it's beautiful!" Lillie said with genuine admiration. She stared hungrily at the new dress her mama had made her, sewn from the fabrics of other older garments that had long ago met their end. Some of her other dresses had been pieced together from the rough fabric of the large bags that flour was often sold in, because fabric was fabric and, much like with food, not a scrap went to waste. Lillie could hardly push down the excitement that rose up in her throat as she eyed the newly polished hand-me-down shoes her mama had placed on the floor under where the dress was hanging.

"Well, it's no work like Mrs. Mary can do, but I'm glad you like it all the same, Lillie," Lillie's mama had replied, a small smile playing on her lips.

"It's perfect, mama. Can't I wear it now? For dinner, maybe?" Lillie's face lit up with anticipation, and her seven-year-old hands wanted to rip the dress from the hanger and toss it over her head right that moment.

"Nah, Lillie. It'll get ruined soon enough, and I don't want that happening before it even makes it out the door. Soon, baby girl, soon."

Lillie's mama swayed back and forth slightly in her rocking chair and gave Lillie a look that told her she understood, but also had meant what she said. Lillie knew enough not to push it.

Lillie's face fell, her gaze hitting the rotting wooden floor. "I sure wish Josie was gonna be going with me, mama… least I'd know someone."

"I know, Lillie, but the Finn kids got to be going elsewhere. Papa needs Ernest and Vera in the fields, and Eva's gotta help me with Caroline and the new baby coming soon. You'll see Josie after school sure enough." She'd nodded as though that settled that, and she continued mending the clothing she had at hand.

Lillie had nodded back, trying to hide her disappointment, knowing she was lucky to be going to school at all. Most of the other sharecroppers' kids, including her own older siblings, weren't going because their parents were desperate for the extra hands. So that just left Lillie who was going, and even that wasn't written in stone.

Lillie's mama looked up from the hemline she'd been working on and saw her daughter's fallen face. "Come here, girl," she said, beckoning Lillie into a warm embrace and stroking her back with her tired, calloused hands. Her mama's swollen belly drew a wedge in between them, but Lillie never minded. Any time with her mama alone was as special as catching a shooting star racing across the night sky. So, even if she had to share it with the little one yet to be born, Lillie just tried to enjoy every moment.

"Lillie, life just happens to some people different than others." Lillie's mama gently ran the back of her hand over Lillie's cheek. "That's just how it is, Lills, you'll make due." Lillie could sense the unsettled feeling in her mother's voice, and she sensed her mama wanted more than what she currently had to offer her children. Though she always made it sound as if she were completely satisfied with life on a farm, Lillie could tell she had an itch to be somewhere else, doing anything other than what she was doing. It was like she wrestled with who she was and who she wanted to be; and though she somehow knew deep down that the two might never meet, she still couldn't quite settle. She put on a brave face, but it didn't fool Lillie.

"Mama?" Lillie pulled out of her mother's hug and ran her fingers over the baby bump that projected outward at an awkward angle. Her mama giggled at the light touch and swatted Lillie's hand away.

"Yes, Lills?" She smiled down at her daughter with tired, weary eyes.

Lillie's hands fell south and landed on the garment her mama had been mending. She played with the fabric of the clothes in her mother's lap and eyed every line of stitch work.

"Can you show me how to sew like that?" Lillie asked. Her eyebrows arched upwards, hopeful she'd say yes, and that she might get more alone time with her mama in the process.

"Ah, Lillie, if I had the time, child. I'm about to be even busier once this baby comes. You ought to be asking Mrs. Finn. I'm sure she'd show you a thing or two here and there when you're visiting. Then maybe you can help me with some of this instead of some of the farming chores." She gestured to the pile of clothes that needed tending to.

"I wouldn't wanna bother her, mama." Lillie shook her head back and forth quickly, disappointed that her mama had said no, and thoroughly embarrassed at the thought of approaching Josie's mama.

"Lills, child, somehow I don't think you'd be a bother at all." She patted Lillie's back and shooed her off to bed shortly after.

Some years down the line Lillie realized what a gift her mama had given her that day by turning her down, though it hadn't felt like that at the time. Her mama knew she didn't have the time Lillie needed, so she pushed her to a place where she knew she'd be better loved. It was her mama's way of trying to get Lillie's foot out of the barn door.

Lillie hesitated for a few days, thinking about what her mama had suggested, but then she finally decided to be brave. She approached Mary Finn one afternoon as she was sewing on a button that had come loose off of Josie's sweater. Lillie stood tentatively in the doorway watching Mary's fast-flying fingers, and she was so mesmerized that she almost forgot why she'd come by. When Mary finished securing the button and cutting the thread with a small pair of scissors, Lillie saw her opportunity.

"Mrs. Finn?" Lillie said softly, trying both not to disturb her and to get her attention all the same.

"Oh, hello there, Lillie Mae. I didn't hear you and Josie come in! You're both usually such a ruckus!" She grinned at the small girl, but then noticed the blushed state of her small cheeks. Lillie was looking at the ground and wringing her small hands together into an imaginary knot.

"Oh no, Mrs. Finn, I, uh, Josie's not, I mean..." Lillie took a deep breath. "What I meant was that it's just me here..." She managed a look up at Mary's face, searching for a reply. "If that's okay..."

Mary's eyebrows flew up in surprise. "Lillie Mae Garrett, you are welcome in this house at any time, girl. No need for a reason!" Mary had a particular soft spot for Lillie. She'd noticed early on that there was something different about Lillie. It was probably the same thing that had drawn Josie to Lillie, something that neither Josie or her mama could ever put a finger on, and neither ever mentioned. Lillie had a little bit of light about her, a simpleness, and a sense of contentment that Mary mostly ever only saw on older folks that had lived a while. Somehow this awkward seven- year-old with unruly curly hair and curious eyes had figured out something many folks never did: how to be happy right where she was.

Sensing Lillie's discomfort, Mary patted the small footstool next to her chair and motioned Lillie her way. "Come here, girl. I think, though, you might have something on your mind?"

Lillie gulped a little too loudly and tried unsuccessfully to talk her cheeks into any shade other than beet red as she made her way towards the stool to sit.

"Well, I was noticing how good you are with that there needle and thread, and I was wondering if you might show me some time how you do all that," she said, motioning with her hand towards Mary's pile of handiwork. Quilts, dresses, socks, and linens all mounded together in a beautiful tapestry of fabrics and colors. "I asked my ma, but she said..."

Mary interrupted her. "Lillie, if you got the fire to learn, then I got the time to teach you. Besides, you'd really be doing me a favor. I could use a little help every now and then. I think you'd be an amazing assistant."

Lillie's face turned from red to beaming. "Really? Me?"

Mary placed her long arm around Lillie's tiny shoulders and pulled her in tight with a loving squeeze. "Lillie Mae, I couldn't think of anyone else I'd rather have, actually."

The truth was that Mary's own children had shown absolutely no interest in her work, and found most of her clientele too stuffy and difficult to work with. So Mary was tickled to her toes when Lillie had asked.

She found Lillie to be an eager student who couldn't seem to take her eyes off Mary's hands as they weaved up and down and her fingers moved in and out of cottons and linens and silks. Lillie loved how Mary made something so beautiful out of something that started so plain, and Mary loved that someone as plain as Lillie saw something so beautiful in her work.

Over time, Mary instilled in Lillie the value of a strong stitch and the art of biting one's tongue. She showed Lillie how to tailor a suit so that it looked as if a man was born to wear it, and she showed Lillie how to wear her own kind personality as if it were a fur coat to be treasured. If the school house was a place for learning about letters and counting, then Mary Finn's sewing shop was a place for learning about life and people. The lessons Lillie learned in Mary's little one-room shop on the northeast corner of Cedar and Main eventually became her survival guide, her only escort in a world full of madness, a beacon in the stormy night that would, in due course, become her life.

Lillie sat silently with her thoughts as Josie's carefree driving bumped her along the dirt road towards home. Josie's singsong voice sounded like sweet background noise, like someone had a radio on, but just ever so softly, quiet enough she couldn't quite make out the words. Lillie felt a bit unsettled, as she rarely ever let herself visit the past. She hardly saw the point, and she quite often found what was right in front of her much more interesting anyway. Likewise, she rarely thought about her destiny; and it suddenly occurred to her that it was a strange phenomenon not to give your future any consideration.

Lillie never had. What was destiny if not an already written life? If it was meant to be and God willed it, then who was she to question it? Though her mother had pushed her in Mary's direction, perhaps with the hope of setting her daughter free from farm life, Lillie had never had any intentions of pursuing anything more than mastering the art of dinner, sewing a flawlessly strong stitch, or perfecting the craft of canning the crop for the winter. She had started her work with Mary only moments after finishing school, and never thought twice about the path she might take after that. She'd learned from Mary that she could choose how she felt, that she was the owner of her emotions. But somehow, in all the time, and all the chats, and all the teaching, Lillie had failed to learn that she could choose her life, too. It was a crucial lesson that Lillie would come to regret missing.

This was the first time Lillie had given any bit of thought to what might happen to her, and an odd feeling washed over her body. What was she doing with her life?

Josie's truck ground to a halt on smooth new brakes, and Lillie found herself sitting in front of her parents' small, canary-yellow house. Her eyes were fixed on some small point on the pristine dashboard, and she was confused as to what Josie was chattering about. She couldn't even recall most of the ride home, come to think of it, and it was a frightening, unsettling feeling for Lillie, whose mind rarely wandered like that.

"Lillie? Lillie Mae! Girl, where is your mind at these days?" Josie spat out, exasperated. "If I didn't know better I'd guess you hadn't heard a word I'd said!"

"Oh, Josie, I'm sorry. I'm just tired, I suppose. I guess I could use a good day's break." Lillie opened the truck door and swung her short legs out with ease. Her feet hit the gravel driveway, and she turned around with a weary sigh and looked at her friend. "I'm real happy for you, Jos. Matthew seems like a fine man. I'm glad you're so happy with it all." Lillie pulled the corners of the collar of her coat together as she felt the cool air wrap its arms around her.

Josie's face softened as she looked at her tired friend and said, "Ah, Lillie, get some sleep. Spring's coming soon, and when the flowers bloom so do all the cute boys!"

Lillie laughed a tired chuckle at her friend's persistence in the boy department and said, "Night, Jos. Thanks for the ride home." She blew her friend a kiss and turned towards the house. She started up the gravel walkway as Josie's truck pulled out of the drive.

An ice-cold chill hit the side of Lillie's face and caught the bottom of her skirt, lifting it slightly in the air. It ran up and down her spine and raised goosebumps all over her cool white flesh. She wrapped her arms around herself and shivered a deep tremble, but not because she was cold. She shivered because of the bone-chilling suspicion that change was coming her way. Whether or not she was in want or need of it, it was imminent and approaching rapidly. Lillie looked upwards towards the clear winter Kentucky sky and stood there hugging herself, taking in the great celestial body that spread before her in all its glory. She exhaled a heavy deep breath and closed her eyes; then, in a whisper barely audible even to herself, she said, "I hear you, Lord. I'm ready."

Chapter Six

Catherine
Hazel Park, Michigan
Fall 1936

I wore a modest dress the day I married Jack, but it was made of fine silk and lace. It was borrowed, of course, from my mother's cousin June, whose dress had taken longer to make than her wedded bliss had lasted. I didn't care, though; it was new to me, and quite possibly the most exquisite fabric I'd ever felt. The ivory silk *crepe de Chine* was the exotic creamy white of an elephant's tusks and had a polished delicacy about it. My cousin June's father had spared no expense when he'd had it made in New York some ten years before, and I was more than happy to be the beneficiary of such quality taste. Everyone said how it complimented my steel-gray eyes and let my wavy locks take front stage, and I'll have take their word for it because all I really remember is how it made me feel. Hand-rolled silk rosettes graced the uneven hemline and swished against my lower calf as I walked, and I couldn't get enough of the sensation. The v-line of the neck showed just enough of my pale skin, but was cinched modestly with a hand-tied bow. More than anything, I was draped in happiness, the exquisite dress completed by a lovely, yet simple, veil that my aunt Rachel had begrudgingly purchased for me.

Our romance had taken off at a blinding rate, shocking not only ourselves, but most of our relatives as well. Aunt Rachel had earnestly, and quite selfishly, tried to dissuade me from my decision to marry Jack, but I could not be swayed. I wish I could say that Aunt Rachel was looking out for me, that her concern was genuine, but the truth is she was just looking to keep her free helper.

I, on the other hand, was looking for the exit, and Jack was my emancipator and champion, my white knight on the proverbial steed. He offered me adventure and a sense of freedom I had never known. He made Hazel Park, Michigan, feel more like Paris, France, or New

York City. He knew things I'd never heard of, things I never knew that I didn't know, and he opened doors inside me that I knew could never be shut again. It all happened in what seemed like a fraction of a moment.

Just six months had passed since I had opened my aunt's door to let Jack in with that hideous oversized chair, but I hadn't needed to think about it long when he'd offered up marriage. We had spent nearly every day together since our first date at the downtown dance, where I had shown him my finest Kentucky dance moves learned in barns and on dusty wooden shack floors. He, in turn, had swept me off my feet with his much more refined moves, moves he'd picked up from attending private school dances and city galas. He was debonair and charming, and I was a farmer's daughter looking for anything other than what I had known. He was refined yet adventurous, and I was feisty, and what some may call a bit plucky, and somehow it was a perfect pairing. Like a little bit of salt to go with your sweet, we seemed to bring out the flavors in each other, and together we created a wonderful palate of vivaciousness.

On the day I married him in August of 1936, I was ten days shy of my eighteenth birthday, and Jack was nearly thirty-two. I had been right on the day I'd met him in guessing he was older than me, but somehow that all faded away the more I got to know him. I didn't see a older man, I just saw him. While my parents didn't necessarily approve of such a hasty union, or of the large age gap, they also didn't exactly object. Aunt Rachel had brought mom and pop up by train for the ceremony, which, besides buying my veil, had been the only kind act she'd ever sent my way.

My humble parents sat amongst Hazel Park's higher society, incongruous with the handmade doilies and Italian glass vases filled with fresh-picked local flowers. God bless them, my mom and pop appeared to take no notice of such people or details. Pop told me later that they could only see their beautiful daughter, radiating love and looking as light on her feet as a feather—light like the French spun silk felt on my tiny hips.

In the end, my folks were satisfied with their youngest daughter's choice, and they bid us all the splendor that affairs of the heart can bring.

I had never even dated a boy before Jack, though it wasn't because none had been interested in me before him. I think deep down I always knew I wanted more than what the farmer's sons of the world had to offer. I felt incredibly blessed to have found such a good, kind, and hard-working man on my first shot at love, and also that he offered such an appealing way out of my aunt Rachel's home. I really loved him, with as much as an eighteen year old can know of love, and I felt truly happy when he placed that ring on my finger under the watch of a gangly Catholic priest. Before God and the church, my parents and his, and a room full of near-strangers, I vowed to love Jack until I drew my last breath. I intended to make good on that vow, too.

I knew I had no need to worry for my future with Jack, financially or otherwise. Jack's folks owned a furniture store in downtown Detroit that covered the gamut of anyone's needs so completely it was doing well despite the recession. Old and new, custom and antique, they sold it all. Jack had worked there from a very young age until his father asked him to become a partner in the family business some seven years before. I found out a few months after meeting him that Jack hadn't delivered furniture for over five years before the day he brought my aunt her chair. The shop's delivery boy had fallen ill, and Jack delivered it himself so as not to disappoint one of the Edens' best customers. After hearing that story, it almost felt like fate to me. Jack never delivered furniture anymore, yet he had, to me. I never gave men much mind before then, yet I had, to him. Fated to be together forever, or so I thought.

We started our life out better than most young couples, due in part to how established Jack already was. He wasn't new in his business, he had some money already saved up, and he knew the city of Detroit like the back of his hand. Our whirlwind courtship led to a whirlwind in the first few years of marriage. We bought a house in an up-and-coming suburb called Roseville, just east of Hazel Park and still close to downtown Detroit. Our small home was just blocks from the edge of Lake St. Clair, and we spent our summer months basking in the sun on its shores and playing in the cool waters of the numerous coves that dotted the margins of the picturesque scene. I could literally walk down to the docks in the summer any time I felt a need for a dip. Both the water and the people were always welcoming.

Jack was considered to be up there in age, as far as a first time father was concerned, but it didn't seem to bother him. Or I guessed it didn't bother him because, to be honest, we never even talked about it. We did all the same things that other young couples were doing. We frequented restaurants, we danced until our feet and our knees felt like jelly, we drank until the entire world was funny and the air smelled of roses and perfume. I was just enjoying my freedom for the first time in a long time, and it was a different freedom than what I had known in Kentucky. The air was saltier, and the vibe of Detroit was sassier. It seemed like it fit me like a glove, and it seemed like Jack had ordered up the world just to fit my liking. We didn't question much, and every day seemed to be a new adventure. I was simply happy.

Chapter Seven

Lillie
Tuesday, August 11, 1953

Lillie didn't have to wait long after her car ride home with Josie to find out what the universe had in store for her. A few weeks later, when February of 1929 had just turned to March, she ended up working late due to a particularly difficult client named Mrs. Prink. She had been especially picky this evening, and that had unknowingly changed the whole course of Lillie's life.

"Now don't you think this is just a tad too big, Lillie? I'm sure it was tighter when we'd done my first fitting," she said.

Lillie thought that if she was to find any more fabric to take in she'd need a magnifying glass to do it. Never mind the fact that Mrs. Prink had to wiggle herself to and fro to get the garment over her voluptuous torso in the first place. Mrs. Prink was never satisfied, even if Mary or Lillie did exactly what she'd asked. Sometimes she'd make up problems just for a reason to make a fuss and would say something like, "I don't know Mary, there just isn't enough lace showing, I'm just sure we talked about more lace showing. I couldn't possibly wear that dress as such!" Ever the stewards of professionalism, Mary and Lillie would respond in turn with "Mmm-hmmm, yes, I see, Ma'am. Of course, you're right. I'll see to it straight away. Tomorrow okay for pick-up?"

That night she was in top form and spitting arrows. "Mary's still under the weather, eh? Pity, really, surely she'd have had this hem right," Mrs. Prink said as she stared adoringly at her own reflection in the long mirror. Mrs. Prink had a particular fondness for Mary and a slight aversion for the sharecropper's daughter turned seamstress, even if Lillie's work was often times more intricate and of superior quality to Mary's. Yes, even in the case where the protégée had surpassed the mentor in skill, Lillie would never be able to outclass Mary socially.

"Yes, Ma'am," Lillie had responded kindly. "Surely."

The people who make you turn the other cheek are the ones who need you the most. Mary's words reverberated in her head. It was something she had recited to Lillie over and over. "Most folks don't even know they are throwing punches," she'd say. Mary's other favorite phrase was "We all pull up our skirts the same way, some people just have more lace showing when they are done getting dressed than others!" It had always made Lillie laugh, though she wasn't sure quite why. She supposed that Mary was trying to tell her that the only difference between people like Mrs. Prink and herself was perhaps a tad bit more of fancy on her dress. Give respect, get respect—everybody was the same in Mary's eyes. It was because of Mary that Lillie had learned how to deal with Franklin's top-drawer blue-bloods like Mrs. Prink, and anybody else who looked down their nose at her.

"You got to look pass your reflection in the glass, Lillie, and see them. Most folks are the same. Everybody just needs a little bit of love, a little bit of time, a little bit of attention. They just need to be seen." That was perhaps the one bit of advice that reflected who Mary was all in one moment. Mary really saw people, and she taught Lillie how to do the same.

"What if they don't see me back, Miss Mary?" a once wide-eyed ten-year-old Lillie had asked her.

"Well then, you just keep staring at them long enough until you see them standing there in their undies. Something so equalizing about folks in nothing but their underthings!" She'd laughed then, and pulled Lillie in tight for a big hug. "Lillie, you'll do just fine. Just remember who you are, even when they can't see past the glass image. You're just as good as any old fool who walks through that door. It doesn't much matter if they see it right away, what matters is if you feel it." Mary thumped Lillie's chest gently with two fingers. "In here, child, feel it in here."

Lillie thought about moments like those all the time, and she smiled to herself, remembering Mary's words, as she closed the shop door. She toyed with the key and lock until she was satisfied it had caught, then headed south towards Main Street, her mind heavy with just how she was going to take in any more fabric on Mrs. Prink's dress without the seams splitting. She thought about lying for a moment and just telling her she'd taken in the seam, but somehow Lillie didn't have it in her for even a little white lie.

Her arms were full with her satchel on one side and a mound of fabric on the other, and she fiddled with the ends of the cloth with unease. She crossed over Main and turned right down Cedar Street and headed towards W.S. Roark & Son General Merchandise Store to pick up a few items for her mama before going home, though she wasn't sure how she was going to carry it all. Mrs. Prink's painstaking demands had caused Lillie to miss her ride home, so she would have to walk the two and a quarter miles to the farmstead. The winter sun was quickly fading behind the hills, and watching it and its warmth disappear made Lillie regret not having worn an extra layer that morning.

She distractedly dodged a bit of traffic crossing College Street and waved apologetically at a motorist who nearly hit her. She was so entrenched in thought about her stitch work and Mrs. Prink's unrealistic requests that she completely forgot that the sidewalk running in front the general store was grossly uneven. She felt her toe catch on the break in the pavement just a moment too late, and she felt momentum pulling her forward and down. She instinctively let the fabric bundle go flying and she reached out to try to catch herself with her one free hand, but instead of saving herself from a nasty tumble, she was captured by the strongest grip she'd ever felt. The large, solid hand grabbed her under her upper arm and pulled her upwards slightly, just enough to save the skin on her palm and soften the blow to her hip. The hold on her arm surprised her more than the fall, and she let out a hefty, "Good Lord!"

"Nah, most people just call me Clay," came the response, and Lillie instantly laughed. She looked up from the ground where she was safely seated on her side, and her large brown eyes came to rest on the most intriguing face she'd ever seen. It wasn't a handsome or attractive face, nor was it vile or revolting. It was simply unembellished and ordinary, much like her own. In that moment between her laughter and her first glance at him, she knew. She knew she'd spend years staring up into that plain face with the muted smile that belonged to a tall and gangly gentleman with a large tuberous nose and long, wide ears that poked out just so. Clay had scooped Lillie off the sidewalk that day with the ease of a banker collecting a debt. She found her footing and stood as she smoothed out her dress as best she could. All the while she was sneaking peeks at the man who'd rescued her from a bad spill.

"Ah. Well then, you're even prettier standing upright," Clay said boldly.

48

Lillie felt a sensation she'd never known before. Her heart rate increased, and a feeling of warmth rose from her shoulders up to her cheeks. Boys had never paid her much mind in the past—but then, Lillie hadn't paid them much mind either. This man, though, was looking right at her, and she thought to herself that he saw her. He really saw her, just like Mary had talked about. Her breath quickened, and she felt moisture spread across her forehead and above her thin top lip, and even though the evening air was cool, she began to sweat. Lillie was speechless, and it was a rare occasion that she was without the right words. She finally managed to sputter, "Uh, um, thanks for breaking my fall. I guess I might'a busted a hip or something if you hadn't caught me."

"Nah, you're pretty close to the ground," he said, nonchalantly commenting on her short stature. "And besides, looks like you got yourself a good amount of cushion there anyhow." Clay reached down and patted Lillie's side, squeezing her just a bit as he touched her. While most women would have scolded him about how he ought not to touch or insult a lady like that, Lillie just laughed a ebullient laugh and wiped the perspiration off her forehead with her fingertips.

"True enough, I suppose," Lillie said between her laughter and her surprise at his boldness. "My mama always thought it was funny that I could barely reach the table, but I could always find a way to fill my tummy up full anyhow!"

Clay chuckled back, "Well, I like me a women with some plumpness. As I said before, name's Clayton, Clayton Woodard. Folks just call me Clay, though." He nodded at her, making their meeting official.

"Lillie Garrett. Nice to meet 'ya." She nodded back at him and smiled a smile that she couldn't seem to wipe off of her face. She felt like it had become permanently glued in place.

"Garrett, huh?" Clay paused a minuted and knitted his eyebrows, thinking. "Your family work the Finn farm?"

"Yup, my folks have been with the Finns for about twelve years now. Why? You know 'em?"

"Nah, just heard of 'em. Good people, I hear, the Finns." When Lillie nodded in agreement, Clay took it a step further. "They pay well, eh? Heard they let you keep half'a your crop earning. Must be mighty nice, I reckon."

Lillie hemmed and hedged uncomfortably as she felt her smile start to fade. She glanced at the ground and shuffled some dirt with the toe of her shoe. She cleared her throat and looked Clay in the eye. It was considered quite rude to be discussing money, but here this man just asked like he'd wanted to know the time of day. She suddenly felt very protective of the Finns, though she wasn't sure what she was protecting them from. At the same time, she admired Clay's boldness. It made her tummy flutter a bit.

"I suppose they are more generous than most… but I always leave all that to my daddy. I take it you work a farm also?" Lillie changed the subject; she didn't want the conversation to end, but she didn't want to get into a discussion on Josie and Mary's family either.

"Yup, expert farmhand, honorably tilling and plowing till my hands bleed, at your service, Ma'am." He sketched a low bow in Lillie's direction, as if he were a magician about to introduce his next trick. "Except we been working old man Adam's farm 'bout six or seven miles on the north side of town. Lived out on Harris School Road before that." No wonder she'd not seen him before, he'd likely been schooled in one of the small schoolhouses on the west side of Franklin. "Damned ole cuss of a man, that one is…"

Clay was brawny and feisty and everything that Lillie was not. He aroused her curiosity as if he were a priceless sculpture in a foreign museum, but Clay Paul Woodard was a piece of work of a different kind. And what Lillie didn't know was that looking up at his plain and ordinary face would quickly turn from a gaze of intrigue and love to one of tolerance—and, eventually, horrifying terror.

The reason Lillie knew that Clay was to be her husband someday in the very moment that they met were an enigma even to herself. Maybe even God knew no one else was built to take what Clay would eventually dish out. Maybe he knew that Lillie was the only one who'd be able to find the good in Clay. Even as he stood before her, flawed to the core, with the core itself rotting from the inside out, she hadn't seen his rotten bits. She'd only seen the red, shiny apple.

If she'd only known what a twisted path her life would end up taking, she might have made a choice to walk right past Clay that, day instead of idly accepting her tragic fate.

And the wind of change gently played once again with the hem of Lillie's skirt as she stood face-to-face with her future.

Chapter Eight

Catherine
Roseville, Michigan
June 1939

Things can change pretty quickly, and in the blink of an eye Jack and I were living a whole other kind of life than the one of those early years. I suppose it started when we made a trip to Franklin to see my mom and pop. That must have been around 1939, because we had been married almost three years by then and I'd figured a short jaunt home wouldn't do us any harm. My mom had been asking for a long time about when I was going to bring my new husband home to meet the rest of our family, and I somehow had put her off every time with some excuse or another. Jack was mine, and I guess I had wanted to keep him separate from the old place. Perhaps back then, though I'm not now, I was a tad embarrassed of where I'd come from. Though it seemed like a harmless decision at the time, that visit changed things for us more than I could ever have anticipated.

I drove into Franklin with Jack by my side, and though it looked just the same as I'd left it, it felt completely different. It was as though someone had left the backdrop the same but changed out all the scenery. Even the air smelled different. Instead of the fresh country air I had always remembered, it just smelled old and musty. I was prepared for it to feel a bit different, as I had been away for quite a few years at that point, but I wasn't prepared for what I found at my parents' house.

We pulled into the dirt driveway, and I knew from the moment I laid eyes on my mom and pop's home that something wasn't right within. The outside whispered at the secrets that lay inside, and it wasn't telling a very nice story. Weeds poked through the small concrete slabs that made up the walkway to the front door, and it was apparent that they weren't satisfied with just taking over there. They had invaded my mom's flower beds and were scattered all over the grass as though they'd been purposely planted there. The shingles were missing in several places, and the paint was sadly chipping off most of the siding of the house. To be honest, it looked abandoned, and I thought for a moment that perhaps my mother had forgotten to tell me they'd moved; but then I saw the curtain pull to the side and my mother's small face peeking out at us. I had the sinking feeling that I shouldn't have come, or perhaps that I should have come sooner—but, either way, it was too late. She'd seen us, and there was nothing left to do but hide my shame and hold my husband's hand as we walked over the weed-covered pavement up to the door and knocked.

My mother was not the mom I had seen just a few years prior at my wedding. She had aged significantly, and walked in the stooped way that I think of old people walking. She was in her late forties, but she looked at least sixty. Her auburn hair had turned completely white, and her smile lines had been etched in as if someone had purposely drawn them on for a more dramatic effect. I wasn't at all sure how it was possible that someone could age that much in such a short amount of time, and she looked so frail that I was afraid to hug her for fear of breaking something.

As I embraced my mom, my eyes met my father's over her shoulder and he quietly nodded at me, acknowledging that what I was seeing was indeed real. Then he raised his eyebrows and gave me three small nods, and I knew he was at a loss for what to do to help her. He stepped forward and pulled me into a hug and whispered in my ear, "My, how we've needed this. How we've needed to see you." I said nothing; it was the first time I'd ever felt that needed by them, and I had no idea how to respond.

My mom pretended all was well during our visit, and she bustled about as any host might do. I could tell she'd cleaned up for us, but the inside of her home told just as sad a story as the outside had. The corners held dust bunnies and the baseboards were dirty and scuffed, things that were once considered abhorrent by my mother's standards back in our small farm house. My mom had given up. She'd quit living and she'd started dying even more than she had when my brother had died, although nothing was really wrong with her medically. Migraines, my pop told me later that night, bad ones, ones that would lay her up for days, apparently. Dr. Goodwin down at the hospital couldn't seem to help her get a handle on them, and everything he'd tried had just sedated her to the point of stupor.

My pop had to work, and my two sisters who were still living in

Franklin had their own lives in such messes that they couldn't really help my mom even if they'd wanted to. I was in my parent's home less than twenty-four hours and I knew what had to be done. I knew I had to ask my husband for the biggest favor I'd ever asked of him, and for the first time ever, I had no idea how he'd react. It was also the first time I'd been afraid of him.

We moved my parents up to Michigan two months after our visit home, and they surprised us with how nicely they settled in. They were staying with my aunt Rachel as a temporary solution, though I never could understand how my mom and pop could stand her. It was sort of the only option, and I think they knew that so they didn't make much fuss. Besides, Rachel was my mom's sister, and she probably knew how to handle her a lot better than I. My home was too small, and besides that, while Jack had agreed it was indeed best to get my folks out of Franklin and get my mom some better help, he had been adamantly against them staying with us. I was so happy he'd agreed to help move them that I took the deal, conditions and all.

I was surprisingly thrilled to have my mom and pop near me again, and I hadn't realized how much I'd missed them until they were around again. Michigan seemed to agree with my mom, and she slowly seemed to start feeling better. Her migraines came less and less, or at least she let them beat her down with a little less vigor. Perhaps it was the change of scenery, or fewer allergens, or maybe even being near her sister Rachel and her beautiful home—though God only knows why she'd enjoy that—but it changed my mom in some way. Though her hair remained the white of a lady many years older than she was, my mom's face softened somehow and relaxed, and the deep furrows of her wrinkles were less visible. It had been a good decision for them to come back with me.

The toll it took on my marriage, though, is a whole other thing entirely. We had been free of obligation up until then, free to do whatever we'd wanted. Suddenly we were driving my mom to doctor's appointments and hair appointments, and taking my parents to the beach with us on weekends. We fell into a more domestic situation than either of us had ever talked about. Instead of theater shows and movies, we stayed in and caught radio shows with my parents. Instead of late nights dancing and drinking, we were entertaining my parents over very traditional family suppers and playing rummy. And boy those suppers changed everything in a way I never knew a meal could do.

Every few times we'd have them over, my mother would look Jack in the eye and ask him, "So, Jack, when are you going to give my daughter some children? She's not getting any younger, you know."

Jack, the charming man he was, would shoot back kindly, "Now Mattie, I think it's me who isn't getting any younger, and I'm quite sure the time will be right soon enough." Then he'd tip back his whiskey a little harder than I thought was necessary and pour himself a second round. The mysteriousness of it would appease my mom until a month later, when she'd ask again.

Month after month this went on until one day, a little over a year after they'd moved up to Michigan, my mom's question planted a seed in my mind as well. When would we have children? I was already twenty-two and had been married for four years. It was almost unheard of not to be at least trying to have kids where I came from in Kentucky, though Detroit seemed a bit more lenient about such things. It made me wonder what Jack really thought about children, and why we hadn't ever really talked about it.

I mulled over the thought of children for a few months before I approached Jack, because I knew it wasn't going to be a short conversation, nor an easy one; otherwise he'd have started it up himself some time ago. I had wondered, too, if there wasn't something wrong with me anyway, as we hadn't exactly *not* being trying either. Our romance had blossomed fast, and for the first few years the fires had run as hot as coal. All Jack had to do was brush his sweet full lips over mine and I was a mushy mess of a woman, the kind I'd sworn I'd never be. So, between the fact that it hadn't accidentally happened, whether in conversation or in actuality, I wondered what Jack really thought about me becoming pregnant, or if he ever thought of it at all. I suppose it's something we ought to have discussed prior to exchanging vows, but to be honest, at that time in my life it had been the furthest thing from my mind.

So I sat on my thoughts until I was sure myself what I wanted, and was also sure of the words I wanted to say; and finally, one night in late February of 1941, it just seemed like the perfect moment. My folks had been over for dinner again, and the more they were around the more sure I was that family life was where my heart was. I loved cooking for them and for Jack, and I loved having my house full of the people I loved as well. The nights when it was just Jack and me felt empty somehow, like the ghosts of our future children were wandering the room wondering when we'd give them life and a place at our table.

That night I felt them linger there, those figments of my imagination, as I lay with my feet in Jack's lap while he massaged my soles with his thumbs. We had lit a fire; the temperatures had just screamed for the toasty crackling of it, and I wanted it to be a nice and calm environment for what I had to say to him.

Like so many things in life, your best intentions don't always mean you will achieve the result you are looking for. In fact I'd blown my whole speech right from the start by absentmindedly blurting out, "Jack, do you ever wonder what our children will look like?" It was as if someone else in the room had said it, but it was me; and the minute I realized what I had asked I knew I'd had too much wine, and I wished I could take it back.

I felt his whole body stiffen under me, and he stopped rubbing my feet and stared at me like he'd never seen me before. Like I was some stranger who'd walked into his house and asked him what size boxer trunks he preferred. Then he slowly broke into his million-dollar Cheshire cat grin and started laughing. "Why like me, of course!" I relaxed a little bit with his laughter and familiar sense of humor and was so relieved to find he wasn't mad to talk about it. And in my confusion over his unexpected reaction, the rest of my speech flew right out of my head and I blurted out my next big blunder.

"So we can try, then?" I pushed myself up on my elbows to look at him, and my eyes felt wide and bright like when a child stands in front of you anticipating what gift is in the pretty box with the big red bow on top. I felt Jack stiffen again, but this time he gently removed my feet from his lap and got up to cross the room to the small wet bar we had in the corner. He didn't say a word, and I sat there watching him pour his heaviest glass of whiskey yet and gulp it down in five large swigs. He placed the glass down harder than he'd meant to, and it made a loud bang that startled us both. This was the reaction I'd expected, and I wished I had had more and not less wine at dinner.

He turned around slowly and crossed his arms in front of him like a businessman who wasn't going to budge a bit on a deal. "Well now, Catherine, I didn't exactly say that, did I?" We stayed like that in silence for what felt like forever. Him leaning into the bar with his eyebrows twisted in a knot and his arms across his chest and me sitting on my knees on the couch ten feet away, the coffee table, some knickknacks, and a rug lost in the abyss in between us. The clock on the wall broke the silence when it chimed the ten o'clock hour, and it busted open my signature feistiness and dumped even more out of my mouth.

"Jack Edens!" I was screaming, and I was scaring myself. "Are you telling me you don't want children? That you married me knowing you didn't want children?" The pitch of my words had risen significantly as I spoke, and I sounded like a small child begging for a lollipop. I stood myself up then and felt my fists balling up at my sides, and I was starting to lob more words at him when he surprised me by bursting into the loudest laughter I'd ever heard. Laughter that I did not find amusing.

"Now you're laughing at me," I'd said. "Perfect, just perfect. Here I am trying to talk to you about having children and you're laughing at me." His laughter just continued, and it looked as though he was trying to say something in between his heavy breaths but just couldn't form the words. I was angrier than I had ever been at him, and a wet hen had nothing on me that night. I was also paralyzed. I mean, what do you do when the man you love just laughs himself silly while you're trying discuss a big part of your future? For a split second I thought about throwing something at him, like the glass ashtray his mother had given us as an anniversary present last year, but I decided I could keep some kind of dignity about me even in the face of complete and utter humiliation.

"What on earth are you laughing about, Jack? I mean, seriously." I was demanding an answer now, and with his face as red as the brick surround on the fireplace, he wiped his eyes and then threw his hands up in the air in surrender.

"Oh, Catherine, you ought to have seen yourself just now, I've never seen you that upset!" He started laughing again until he caught my glare and said instead, "It was just cute is all, you were cute." Then I was the one confused and crossing my arms. I had never felt so puzzled in all my life. What on earth was happening here?

He slowly crossed the room towards me with his hands up, I suppose to potentially protect himself from my wrath, and he pulled my arms out of their angry crisscross and held my hands in front of us. "If you want to try, we can try. I've got no problem with that, love." I felt the air leave me, and then I was the one laughing and hugging him and crying. I'd definitely had too much wine, and my next thought had been, *what better time than the present to start giving it a whirl?* That's how it was with Jack and I. Fire and ice, wind and rain, laughter and tears. And then, eventually, just the tears.

Chapter Nine

Lillie
Tuesday, August 11, 1953
8:30 p.m.

"I don't know, Flora. Seems as though my father's more in love with him than I am!" Lillie's nurse said to another young nurse.

"He's a good man, Elizabeth. We should all be so lucky. He'll get you outta this hellhole in a minute! I heard he does a lot of work out of Nashville. Nashville, Elizabeth! Can you imagine?" Flora was obviously taken with Elizabeth's new beau, though she'd never even met him.

"I know it. He actually took me down there a couple weekends back. It is a nice city..." Elizabeth's voice trailed off as if she immediately wished she hadn't shared with Flora, the hospital's biggest gossip.

"What! Why on earth would you not tell me that? Oh, he's getting serious alright. You need to get on board, girl, 'fore that train leaves without you!" Flora snapped at Elizabeth, and then Lillie heard a name being called with an angry shout.

"Flora, really! It doesn't take two of you!" It was the shift supervisor, and she wasn't happy. Lillie heard Flora's heavy feet swiftly lead her away from her bed and down the hall.

Lillie heard the young girl sigh. The nurse with the kind and gentle hands. Hadn't she given Lillie a bath last week? Lillie couldn't remember exactly, but she was sure she'd liked her. So her name was Elizabeth. Lillie couldn't quite remember before.

The young nurse spoke again to the almost empty room. "But what if I don't like where that train is going?"

Lillie heard water being poured from a pitcher into a basin. Elizabeth was going to bathe her again, Lord bless her. Maybe she could drown the ants. Lillie felt her sheet being pulled back and her thin gown being partially removed from her arm. The warm air hitting her skin felt better than the scratchy sheets, and Lillie was grateful for the little bit of reprieve that it offered. She felt Elizabeth take a cool cloth to her shoulder and under her arm, and Lillie pictured a million tiny ants washing out to sea on a large foamy wave. Drown them. Please. One by one let them drown.

"I suppose they are right, though, he is a nice enough man," Elizabeth sighed as she spoke to Lillie's sleeping face in a quiet voice. "My daddy must know better than me." She pulled the cloth gingerly over Lillie's elbow and down towards her hands. "But Nashville? Can you imagine?"

"Don't," Lillie whispered. Elizabeth jumped a foot backwards, hitting the tray that held the basin and causing the water to wobble gently up and down the sides of the bowl like a clock pendulum. Some water hit the floor with a large plop and made its way towards the bed on the uneven white penny tile.

"Oh, my gosh! I'm so sorry, Miss Lillie, did I hurt you?" Elizabeth approached the bed cautiously and placed a kind hand on Lillie's gnarled knuckles.

"No, child." Her eyes fluttered open and she stared at Elizabeth's face. It was beautiful and young, and carried none of the scars that Lillie's did. It was innocent, and Lillie could see the hope she held for her future, a future that Elizabeth thought about all the time; and Lillie couldn't help but think about what a contrast that was to how she had been at Elizabeth's age.

"No, don't do that." She hadn't spoken for days, and her voice came out in a garbled murmur.

"I can just wash your face, Miss Lillie, and be done, if you want." Elizabeth knitted her eyebrows with confusion and concern and then searched Lillie's eyes for an answer. She never liked to cause discomfort even though it was often part of the job, and Lillie had been through so much already.

Lillie cleared her throat with a wild hacking sound that made Elizabeth cringe slightly. "No, I like the bathing." Lillie sighed and caught her breath. Where had all the oxygen in the room gone? She looked Elizabeth in the eye and said, in the clearest voice she'd heard come out of her mouth in a long time, "Don't let life just happen to you."

Elizabeth stopped moving. "How do you, I mean, hmm? How do you mean?" she asked through a cracked voice. Was it possible Lillie had heard her before?

"That boy. Nashville. You be sure about both 'fore you go ridin' off into the sunset. It's a long life, Elizabeth, or at least it should'a been." Lillie held Elizabeth's gaze as she continued to study her young face.

"I'm sorry, I didn't know you could hear us, me, I mean. I didn't realize..." her voice trailed off as she thought about all the other various conversations the staff had shared at Lillie's bedside the last few days. And all the comments the others had made at Lillie's expense. Elizabeth drop her hands by her sides and hung her head.

"It's okay," Lillie said quietly.

"No, it's not. All those things we said, we were just making conversation. I really am so sorry." Elizabeth found the short white stool meant for the doctors and slid it up by Lillie's side. She took Lillie's hand and sandwiched it between her palms. "Truly..."

"They weren't lies, Elizabeth." Lillie closed her eyes and tried to slow her quickened breaths. Really. Where had all the air gone? She imagined some swirling vortex in the ceiling, sucking up all the oxygen and spitting back black smoke. At least it felt like black smoke in her lungs, burning them with every inhale.

"How do you mean, Miss Lillie?"

"What you said about me," Lillie explained. Goddamn burning. "None of it is lies, so what 'ya got to be sorry for?" She took a deep breath in and opened her eyes again, turning her head gingerly in Elizabeth's direction. "You were just speaking the truth, and you ain't ever have to apologize for the truth."

A small smile found Elizabeth's small thin lips. "My mama used to say something like that," Elizabeth said. "She said there are three things that can't be hidden—the sun, the moon, and the truth. Said she'd heard that somewhere, some old proverb or something, and it had rung so true that she never forgot it."

"Your mama," deep breath in, "is a smart woman," deep breath out. Lillie stared up at the ceiling, trying to pace her breathing.

"Was. She sure was. She passed some years back." Elizabeth placed her a hand lightly on Lillie's chest. "Easy now Lillie, easy. Just in and out real nice-like. Here, like me..." She breathed with her for a few moments and continued on when she thought Lillie's breaths had calmed. "I can hardly remember her some days, but then something she used to say just wiggles its way back up and its like she's standing right before me shaking her long, skinny finger in my face with her dirty dishtowel in the other hand. Lord, she was beautiful..."

"So sorry, child." Breathe. "Shame." Why did it burn so? "Would your mama have liked your fella?" Lillie asked Elizabeth. Big billowing smoke in her lungs. It would choke her soon.

Elizabeth laughed. "I think mama would'a liked any fellow who took me off their hands. There's ten of us, 'ya know!"

Lillie chuckled weakly. "I right felt like that some days." Breathe. "But then the next day you want to hold 'em tight and never let 'em go."

"I can imagine!" Elizabeth shifted uncomfortably on the narrow stool and softly cleared her throat. "She died here. Well..." she gestured to the room next door, "in there actually. She got the fevers two days after having my youngest sister, and was gone in just a few days. Infection took her fast. It was awful..." Elizabeth stopped herself and stood up quickly, wringing her hands. "Oh, listen to me, Miss Lillie, I'm just rattling on about my sorry life when you are lying here so uncomfortable."

"The bathing helps." Lillie lifted her hand slightly off the bed and motioned towards the basin. Drown those damn ants and the smoke, Lord plug that vortex. Please Elizabeth, please.

"Oh certainly! Long as you like, if it feels good."

Lillie was getting sleepy. "Does feel good, it does, it drowns them..." her eyes closed slowly.

"Drowns what?" Elizabeth looked down at Lillie's face and realized she fallen back into sleep. She stared at her. A simple face, uncomplicated, and straightforward, and honest. A face you like pretty quickly once you get to chatting with it. A face too old for its forty-four years. She ran her hand over Lillie's matted hair and down the side of her cheek. Huh, so soft. Soft for a face that had seen a rough life, an unexpected find for sure. And curious, Lord, was this woman curious. What on earth had happened to her?

Elizabeth's thoughts raced from her mother's memories to the mother of seven lying before her. "Just sleep, Miss Lillie, and I'll drown whatever needs drowning for as long as you need. I'm not going anywhere."

Chapter Ten

Catherine
Roseville, Michigan
December 1941

Later in the year, some ten months later, to be exact, our whole world changed. It's funny how the question "Where were you when you found out?" has such a different meaning depending on the subject matter. Oh, how I wish I were talking about a pregnancy and a subsequent bundle of joy. I remember the day our world changed because anyone who is alive and was over the age of five at the time will always remember it too.

It was a Sunday, and I was home alone because Jack had decided there was one thing or another that needed to be worked on in the shop. It was a tactic he'd been employing the last few months to get out of dinner with my folks again. It was just after 2:30 in the afternoon and I was vacuuming my living room for the second time that day, probably out of boredom, or a need to occupy my mind with something other than why I wasn't pregnant already. Either that or I was trying not to think about how much Jack's drinking had taken a turn for the worse. I can't really remember why exactly, I just knew I had to have really clean carpets.

I had the radio on in the background, and though I couldn't make out what was being said on the afternoon show because of the noise of my Hoover, the fact that it was on made me feel a little less lonely. It was December and cold out, with the first of the season's good snow on the ground, which made going outside extremely unappealing. Unless, of course, you are Jack, and your in-laws are coming over in a few hours, because then it's perfectly normal to trudge out in the bitter cold. I finished vacuuming the rug in the living room and shut off the switch, and as I grabbed the cord to wrap it up, the chatter on the radio clicked on in my head like a light.

"*Hello, NBC. Hello, NBC. This is KTU in Honolulu, Hawaii. I am speaking from the roof of the Advertiser Publishing Company Building. We have witnessed this morning the distant view a brief full battle of Pearl Harbor and the severe bombing of Pearl Harbor by enemy planes, undoubtedly Japanese. The city of Honolulu has also been attacked and considerable damage done."*

I dropped the vacuum cord on the floor and stood motionless as the announcer continued. *"This battle has been going on for nearly three hours. One of the bombs dropped within fifty feet of KTU tower. It is no joke. It is a real war."*

America was at war. There was no doubt in my mind, how could there be? Still, I didn't want to believe what I knew to be true.

My older brother, my *only* brother, was stationed in Hawaii with the Army Air Corps as a mechanic, and though I wasn't sure exactly where he was, I knew there was a distinct possibility he was in danger. People were dying in Hawaii as the minutes ticked by. They were dying on American soil, and most of them were sailors just docked in a quiet harbor, enjoying the peacefulness of a beautiful Sunday morning. One of them could very well have been my brother. I remember standing there, frozen to the shag rug, feeling unable to breathe and feeling like the world around me was literally crumbling. All I could selfishly think was how my mother couldn't possibly survive the loss of another son.

I'm not sure how long I stood there, not moving and just listening to the crackly static of the man on top of the advertising building who was giving us his firsthand view of what was happening.

"The public of Honolulu has been advised to keep in their homes and away from the Army and Navy. There has been serious fighting going on in the air and in the sea. The heavy shooting seems to be…a little interruption. We cannot estimate just how much damage has been done, but it has been a very severe attack. The navy and army appear now to have the air and the sea under control."

A telephone operator interrupted him then in order to place an emergency call, and I hadn't even realized I had tears running down my cheeks and onto my clothing, wetting the front of my dress. I suddenly heard a frantic knock at my door, and it brought me out of my trance and into another sobering reality. My neighbor Susan, whose cousin Gene was in the navy and docked in Hawaii often, was beside herself with grief. I opened my door just a smidgen before she embraced me hard and started sobbing. I led her from the doorway to the couch where we sat down, holding hands and crying. Neither of us made a move to turn down the radio even though the announcements were so gruesome.

The official broadcast that came later confirmed it.

"We interrupt this program to bring you a special news bulletin. The Japanese have attacked Pearl Harbor, Hawaii, by air, President Roosevelt has just announced... A Japanese attack upon Pearl Harbor naturally would mean war. Such an attack naturally would bring a counterattack, and hostilities of this kind would naturally mean that the president would ask Congress for a declaration of war. There is no doubt from the temper of Congress, that such a declaration would be granted."

Jack came home some time in that hour and immediately turned up the radio, which prompted me to walk Susan home and sit with her there until her husband arrived back from his job at the hardware store a few moments later and I felt it was prudent to leave her. When I came back to my house I was struck by the obvious odor of alcohol that lingered in the air and wafted off of my husband's skin. He had no more been at the store than I had—and yet, in that moment, I didn't really care where he'd been. It just wasn't important. The chatter on the radio translated to vivid images in my mind of what had occurred, and it wasn't long before I had to leave the room. It seems it was as bad as the original radio announcer had said—and possibly even worse—and my brother lingered in my mind. I didn't have the heart to call my mom. I just prayed she was perhaps napping and hadn't yet heard.

I busied myself in the kitchen, trying to pretend it was just a Sunday like any other and that the bombing of Pearl Harbor was just a mistake, an isolated tragedy. I willed my brother to be okay. As I began chopping the onions and carrots for my beef stew, I knew it meant our men and women were going to be asked to do things that would change their lives forever, and I had no idea just how much it would change mine as well.

My immediate concern beyond my mom and brother was Jack and whether he'd possibly be drafted if it came to that. He'd already served two uneventful years when he was just nineteen, though he hadn't gone further than a few states over for his training and duty station. At least that would buy him some time. Jack always joked about his time in the army and said it was his dad's way of not having to pay company money to get him up to snuff to help run the family business because the army would do that for him. A few years after he'd gotten out, Jack was asked to be a partner in his parents' business, and his life had been the furniture store ever since. He hardly ever talked about his service time, or why he had decided that two years was enough, but I would find out soon enough. I would find out more than I ever wanted to know.

The word soon came that my brother was okay, and with the news came mountains of relief. I think my mom all but collapsed upon hearing he was fine. Still, I worried. Like every other wife and mother and sister and daughter on my street I worried that the man in my life would be forced to go overseas and fight an inconceivable monster of an enemy. I worried I'd be widowed if he went, but on the other hand, I worried I'd be divorced if he didn't. I was worried about the war brewing overseas and the war beginning to brew in my home as well. Things weren't quite as rosy as they had once been in my marriage. There were a lot of reasons, I suppose, but it started with my lack of ability to get pregnant, or at least that's what I thought started it. At first trying to have a baby had been fun, as any young couple could imagine, and we made good sport of it. In fact, if relations with your husband could be a sport in the Olympic games, we'd have surely won gold. However, seven or eight months into our efforts we had started to find it a tad tedious, and not such a fun game anymore.

I came from a long line of fertile women. Both of my grandmothers had ten children, and my mother had seven. There were no miscarriages or stillbirths to speak of, which in those years was nearly unheard of. Many of my mother and grandmother's friends had experienced either one or the other, and repeatedly. So I was absolutely convinced that it wasn't me, and couldn't possibly be anything other than a problem with Jack. He was the older one after all, almost thirty-seven years old, and I was only twenty-three. But how do you tell your very confident and masculine husband that you think there is something amiss with his ability to father children? No matter how delicately you approach it, it doesn't tend to go over well.

"Jack," I'd said one night at dinner about a month before the news of Pearl Harbor had broken, "Do you think maybe a doctor could help us?" I was tired, and my face showed it. I had bags under my eyes where none had ever been before, and I could feel the fight in me starting to slip. No one had ever told me that making a baby might be so much work.

"Help us with what?" He'd been smug and tried to blow off the subject before I even got started.

"You know with what. Our bedroom problems." I hadn't been able say it out loud because then it was really a problem.

"We have a problem in the bedroom? Ask anyone around, Jack Edens has no problems when it comes to the bedroom." He tried to make a joke of it as he smirked at me.

"Jack, I'm serious. Maybe you could go to the doctor? See if they think something is wrong? I mean, it's been nine months already and nothing…and all the years before that too." I really just couldn't say it out loud. I couldn't say, 'And I'm still not pregnant.'

"Oh, Catherine, you worry so. It will happen when it happens. It's in God's hands darling, nothing a doctor is going to change." He seemed done with the conversation, and I had the thought that it seemed a bit desperate for a very non-religious man to reference our great Creator's master plan.

"In God's hands? Really Jack, I…" He interrupted me then, something he rarely did because he considered it the rudest of poor manners, and simply said, "No, Catherine. I will not see a doctor. But feel free to have yourself looked at if you are that concerned." He left me sitting alone at the table then, his plate half full of mashed potatoes and meat-loaf, and I couldn't touch another bite. Something was more wrong than I had thought, and I'm not talking about our inability to procreate.

I didn't push him on the topic, but I also didn't see a need to have myself "looked at" as Jack had suggested. My monthly cycles were as right as rain; every twenty-eight days when my menses started the disappointment crushed all of my hope. It just couldn't be me. So I focused instead on wooing him every month, and he responded in a way I never imagined. He would indulge me and then get up, get dressed, and drink by himself long into the night. This went on for many months, and the tension around the subject of having children grew as much as the tension around the idea of Jack being drafted. I lived in a state of fear daily and then a state of utter disappointment every month when I would start to bleed. I just couldn't believe what was happening—or not happening, I suppose.

And then something did happen. Two things actually. Two things that sent Jack and me on a collision course with disaster and then on another road out of Michigan. I suppose I'll start with Jack's best friend, because that is the lesser of the two painful memories for me. Jerry Graham had been in Jack's life since the two were nothing but two feet tall, and had been a part of our lives since the beginning of our romance. He was like a brother to me in many ways, and I had the utmost respect for him and his family of five. Jerry and Jack had been neighbors their entire lives and Jerry had ended up owning a mechanic shop just a block from the Edens' furniture shop, so the boys often shared their lunchtime in downtown Detroit together.

That was, until Jerry's draft letter came, requesting politely that he report for duty. Jack had the advantage of having previously served on his side, which put him down at the bottom of the list of possible draftees, but Jerry had never served. He'd never even left Detroit before. He did obviously leave eventually, though. In the fall of 1942, the Fifth Air Force swept him away in the wind. In the spring of 1943, just after the Battle of the Bismarck Sea, there came a knock on the door, just as it had come to thousands of doors across the country, and with it came a telegram.

If Jack had been beside himself when Jerry had left, then he was outside of himself when Jerry was killed. The stiff drinks that once made our forced lovemaking bearable for him eventually turned into a way to ease his worry over his best friend being overseas, and then became a way to drown his grief entirely. I watched it slowly progress. One drink became two, then the first drink was earlier in the day than the day before, and I found myself waiting for the day Jack asked for whiskey instead of orange juice at the breakfast table, because I was just sure it was coming.

The other thing that happened nearly killed me and almost shoved my already struggling marriage into the grave headfirst. It was about a month after we'd attended Jerry's funeral, and a few months over two years since Jack had agreed to try to have children. That night when I'd screamed so passionately at him seemed like decades before. Now I was just trying desperately to cheer Jack up from his all too familiar morose inclinations. I'd gone to the supermarket to find something to surprise him with for dinner. I went there for steaks and I came home wanting to pull up stakes and run as far away from Jack as I could. Life can change so very fast, and all you think you know can be challenged even by something as simple as trip to the grocer's for a cut of beef.

When I arrived at the shop it was a bit crowded, and the meat counter was particularly packed. I took a number off the board and decided to wander down the other side of the aisle where they kept the oils and spices. I thought maybe a new flavor could jazz things up. As if that's all my marriage needed, a new rub for the cheap cut I was about to purchase. If the saying that the fastest way to a man's heart is through his stomach was true, then I was at the least going to try to take the fast track, and I needed some new and amazing spice to get me there. I was lost in the assortment of tiny bottles from which to choose, and I needed something far beyond my standard allspice and salt and pepper. As I looked up and down the small spice section for something exciting, I heard a very familiar voice, and it struck me as odd because she was almost whispering. I soon found out why her tone was so quiet, and it wasn't because she was discussing politics with her girlfriend.

"Good Lord! That's horrible! Do you think she knows? Well, she's a smart woman, she must know." They had my attention. I mean, anytime someone is whispering I think it makes you more and not less likely to try to tune in and overhear something juicy. It's got to be good if they are trying to be that shushed about it.

"But why the ruse, then? Why wouldn't she just be honest about it?" It was my neighbor, Sally. The one I'd embraced so heartily when she stood on my doorstep on the day Pearl Harbor had been bombed some eighteen months before while we cried because she thought she'd lost her cousin and I thought I'd lost my brother. Turns out she hadn't; he'd also been spared. I had almost stepped around the aisle to say hello and perhaps to see who they were discussing when I heard exactly who they were talking about.

It was Ruby who spoke next, Sally's sidekick and another of my neighbors. "Well, maybe she doesn't know. I mean, Jack Edens. I never would have guessed he'd be the sterile kind. I mean, he's just so manly!" Her tone had risen, and Sally made a shushing sound as my knees went weak underneath me. What had she said? Sterile? What did that mean?

"It's true," Sally continued. "My cousin Gene who's been in the navy forever heard it from his buddy who knew Jack from his army days. Apparently Jack was medically released after having got the mumps in his barracks." My blood ran cold, and I had to grip the shelf to stay standing. He'd never mentioned to me that he'd once had the mumps, nor that his leaving the army hadn't been his own choice.

"But I don't get it, Sal, why would that make him infertile? The mumps. My brother had it once and he's got five kids." Ruby was rubbing salt into a quickly opening wound.

"Well, I guess it's really rare, but sometimes when boys get the mumps it makes their…" She stopped, perhaps finally realizing that her location wasn't exactly appropriate for such a topic. I silently willed her to continue, my knuckles white from gripping the shelving unit so hard. I had to hear the rest. She continued, and I had to really strain to hear because she had lowered her voice significantly. "Well, sometimes their manly parts get just as hot and swollen as their airways, and though I guess it's rare, sometimes it can leave a man sterile."

"My goodness, that's awful. But how does Gene know that Jack's the one who's sterile? Maybe it isn't Jack. Maybe Catherine's the reason they haven't had a baby yet."

"Well now, Ruby, that's the other part to the story. Catherine's not the first woman that Jack's had this problem with. Apparently Jack had gotten himself tested after his first wife couldn't conceive."

She kept talking, but all I heard was a muffled sound in my ears like someone had covered them with earmuffs, and all I saw was a blackness that started around the edges, a blackness moving in towards the center of my visual field. All I tasted was my bile rising in my throat; and all I felt was nothing and everything. Then I felt pain as I hit the hardwood floor with a huge cracking sound and the two gossiping hens finally shut up.

Chapter Eleven

Catherine
Roseville, Michigan
May 1943

How quickly we unraveled then, Jack and I. Fire and ice quickly become a solid iceberg. I hadn't asked Jack about it right away, mostly because I didn't really know what to say, and I wasn't sure if he'd be honest about it anyway. It wasn't just his deceit that bothered me. His family knew as well, though perhaps not about the infertile part of things; they surely knew he'd been married before, and yet there had never been a word said about it. I was shocked too that my aunt Rachel hadn't known, given that she knew the background of just about every person around. How could she not have told me? It turns out that Jack was more a master of concealment than I had thought.

I set out to prove Sally and her cousin Gene wrong. I went down to the county records office and researched everything I was allowed to, but I couldn't find any evidence that Jack had been married before. Surely it was a mistake. I tore apart my own home too, looking for Jack's discharge papers; and while I was looking, I noted that I couldn't even find my marriage license. Come to think of it, had never seen it to begin with. I wasn't quite sure why Jack would hide it from me. I remembered filling out my part of the marriage application, and I do remember I had signed the actual license on the day of our wedding, but I had never seen Jack's part of the application. He had insisted on taking it to the courthouse in Detroit. I never knew I had a reason to find that odd. Thinking back on it now, though, it gave me an idea for what to look for next and I requested a copy of the application we submitted some seven years prior. It told the part of the story I had obviously not been privy to.

Jack came home that evening to find me sitting quietly on the couch, gripping the paper I'd found. After spending a long and emotional day sifting through documents and finally finding what I had been looking for, I hadn't felt like cooking supper. His eyes swept the empty dining room table and then landed on me like a rock. He knew something was wrong, but instead of being a man about it, he tried to pretend it was normal to find me where I was.

"Ah, a night out I see. Good idea, though I wish you would have warned me so I could make us reservations. Friday nights it's hard to get a table before eight P.M. or so..." His voice trailed off, and he let go of his ruse that I'd planned a night out. It was probably the look on my face, or the way I was slumped into the couch like I was a part of the fabric or the throw pillows. I hadn't moved a muscle since he'd come home, not even to look at him. I heard him set his briefcase down on the hardwood, and he took a seat opposite me in the antique armchair he'd inherited from his grandmother.

"Catherine? What is it? Is that a telegram? Did someone else... did someone...?" He thought it was another war death, and to me what I'd found was just as bad. It could mean the death of my marriage.

I finally spoke very quietly, which was the complete opposite of what I felt inside. Inside I wanted to explode. Inside I wanted take him by the shirt collar and lead him out of the front door on his rear end. Inside I felt anything but calm. So it sounded like someone else other than myself talking as I said, "No, no one has died." I paused. "Yet."

"What does that mean?" His age showed deeply on his face when he frowned, and if I didn't know better I'd think he was afraid of me, or at least what I had to say. It felt good to have him afraid, and it gave me the strength to do what I needed to do.

"Can you tell me, please, who..." I stopped. I couldn't do it. But I didn't have a choice, I couldn't live with this lie in between us for another day. I took a deep breath. I had planned on toying with him a bit, making him squirm as I asked him who Cordelia Edens was, making him sweat it a little bit, but I decided that was who he was, and not me. I wasn't the game-playing type. So I continued with a more straightforward approach.

"I heard some talk the other day. At the supermarket of all places, and from Sally of all people. I overheard her telling Ruby Maxwell that her cousin Gene said he knew you from your army days. He said he remembered you having the mumps and having trouble conceiving with your first wife because of it." I watched Jack's face drain of color and his hands grip the side of the chair. I just continued because he obviously didn't know what to say about it. "Well now, I didn't want to go thinking the worst of things and I know gossip is sometimes just gossip, but this seemed to explain a lot. Like why I can't get pregnant. And why you don't talk much about your army years, or the few that followed. Why a man of your intelligence and good looks hadn't married before the age of thirty-two. I guess I made some assumptions that you never felt a need to correct."

He just stared at me, pale-faced and sweaty, a sight, a look I had never before seen. I had imagined him getting angry and yelling and he was neither, and I didn't find that comforting at all. He wasn't even going to deny it because if he was, he'd have done it already. I needed him to talk, though, to fill in the holes in the stories he had told over the years. I had just assumed he'd gotten out of the army and gone right back to work for his dad. I had assumed the only place he'd ever lived was Michigan—that is, until the paper in my hand told me differently. I needed to get him talking, so I threw him a bone and offered him a place to start.

"Jack, why were you in Missouri?"

I felt the wind blow out of him in one long breath, and I realized he was tired too, of his own lies. Finally he asked, ever so meekly, "How do you know about Missouri?"

I stood up and handed him the paper. I sat back down and waited with my head held high and my eyes dry. I wasn't going to give him the satisfaction of knowing how much he'd broken my heart. "I guess I know why you insisted on turning in our application."

I'd handed him the paper that he had turned in requesting our marriage license in the state of Michigan. Under the groom's portion he'd answered "yes" to whether he had been previously married, listed "Cordelia Edens" as his prior wife, and had written "1925–1929" as the dates the marriage had occurred. He'd also written in "Missouri" under the question of where the marriage contract had been dissolved.

"I was twenty years old, Catherine, and a mess."

n"You aren't twenty anymore, Jack. You're thirty-nine. I think it's time you cleaned up your messes." I wasn't giving him an out. I wasn't mad at all that he'd been previously married, but I was mad as hell that he was too much of a child to own it.

"I'm not sure where to begin. I…" He stopped, and his face softened with grief. "Catherine, I'm so sorry, I never meant to…"

"Don't. No way, buster. Don't do that. You want to apologize? Then you make it right. You tell me straight right now, and then I get to decide what to do with it. You don't get to choose how I feel about it."

Jack nodded and then loosened his tie. He got up then, startling me, and I thought he was going to leave, but instead he crossed the room to the bar and poured himself a double. Of course, he couldn't do anything without the amber stuff anymore, so it didn't surprise me he needed it now.

He took a large sip and then turned around to face me. Then he slunk to the floor and sat there, knees bent, leaning into the bar cabinet as he started to speak. "It's true. I left the army because I'd caught a bad case of the mumps. It had left me pretty listless, and the doc wouldn't re-up my contract seeing how weak I was. I was a failure as far as my dad could tell, even though it wasn't my fault catching the mumps, and I just couldn't go home right away. I was stationed at Fort Bragg in North Carolina, not too terribly far from home, but I just couldn't go back right away."

"Well, Missouri isn't exactly on the way. How did you end up there?"

"I caught a ride up north with a buddy to see the big city. New York, 'ya know? I'd never been, and my buddy was from Brooklyn so it seemed like a nice road trip before going home to face my old man and my life here. Anyhow, I met Cordelia there. She was out from Missouri visiting family, and I met her one night in a bar. Cliché right? Military guy meets pretty young girl in a New York City bar and falls in love? Well, ex-military guy, I guess…"

He was trying to make light of it, forgetting that I was listening to my husband talk about his first wife that I had known nothing about for the seven years I'd been married to him. I wasn't feeling like laughing.

"Anyway, she'd been staying with her aunt for a few weeks and was heading home. I had overstayed my welcome with my buddy, and he had to get back to post anyway and well, she invited me to come back and escort her home. I really wasn't ready to come back here yet, so I did what any dumb twenty year old would do. I followed a perfect stranger across the country."

"And what? You just married her? Just like that?" It sounded a lot like our own quick courtship, and it unsettled me.

"Yes, but I had reason to. Or so I thought. A month or so after meeting her, Cordelia had told me she was late, as in pregnant late. She came from old money and a well-known family and she was completely panicked. I thought I was in love, and so I did the right thing. We were married very shortly after."

"But I thought, so you are able to have, I mean…?" I had a hint of hope that floated in, even though the thought of laying with Jack at the moment made my stomach turn.

"I'm not finished, Catherine." Jack sighed and rubbed his face, willing himself to go on. "Three months later she started to bleed. I mean badly, and they couldn't stop it. She lost the child. And I know now, but I didn't back then, that the baby was bigger than it should have been, I mean it was big enough for her to hold. I just was so young I didn't realize what that meant."

"It wasn't yours…" and Catherine knew what that meant too.

"No, it wasn't. She'd been pregnant before she ever went to New York City. She went to find some unsuspecting fool like me, and she found him. After she lost the baby she was beside herself with grief, and begged to try again as soon as we could. We tried for the next four years and it was horrendous, until finally something clicked with me. I had forgotten that the army doctor had told me sterility was a possibility in my case, because it had gone to my man parts. I guess I just hadn't heard him at the time because it wasn't the biggest thing on my mind. I was twenty-one and getting out of the army. Children were the last thing I was thinking about when he said that."

"So it's confirmed then? By a doctor?" I was holding my breath, still hoping it wasn't true.

His eyes were painfully hollow as he continued to speak. It was as if he couldn't stand to be present in his mind when he uttered his next words.

"Yes, Catherine. I finally saw a doctor. After they confirmed what I had suspected, I put two and two together with the baby she'd lost. Our whole marriage had been about trying to replace that baby, and it hadn't even been mine. When I confronted her about it and then told her my news, she all but packed my bags for me and locked the door behind me. There was no discussion, she just wanted to move on with her life, and I guess I knew I needed to as well." He paused, taking a moment to take in what he'd just told me. I was speechless and couldn't move as he continued.

"I went back home to Michigan then for the first time after leaving the army some six years before. I needed to face my dad and to start a new future. I barely made mention of the fact that I'd been married to my folks, and I never told them I was also infertile. The army and the marriage as failures were enough for them to try to accept. I think

I knew deep down from the start that it was all a mistake, and it was one I didn't want to carry into my future. I just never talked about it. I went back to work for the old man, and he made me a partner two years later. I put my head down and worked hard and played hard. I gave up the idea of marrying again, to be honest. And then a few years after that, I met you."

The rest of that night is sort of a blur. He cried for the first time ever and he begged me to stay as I started packing my bags with no particular place to go. I couldn't picture showing up on my aunt Rachel's front doorstep and I certainly wasn't going back to Kentucky to be with my sisters. I settled instead for me in the bedroom and Jack out on the sleeper sofa, though I thought about asking him to leave altogether. I was so terribly conflicted because I loved him and I had pictured us growing old together in this town. It wasn't as though he'd cheated on me or blown all our money at a poker game. Don't get me wrong, what he did was just as bad in some ways because he'd broken my trust. No, more than that, he hadn't trusted me enough with the truth from the beginning. He had never trusted me. How do you fix that? How do you rebuild a trust that was never really there in the first place?

I racked my brain about it and prayed for some sign as to what to do. Stay or go? If I went, then where would I go? If I stayed, then how could I forgive him? More than that was the issue of having children, which, for the first time in a very long time, was something I just couldn't even think about. I was overwhelmed by what I felt and didn't really have anyone safe to share it with as most of my friends were much like Sally and Ruby, gossipy. So we went on about our lives for many weeks in basic survival mode. Two lonely drones going through the motions, minus the pretense of trying to make a baby. Two icebergs at a standstill. Most days we were barely speaking.

That is, until one Sunday morning, when out of nowhere Jack had an idea that started with a very simple question. "Catherine, what do you know about California?" he asked with an impish grin.

"California? What's in California?" I wasn't at all sure where he was going with this. It was the first time he'd talked to me in two days.

"Opportunity. That's what. Opportunity abounds in California," he read to me out loud from the paper. He said he could just feel the pull of the endless sunshine and warm Pacific waters. "Why couldn't we open a shop up in downtown Los Angeles? This whole article is about the revitalization of the downtown Los Angeles area, and now is the time to get in on it!" He spent over an hour salivating over the feature photos of handsome young men and dazzling young women, smiling and happy, adventurous and successful, and I could tell he wanted all that and more.

I didn't say no. In fact, I didn't say much of anything. I just watched Jack sip his coffee and eagerly flip through the black-and-white pages of the paper, trying to find out as much as he could about the west coast lifestyle. While watching him I had an epiphany of sorts, and I suddenly knew that the answer to my question was really very simple. How do you rebuild something that you never really had? You don't. You just start over from scratch.

Chapter Twelve

Lillie
Wednesday, August 12, 1953
7:30 a.m.

The room was hot and stuffy again, and Lillie could hear the fan ticking its way back towards her face. Five, four, three, two—ah. There was her air. The smoke was gone, and she could breathe again. She felt a slight draft floating over her body from somewhere other than the fan. Lillie deduced that it was probably morning time again, given the light filtering in through the windows, and she supposed that she'd slept the whole of the night. Elizabeth had cleaned her well while she'd been asleep and had propped her head up on a few pillows. Lillie could see the window across the room from the new angle, and she was happy to get a glimpse outside again. She watched the slight wind hit the late summer trees that were heavy with leaves. Even the trees were withering in this heat, begging for fall to come so they could shed some of their bulk.

She heard a *whit-chew, whit-chew* followed by whistling and an incessant *purty, purty, purty* sound. She couldn't quite see its owner, but she knew the bird. A few sharp clicks and she was sure. He was calling his mate. She closed her eyes and listened. How many times had she woken to that sound? Hundreds? Thousands? It all seemed so long ago, and yet the *whit-chew, whit-chew* of the Kentucky cardinal, often known as the red bird, was as much a part of her day as was supper. The silly birds that don't go anywhere for winter, that flew in small packs over frozen ponds and untouched fields of pure white snow. She always thought it was funny how most folks didn't know the female wasn't the vibrant scarlet of her counterpart. They were brown and plain and sparrow-like except for the shock of muted red down their wings, tail, and crown. Unexpected and surprising.

Maybe the female would come and answer her fellow. Maybe Lillie could see one again. She lifted her head a bit and looked hard out the window. Her vision was blurring in and out, and she wasn't sure what was what anymore. She had just about given up looking when something happened that shocked her into a painful fit of giggles. Boldly, swiftly, and right through the half-raised oblong window came a tiny bird, not yet fully grown. It landed its small body on Lillie's bedside stand and sang her a melodious *purty, purty, purty* as it wobbled back and forth on the edge of the tiny dresser.

"Why, hello there, girl! What 'ya doing inside?" Lillie put her hand out slowly, and the bird didn't flinch. For a moment she forgot where she was, that her body ached, that her time was near. She moved her arm across the space between the bed and where the bird sat looking at her. The only thing she saw in the room was that tiny, beautifully-crafted red bird. When Lillie's short stubby fingers unfurled painfully and extended in the bird's direction, it gladly hopped on. She was dreaming, surely. Birds were usually so dang squirrely and, unless you had food that interested them, they'd fly away on account of a sneeze. Not this one. She wanted to see Lillie as much as Lillie wanted to see her. Lillie cupped her hand to make her a place to sit and slowly brought her arm into her chest.

"What's your story, little one?" *Whit-chew* was the answer. "Now we all got a story, even if it's a sad one." *Cheer, cheer, cheer* chirped Lillie's new friend, and Lillie half grinned. "You been over to my farm? Did Clay send 'ya? Ha, never could do his own dirty work." *Cheer, cheer.* "How's my kids, pretty one? Hmmm?" Small tears formed in the corners of Lillie's eyes as she asked. "How's they doing? If you'd keep an eye on 'em for me, I sure would be mighty grateful." The bird looked at her and hopped back and forth between her two stick legs. "I'll take that as a yes, then!"

"WHAT ON EARTH!" Lillie's moment shattered in an instant. The older nurse was back. Feva? Flo? No, Flora.

"What are you doing, Miss Lillie? You can't bring that bird in here! They carry all sorts'a disease!" She advanced towards Lillie, who protectively cupped her other hand around the bird.

Lillie laughed out loud and startled Flora. "Ma'am, what you think? This little bird here gonna kill me with something worse than I already got?" She laughed so loud her chest movements shook the bed and Flora stopped in her tracks. "Besides, I didn't bring her in, she came in... to see me."

Flora's face softened as she realized it was the first time she'd ever

78

heard Lillie laugh. "Miss Lillie, you know you can't keep her, right?"

"I know. Can't take much with me where I'm going, I guess." Flora cringed at her words, and Lillie looked at the bird in her hands. "Can't keep a free spirit caged up anyhow, that I ought'a know." She slowly moved her hand towards Flora and offered her the bird. "Here, take her. Let her go."

Flora gently scooped the bird into her hands and held onto her with a slightly firm grip. "She's a bold one, eh? Coming on in like that through the window. And she's pretty, so pretty."

"Yes," Lillie said as she let her hands fall back to the bed. "She reminds me of someone."

"Oh? Who's that?" Flora inquired.

"One of my sisters." Lillie's grin widened and filled her cheeks with color. "We called her Little Red."

"Little Red, eh? That's an interesting nickname!" Flora laughed a little and peered down at the tiny specimen in her hands.

"Well, she's little, 'ya see. Tiniest of our whole family, but with the biggest spirit. So us kids in the family we nicknamed her. Lord, she was a beautiful child."

"Where'd the red part come in?" Flora knitted her brows, looking puzzled.

"Well, my whole family's got brown hair. Kind'a like that bird's body color. A real buffy dull color, 'ya know?" Lillie smiled, thinking about her brothers and sisters again, and the image of them lit up a place in heart that had lain dormant for some years.

Lillie continued after a short pause. "But, my little sister, she done got the reddest head of hair you ever saw! She wears it real short, it's real wavy-like, but you can't miss her if you tried. When I was growing up people would see our family coming and they wouldn't pay us no mind, and then they'd see her head'a hair and couldn't help but stop to say something about it. Lord, how she professed to hating it, but I saw her little smile when folks would talk about her." Lillie's mind wandered back to a younger version of her sister's face with that secretly hidden grin and that not-so-hidden twinkle in her eye, and her heart ached suddenly with missing her.

"Well, Little Red makes sense, then," Flora said. "And that's a fine name for this little one here too!" Flora held the bird closer, inspecting her wings and tail color. "Teeny tiny, mighty fine, and mighty bold!"

"I wish I was more like her," Lillie said her smile fading.

"Who, the bird? They just flying round with no particular place to belong. Adventurous, I guess. We could all use a little adventure." Flora looked at the little bird knowingly, like she too wished she was a little bit more free.

Lilly laughed, "No, not the bird, though she's lovely. My sister. She's something pretty amazing."

"Mmmm. Sure she is, Miss Lillie." Flora gave Lillie a smile and headed towards the window.

She slid the bird off her hand and onto the window sill. Flora made a small shooing notion to get her to leave, but she didn't move. Suddenly, the bird flapped her wings fervently and she flew back to Lillie, landing smack-dab in the middle of her large chest. She looked Lillie boldly in the eye and then, a second later, was off again, flying out the window towards the heated morning sky.

In that second, sitting bravely on Lillie's chest, the little red streaked bird planted a tiny seed in Lillie's mind, and it slowly started to grow.

Lillie thought about that bird all day, and strangely enough all she wanted to do was tell Elizabeth about it. All she wanted to do was tell Elizabeth a lot of things. She'd been silent for so long she was struggling to find her voice. But, with every breath, she knew her time was running out. Even the little bird had confirmed it.

Elizabeth tiptoed into the room later that day, trying not wake Lillie. She looked paler than yesterday, and her face was more sallow. Elizabeth didn't know how she was still breathing, really, and she thought about how amazing it was that the human body could hang on if the mind wasn't ready to let go yet.

"Elizabeth," Lillie said startling the young nurse. "I'm glad you're back."

"I'm on a four-night stretch. Day two, here we go. At least it's not so busy, being summer and all. Come fall we'll be having lots of mamas having babies, and then comes all the winter sickness. I like working the summers, even though it's a fright hot!" Elizabeth replied cheerfully.

Lillie smiled at her lighthearted chatter. It was nice to hear a young person's voice again. "Did you hear I had a visitor this morning?" Lillie was lying on her back again with her head still propped up on the pillows. She raised her head a little and looked with anticipation towards Elizabeth. The sun was greeting the horizon behind her in the window, and the room grew darker by the minute.

Elizabeth raised her eyebrows, and her face showed her surprise. "Really, Lillie? Did one of your kids come in?" How she hope for Lillie's sake that that was the case. She reached up and pulled the chain to turn on the naked light bulb that hung precariously from the ceiling.

Lillie shielded her sensitive eyes from the glaring glow. "Nah, I don't be expecting I'll see them again," Lillie responded matter-of-factly and without too much emotion. Elizabeth felt her heart fall a little, and her initial hope washed away like bubbles down a tub drain.

"Here, Lillie. Let me just look you over real quick then I'll turn that light off and use the wall sconces." She retrieved a wash towel from the stack in the cupboard, folded it in half, and placed it gently over Lillie's eyes. "There, is that better? Now what about your visitor, then?"

"Well, I had a little bird come see me!" Lillie was beaming from beneath the cloth, and Elizabeth was shocked at the glow in Lillie's cheeks that hadn't been there just moments before.

"Ah, yes, right. I had heard that." Elizabeth adjusted the shades down some. Most nurses didn't care, but Elizabeth hated exposing someone during an examination and having the possibility of someone on the street seeing something they ought not to. "Flora said the bird was a pretty little thing. Flew right in and went right to you! That must'a been a sight!" Elizabeth's face softened, and she started gathering linens for Lillie's bed bath from the nearby cupboard.

"Was it ever! You know what it means when a bird flies in a window, Elizabeth?" Lillie asked. Lillie lifted the washcloth off of one of her eyes and peeked at her nurse.

Elizabeth knew, but she shook her head full of dark curls anyway. "No, Miss Lillie, what do you think that means?" Elizabeth's gaze turned downward. She didn't want to look at Lillie, she wished she'd keep that cloth on her face.

"Means someone's gonna die soon." Lillie had a little twinkle in her eye as she searched Elizabeth's face for a reaction.

"Hmmm," was all Elizabeth managed quietly as she fussed with folding a towel she had just unfolded.

"Sure hope today isn't your day, Elizabeth!" Lillie belted out loudly.

"Miss Lillie!" Elizabeth spat out, exasperated, but she stopped and started laughing when she caught the mischievous look on Lillie's face. "Miss Lillie, that's not funny!"

Lillie laughed a big throaty laugh. "I'm sorry child. My mama always said a little humor on a dark day will make the clouds disappear."

"Well," Elizabeth said as she came over and turned down Lillie's sheets, "Your mama is a smart woman!" She swatted playfully at Lillie's arm and said, "But you're still not funny!"

Lillie lay back and waited quietly while Elizabeth assessed her body. Her touch was compassionate and patient, and Lillie was grateful. There were moments when she felt like she was just existing, but this wasn't one of them. Elizabeth made her feel as if she still mattered, as if the state of her dying body was important. She listened intently to lungs that Lillie knew were slowly filling up with fluid, and she concentrated hard on a heart that was working too hard to push around all the toxic sludge that was her blood now that her kidneys were shutting down. She took particular note of the state of her skin, her color, the swelling, the painful parts. She poked and prodded with sweet-mannered fingers and asked simple questions about Lillie's pain, about her cognitive abilities, and about her strength. Lillie knew she had to do all that—it was her job, and other nurses had done the same—but Elizabeth never made Lillie feel like a dying body on a thin mattress in a lonely hospital. She made her feel like a person, a mother, a wife, a friend, and a woman. She extended her the dignity that Clay had stripped away from her when he'd left her at the street.

"Can I take a peek at your back, Lillie? I'll just roll you real gentle-like." Elizabeth motioned a roll with her hands.

"Can we skip it today? Ain't nothing hurting no more back there." Lillie was tired at just the thought of moving. She was quite comfortable just where she lay.

"Sure, Lillie, whatever you want." Elizabeth continued her assessment, and when she was done she turned off the bright bulb as promised and turned on the softer wall sconces. Lillie removed the washcloth from her eyes and watched as Elizabeth's small frame wandered over towards the utility sink in the corner of the room. "Do y'all have oil lamps, Elizabeth?" she asked trying to keep the hope out of her voice.

Elizabeth stopped and thought about it a minute before answering. "Hmm, I'm not sure. I haven't seen one here before, but that doesn't mean they don't keep them in the supply room in case the electricity fails. Why do you ask, Lillie?"

"I just always like one by my bed is all. No big deal, though. Just wondering why I ain't seen none here." Elizabeth knew why. Most folks had tucked theirs away to be used only for emergency gear as, years ago, house by house, everything had been fitted for electrical.

Elizabeth turned back to the sink. "I'll look around, Lillie," Elizabeth said as her curiosity piqued at how it was that Lillie must live day to day. She turned the X-shaped silver knob and ran the water for a few minutes as she felt the temperature of the water from the sun-warmed pipes with the back of her hand. "I hate how in the winter you have to wait forever for warm water and in the summer, all you get is warm water when all you want is cool." She ran her fingers under the steady flow and asked, "You like it a bit cool, right, Lillie?"

"Yes, please." Lillie could feel the ants returning, but she'd had a bit of fun this morning in her mind pretending she was squashing them like the spiders in her and Josie's childhood games. *Hey Lills, I'm the biggest meanest spider you ever did see, and I just caught you in my web. When I catch you, Josie Finn, I'm a gonna squish 'ya with the back'a my heel.*

Lillie was quiet for a moment and then said, "At least y'all got running water, no matter how hot or cold it is."

Elizabeth thought she'd remembered something about Lillie's family being farmers. Somewhere on the west side of town. "You have a well, Miss Lillie?"

"Yup. I know most folks don't like the taste of it, but I like knowing my water's coming from the earth and ain't been traveling too much through some man's pipes." Lillie could taste the water at her home now. Sometimes salty, sometimes sweet. Sometimes it just tasted like the earth that surrounded it. Lillie figured it was God's way of giving them whatever it was their bodies needed that day.

"You know, one time I brought up some water and took a sip and it tasted just like I imagine car oil might taste," Lillie said. "Turned out some of the local teens done crashed a car on the farmlands next'a ours and the gas tank done busted open like a squashed orange. It spoiled our water and everybody else's around us for a month!"

"How'd you get your water then, Lillie? Can't go a month with no water!" Elizabeth couldn't imagine such chaos over water. She lived in town and simply turned the knob on the kitchen sink when she wanted something to drink or cook with.

"Well, I walked over to my friend's place, about two or so miles to the west of us 'cause I figured theirs was probably safe, and I struck up a deal. She and her husband let me and my young'ins come by every couple days with big ole buckets, 'ya know those three gallon ones? Anyhow, she let us pump up what we needed as long as we didn't ask her to help carry it back. Lord, how it killed my back. In exchange, I promised to do some sewing for her. She never could throw a stitch."

"You sew, Miss Lillie?" Elizabeth filled a small pitcher for drinking water for Lillie and then filled the round deep basin up half way. She shut the water off and thought about what it would be like to have to go outside every time you needed a bit of water.

"I do. Well, I did, I guess. Was pretty good at it too. Used to work at a shop on the square as matter of fact, but that was some time ago." Lillie looked down at her swollen, disjointed hands and wished she could feel her fingertips again. "Can't sew when you can't feel your hands no more and can't see real good. Might stitch up your finger and not even notice!"

Elizabeth laughed. "Suppose that's so." She pulled the rolling table close to Lillie's bedside and placed her towels and basin on top. Lillie watched as she pushed a washcloth into the water and pulled it out, repeating this several times and then eventually wringing out the water so she didn't make a big mess. It reminded Lillie of doing the laundry. The farmer they worked for had a motor-driven wringer washer with a big, deep cast-cement wash tub. It was large and white and beautiful, and Lillie'd heard it held some ten to fifteen gallons of water. Lillie never had enough nerve to ask the farmer's wife, Mrs. Adams, if she could maybe use it on occasion. She just used her old hand-cranked wringer that was clamped onto the side of a round metal washtub, and she only had that because Mrs. Adams hadn't a need for it after her motorized one had arrived from Sears. Before that Lillie had used a good old fashioned galvanized tub and scrub board to clean her family's clothing. Even after the hand-me-down wringer contraption was given to her, Lillie would often pull out the old scrub board and tub and get her hands good and wet. She found the repetition calming, and it brought her back to her childhood days of sitting on the back porch with her grandmother while she washed the linens or scrubbed the dirt off her father's clothing. Back and forth with the fabric and soap, up and down the metal ridges, in and out of the water. There was just something therapeutic about cleaning clothes the old-fashioned way.

"You know how to make soap, Elizabeth?" Lillie was curious. The girl's hands ran up and down Lillie's legs as she started to bathe her, and they were soft like Lillie remembered silk being. They certainly weren't the hands of a farmer's daughter.

"No, Ma'am. My daddy works for the city council, and we just buy most of what we need at Roark's. You make your own soap, Miss Lillie?" Elizabeth raised her eyebrows in surprise. Hardly anybody made soap anymore.

"Oh, Lordy, yes. We only do it once or twice a year, though. You make it just after they kill the hogs, and then more in the summer if you got enough stuff to do it."

Lillie thought about the bucket of lard under her sink. Her soap bucket, she called it. She carefully drained all the fat from her cooking into it and then sealed it up tightly. And then there were her barrels of wood ashes she saved all year that she turned into lye when the time came. All her savings. Would Clay know how to take all that grease and all those ashes and turn it into soap? She hadn't shown her girls; it was just too dangerous with all that hot fat and skin-eating lye. She just had her boys take her big kettle into the barn and she'd set up there where the kids couldn't accidentally tip the hot liquid over on themselves. Besides that, she didn't like fishing insect bits out of the mixture, and she didn't want her cows thinking it was some sort of trough.

"You use meat scraps, right? And the fatty bits?" Elizabeth had heard of it before, but had never seen soap being made. She'd just unwrapped whatever brand they had on sale at the store and lathered up.

"Yup, that's right. It's tricky, though. It take a whole lotta ashes, lot more than you'd think. And you got to get the amounts just right, otherwise you just get the fat rising and the lye sinking and turning all syrupy-like. Most folks nowadays done give it up, just buy or trade for it. But that's fine by me 'cause I always got something they want, and then I can trade and get me something they got. Something we might need. I just got to making big batches of it." Lillie was surprised at how good she felt. Thinking about her home was numbing some of her discomfort, so she kept talking.

"You ever use soap made from ashes and pig fat, Elizabeth?" Lillie looked at the girl who was listening to her with intent interest as she bathed her moribund body.

"No, I guess I haven't." Elizabeth dipped the washcloth back in and out of the water and ran the cake of soap the hospital had provided over Lillie's other leg. She had actually never given much thought to soap before now. It just showed up on Tuesdays on the back of a big truck with the rest of the grocery store items that were trucked in and made its way onto the store shelf. Where it came from was not of concern.

"Wasn't much good for washing yourself, though. Mrs. Adams, the farmer's wife who lives some few hundred yards from us, she like my lye soap fine enough for dishes and clothes and housework and such, but she always got her some store-bought stuff for washin' her hair." Lillie had always wondered what that must have been like. Her soap was a good multipurpose tool for just about everything, but it didn't lather real well, and her hair always felt greasy and dull.

"Lillie, can I ask you something?" Elizabeth's cheeks turned red, and her face became pensive. She stopped rubbing Lillie's calf and said, "It's kind'a personal, but I have always wondered about something."

"Elizabeth, you can ask me anything. I got nothing to hide no more," Lillie said as she watched Elizabeth's forehead relax and her color start to return to normal.

"Well, I was wondering…most of the kids in school who come from the farms…well, they had real short-like hair, even the girls. It was cropped right close to their ears. My brother, Thomas, always said it was on account of lice, but one girl told me they just couldn't afford much shampoo." Elizabeth fingered her long curly locks that were tucked under her cap, and her scalp started to itch for no good reason. Oh, the mind is easily suggestible.

Lillie laughed. "A farm girl's nightmare. We got lots a critters big and small out there in the fields. It was a little bit of both, I guess. I always kept my hair back real tight and kept it covered, but it was just easier for my girls to keep it short. They've had lice a time or two for sure, and when you don't have running water or any soap that makes a good suds, you just better to chop it off. Ain't none of my girls gonna win no beauty contest for sure, but it's a ton easier to get all the nits out if there ever are any!"

"I'm sure they are precious children, Miss Lillie, head lice and all," Elizabeth said. She dried off Lillie's legs with a scratchy white towel and came up towards Lillie's head. "Do you want me to wash your hair, Miss Lillie? With the good soap, maybe?"

Lillie looked up Elizabeth and tiny tears flooded her eyelashes. She slowly reached for Elizabeth's hand and gave it a good squeeze.

"I sure would like that…" she said as she let her words trail off, a rogue tear running down her face. She closed her eyes and tried to relax as Elizabeth helped her lift her head and place it over the large basin. She felt delicate fingers run through her oily, straw-like hair as Elizabeth untangled the looser knots that had formed while she was lying in bed.

She kept her eyes closed the whole time, savoring Elizabeth's merciful touch, the cool water running over her scalp and through her tresses, the bubbly soap that smelled like lavender. She pictured the little stream behind her home as a child, the cool water rustling over the rocks and flowing into tiny ponds. She pictured Josie, Mary, and her mama. She pictured her kids running around the fields, diving into the wash bucket on Saturday bath night, and fighting over whose turn it was to go first while she tried to keep the fire going to keep them warm enough. She pictured Clay. She lingered there on his face for just a second, but quickly replaced his image in her mind with a smaller, kinder one. A tiny bird, with a brown body and shocking red wings and tail. She was falling asleep slowly and peacefully as she remembered what the bird had told her to do. She could do this. She could. She just had to.

Chapter Thirteen

Catherine
Los Angeles, CA
July 1943

Buses and cars flew by on the freshly paved street in front of the tiny shop we had secured on Temple Street. Our street, and every other in downtown Los Angeles, was alive and teeming with possibility. The big city that had been in a deep and dreary slumber through the depression was now awakening with a renewed liveliness. The lights that had been dark for so long now burned brighter than they ever had, and the eagerness of the city's occupants was almost palpable. It was early summer, and I certainly felt the warmth of it in every bone in my body. Everywhere I went the smell of freshly-made bakery breads filled the air, and it mixed nicely with the salty scent of the sweat pouring down the backs of the hard-working men and women who were bringing Los Angeles back to life. Our shop, like many others around us, was in need of some major care and renovation, and we were more than happy to tend to our new family member. It was as if our life in Michigan had never even occurred, as if all the lies had never been told, and as if the reality of my inability to have children with Jack didn't matter. Jack and I had started over.

I scraped away at old English rose wall paper that reminded me of my aunt's wingback chair, while Jack was busily replacing roof shingles and patching leaky pipes and creaky floorboards. I spent hours cleaning away cobwebs and sweeping dirt from tiny corners that I hadn't even known were capable of holding such filth. As we cleaned and repaired, it was as if we were clearing out all of our own cobwebs, dusting off all of our demons, and casting them into the waste basket along with the rest of the debris. It was cathartic, and we were both coming alive like the city was, and our excitement was also palpable. I finally felt like we would be okay, that no matter what, the vows we'd taken so many years before would, and could, mean something, even if they hadn't been based on truth in the beginning.

We didn't talk about many serious things. We just danced around it and found comfort in being playful with one another. I think we just didn't know what to say, and were tired of all the same old talk anyway.

"Jack! I found the biggest roach yet! Surely it rivals the mammoth one you found yesterday." I'd covered it with a glass from the cupboard because I hated the crunching sound it made when you squashed them. Jack could do it for me.

"Nonsense, darling. That one yesterday was a beauty!" he replied, scooping me up in his arms for a long, hard kiss, and then taking care of the roach for me like a hero saving a distressed damsel. My knight was back and I was all too willing to let him take that lead. Yes, it was almost as if nothing had ever happened. Almost.

Dust and muck covered both of us from head to toe, and we didn't care. This was our time and place to start an amazing new life, and we reveled in every blister and sore back, every broken fingernail, every tension headache. We blinked, and within a few months we were able to cover the rent on both the shop and the small apartment above it with plenty leftover for a bit of fun. Jack had been right, a used furniture shop was apparently the perfect business to open in a time of renewal.

Los Angeles was more amazing than the paper had made it seem, and I was a happy and captive audience. I felt lured by the beauty and excitement exuding from every street corner, and I was especially taken by the women of the city, who were dripping with sophistication and form-fitting clothing. Skirt hems were considerably shorter than what you might find in Detroit, and dresses clung hungrily to curvy hips. Bust lines plummeted shamelessly, showing breasts that had no intentions of feeding babes and comforting toddlers. Heel heights grew by such leaps and bounds that most of the male population seemed to shrink overnight. These ladies were vivacious and cunning and undaunted by challenges, and I was mesmerized. They'd just survived a hellish decade of deprivation and were walking into the next one with the attitude that they had nothing to lose. Even the war overseas didn't seem to stop them; it in fact invigorated them more as they ante-upped to help America's war heroes. Time was healing them all, and it was healing Jack and me as well.

But sometimes fate intervenes and your white knight goes astray.

Five months prior we had celebrated our eighth wedding anniversary in our tiny apartment, which we'd finally finished renovating above the store. We'd made fast friends with another young couple who lived a few blocks away, Len and Betsy Piper, and had spent much of the recent holiday hustle and bustle hanging out with them as well. New Year's Eve came and went, and we rang in 1944 with a bang and a kiss and all the hope that a new year brings. We finally felt like we had what the paper had promised. Yes, we had it all. Jack and I were on the way to easier times, and I had made a true friend in Betsy. We had hit it off right away, and I was so grateful for her. She was fun and authentic and completely trustworthy. She was about as far from my "girlfriends" in Michigan as could be. We both adored picture shows, and since Jack said he could take them or leave them most nights, we two girls would often venture out on our own. One night, early in February, we decided to catch a show together, and little did I know I'd get a show of a different kind.

"Are you ready, Catherine, darling?" Betsy had called through the hollow apartment door. "Mr. Gable awaits, dear, and I never like to cause him delay. He's just so dapper, oh, and so impatient!"

I laughed and then threw open the door with a grin. Betsy should have been in the movies for all the theatrics she threw around. God, how I adored her. I finished pinning on my hat while she stood in my doorway looking like a movie star. "I think you're the one who is impatient, Miss Betsy!" I ribbed. "It takes some time to look this good, darling, and Clark will always wait for me," I said with a grin.

"I am just so aflutter about seeing him at the El Rey. What a thrill! Thanks for coming with me. Len said he just simply couldn't stomach another romantic film, even if Myrna Loy and Jean Harlow were in it," Betsy rambled. She liked using words like aflutter, darling, and dapper, and I'd started to pick up the habit too. She said they were as essential to a steady romance with your husband as kissing and, though I found the words slightly pretentious, somehow, when they came from Betsy, they were indeed quite darling.

"His loss, my gain. Plus, I'd rather have you on my arm any day than Jack. Just don't tell him that!" Betsy was like the sister I used to have and had lost when Lina had married and left.

We both laughed as we headed for Wilshire Boulevard and the twinkling lights of the El Rey. We hadn't seen a movie yet in the new theater, and though it was farther than our usual playhouse we were more than willing to make the trip. I don't actually remember the story line now, but I do remember us discussing which woman we'd rather have been if we could be side by side with the dashing Clark Gable on the big screen. We were giggling like school girls about it as we linked arms and left the theater, stepping out into the the chilly evening breeze. We headed east towards a cafe, and I was asking Betsy what we should do next with our evening, when Betsy suddenly stopped short. I caught myself just in time before I tripped over her.

"Good Lord, Betsy, what in the world are you…" I heard my voice trail off as my eye caught what Betsy's had already seen. I stopped dead in my tracks and my arm fell away from my dear friend as I stood there, speechless. There, across the busy street, was my darling husband Jack and a lanky blonde woman with a stylish bob whose arms seemed to wrap around him twice over. She nuzzled his neckline and whispered something in his ear. When his laughter hit my ears I knew I wasn't mistaken. That was the laugh he reserved for me, for our private jokes and intimate moments. It was the laughter of anticipation and lust. It was the laughter that had just recently been mine again. Of course, that was when my husband had been mine alone.

I watched silently as he slipped a sexy arm around the small of the girl's back and pulled her into him. He hadn't seen Betsy or me, and neither one of us made an attempt to get his attention. Betsy silently took my hand and gave it a squeeze as we watched Jack and his lady friend head west towards Burnside Avenue.

After a few minutes had passed of me staring after Jack and not able to move, Betsy said, "Catherine? Darling, what can I do?"

I felt the air exit my lungs involuntarily and instantly thought of the 'until death do us part' vow of my marital covenant. The one I'd clung to for the last year as if it were a life vest. It was part of the reason I'd given Jack a second chance after finding out about his lie, but with one last look and one last breath my love for Jack died right there on the corner of Wilshire and Dunsmuir Avenue. And that was all the death I needed to justify what I knew I had to do. "Take me home, Bets," I'd said, "I have some packing to do."

I entered the apartment that, just hours before, had felt like my happy home, and stood in the middle of my bedroom. The bedsheets were still tussled from the nap we'd taken together earlier, and my reading lamp was on, waiting for my return. I've always hated walking into a dark room. My new dresses hung neatly next to Jack's freshly pressed shirts and the hemlines flirted with my new red heels on the closet floor. Everything was so fresh, and the room oozed with anticipation.

As my eyes took in the room, looking for Lord knows what, they landed hard on the Hemingway novel on my bedside table. I'm an avid reader, and was quickly introduced to the beauty that is Hemingway when we'd moved to Los Angeles. Hemingway was another man who sent Betsy all aflutter. I never dog-ear the corners, or use paper for bookmarks to keep my place in my books. Much to the chagrin of most other book lovers, I like to flip my books wide open with the typeface down and the binding creased and stressed. I just love the way it makes the cover lay out, sort of like a man's handlebar mustache. I guess I always felt like the story stayed alive if the book remained open, and until I am ready to let go of the magic of a tale, I never close my books.

That night, though, it lay strangely closed and set, its ivory cover reminding me of my wedding dress. It's like the book knew it needed to be ready to go, that the chapters of Jack and Catherine had already been written, and our story had come to an end. I remember I fingered the spine, then cradled the book to my bosom as I knew the journey was finally done.

There was no time for tears, though. I didn't want to be there when he got back. I quickly tossed the novel into my suitcase along with my clothing, and hastily began packing the rest of my things. When I was done I found a small slip of paper and scribbled my husband a note. It simply said, "I know. I saw you. I hope you find the happiness you seek, it just won't be with me. I'll take care of the paperwork." I signed it without sentiment and placed it on his pillow. I took one last look around the small dwelling that had held so many hopes and dreams, and I sighed a very heavy breath that sounded every bit as tired as I felt. I grabbed hold of my luggage and walked slowly over the threshold, closing the door behind me.

I took just a moment to stand there, eyes closed, taking in what I was doing and assuring myself that it was the right decision. For the second time I knew I'd never be able to see him the same way again, and there was no more starting over. He was simply lost to me. I walked forward towards Betsy's apartment, with what Jack might have called my typical Catherine tenacity, and I never looked back.

I stayed with Betsy and Len for a few days, mostly because I wasn't sure what my next move was supposed to be. I don't remember crying much; but then I think I was just so exhausted from the eight years I'd spent on the Jack and Catherine emotional roller coaster that I had nothing left for making tears. Eventually I decided the best thing to do was to go back to Michigan and get the paperwork started in person before I gave myself the opportunity to see him again. My mind was made up, but the heart can be a trickier thing.

I purchased a one-way ticket back east, and arrived on my aunt Rachel's doorstep in a state of quiet surrender. What could I do but knock? I had nowhere else to go, and though I had money, I knew many landlords would find it hard to rent to a married woman who had just left her husband, no matter what the reason. I also knew my news would be ill-received by my family, particularly Aunt Rachel, who would fret over what sort of mark it would leave on the family name. I wasn't sure what mom and pop would say. I'd never shared with them the news of Jack's first marriage or his deceit, so I knew they would be hard-pressed to understand why I couldn't try a little longer. To be honest, I really didn't care what any of them thought. I just needed to be free of him.

My reception in Hazel Park, Michigan, was just as bad as I'd expected, and just as cold as the winter days that filled the yards and streets with ice and snow that early March. Instead of support, I felt chastised. Instead of a safe haven, I found a hostile environment where both my family and Jack's family attempted to dissuade me from my choice. I had done nothing wrong but fall for a wolf in sheep's clothing, and I felt punished by those closest to me. I was only trying to redeem my mistake, and no one could see it that way but me.

The only exception to the battering that I felt was perhaps my mom and pop, and though I wouldn't say they gave me a pat on the back and a golden nod, they were largely quiet about it. While I could tell my mom did not approve, she knew me well enough to know that I had made up my mind. My pop had given me a hug and welcomed me back but had never mentioned a word about any of it. He acted as if I'd returned from vacation and he'd been expecting me, and I took his silence as the only approval I was going to receive.

Not everyone was as reserved about their opinions. The more people I spoke to, the more energy it took to maintain my composure; and three weeks into being home it took me everything I had just to remain calm.

Even some of my better girlfriends were of no help, a twist I hadn't expected. "Surely you were mistaken, Catherine," one friend had said to me over coffee. "It was probably just a new friend. Jack would never do that!" But I knew what I had seen, and all I could do was shake my head no in response. Jack's mother was perhaps the icing on the cake, and had pleaded her son's case quite heatedly on his behalf.

"Darling, please, we mustn't make a mess of things over something so small. How will he ever remove that smudge from his reputation?" she'd said, and I wondered what she'd said to him after his first marriage debacle. In my book, his reputation was ruined long before he ever met me. When I thought her pleading couldn't get any worse, she continued and said, "Besides, all men wander eventually, it's in their bones, dear."

I responded in kind by saying, "So you'd have me live a lifetime with a man who is a liar and a cheat just for the sake of his standing? I'd rather live a lifetime alone, Ma'am, than endure the embarrassment of being married to such a man." I was done being nice, and so next I went for her jugular, mostly because of her insinuation that all men were as crass as Jack and that I shouldn't get so upset over it. I felt myself start to sweat as I spat words at her with much more venom than she probably deserved. She was, after all, just trying to protect her son. "For the record," I said, "My father never disgraced my mother as such, so perhaps Jack's is just a family affliction."

Every biting comment I heard and every plea that was made to try to fix it made my spine crawl, and I began to feel anger like I'd never felt before, even when I'd lived there as a teenager. It haunted my sleep and made me restless and irritable like I imagine caged animals must feel at the zoo. It was turning me into someone I knew I wasn't, and yet I felt helpless to stop it.

Funny enough, though, the person who changed my course away from a life filled with bitterness was my aunt Rachel. I had filed what paperwork the county required for a divorce, and I'd started looking for a job as well, because the money I had brought with me wasn't going to last long. I knew I wouldn't last long either under Rachel's roof, even if my parents were there right alongside me this time. Her house held too many memories, and with every passing day I began to feel imprisoned again, and angrier. Just as I began to wonder how it was I was going to break free once more, Aunt Rachel made it such an easy choice.

It was a Sunday, and I'd been staying with Rachel and my parents for almost two months. Easter had passed without me really even realizing it, and spring wasn't too far off; though for me, I wouldn't have care if it stayed winter for a bit longer. I felt frozen inside, and the weather suited my mood perfectly. I wasn't ready to defrost yet, or frolic in spring dresses and delicate sandals. I wasn't ready to frolic at all, because all I really wanted was a job, or anything really, to keep me out of the house during the day.

I had just sat down with the paper and a cup of coffee and had my pen in hand to peruse the want ads once again, and I was starting to feel slightly discouraged. I basically had no skills to tout on an application, and was quickly becoming dismayed by what my resume might look like—never finished high school, was a nanny and housemaid for an ungrateful relative, kept house for a lying and unfaithful husband. Somehow I didn't quite think businesses would find the value in any of that. I sure didn't.

As I felt my mood shifting down deeper and deeper, my aunt Rachel came in the room. She hesitated when she saw me, as if I were a surprise that she wasn't expecting. Then her eyes took in my long pajamas and slippered feet.

"Catherine, dear. Whatever are your plans for today?" I will translate for you; in other words, aren't you going out somewhere?

"Why this, actually. It's chilly out today." I smiled sweetly and gave her nothing. I actually had plans, but she didn't need to be privy to them.

"I see." She paused. "Well perhaps then you could do me some favors. I think that the…" I cut her off before she could ramble off her laundry list of things to be done that were beneath her to actually do.

"Actually, I'm looking for a job." I rustled the paper as if to say, see? I'm busy.

She smirked at me and put her right hand on her small hip. "Oh?"

"Yes, well, I figured I'll need a place of my own soon, and I'll need an employer to list on my rental application. So, anyway, I'm looking." I'd been looking for weeks, actually, but every advertiser I'd called that listed a decent salary had been kind, but had politely turned me down, citing a need for someone with experience. With every phone call I wondered more and more how I ended up in this place again. Stuck in Rachel's house.

"I see. Well, Catherine, I'm not sure what you expect to find, given that you've no education to speak of, nor skills." My aunt Rachel might be a terrible person, but she was smart, and wise about the ways the world worked. I just found it terribly ironic that she was the one to point those things out to me when she was in fact the reason I had neither. I had come to her at fifteen for schooling and opportunity and had left her with nothing. She fueled the fire in me with her next comment, and the anger that had been just under my surface almost exploded. "Too bad you never completed high school, Catherine, it would have opened so many doors for you."

I dropped the pen out of shock, and all I could do was stare at her as I sat trying to swallow the indignation that was rising in my throat. I opened my mouth to speak, and was surprised by what I said back to her.

"You couldn't be more right," I stated frankly, and not because I was playing along, but because she was right. Aunt Rachel may have been the reason I didn't complete high school all those years ago, but she wasn't the reason I hadn't done it since. I could blame Jack, I suppose, but the truth is he would have supported it; and had I taken it upon myself back then to pursue it, in the end I wouldn't be in the position I found myself in currently. I was unemployable. I knew what I needed to do, and though Aunt Rachel's intention that day had been to degrade and humiliate me, she actually was the just the catalyst I needed.

She hadn't replied to my comment because I'm sure it was the first time ever that I'd conceded her opinion. I usually either ignored her or changed the subject to avoid a disagreement, but I had never told her she was right before. I folded the newspaper, tucked it under my arm, and crossed the room to where she stood. I placed a gentle kiss on my cold aunt's cheek and walked down the hallway towards the front hall. If I would have looked back at her I would have surely seen the confused look on her face as she stood there unmoving. She surely had no idea what had just happened.

I headed towards the foyer area and picked up the phone receiver, hoping the line was free. We shared a party line with three other neighbors, which meant that while we each had our own telephones, we shared one line. A nosy person might find much joy in being able to listen in on the goings on in the next house, but I just found it ever so frustrating that you had to keep your conversations short and coded for privacy. That day, though, I didn't really care if anyone listened in, I just wanted the line to be free. As I placed my call through to the operator I could feel my mood lighten, and as I waited and waited for my friend to pick up on her end, I felt my pulse quicken.

"Hello?" Betsy Piper's voice was strained and frog-like and I knew

I'd woken her up.

The operator broke in, "Ma'am, I've got a Catherine Edens on the line. Do you wish to accept?"

"Of course!" Betsy was awake now. I hadn't called her since I'd left, and though I'd written her once I was sure she'd been worried.

"Catherine! Darling, are you all right? How are things?"

"Horrible, Betsy, but not for too much longer." I was so excited I didn't know where to start or how to ask her for the favor I needed.

"Where are you? When are you coming back? We miss you terribly." Betsy had the kindest heart, and was always so sincere. I could hear how much she'd missed me.

"Well, Betsy, can you pick me up in a few days? I don't have the details yet, but I'll be coming by bus." I could hear her delight almost instantly, and it was the first time I'd felt welcome in many, many months.

"Of course, darling!" She practically squealed it. I heard her cover the receiver and yell over her shoulder, "Len, Catherine's coming back!" and then to me she said, "Oh, I'm ever so excited! I'll be there, you just send me notice of when and where!"

"Thank you, Betsy. You are such a gracious friend. Might I stay with you for a while until I sort a few things out?" I knew what she'd say, but still I had been nervous to ask.

"Do you really need to ask, darling? If you can stand my Len, then you are more than welcome in our home." I could almost hear her smiling, and my heart felt ever so full.

"Thank you. Listen, I've got to go and keep the line clear, but you really are a lifesaver, Betsy." I paused and then added, "Oh, and Betsy, one more thing?"

"Yes, Catherine? Anything."

"It's not Catherine anymore. It's Cate. I think I'm done being Catherine Edens."

"Of course you are, love, of course." I hung up the phone and stood there for a moment thinking about what I'd just set in motion. When I finally turned around I jumped a bit when I found myself face to face with my aunt Rachel. Apparently it wasn't just the neighbors being nosy that one needed to worry about.

We stared at each other, and then she spoke first. "You're leaving?" she asked with an intonation of surprise. I couldn't read the expression on her face, but it wasn't the delight I'd expected about my departure.

Then it hit me that, of course, she wasn't excited. It meant she'd lost her free help for a second time, which was all I'd ever really been to her. She thought she had me for good this time. What a sad pathetic person I must have looked like to her the day I'd come back.

"Yes, I'll likely leave tomorrow. There are buses out to Los Angeles every day now, I hear. You all will get along fine without me, I'm sure."

"Yes, but Catherine, whatever will you do there?" She'd replaced her surprise with her typical affect and was smirking again. As if I wasn't capable of taking care of myself.

"Whatever do you mean, Aunt Rachel? It was your idea after all!" Now I was the one smirking and reigning in my sarcasm as much as I could before I took it too far.

"What? I never suggested you leave. I..." She was stuttering and unsure of herself, a first for the poised and elegant lady of the house.

"Oh, not that. That was my choice, of course. To leave that is, though you all have been ever so welcoming and understanding of my... what do you all call it? My mistake, is it?" The devil was on my shoulder now, and I couldn't shake him.

She ignored the poke at her and said in demanding tone, "Well, what was my idea, Catherine?" She furrowed her brow, running our conversation through her head and trying to figure out what it was that she'd said to prompt my bold actions.

"School, of course. I'll be going back to school. Southern California has some of the finest." I paused for effect as she took in what I'd said. "So, thank you again for suggesting it." I turned from her then and started to walk away, but that time I stopped and looked back at her over my shoulder. The surprise that held her face hostage was worth every moment I'd spent in her unkind and judgmental presence. The big picture window at the landing of the staircase caught my eye, and I noticed the first signs of spring outside, as if they had just shown up that morning for me. I felt the ice inside me melting with every step I took up to the second floor, and by the time I reached the top, I felt as light and fresh as the new leaves that were budding on the trees. And, God forgive me, I couldn't help but strut ever so slightly as I made my way to my room to start packing.

Chapter Fourteen

Lillie
Wednesday, August 12, 1953
11:15 p.m.

Lillie woke up several hours later with a feral scream lodged in her throat. She was moist with perspiration and howling on the inside. Her breaths were quick and panting like the wild dogs' that roamed the property around her house. The room was inky and dark, and panic poured into the holes of her deteriorating brain like honey on a honeycomb. Finally, the soupy air slipped past her vocal cords, and Lillie heard herself hollering, "My baby, my baby. Please, somebody help him! Please, someone!" She tried to sit up, she was sure he was here somewhere. Where had he gone? Her arms ached and felt excruciatingly empty. She heard footsteps moving with purpose. A woman's heels on a hard tiled floor. Faster and faster, louder and louder, until she felt a calm touch on her forearm.

"Lillie." Elizabeth stood at Lillie's bedside, concern plastered on her face like heavy makeup. "Miss Lillie, it's okay. Wake up a little bit, Miss Lillie. You're okay." But Lillie was awake. She could see Elizabeth just fine, even if her blurry vision made the details vague. Where was he, damn it? She was getting mad. She felt the anger rise in her chest until the heat of it pinched her cheekbones red. She wasn't done holding him yet.

"Margaret, please, give him back. Give me back my boy." Lillie was screaming now, and Elizabeth was doing her best to shush her. She didn't want the administration getting wind of Lillie's delusions again.

She had heard the stories about Lillie and the nonexistent baby, and while Elizabeth had seen Lillie in other states of confusion, she hadn't witnessed one about her boy. Two weeks prior, this had gone on for days. Lillie had wept and begged and wandered around searching for him. That was when she was still able to walk, and that all seemed so long ago now to Elizabeth. The director had discussed moving Lillie over to the Western State Hospital in Hopkinsville. The insane asylum, the madhouse, the funny farm. That's where the director thought the "farmer's wife" should go. That's where she thought this tired, anguished, and fading mother should be sent. Elizabeth and a few other nurses had fought hard against it.

"She isn't crazy," Elizabeth had pleaded to the conservative head nurse and the paunchy head doctor. "Her mind is just affected by the diabetes; she's real good sometimes, honest." Elizabeth had fought earnestly. She was sick at the thought of Lillie there lying among the insane. "Please don't send her to that place. She'll die alone." It had taken several of them saying the same thing to convince the two elders to allow Lillie to remain, but in the end they had agreed. The head nurse had added coldly that it wasn't worth the hassle of transporting her anyway, she'd be gone soon enough.

It took several minutes of trying to convince Lillie to calm down before her labored breathing slowed. Tears poured down her face and into her hair and her pillow as her eyes pleaded with Elizabeth. "Please, Margaret, please. Can I just hold him one more time?" Elizabeth's heart split into a thousand tiny pieces for Lillie, but she didn't know how to shake her from her delusion. She thought hard about her lessons from school regarding dementia. What was the proper thing to do again? She just couldn't recall, and she didn't want to alert Dr. Hunter to her condition by asking for a medication order.

She took a deep breath and decided that if she couldn't convince Lillie that there was no baby, that she was in fact alone, then she'd just give her what she wanted. Elizabeth ran down to the children's ward on the floor below. Her feet skipped nimbly down the limestone staircase, and she almost took a spill on the last few steps. She steadied herself with her resolve and kept going. She flung open the door to the little playroom near the nurses' station, the one the elders from the Presbyterian Church down on the square had donated money for. She tore through three toy boxes before she found what she was looking for, and somehow managed to avoid unintentionally alerting her co-workers to her mission of mercy. She clutched the item in her hand as she ran hard up the large staircase that split the building into two wards on each floor. Finally she reached the open bay of a room where Lillie lay alone and sobbing, the only patient on the ward on a hot August night.

"Here, Lillie, here." She placed the porcelain-faced baby doll in the crook of Lillie's arm and tucked her hand around the soft cloth that formed its body. She took a step back from the bed and prayed hard that her idea worked. This could go either way, and she knew she was taking a chance.

"Oh, Margaret, oh goodness. Thank you so much," Lillie wept. She ran her fingers over the doll's head and down her well-worn dress. "He's so beautiful. So, so beautiful." Lillie calmed as she tried to rock the baby back and forth. A small hum, almost inaudible, escaped her chapped, dry lips and Lillie sang her son a well-known lullaby.

> Go to sleep, my baby, close your weary eyes
> Angels are above you, peeking through the skies
> Great big moon is shining, stars begin to peep
> And it's time for little Nathan to go to sleep.

She closed her eyes, stroking the doll's face to her silent melody. Within minutes she felt her body drifting back into the darkness, back to the painless sleep. Her arms felt full and her heart felt lighter. She'd have to remember to thank Margaret in the morning.

Lillie woke up several hours later clutching the baby doll to her bosom. How on earth had that gotten there? What was happening to her? The room was lit softly by an old oil lamp like she used in her home, and she could make out the silhouette of a woman sleeping in a chair next to her bed. She was sitting sidewise and curled uncomfortably in a ball, her knees tucked into her abdomen.

"Elizabeth?" Lillie whispered, and Elizabeth didn't stir. Lillie's nose felt stuffy, and she felt phlegm hit the back of her throat. Her eyes felt swollen and puffy and tired. Lord, she felt tired. Had she been crying? She couldn't remember, but the viscous mucus was building a hefty cough in her throat that she couldn't help but release. The noise of it woke Elizabeth from her light slumber, and she jumped up quickly to tend to Lillie.

"Are you alright, Miss Lillie? Do you know where you are?" Elizabeth tried to determine if her new friend was alert again, or if she had averted disaster for just a few short hours.

"I'm alright. Is this your doll? I don't reckon I need it." She handed the doll to Elizabeth and tucked her arms under the covers. She was cold, and her skin felt raw against the air circulated by the lonely fan.

"Right as rain again, I see." Elizabeth sighed inwardly.

"What do you mean? Was I not okay?" Lillie was confused, and her face showed it. She knitted her brows and tried to recall what happened. All she recollected was a sad, sorrowful wisp of dream that left her feeling even colder.

"Never mind, Lillie, it doesn't matter. Are you cold? Let me get you another blanket." Lillie's internal thermometer was going haywire, and Elizabeth knew that wasn't good.

"Nah, tell me. Please. Was I not okay?" Lillie implored Elizabeth for the truth. What had she done?

Elizabeth covered Lillie with a thick woolly blanket that smelled of the oak chest of drawers it had been lying in for the last four or five months since the winter. She smoothed it out and tucked it up under Lillie's chin. "Well, Lillie, it's sort of a long story. I don't mind telling, if you don't mind listening." Lillie nodded, and Elizabeth continued. "Well then, it started a couple weeks ago, I guess. Flora had taken you in a wheelchair out to the center yard. She said you seemed restless and agitated, and she thought you could use some fresh air. Sometimes staring at four walls from a bed will do that to a patient. She sat with you awhile, but then she got called inside to do something right quick. When she got back to you a few moments later she found you..." Elizabeth stopped, not sure how to go on, how to say it without embarrassing Lillie.

"Elizabeth, really, it's okay. I want to know." Lillie caught Elizabeth's eye and didn't let go. She held her there, showing her she wasn't ashamed of whatever it was that she had to say. She was done being ashamed.

"Well, she came back and found you rocking an imaginary baby in your arms. You were humming at first, and then crying. You were crying real bad, Miss Lillie. You were begging God to help him, to make him breathe." Elizabeth saw tiny tears forming in Lillie's eyes and, as she hesitated, she saw Lillie nod her head, prompting her to continue. "Well, Flora didn't know what to make of it. You hadn't done anything like that before, and she couldn't seem to get you back to reality. She took you back to the ward, but you just wouldn't settle, Miss Lillie. You cried for hours, until finally Dr. Hunter came and gave you a shot of something that knocked you out for a good while. But for days afterward you would just wake up and cry. You'd cry about your son, and you'd beg the staff to help you find him."

"Huh. Is that so...?" Lillie was quiet. She'd held together so well after the actual event, and now it seemed her body needed to grieve. It had been many years since then, and she was still holding on, still looking, still feeling the absence.

"They were trying to send you away from here. The doc and head nurse, that is. To Western State. But we all talked them out of it, and it's like you knew it too. Your crying episodes stopped suddenly, and you were... well..."

"Right as rain?" Lillie gave Elizabeth a small smile and mouthed a thank you. "You probably guessed there's a story there."

"It's okay, Lillie. You don't have to explain." Elizabeth tried to hide her curiosity in her statement of compassion, but Lillie knew she wondered. Who wouldn't, with such outrageous outbursts?

"Well now, I don't mind telling you, Elizabeth, if you don't mind listening." She wiggled her arm out from beneath the sheet and beckoned Elizabeth towards her. She was quiet and calm, and Elizabeth sensed Lillie needed to tell the story as much as she needed to hear it. Elizabeth pulled her chair closer to the bed and accepted Lillie's offer. Hand in hand, in the glow of the old lamp and the mid-August moon, Lillie told a story that gripped Elizabeth's soul and never let go.

It was May of 1945, and Lillie was thirty-six years old. The pains had come in waves, crashing into her like the sea slamming into a rocky cliff. Lillie closed her eyes and felt them burn with her tears. She found the most radiant image she could think of and held on to it for as long as she could. Heaven, or what she thought might be like there, far up beyond the skyline. She pictured all the details, both the minute and the obvious. She tried to feel the texture in her hands, the smell in her nostrils, the taste on her tongue. Concentrate, damn it, stay with it.

And then it was gone. She let her eyelids rest together for a moment, feeling herself breathe. The air was viscous with discomfort, and she felt like it was filling up her lungs from the bottom to the top as the air entered and exited her throat. Slowly the room came into focus, and it looked strangely different to her. Things were hazy and not making sense. She placed her hand gently inside her sister's palm and turned her head away towards the window. Through the withered glass pane she stared tiredly at the dark tobacco field that had sustained her family for years. It seemed lonely this night, and colder than usual for the late spring.

The pains came again, closer now, and more powerful. She felt them wrap around her rhythmically from back to front and down subtly into her thighs. She closed her eyes and searched for that beautiful place again, but found it more and more difficult to get back there. She lay on her side and cradled her head in her hand, her cheek in her palm. She draped her other arm across her chest and pulled her knees into her abdomen. She began rubbing her feet together, slowly and rhythmically, kneading away the pain.

"Slow now, Lillie. Slow it down." The midwife spoke as from a hundred miles away.

Lillie's eye flung open and zipped wildly around the room. She had a hard time focusing on the faces in the room—they were blurry and indistinct. Voices were all they were; voices that she could hardly hear. Her breath quickened, and the pain became a constant dull ache that quickly built into a mounting inferno. Her body was not her own any longer, and whatever control she'd had was slowly slipping from her grasp like a vase falling through wet hands towards a tiled floor. She heard her resolve hit the earth with a crash. And there it shattered, breaking the silence. She heard a loud scream fill the room, and was confused as to who was making such commotion while she labored. Her bottom began to feel heavy as the tissue slowly stretched. She cried out in agony, "Margaret, please!" Her tears found her cheeks in a well-known path and she let them fall, freely hitting the sweaty sheet underneath her. They were warm and familiar and provided an odd comfort, like an old friend coming round for coffee.

"Almost there now, Lillie, almost." Margaret's voice was even and collected.

The pain was back, and shrouded Lillie like lightning. It came like a moment of inspiration often does—fast and furious, without any forethought, without any warning. Its current was strong, pushing, pulling, contorting. It was too strong, terrifyingly strong. It invaded, overtaking every one of her common sense cells.

But she knew this pain: they'd met many times before. In the very spot she lay now she had greeted it over and over. It was the same coverlet under which she cowered now, and the same placid view out the window, and the same women in attendance. Four daughters and three sons were born in this very place, one of whom was born still. Paul. Sweet Paul. She hadn't known beforehand and had waited and waited for him to cry. And then she'd seen him, cord still attached, white and still, swollen and dead. She had spent moments that felt like years just waiting to hear him cry. And she spent years that felt like moments waiting for answers, waiting for calm, waiting for something. Her youngest girl had followed, healthy and fine, but quiet and reserved, carrying the soul of her lost brother into the world on her unknowing shoulders. She was just shy of turning one.

And now Lillie lay waiting again, writhing, knowing it was coming. She was almost done. She would soon meet the person who had wiggled inside her and pushed so far up into her rib cage that she could hardly breathe. The child who had hiccuped so hard every evening before bedtime that the jostling was visible from the outside. The child who had carried heavy and low for some time now and had caused her back to ache from the overcurvature of her short spine. The child she already knew and loved. Soon she would hold the life in her arms that she now held in her belly.

"It's coming, Margaret," cried Lillie, the tears flowing freely now.

She pushed into the pain, hard and deep and with everything she had. She found relief in the pushing, and a sense of renewal as she moved the baby down fast. Lillie felt herself spreading, hot and fiery, like her pelvis was being drawn and quartered. The dark head of hair emerged from its hiding place and followed the well-known path towards the dawn as Margaret readied herself. Lillie's last four had come so fast that if Margaret had stepped away for a moment she would have missed them.

Lillie's pelvis spread, and the pain spread with it. She arched her back with surprise, bringing herself to an upright position. She placed her feet apart and curled her shoulders and chin towards her navel. Lillie bore down, and her son crowned.

"Lots of hair, Lillie! Again, go again!" Margaret's forehead was damp with unease, and she used the crook of her arm to wipe it away from her eyes. The boy's head emerged and Lillie cried out in both pain and relief.

Margaret wiped away the mucus from the child's nose and mouth as best she could with a towel, and helped him rotate his face towards Lillie's right thigh. She placed her hands on either side of his head and pulled down, gently attempting to guide his right shoulder under Lillie's pubic bone. She felt too much resistance, so she applied more pressure, and more. The boy didn't move.

"More, Lillie! I need more! Now!" Margaret shouted, her voice filling up the quiet space with her trepidation. Panic nearing hysteria filled Margaret's mind. Perspiration poured down her face with her efforts, and still the boy would not move. Lillie lay on her back and grabbed behind her knees, pulling her legs upward and outward. She bore down again, hard, and harder still, pausing only for a short breath. She felt it; Lillie knew he was stuck. She pushed with every ounce of vigor she had, willing him to free himself, begging God to help her release her child, visualizing her baby slipping past and crying angrily at the chaos of it all. Lillie pushed and Margaret pulled, maneuvering as she'd been taught. She attempted to push the boy back to pivot his shoulder and dislodge it from where it was wedged under Lillie's bone. He was too large, he filled up every space in her flesh. Lillie's tissues tore under the strain, freeing a steady flow of blood; but it was not enough to free him. With all of her knowledge exhausted, Margaret did the only thing she knew to do.

"I'm sorry, Lillie." Margaret found the baby's small clavicle and pushed hard until she heard and felt the pop. It was enough to allow him to pass under. It was enough to get him out. Lillie felt her child leave her body and collapsed backwards into the bed in a heap. She had done it, she was done. It took only seconds to register the silence. She waited for the cry, waited for mercy, waited for something, for anything. She looked down between her legs and saw her son Nathan for the first time. He lay on the warm, wet sheet, big and beautiful—white and still, like her Paul.

Chapter Fifteen

Lillie
Wednesday, August 12, 1953
11:45 p.m.

"There was nothing to be done, he'd already been gone for a few days," Lillie said. A steady stream of tears trickled down her face. Elizabeth sat silently wiping at her eyes with her free hand, trying to be strong for Lillie. "Two boys I lost. Two."

"I'm so sorry, Lillie," Elizabeth said, and she was. She was at a loss for words, as people often are when dealing with such delicate topics. "I'm not sure I could have gone on after that," Elizabeth said softly.

"You think that, but what choice did I have? Weird thing is, time don't stop when a baby dies. Feels like it ought to, but it don't. Sometimes it don't even slow down. Life just keeps on going with or without you." Lillie squeezed Elizabeth's hand and then let go. "Elizabeth, I'm real tired now. I think I might just sleep a bit."

Elizabeth wiped her eyes with the back of her hand and said, "Sure, Lillie. You go on now and get some rest." She watched as Lillie drifted off and had a new-found feeling of respect for her. She might be lying there dying, but she was a survivor. Elizabeth tucked the blankets in around Lillie's chin, turned down the oil lamp a bit, and then headed downstairs for some fresh air.

As Lillie's mind meandered through the stages of sleep, she started thinking about the moments that had followed that horrific affair. She had blocked it for so long, pushed it down, pretended it hadn't happened. Now it was here, in front of her, and she couldn't help but revisit her memories. They were as crisp as the cool spring night on which Nathan was born.

Margaret had tended to a small tear that Lillie had sustained while pushing, while her sister Caroline tended to the baby. Caroline gently wiped him down from head to toe, sweeping in the folds of his flesh. She dried his hair with a soft cloth and smoothed it down over his tiny forehead with her fingers. She took the swaddling cloth and bundled him as she well knew how to do, and handed the boy to Lillie. Lillie stared at the round face in disbelief, and the tears found her cheeks once again, flowing without restraint. She sobbed gutturally as the other women in the room faded away to nothingness. There was only Lillie and her forever sleeping angel.

Even Clay's intrusion into the room didn't register as he barged in and spat out the ugliest thing he could think of. "Goddamn, she's gone an kilt another boy. Ought'a be jailed, that Goddamned woman. Useless, Goddamned useless I tell you!"

Nathan would have been nothing like his father. He would have been kind, and gentle. He would have been generous and loving. He would have been her.

Lillie held her son for hours in the crook of her arm, snug at her warm bosom, close to her beating, anguished heart. She gave no thought to Clay or her other children. There was only her and Nathan for a few, but precious, moments. She sang him a lullaby, soft and low. She sang him a song he would never hear with his tiny ears; a song he would never feel in his tiny silent heart. It started with *Go to sleep my baby, close your weary eyes*, and ended with a fresh river of salty tears. Lillie held him and held him, stroking his perfect face, until both her arms and her heart ached so much that she could no longer bear the burden. Wearily, she gently placed a kiss and a blessing on his tiny cheek and put her son once again in Margaret's capable hands.

Nathan was the largest at just shy of sixteen pounds, a gruesome result of Lillie having the sugar. She hadn't known it then, but had suspected after her last two babies had been so large, and her feet and hands had started going numb. Truth be told, Clay knew Lillie was sick long before the actual diagnosis, years later, but he hadn't wanted to take her to the doctor in town.

"Bunch'a lying thieves they are," he'd snarled. "They invent a new illness if they thought it'a get 'em some 'a my green!" Money was most of it, but it wasn't the whole story. Clay couldn't see past what was happening right in front of him. Taking Lillie to town meant time and it meant effort. It meant he'd have to pick up some of her part. He never saw that not helping her in the present meant that she might not be there in the future.

Clay allowed Lillie two days to rest and then his tolerance for her 'laziness' wore out. Three days after the loss of Nathan, Lillie was up and about, tending to the household chores. Two more days and she was expected to resume her full workload in the garden and on the farm, while the soil over son's grave hadn't yet set.

Lillie was exhausted. She just existed most moments, trying to pretend it was meant to be, that she just needed to accept it. Her heart told her otherwise. Her body ached, and she felt as though she'd been trampled by a herd of cattle. Her soul felt like it could lie down in the tobacco field and never wake back up, but Lillie didn't let that stop her from taking the time to send something Margaret's way. The aging midwife only worked *pro bono* for the Woodards because she had a warm spot in her heart for Lillie, and felt grievous that she had to put up with Clay. Plus, Lillie was always so genuinely gracious and grateful. Even after her first son Paul had died, thoroughly engulfed in her grief, Lille had sent Margaret a gift; and this time was no different.

A week after she gave birth to Nathan, Lillie waited until Clay had gone out to the fields for the day so she'd be assured a few hours peace. Clay clomped around the kitchen, leaving a mess in his wake and biscuit crumbs on the table. Then, without so much as a goodbye, he plowed out through the door and hopped down the steps. The screen door slammed shut with a bang on its rusty hinges, and it seemed to say "good riddance." Lillie cringed at the noise and then peeked out the little window beside the stove, watching his distinct heavy-footed step lead him to the big red barn just over the hill. She stood, ever so quietly gripping the table with her eyes closed, and wished Clay away for a while. Lord, let it be a long day. When enough time had passed that she was sure he wouldn't return for some forgotten thing or another, she got to work.

She kneaded the dough with her rough and calloused hands, rolling and rolling it until it was just so, infusing love with every motion. While the dough was left to rise, she picked out the finest of her canned goods. Jellies, green beans, tomatoes. May didn't leave Lillie much in the way of fresh crops, but for her babies that had been born during the harvest times Lillie had given fresh goods like corn, carrots, cabbage, or apples. She'd washed the earth off of them with tender care and dried each piece as if she were polishing the finest of silver for the highest of royalty. This time, though, with only canned goods to give, she gently brushed the cellar dust off her jars and then wiped them clean until the Kerr name on the glass sparkled nicely.

All the while that she was preparing her gifts, she would have Margaret in her head. Margaret's kind and capable hands. Margaret's warm and inviting dimples. Margaret's sincere embrace. She pictured Margaret's old and weary face, marked with too many babies born, too many babies and mothers lost, too many burdens to bear, and Lillie would smile. She'd smile a Margaret smile, as she bundled the shiny vegetables or the glistening jars in with the warm bread, and she'd tuck in a kind note with a keen sense of appreciation conveyed. Lillie hoped that Margaret knew how much she was grateful. Even though she hadn't much to give, she gave what she had, packaged it in the pretty paper of love and topped it with a vibrant bow of gratitude. And every time one of the young'ins would come running, saying, "Miss Lillie's baby is a comin'," Margaret would get to going too without any thought of what she might get in return.

It hadn't always been that way, where Lillie had to hide who she was from Clay. In the beginning it had been nice, and she'd had nothing but the greatest of hope for her marriage. It was like Lillie had two husbands—the one she'd married and the one she'd ended up with—and somewhere in the middle he'd morphed from a husband to a tyrant. Maybe the mean Clay had been there all along and she just hadn't seen it. She'd just seen a man, like any other man, in need of care and love, a family, and a wife.

Elizabeth came back around midnight to check on Lillie and found her awake, staring complacently at the dimly glowing oil lamp that Elizabeth had scrounged from the bottom of a dusty box in the basement supply room. She had picked the prettiest one out of the bunch and cleaned it meticulously until the white porcelain bottom looked new and the brass was as free from patina as she could get it. There was enough wick left for a few evenings' use, and Elizabeth knew that was all she'd really need. The satin glass was scratched a bit, but the brass knob turned freely and easily. Elizabeth figured it was safe to use, and she would just hide it at the end of her shift. No sense drawing attention to the fact that she was blatantly breaking the rules for Lillie.

"Can't sleep, Lillie?" Elizabeth prodded. Lillie looked exhausted, like she hadn't slept in weeks. Her face was swollen, and tiny red-streaked veins danced in the whites of her hollow, sunken eyes.

"Nah. My mind been wandering round like a stray sheep. Strangest thing. It never done this before." Lillie shook her head a little with a subtle look of befuddlement. "Odd not to have control of your head."

"I'm sure it is. Got to be confusing." Elizabeth could only imagine that it must feel like a foreign invader coming in and staking claim to your land and taking control of your mind. She could almost picture tiny soldiers marching along the ridges of the brain, toting a rifle in one hand and a long pole with little flags on top in the other hand. They'd stop, randomly pick a region that they liked and then slammed the pole deep into the tissues, commanding their attention and taking over control of their function. Broca or Wernicke's area conquered in one foul swoop. Odd, indeed.

Lillie shifted slightly so she had a better view of Elizabeth. "You know, ever since I was little, I never did think much of the past or future. It might sound strange, but I never did. I just only ever saw what was happening that day. Only time I ever thought about what was to come was when I was planning for supper, or what we might need throughout the year." Lillie rubbed at her eyes. They burned something fierce. "'Ya know, I never got what folks meant when they say they daydreaming or letting they mind wander. Never did get that till now."

"Must be kind of nice, though. I mean to always just be in the moment." Elizabeth was envious. Thinking about her past and her future often felt like a heavy dark cloud hanging low over her, following her around and taunting her as the clock ticked by. Tick, tock, choose. Tick, tock.

"I'm sure doing enough wonderin' now to make up for all the years of not. Sort of, um... what do you call it when something is all kinds of twisted?" Lillie scrunched up her face as she tried to recollect the word she wanted. It was in there somewhere, tangled up with all the other things she knew that she knew.

"I'm not sure what you mean, Lillie," Elizabeth said. She fussed with the sheets on Lillie's bed, although Lillie hadn't asked her to.

"When I was growing up the preacher was always talking about how if you just stop and be grateful for the moment you are in, that's the key to happiness. I always just thought, well, of course, don't everybody do that? Now then, look at me. I done lived my whole life like that, being grateful and forgiving daily. Look what happiness that done brought me!" A little bit of anger permeated Lillie's voice, though she wasn't quite sure what she was angry about.

"Ironic. That's the word you wanted. Ironic," Elizabeth said decisively.

"Yeah, ironic. Lord, help me, I'm a fool!" Lillie spat the words at the air in front of her as if it would make them less true.

"Lillie, you're no fool. The way you see the world is a gift, really." Elizabeth pulled a chair up next to Lillie's bed again, a situation they were both quickly becoming accustomed to. "I figure, though, that we need a bit of both learning to live in the moment, and also stopping to look up every so often to see what the rest of the world is up to." Elizabeth was as much asking as she was telling.

"I reckon so. It's like God forgot to give me that last part, though. Like he left that outta my bones and replaced it with blinders." The irritation had left Lillie's voice, and she felt her tears rising again. "I'm not perfect, Elizabeth," Lillie choked out. "I made so many mistakes by being that way. By not looking up. I just couldn't see then, but I do now. So many mistakes." Lillie closed her eyes. If only Elizabeth knew, if only she could see what she'd done by not doing anything.

"Lillie, remember how I told you my mama died? And that I don't recall too much about her except some of the things she'd say?" Elizabeth rubbed her hands together nervously. She hardly ever spoke about her mother, yet here she was bringing her up twice in as many days.

"Mmm-hmm. Your mama the one who said the thing about how you can't hide the truth? I remember," Lillie said.

"Yes. Well, when one of us got in trouble for something or other, she'd always say, 'we all make mistakes child, now what you gonna do about it?'"

Wasn't that what the bird had told her? Little Red. Hadn't she said the same thing?

Elizabeth looked at Lillie and waited for some sort of validation. Some sign that her mama had been right. When Lillie didn't say anything, she continued cautiously. "Or when we'd fall down and skin a knee or bust open our palms, she'd always say to us, 'Well, it looks like you're okay then. Now you can sit there crying about it, or you can hop back up and go clean yourself up.' She always helped us, don't get me wrong. She'd bandage and kiss whatever needed kissing, but I still always thought it was kind of heartless. I wanted once for her to just pick me up, to not make me scramble off the floor." Elizabeth stopped and paused a second, thinking hard about what she wanted to say next. "But I understand it now. Life's gonna knock you down for sure, and there ain't always someone there to pick you up." Elizabeth shot out her words in rapid succession. She was worried she'd offend

112

Lillie. Who was she but a young girl giving an older woman advice?

Lillie had heard this before, and she knew it in the heart of her being to be true. Mary's face came into focus in her mind, and she wondered silently if perhaps Mary Finn and Elizabeth's mother had been friends.

Mary's similar advice had come so many years earlier. When Lillie had just turned nine, her little brother Samuel, who was twenty-one months old at this time, fell quite ill. Samuel had been born shortly after the Garretts had moved to Franklin, and Lillie's mama had called him their good luck charm. He seemed to fill their small house from day one with a lot of laughter and good-hearted smiles. He'd started out late in February of 1918 with what seemed to be a simple head cold, but it quickly became apparent that it was instead the flu. With quarters as tight as they were, he'd passed the virus along to his sister Caroline, who was just shy of five. His fever soared and plummeted for days, and Caroline seemed to match every move. Ice baths and warm blankets, steam tents and gently tapping his back and chest to clear airways of the heavy congestion. Days and days of both children riding the roller coaster of a flu; only when Caroline's body started to fight it off, Samuel's body didn't follow suit, and he had ended up with bronchial pneumonia. For six days he lay under the watch of Lillie's parents and a very concerned family doctor, but in the end it was too much for his small body to fight, and it consumed him. His loud and laborious breaths simply stopped one night while Lillie's mama held him to her chest and begged God for mercy.

Lillie's family was devastated, and her mama had been inconsolable for weeks. She was also three months along with another baby, and between being consumed by her broken heart and her body's exhaustion she couldn't get out of bed long enough to comfort her grieving children. Lillie had stayed at home, trying to make sense of it in her head, not wanting to bother her mama or siblings who seemed just as caught up in their grief; but eventually she turned to Josie and Mary for solace. She ran all the way into town with tears streaming down her face, feeling like the world was crashing down around her as she flew down one dirt road after another. She collapsed in Mary's lap in the middle of the sewing shop on a Wednesday afternoon and buried her face in Mary's skirt. Lillie remembered feeling like she'd never see the beauty in anything again, like she'd never be able to feel the sun shining on her face again without her brother Sam.

Mary stroked her head for a long time before she said softly to Lillie, "Child, your character ain't determined much by how you act when you're happy. Anybody can do great things, say the right things, and be nice when they're happy, when life's going well. That don't show much about who you are. What determines who you really are is what you do when life treats you badly. Who you are when you feel terrible inside. Who you are when you get knocked down. 'Ya see, Lillie, everybody falls, but not everybody gets back up." Lillie lay there for what seemed like forever in Mary's lap, and Mary let her. Patiently she let her stay there, letting it sink in. At long last Lillie got up, kissed Mary softly on the cheek, and slowly made her way home.

"Lillie? You still awake?" Elizabeth asked. Lillie had closed her eyes while thinking about Mary and her precious gift of words. How many times had that little piece of advice saved Lillie with Clay? How many times?

"I am. I am." Lillie stared up at the ceiling. The room was so dark, but it felt safe, like wrapping a big thick blanket around yourself in front of the fireplace.

"Miss Lillie, my point is that you might'a made mistakes. We all do. But it sounds like you always got back up. Even in here, while you feel so terrible. You could'a been nasty with us, you could'a broke down weeks ago, but you didn't. A lot of folks do. You got some inner strength, Miss Lillie. That's what matters, isn't it? Not the mistakes you made, but that you kept going?"

Lillie sighed. "You're right, Elizabeth, I have been getting back up. I've been getting back up for years, and there's something to that, I guess." Lillie paused thinking about her next sentence. "But that ain't the same thing as getting back up and doing something. I might'a got back up, but I just stood there and waited for the next blow." Lillie thought about how, when life had turned sour, through no fault of their own, Clay had changed. He'd let it eat him up and it had turned him into a monster—and she had just stood there and watched.

Lillie took a long deep, contemplative breath. "I'm not sure that's what your mama meant, Elizabeth." *I'm not sure that's what Mary meant.*

"Miss Lillie, I sure am glad they didn't send you away to Hopkinsville," Elizabeth whispered gently.

"Me too, Elizabeth." Lillie turned and looked at her new friend's silhouette. "I think we have a lot to teach each other."

Chapter Sixteen

Cate
Los Angeles, CA
April 1944

My parents didn't fight me on my choice to leave again. I'm not sure if it was because they knew it was the right decision, or if it was because they were happy to have dodged the bullet of what would have exploded between Aunt Rachel and me had I stayed much longer. My dad even seemed a bit excited about my new adventure back to Los Angeles and said that when he'd saved up a bit maybe they would come visit. Though his offer sounded nice, I wasn't putting money on it. As far as Jack was concerned, he'd been kind in one last act by not contesting anything, and he even sent me a good chunk of the first year's profits on the store with a short note saying I'd done half the work, and I ought to have half the money. I almost sent it back to him on principle, but then realized he was right, and it was, indeed, money I had earned, in more ways than one.

I stepped off the Greyhound bus and hit the ground running upon my return to Los Angeles. The Pipers were ever so kind in opening their home, but I felt a need for a bit more freedom and didn't want to burden my friend for very long. I was extremely lucky to find work right away with the help of Betsy's husband, Len. Len worked at the North American Aviation plant, on the southeast side of the Los Angeles Municipal Airport, which was very convenient as it was just on the northeast corner of Imperial Highway and Aviation Way. He had given me a good recommendation and set up an interview for me, without me even prodding, and I was more than thrilled with the opportunity. The plant's location made it a well sought-after place to work, and I was lucky that I was allowed to even sit for an interview, much less that I actually get a spot on the assembly line, with my inexperience. It seemed like folks in Los Angeles were willing to take a bit more of a chance on people than in Michigan, and I knew instantly that I was in the right place.

North American Aviation was a massive operation, and was staffed by numerous female workers who weren't just filing paperwork or cleaning. These ladies were Rosie The Riveter in the flesh, and were making and assembling B-25 'Billy Mitchell' bombers and P-51 Mustang fighter planes, amongst other things. It was all the war posters had advertised, and more. They were welding, assembling fuselages and engines, running lathes, and machining small airplane parts. They were cowlers, making covers for the airplanes' engines; riveters, inspectors and supervisors; and, though the pay might not have been equal, they were seen as just as important as their male counterparts. They ate lunch side by side with the men, sharing stories and offering work advice. What struck me the most was how the women wore slacks, simple button-down blouses, and penny loafers instead of long skirts and high heels. There was just something so appealing about it, and the place felt magical to me. It was liberating to see, and I again just knew I was supposed to be a part of it somehow.

The plant was enormous at almost 160,000 square feet, and the main hangar, where the final assembly and storage of the planes occurred, was the most impressive thing I'd ever seen. There were row after row of shiny, perfectly put together aircraft, made by the hands of local men and women, and meant for our nation's finest overseas.

As large as the company was, you'd expect some degree of chaos, but to be honest it was as organized as anything I'd ever seen. You could simply smell the sweat and metal; you could hear the powerful tools used to create the bits and pieces that made a plane; you could feel the workers' pride the moment you entered the facility. The workers weren't carrying guns or trekking through foreign lands, but they were fighting the enemy all the same, and what they were doing mattered. It felt so good just to stand and watch them at work that I couldn't wait to get my hands on a rivet gun and help. They put out such an amazing product in the P-51s that Britain even purchased some of them and first used them in the raid on Dieppe. As it turned out, the Mustang was the only American made plane that the British flew during the entire war, which was a testament to its quality.

So, much to my delight, I was hired fairly quickly, though not as a riveter or on the big assembly lines as I had hoped. There were size requirements due to the heaving lifting that was necessary for some of the assembly, and I was considered to be too small. So a

Rosie I was not, but I found my place on one of the sub-assembly lines making small parts and learning about all kinds of machinery that I hadn't even known existed. I started on the chucking machine, which is just a spruced-up name for a lathe with a chuck piece on the end. It made the threads on the rivets and the inside of bolts. When I proved myself worthy of working with the small things, I was entrusted with punching the rivet holes in the frames of the B-25s that would be assembled elsewhere in the factory. Eventually I was trained to inspect some of the electrical sub-assembly parts before they went to the line for installation. I learned so much in such a short time, but what I didn't know was that this knowledge would become an invaluable business asset later in my life as well.

I started working at the plant in early May of 1944, when I was twenty-five years old. In all of my working years to come, and I had many, none could ever stand up to that year I spent working at the war plant. Maybe it was because it was the first money I'd ever made for myself, or because it was the first time I had ever had a real job, but it felt like more than that. I was doing something important, and I felt needed and appreciated for something other than putting dinner together and getting it on the table in time. It was my time for renewal, and to see what I was made of, on my own, and I took up the challenge with a fiercely willing heart.

Though the paychecks were indeed nice, the camaraderie I felt with my co-workers was priceless. I was welcomed by the women on my assembly line like I'd been with them since day one. No one asked me about my marital status, and not because they didn't care, but because it didn't matter to them. The world was changing, and these gals were changing right along with it. I remember the day the girls in my department found out I'd been married. I hadn't mentioned it to a soul because, again, no one had asked, and I didn't really feel like dwelling on it. We were too busy chatting about politics, or social events, or baseball even, for that matter, to concern ourselves with each other's social standing. I felt planets away from the life I had known in Michigan—but when my 'secret' finally did come out, the response I received was not at all what I'd expected.

We were sitting outside near the flight line in late June with our lunch pails beside us and were enjoying the free bottles of Coca-Cola that the plant managers had handed out as part of the flight show day. A few times a month the company took the new planes out for test runs, and it gave the employees a chance to see the fruition of all of our hard work. I can't tell you what amazement it brought to see something in the air that I had been a part of making. It was a wonderful way to pat us all on the back.

It had been a warm day, but none of us seemed to mind too much. It was nice to be outside and out of the lunch room, and the colas helped to make the creeping temperature seem a little less torturous. Claire and Macy, two of the gals on my line who eventually ended up being my roommates, had been discussing their plans for the weekend.

"Seriously, ladies." Macy had a flair for the dramatic like my Betsy. "Three little letters just may change your life. U-S-O. Eye candy, girls. Eye candy." The lot of us laughed, and I could picture Macy lighting up a USO dance like sparkling Christmas decor on a front porch rail. She just had a shine about her. She stopped for a second and sipped down some cola and made the loudest, most theatrical, "Ahhhhhhhh" sound she could muster.

"Good Lord, Macy, really," Claire teased her friend. "Next thing you know she'll be belching us a song," she said as she grinned.

"Oh, a serenade is what you're after? Well, in that case..." Macy was drawing in a large breath like she was about to belt out an opera when Claire busted out laughing and said, "MACY ANN, don't you dare!" and sent Macy into a fit of hysterics.

Through her laughter Macy said, "Geez, I was only teasing, Claire! But I am working on belching out the Star Spangled Banner for next time." I was falling in love with these ladies fast, and it felt amazing to be around real women, who weren't afraid to blur the social lines a little and just be themselves. I had no idea how much I had been holding back until I met true authenticity, and day by day the real me crept out a little more until I knew I would never hide her again.

I was holding the Coke bottle between my hands and watching it sweat a little when Lana, an inspector on our line, asked, "Do you all remember the first time you had a Coke? I sure do. The bubbles scared me so much I spat it out all over my momma's dress, which didn't make her too happy. I didn't get to have one again for quite some time!" We all chuckled at the thought of Lana, probably the most conservative of our crew, spitting anything out of her mouth.

"I remember my first sip," I said without any of the thespian flair that Macy had put on before.

"Oh yeah, Cate? How old were you?" It was Macy, and I knew why she was asking. I hadn't really shared much about anything, and I think they were all curious as to my age amongst other things. Not curious in a judgmental way, though, just curious in a 'I'd really like to know you better' kind of way. Up until then I hadn't really said much, I'd just listened.

"I was quite young really, maybe five or six, but I remember it. We lived in a really small house on the outskirts of town and had to walk quite a way to get to the general store from our house. It was probably only two or three miles, but it sure felt like ten sometimes, and my pop had really long legs so I pretty much ran alongside him the whole way. I remember it was really hot that day, so it must have been summertime, and I remember feeling so thirsty by the time we hit the store that I felt like I'd swallowed all the dirt from the road on the way in." I looked around at all the girls nibbling their sandwiches and sipping their sodas, and it struck me how attentive they were being. I'm not sure I'd ever really been listened to that way before, and it gave me a boost to continue.

"Anyway, I'd heard about the soda fountain drinks before, but hadn't tried them. That day, though, there happened to be a Coca-Cola sales representative in the store who was giving out samples and marketing the easy-carry six pack. They'd come out with the contoured glass bottles a few years before and they were just reaching the small mom and pop shops like in my town. I took one sip, and I swear I thought God had poured some of his heaven in my mouth. All I could tell the eager rep was, 'I think I like it.' I think he was expecting a little bit bigger response given the huge grin I had on my face! I must have drunk two whole bottles before my pop cut me off, and oh, how I remember that the walk home seemed a whole lot more fun than the walk into town had been!"

The gals chuckled a bit, and then someone else put forth their story and we took turns listening to each other's childhood memories. It was fun to picture everyone in a younger state, and I think we all enjoyed hearing about where each of us had come from. Most of the girls had come from small towns, seeking out big adventure in Los Angeles, and they could relate to being the last to know about things like Coca-Cola. That afternoon also helped me break out of my shell a bit, and helped to make me really part of the gang.

We were heading in from lunch when Claire and Macy flanked me on both sides. Claire threw her hand around my waist and Macy looped her arm through my arm. It startled me, but I wasn't as uncomfortable as one might expect. I looked from face to face and saw that they both has mischievous grins plastered on their faces.

"Yes, ladies? What is it? I feel like I'm about to be in trouble." I was laughing, I knew whatever it was was going to be fun, with those two.

"You got you a man, Miss Cate?" Macy again, with her best imitation of a back hills hussy.

I snorted, which made us all laugh, and then I said, "No. No man. I used to have one. Was married, in fact, for seven years or so, but, well..." The truth was I was still married, but that point seemed inconsequential.

"Well..." Claire prodded me ever so slightly and squeezed my hip teasingly. "He wasn't man enough for you?"

"Good Lord, Claire! Now who's being inappropriate?" Macy giggled and said, "I apologize for her, she never did have no manners."

"You aren't from the South *Mizzzzz* Macy. Or sorry, should I call you Scarlett O'Hara?" Claire bantered back. "What I meant to say was, what happened to your husband? Unless..." She stopped teasing and her face fell serious. "Did he? Oh goodness, did you lose him overseas, because I am so sorry if I..."

I broke the tension with more laughter and put Claire out of her misery quickly. "No, no. Nothing like that. He's alive and well. Well, he's alive anyway." I felt her relax beside me and take a deep sigh of relief. "No, I just thought he ought to love just his wife, and he, well... he thought differently is all." I wasn't going to go into details, there wasn't a need, really; it was history already written, no need for it to change anything else.

I expected more questions, more poking into things, but the two girls were above all that. Claire just said, "Aw yes, I know a few men who are afflicted with the same thoughts." And Macy gave a big "*Mmmmmmm-Hmmm*. Yup. Me too." But they sealed the deal of friendship with Claire's next comment.

"Good for you, Cate," she'd said. "You deserve better than that."

Those were the only words I had wanted to hear from my friends and family back home, and never had. I had felt shamed in Michigan, but in Los Angeles the same choices made me feel empowered. Funny how a change of scenery and a change of company can give you a new perspective. As I looked from Claire to Macy and took in how accepting they were being, I knew that I'd found two women who I wanted desperately to be my friends. And that they would be part of my history not yet written.

Chapter Seventeen

Lillie
Thursday, August 13, 1953
2:30 a.m.

Elizabeth was exhausted. She had never poured herself into a patient like this before, and a conflict brewed within her between drawing a professional line and honoring Lillie's humanity. More than that, she felt drawn towards Lillie, like a sphinx moth intoxicated by a rickety porch light. Careless creatures, seeking out luminescent inebriation even if it ultimately leads to their own demise, the compulsion ultimately killing them. But Elizabeth felt solidly that Lillie's light was meant to kindle something greater in her, and that it wouldn't harm her, but would make her stronger. That its glow was taking her somewhere she was meant to be heading. Somehow Elizabeth knew she needed to pay attention, to listen, to really see Lillie.

Lillie had fallen asleep again. It seemed like twenty to thirty minutes was all she could handle of being awake before the sandman came to collect her. Elizabeth pulled the covers up under Lillie's chin and tucked her rogue swollen arm up on her abdomen underneath the sheet. Although she didn't wish her further misery, Elizabeth prayed silently and selfishly for more time. There was something that was supposed to happen that hadn't happened yet, and Elizabeth hoped Lillie's body could hold out a few more days so she could find out what it was.

She picked up the miniature milk lamp by its bulbous white base and shook it a little to get a feel for how much kerosene was left. She didn't want Lillie to wake up with the wick burnt out and not know where she was, and the harsh glow of the naked bulbs in the wall sconces seemed to agitate her. Finding the lamp a bit low, Elizabeth headed down the staircase to see if she could find any more kerosene. On her way she stopped at the elongated window on the landing that was raised about six inches, and Elizabeth felt the hot August air pouring in through the stifled opening.

She pulled the lower sash up a little higher so she could look out, which took more effort than she'd expected. The window was large and heavy, and she had to shove it up forcefully until it was high enough for her stand on her tiptoes and lean her shoulders and head out into the unclouded night. She turned towards the southern side of the building and could see the edge of the moon peeking out from where the thick white cornerstones met the flat frieze cornice at the roof line. She leaned out a little further to see it in its entirety and found, as she expected, that it was half full and shining brilliantly in a sky as translucent as glass. The air smelled heavily of late summer flowers and the remnants of the gentle showers that had cleansed their petals just hours before. Yellow hollyhocks and Japanese anemones lined the side of the building in shallow beds, and the moist Kentucky air pushed their sweet fragrances around on soft breezes in the darkness. Elizabeth couldn't see them very well, but she could smell them, and she took a few minutes to relish the sugary sensation of the flowers' perfume as she deeply breathed in the humid night air.

Her body was warm, and her once-crisp white uniform now clung to her curves from the moisture of the day. Even with her hair pinned up under her nursing cap she could feel the little beads of perspiration that clung to her neckline. She wiped away a teardrop of sweat that threatened to roll down her forehead and into her brow. A buzz was filling her head, but she didn't recognize it as fear, or even excitement. It was like the smell in the air that permeated into your bones right before a big rainstorm. All she knew was something big was brewing, and it wasn't the coagulated and nearly gelatinous coffee that her coworkers were making on the floor below. She stood, entranced by the light of the half moon, and enchanted by the sounds and smells of the summer evening. That was, until she heard distinctive footsteps coming up behind her. Footsteps that she knew well. They were light and fast and purposeful on the unforgiving gray stone flooring, and quickly reached the tiles behind her.

"Hey, girl!" It was Rose Cooper. Elizabeth had known her since they were young girls, endlessly jump roping in Rose's front yard while their mamas strung laundry on the lines out back. They'd been practically joined at the hip until recently. "What 'ya doin' hanging out there? Trying to escape?" Rose asked, laughing critically at her friend's oddly positioned body. "The front door is just as easy to exit through, if you ask me."

"Very funny, Rose," Elizabeth replied, irritation dripping from her small words. Elizabeth pulled herself back in the window and slumped against the hard, cool wall. She crossed her arms across her chest and shrugged her shoulders. "I was just thinking, I guess." Her eyes caught the large pendulum clock on the wall at the bottom of the staircase. It was late, much later than Elizabeth had thought.

"What 'ya thinking 'bout with your head stuck out there like some drunkard?" Rose, always dependably insensitive.

"I don't know." Elizabeth looked at the clock again and wondered where the night had gone. She looked back at Rose and said, "I just don't know what I'm doing any more, Rose. If I'm where I'm supposed to be." Elizabeth looked at Rose with eyes that were fishing for a reply she knew wasn't coming. It was like sitting in a boat on a frigid day with no bait on the line and expecting a bite anyway.

"You been listening to that old fool up there?" Rose scoffed. "What do you think she knows? Look where her life got her!" Rose made a disgusted face, clearly indicating just what she thought of the sad old woman dying above them. There it was, the predictable response from her oldest friend, and even though she knew it was coming, Elizabeth's body stiffened as her line snapped audibly in her ears under the weight of Rose's words.

"Rose!" Elizabeth was hot, the outside temperature having little to do with the instant red flush that hit her cheekbones. "She's no fool. I assure you of that!" Rose, always so black and white. Her heart was good, but her spirit was always so angry, only seeing the worst in people.

Rose threw up her hands defensively and raised her high arched brows. "My, my, I've hit a nerve, I see. Sorry, girl!" she responded. And she was, too, because she could tell she'd aroused something in Elizabeth that she feared was a long time coming.

"Ah, Rose, it's just, there's something there. Something special in her. I think she needs to tell her story before she'll really let go." Elizabeth turned and pulled the window down a bit before turning to face Rose. "And I think I'm the one who's supposed to hear it."

Rose placed her hand on Elizabeth's shoulder and pulled her closer. "I always knew you was a softy. You got you a good heart, Elizabeth. But she's gonna die whether you listen to her yappin' or not." Rose's face turned serious as she looked her friend in the eye and said, "Just don't be doing nothing stupid like getting too involved. Folks like that will reel you in like a big ole juicy catfish."

"Rose, I've been playing it safe my whole life. Keeping my distance. Doing my job. Raising my siblings." Elizabeth brought her hand up to Rose's tiny hand as it lay on her bony shoulder. She gave it a couple of soft pats before removing it briskly from her body. Elizabeth took a step back from her friend and looked her square in the face. She could smell Rose's fear at her actions. She'd never been like that before, feisty and unapologetic. "She may well die any second, and I may never know what she lived through or what she's done, but I know in my gut that that woman up there has something left to give. And she's holding on to give it to me."

Rose stood there frozen, and for the first time ever was at a complete loss for words. Her mouth hung open slightly and her eyes betrayed her confusion. "Elizabeth, I..."

As the scent of the hollyhocks hit her palate again and the sound of the night's crickets hit her ears, she knew she'd been listening to the wrong music for a long time. "No Rose, save it. I've got work to do." Elizabeth brushed proudly past her friend and skipped quickly down the rest of the short staircase, leaving Rose with a mess of tangled fishing line and sharp bait hooks to sort through by herself.

She headed towards the equipment room, determined not to stop and talk with anyone else. Damn that Rose. All she'd wanted to do was get a bit of fresh air and see about some kerosene. Plus, she needed to get her chores done before Lillie woke up again. She didn't want to miss a second if she could help it. Her mind wandered down the list of things she was supposed to do before the morning came, and she decided to start with cleaning the thermometers. She removed a clean white cloth from the stack in the cupboard and liberally poured isopropyl alcohol on it until the vapors reached her nose with a sting, a smell she both loved and loathed. She wiped each glass, mercury-filled unit with the saturated cloth and placed them in the appropriate large glass beakers of the same solution. The red-topped oral ones went in one and the blue-topped rectal ones in another. Mixing them up was just not an option.

"What the hell does Rose know?" she said under her breath as she worked. She thought about what her old friend had said and, with some humility, gave it some thought. Maybe she shouldn't get reeled in after all. Maybe Rose was right. Maybe Lillie just led a sad life and was going to die a sad death and it didn't really matter what Elizabeth did in the end. Her life was complicated as it was, and she had enough on her plate. Maybe she just ought to let it go.

Damn it, Lillie. But Lillie wasn't forcing anything on Elizabeth. It had all come about so naturally, and the more Elizabeth listened to Lillie, the more she felt a stirring within her. There was so much she didn't know, so many things her mama had never had the chance to show her. Here was this woman, a stranger, who was willing to share her life's wisdom with her; and, although Lillie wasn't her mother, it was what Elizabeth had felt like she had missed out on with her own mama. In a crazy way she felt her mama's pull in all of this, as if she had something to do with Lillie ending up in Elizabeth's life, confronting her, challenging her, changing her. As if her mama didn't like where she was going and had sent Lillie to try to fix it.

Elizabeth struggled with her conflicting thoughts as she turned her attention to the glass syringes, sighing at the sheer amount of work ahead of her that evening. All she wanted to do was sit vigil at Lillie's bedside and wait for her to awaken, but syringes didn't clean themselves. If she didn't want to find herself standing in front of the head nurse's desk in the morning, she'd better get to cleaning them.

There was one set of glass syringes for injecting medications, and a separate set for drawing blood and other pathological fluids from patients. Flora had collected all the used syringes from the different units earlier in the day, and had been kind enough to remove the needles and set them in the antiseptic solution of phenol and water. Not all of the day nurses were as considerate, and often Elizabeth found herself hiking up and down the three-story annex and the few units over in the main building to retrieve all of the used and dirty items herself. Flora had even been so nice as to leave the glass syringes in tidy rows on the two rectangular perforated sterilizing trays. Even Flora, the house gossip, knew that Elizabeth's time was best spent with Lillie in the next few days.

As she was one of the younger nurses, sterilizing duties often fell to Elizabeth, and it was times like this that she was grateful to the anonymous donor of their two small steam autoclaves. The donor had been kind, but also thrifty, and the autoclaves were used and old and probably left over from earlier in the last decade. They were both different, obviously picked up from separate facilities, which meant the operator had to know the quirks and tricks of each one. The autoclave on the left required a good steady push on the top to seal the lid. The one on the right required that the handle be pulled up and slightly outward in order to achieve its seal. Mixing up which autoclave was which meant a whole cycle of useless cleaning as the units would not seal correctly and the process would have to be repeated.

Red and blue thermometers, therapeutic and body fluid syringes, persnickety pseudo-twin sterilizing units. So much to keep separate and keep track of. Precision and attention to detail had been drilled in during nursing school for even the most menial of tasks, and now Elizabeth understood why.

She hardly ever complained, though. She'd heard the older nurses grumbling heartily and frequently about how all the young, fresh girls had it easy compared to when they started. How they'd had to boil a mixture of water and antiseptic solutions and sterilize needles and syringes with that method for years. She'd heard how tedious and time-consuming it had been, and how, since the syringes were never really stored properly afterward, it was almost sort of pointless unless you boiled them again right before you used them—and well, what physician was going to wait for that?

She plugged in the two square, copper units and adjusted the dials according to what she'd been taught. She heard the units start up and imagined the steam forming slowly, like a cloud of dust kicked out from a back tire on a dirt road. It built leisurely, nearly transparently, and then grew into a cloud of garbled murkiness. She pictured the swirling white vapor creeping up through the small holes that lined the bottom of the instrument tray and delicately surrounding the medical tools in its purifying mist. It cleansed every thing it touched, making it like new again, giving it all a fresh start.

Sometimes Elizabeth wished she could climb in alongside the scalpels, tweezers, needles, and syringes. She wished she could start over, start fresh, be as clean as the day she was born. She wished an obscure cloudy haze would whisk through her life, seep in through her pores, and set her right again. Within seconds her thoughts quickly landed on Lillie. Lillie, who was moments away from the end of her life. Lillie, who she barely knew, but felt like she had known forever. Lillie. What on earth did Lillie have to do with an old copper autoclave in a tiny cove of an equipment room in a small town community hospital? Elizabeth realized she was more tired than she had thought as she struggled to connect the dots between her two lines of thought.

Elizabeth shook her head as she cupped her hands over her nose and mouth as if in prayer. She closed her eyes and breathed in the scent of the harsh cleaning solutions that were harbored in the old oak cupboards that lined the back wall and filled the glass beakers on the shelves. "Lord, I must be crazy." Elizabeth laughed. "And now I'm standing here talking to myself." *Crazy or not, hold on tight girl, here we go…*

Chapter Eighteen

Lillie
Thursday, August 13, 1953
3:30 a.m.

Elizabeth pick up a small washcloth from the heap of linens that sat before her. They smelled like store-bought soap, bleach, and freshly piped water. They smelled like sunlight, hollyhocks, and angel pink angelonia. They smelled like her Kentucky. She matched corner to corner perfectly, as if making the perfect fold would make the rough cloth somehow better. She always assumed that with enough washes, the fabric would give, would soften somehow, but the hospital-grade cloth remained as stiff as the starched white nursing cap on her head. It was rigid and bristly, much like the head nurse who insisted the linens be folded in exactly the same manner every time, and placed just five towels high on any given shelf.

The work was monotonous and repetitive, but, as always, it offered Elizabeth some quiet time to think. Anyway, the other older nurses weren't exactly beating down the door to the laundry services room to help her. In fact, she was pretty sure she'd seen one cranky senior nurse napping in a rocking chair on the children's ward, where surely she thought no one would notice. Corner to corner, smooth it out, corner to corner, pat it flat. Five towels high and not one extra—the head nurse would count in the morning, because somehow she thought it mattered. Elizabeth sat silently, her hands working without needing her mind to direct them. She couldn't get Lillie out of her head. All she wanted to do was shove the linens in a cupboard and go wake her up, but instead she folded meticulous and perfect folds in the weary coarse fabrics that seemed to procreate like an unending mound of vanilla ice cream, or the sloped mountains of Wisconsin.

She didn't hear the footsteps this time. Her friend had learned some stealth in the last few hours, and it startled Elizabeth when she came up behind her and rubbed softly with the knuckle of her index finger between Elizabeth's shoulder blades.

"Hey there," Rose said quietly. "Looks like there's a lot tonight." She gestured at all the sheets, towels, pillowcases, and blankets. "Would you mind if I gave you a hand?" It wasn't Rose's night to fold laundry, but she was sorry that she'd been so insensitive, and it was written all over her freckled-covered face.

"Sure thing, Rose." She patted the spot beside her on the long wooden bench. "I'd love that." She folded two more towels while she contemplated how to bandage the wound that had torn open on the staircase, and how to bridge the divide that had been quickly created with her long time friend. "Rose, I…"

"No, no need, Elizabeth. I get it. Really, I do. Sometimes people come along and you're not sure why, but you just need to know them. Or something like that, right?" Rose sat lightly on the edge of the bench with her knees locked tightly together and her feet perched up on her tiptoes. She rubbed her hands together nervously. She leaned forward towards her friend and said, "I know I'm an idiot sometimes, girl. No need to tell me that. I just wanted you to know I understand."

Elizabeth smiled, and felt her heart warm towards her stubborn and spirited childhood pal. "Well then, in that case…" she bunched up a pillowcase and threw it in Rose's direction, her impeccable aim landing it solidly in her face. "Get to folding, girl." Rose dissolved into her familiar laughter, a gentle uproar that always sounded as hearty a bowl of homemade chicken soup. It was a sound that warmed Elizabeth from her toes on up from the moment it reached her ears. The laughter died down, and the girls worked quickly and quietly, not wanting to upset the calm that had formed between them. When there were just a few items left in the pile and things felt right again between them, Rose said to Elizabeth, "I suspect your friend might be needing to be checked on soon. You go on, and I'll finish up here."

"Rose, I still have to put them away and…" Elizabeth started to protest, but her mind was already walking up the staircase towards Lillie's bed.

"Nah, now go on now. I got it. You may just owe me an ice cream or a drink some time later this week." Rose grinned her cheeky grin and shooed her friend out of the room with the waft of a bath towel.

Elizabeth greedily arose from her seat and practically made a run for the door. "Thanks, Rose, for everything."

"Yup, get on now," Rose replied, attempting to feign irritation at

Elizabeth's continued presence as she began folding the towel in her hand. By the time that Rose looked up, Elizabeth was already gone. She could hear the click-clack of fast and excited feet carrying Elizabeth away from the main building and over to the annex.

Elizabeth slowed herself as she entered the big room called the general medical unit and found Lillie in a confused state. She was picking at the air and the bedsheets with jerky and unstable hands. Lillie was agitated, and seemed intent on whatever it was that she was doing. Elizabeth approached her cautiously, and finally decided it was safe to ask.

"Lillie? What's going on? Do you see something there?" She stood quietly at her bedside, not sure whether to leave it be or to attempt to break whatever trance she was in. Finally Lillie broke the silence.

"Those ants, Elizabeth. They won't leave me alone, and now I can see them on my bedsheets. They're too fast for me to catch. If could only just squish a few." She looked puzzled and uncomfortable, and Elizabeth fell right into character. She knew just what to do about the ants.

"I'll get them, Lillie, if you'd like. I'm pretty good at squishing ants, I had lots of practice over the years on my front porch." Elizabeth sounded convincing, and she hoped Lillie would bite.

"Well, alright then, but can you start with that big one there on near my knee. I think she's the queen ant, and if you get her maybe the rest will get right frightened and go away. I just can't reach her." Elizabeth played along, not having the heart, or the need, to correct Lillie's delusion.

"Oh, you mean this one here? Yes, she's mighty big alright!" She pretended to pick up a sizable insect by her thorax and take a good look at her. "Should we let her go? Outside maybe?" Elizabeth looked at Lillie, who seemed quite relieved that Elizabeth had removed the plump monarch from her linens.

"Nah, squish her," she said with disgust. But then suddenly she pushed herself up on her elbows and yelled out to Elizabeth, "No wait! Don't! Put her out on the ledge there, and maybe my bird will have a mighty fine supper." Lillie lit up at the thought of Little Red.

"That's a fabulous idea, Lillie. Maybe all her little workers will follow suit. I'll just stick her here…" She opened the window across the room so that Lillie could see and placed the illusory ant on the hard stone windowsill outside. "There now. Oh, look Lillie! Here come the rest of them! They are following her. Brilliant plan, Lillie. Brilliant!" Elizabeth clapped her hands and grinned from ear to ear. She turned around to find Lillie smiling a wide, childlike grin that ran the whole course of her wide chubby face. She was missing a few teeth, a fact that Elizabeth hadn't noticed before, but it didn't take away from the sheer delight that Lillie had shown from their little skit.

Lillie relaxed back in the bed, her lips covering her teeth again, but her smile still dancing closely with her cheekbones. "Thank you, Elizabeth. I've been trying to get them to go away for days, but they just keep coming back."

"Certainly, Lillie. Any time." Elizabeth closed the window and came back across the room to Lillie's side. "Now then, are you thirsty, Lillie? Would you like some water?"She started towards the pitcher at her bedside and could tell just by picking it up that the water inside was tepid and sour.

"Nah, actually, what I really want is a cola." Lillie lay on her back, staring up at the plaster medallion that circled around the light bulb on the ceiling.

Elizabeth had already started towards the sink to dump out the warm water and refill it with a cooler version of the same, but stopped short when she heard the word cola. "Lillie, there's no way. That amount of sugar could..."

"What?" Lillie interrupted. "Kill me?" Lillie laughed quietly at first, then louder and louder until her voice filled up the entire empty hall. It bounced off the empty beds next to her and hit the plain and vacant walls that surrounded her. Elizabeth stood frozen, not sure whether to join in or not, and pondering whether perhaps Lillie was further gone than she'd thought. Lillie finally managed to squeak out, "Lord, Elizabeth, I'm dying here, child!" Tears streamed down her face as she laughed, and she didn't bother to wipe them away. "And all's I want is a cola. Ice cold and from the bottle like my father used to get me. I ain't had one in over twenty years."

"What?" Elizabeth stopped. Shock hit her eyebrows, shooting them upwards towards her hairline. "Twenty years?"

"Yup. Ain't no soda pop stands or diners out in my fields. We just drink water, milk, and juice mostly, the kind you squeeze yourself when the local crops is good enough to spare a little. Oh, and coffee and tea when we could get us some. But cola, now that's just milk and honey, and we ain't kin to many luxuries, Elizabeth." Lillie shifted her weight and tried to turn on her side, a feat she was finding more and more difficult as the days passed. She made it halfway up on her hip by pulling herself on the side bed frame, but lost the strength and fell again onto her back.

"Oh, Lillie, wait, let me help you." Elizabeth hastily put the pitcher down and helped Lillie by pushing gently on her hip as Lillie pulled herself in the direction she wanted to roll. Elizabeth adjusted the bag that was connected to the Foley catheter that had taken up residence in Lillie's bladder two weeks before so that the movement didn't put any tension on the flexible rubber tube. She used the draw sheet to ease the burden of Lillie's hefty body and pulled Lillie's bottom hip towards her gently. She took a pillow from the vacant bed next to Lillie's and started to tuck it behind Lillie's back to help prop her more comfortably when Lillie's gown fell slightly towards the bed. The shift in fabric revealed a horrific secret that made Elizabeth gasp loudly. "Lillie!"

"What is it? Something wrong, Elizabeth?" Lillie mumbled into the bicep underneath her head as she tried to catch her breath from the pain of all the movement.

"Lillie, how long has that been there? I mean, the sore on your bottom? I didn't see that yesterday, but then I guess I never did turn you over during your bath 'cause you fell asleep." Elizabeth was sick to her stomach. *Oh, good Lord in heaven.*

"I'm not sure what you talking about. My bottom's been right sore for a bit now, I guess, but then things get so numb that I just stop feeling them after awhile."

Elizabeth stared at the tissue around Lillie's tailbone. She was mortified, embarrassed, and angry all at once, and she felt a lump rising in her throat. All she could think was that this never should have happened. She had taken care of Lillie a couple of weeks prior, for one evening, and Elizabeth didn't recall anything being mentioned about something like this. In fact, now that she thought about it, Lillie had been sleeping the whole night, the effects of a strong sedative in full swing. She was kicking herself now for not having turned her over last evening and realized she'd neglected it as well tonight. But then, Lillie preferred being on her back, and it wasn't often she asked to be moved; her abdominal girth made turning her without Lillie's help slightly challenging for most, and darn near impossible for someone of Elizabeth's small stature. *Excuses,* she thought, *all excuses.*

Lillie's tailbone was the color of raw meat, with layer after layer of skin broken down and necrotic from the constant pressure placed on it by Lillie's consistent back-lying position and the weight of her body shifting on the hard mattress. It had sheared, torn, and been unrelieved of pressure for so long that a three-inch-wide crater had formed where her buttocks met the end of her spine. It was cherry red in the center, and its surrounding ridges were various shades of red, purple, black, and white.

"Lillie, has no one treated this?" Why on earth hadn't someone addressed this gaping wound? Elizabeth didn't understand. Their facility had an impeccable reputation for the care it gave, but Elizabeth was quickly taking note that perhaps that didn't extend to poor farmer's wives who couldn't pay.

"Well, now that you mention it, I do kind'a remember that one doctor looking at it a few days back. You know that real skinny one, with the bald head? I think he said something like *Oh, never mind about it.* Something about *Why bother fixing a dying horse* or something like that. It's okay, Elizabeth. Whatever it is, I can't really feel it."

It wasn't okay, and Elizabeth was horrified. Had Flora known? Or Susan, or Barb? Had her fellow nurses all turned a blind eye to the cavernous trench that was Lillie's backside, all because she was terminal anyway? Apparently, she had already stopped mattering to the world.

Elizabeth understood that some sores were just impossible to stop from forming. Given her immobility and her frail skin that had poor blood flow because of her diabetes, some breakdown of Lillie's skin was to be expected. Elizabeth had seen that Lillie's elbows were fairly chafed and her heels were quite red where they met the bed. She'd given these areas a little extra attention the last two days, cleansing and protecting her bony prominences with skin cream, and propping Lillie's feet on pillows when she could. How did she miss the enormous fissure on her bottom? Surely, if someone had addressed it weeks ago when they first noticed it, it wouldn't have come to this. It might have been red and sore, but it wouldn't be the grand canyon of bedsores that it was now.

"Lillie, I am so sorry. I am so glad you don't feel much of it, but there is quite a large bed sore on your backside." Elizabeth cringed as she got closer to assess the tissue better.

"Huh. Is that so? Well, what can you do, Elizabeth? They're right. I'm going soon anyway, I suppose." Elizabeth couldn't really squabble with that argument, for the truth was that slapping cream and a bandage on it now was like throwing a bucket of water on a raging house fire, slightly useless and inevitably futile. What Elizabeth fundamentally had a problem with was how it had been ignored; how the choice had been made to do nothing about it because of who Lillie was—and what she was fated for.

Fruitless or not, Elizabeth gathered her wound care items and got to work. She cleaned and debrided the dead tissue; she applied ointment and bandages, covering Lillie's raw skin and giving her back her dignity.

Lillie was quiet as Elizabeth worked, sensing that something larger than the care of her wound was occurring. She wasn't dying tonight, and until Elizabeth saw Lillie's breaths become labored and the angels come down for her, Elizabeth would continue to treat the woman before as more than a body, or a patient, or a lost cause.

Elizabeth tucked two pillows up underneath Lillie's side to support her weight and keep her off of the wound. She pulled her gown closed and tugged at the sheets until they were smooth, and then she covered Lillie up to her shoulders.

"Hey, Lillie, "Elizabeth said when she was done.

"Yup?" Lillie looked up at her expectantly.

"I'll bring you that cola tomorrow, okay? You just got to promise to be here to get it." She grabbed Lillie's hand and gave her a small squeeze as if to convey her seriousness.

Lillie grinned and squeezed back. "I think I can do that."

Chapter Nineteen

Cate
Los Angeles, California
Summer 1944

I didn't think I could ever be thankful enough for Len and Betsy's generosity during those first few months back in Los Angeles, but I also knew that I couldn't overstay my welcome. I started looking for a one-bedroom apartment near the Pipers so I'd still have Betsy's support, but a ride on the downtown bus one day made me change my mind. I thought I'd seen Jack standing on a street corner and it made me go breathless. I had wondered what I might say if I'd ever run into him, and all I felt was panic. It turned out to be someone else entirely, but I decided that with the Pipers living so close to our old shop, since I really didn't want to take the chance of seeing him ever again, I had to start looking further out, towards the plant. Betsy insisted I was welcome to stay, but I knew what I needed to do.

Claire, Macy, and I had hit it off fabulously after our initial chat at that air show lunch. So much so that when I mentioned at work that I was looking for a one-bedroom apartment they both lit up like the Empire State building at night.

"Oh, Cate. Fate it is, I tell you. Fate." Macy was Shakespearean this time, and very solemn.

"Fate?" I'd asked. "What is?"

Claire answered before Macy had the chance to go into a monologue. "Well, it's funny you should mention that you are looking for a place because, well, we know of a place who needs someone just like you!"

I was cautious. They both seemed so excited, and I was afraid if they suggested something that I found deplorable I'd have a hard time masking my horror. "Oh?" I said. "What place is that?"

In unison and with the fever of school girls they both immediately squealed, "With us!" They were looking at each other and nodding and assuring one another that they had in fact been on the same page as the other one.

"Really?" I was in shock. It was more than I could have hope for. These were two fiercely independent women who worked hard and played harder. And they were kind, even to almost strangers like me. They were ever so kind.

"Oh, yes, Cate! It's perfect, really. We had a roommate, but she was lured away by a marriage proposal or some such nonsense, and now we just have an empty room and no third roommate." I laughed at the marriage comment, and it made me love Claire just a little bit more.

The proper thing to do would probably have been to hesitate and not act so eager about it, but, to be honest, I was as excited about the idea as they were, and soon found myself squealing with the delight of a school girl. Besides, these gals weren't worried about being proper anyway. I moved in the next week with my two bags and what was left of my old life, and I felt more hope than I'd felt in a long time. I was really doing it. I was almost twenty-six, unmarried, childless, and not too far from penniless—and yet, I had never been happier.

We had some amazing times, Claire, Macy, and I. I could probably write a whole book on the adventures we had during that time, but some of it might be too scandalous to print. Of course now, after living through the 1960s, it doesn't seem like much is off-limits anymore.

Our days at the plant were long and our schedules insanely busy, but we still managed to make time for fun. Macy was a huge flirt and had absolutely no desire to settle down any time soon. The combination of the two made USO dances and the clubs frequented by sailors and soldiers the perfect match for her. Besides that, she called it her patriotic duty to give the boys something to look forward to. I didn't care why she wanted to go, really, as I longed to dance any chance I could get. I was always more than happy to accompany her.

Big band and swing music were the thing back then, and the moves to match the melodies were fast and sexy all rolled into one. I imagine the same dances in Michigan were attended by a more conservative crowd with floor-length skirts and a little less swing, but in Los Angeles hemlines were cropped to the knee, and the more teasing a dress was, the better the swing. The better the swing, the more attention from the boys; so for a while there it became Macy's main objective in life to find the cutest dresses and the highest heels that she could stand to dance in. I'll admit even I got caught up in all of it for a time, and I dare say my closet was pretty dapper, as Betsy Piper might say.

I never went with the intention of meeting men, though. I really just enjoyed the dancing, and it allowed me to really give myself over to the music. I never feel more free than when I'm dancing. I hadn't sworn off men entirely, but I certainly wasn't looking, and after six months of attending dances with Macy and Claire, all the boys started to blend together and look the same anyway. I could see how Macy had attended dances and clubs like that for years and not really made a connection. It was like dancing with the same man, just on different nights, and the loudness of the halls made conversation a difficult task. I sort of liked that about the dances, though. No expectations, just good fun dancing, and maybe a sip or two of an adult beverage here and there. I was relaxed, too, because I knew who I was going home with at the end of the night, and it wasn't anyone in a uniform: it was my two new gal pals. So, I was caught a bit off guard one Saturday night when I felt an attraction to a guy that I just couldn't shake. I was so uninterested in dating that I almost talked myself out of what I was feeling. But, instead, I just decided to let go and see what happened. What happened was not at all what I expected.

I'd been working at the plant for six months and was feeling a bit run down from my long days and longer evenings. In addition to working at the plant, I had forged ahead with my plan to complete my high school diploma. I'd started night school about three months after I got my job, and was told it would be hard to do while working so much and that it might take me a year or more to finish, depending on how dedicated I chose to be. I, of course, took this as a challenge. I'd work alongside my gal pals all day on machinery, then I'd clock out and race to catch the bus to Inglewood High School where evening classes were held. The workload was rigorous, just as I had been warned it would be, but I had upped the ante even more because I wanted to get more than just my diploma. I wanted to attain a certificate as well, for bookkeeping. I knew when the war ended that my résumé was going to need more than 'chucking machine operator' on it, and with all the up-and-coming businesses in the Los Angeles area, someone was bound to need some help. I not only didn't have a desire to look for a man, I also really didn't have the time.

"Cate, come on, lovey. You can't sit and mope on a Saturday night!" Macy was pleading with me because Claire had already turned her down and tucked into bed with a good book and a cocktail. I was curled up on the sofa on my side with my feet tucked beneath me. I had no intention of going anywhere, no matter how much she pleaded. I was exhausted.

I sighed a heavy sigh, and with sleepy eyes I looked up at my dear friend who was dolled to the nines in a red floral patterned dress, a dazzling red belt, and the cutest red shoes I'd ever seen. Not a hair on her head was out of place, and she'd even tucked a large flower behind her ear for flair. She smelled of gardenia and some other fragrance that I couldn't quite put my finger on. 'All dressed up and no where to go' was what her body language read.

"Macy, I'm just so tired. Can I call a rain check? Next weekend, I promise." I felt badly; she looked so beautiful and excited, but I couldn't seem to will myself to get up. I felt plastered to the furniture, and I'd barely gotten my work shoes off my feet before collapsing into the welcoming cushions of the tired and worn-out sofa.

"But I'm all ready to go!" I thought for a minute that Macy might actually stomp her foot and pout, but it looked as though she thought better of it and her face just fell flat instead, her enthusiasm falling to to floor along with her typical Cheshire cat grin.

"Macy, *you* had the day off, darling. I did not, and besides, I have tons of reading to do." It was true, but I certainly wasn't reading any of it that night. I wasn't sure I could even stay awake another hour. My feet ached, and I could hear a warm bath calling my name. Bubbles and sleep, that's all I wanted to dance with.

I watched as Macy's shoulders slumped and she worked her way around the small wooden coffee table to sit beside me on the couch. She gingerly lifted my feet into her lap, and I felt her sink into the cushion back. It was her grown-up version of a pout, and I couldn't help but smile a little at my friend's childishness.

"I'm sorry, girl," I said, because I was sorry, just not sorry enough to go with her. "I'm just not sure I'm up to it tonight. Dancing and twirling, flirting and yelling over the music just to be heard. I can't." Macy perked up at that statement and sat upright, smiling.

"Well, perfect!" Her enthusiasm was back, and I was confused. I had apparently not used the right words of persuasion to get her to let it go. "You can just watch then!"

"Macy, I..." I didn't get my words out because she was ever so dramatically on one knee in front of me as if she were proposing marriage. She had a pleading look on her face as she took my hand in hers and began her theatrical speech.

"Catherine Grace Edens, I do solemnly swear, I will not keep you out late, nor expect anything of you on the dance floor. All I ask is that you allow me to buy you a few drinks and that you agree to escort this lonely gal to the Shriner's Club just a mere five blocks away from here so that I may blow off a little steam. I will forever be indebted to you..."

I laughed then, and blurted out, "You liar, you aren't any more lonely than I am!"

"Okay, okay. True," she conceded. "But I really, really just want to dance for an hour, well, two hours, tops! I promise! I'll have you back in your slippers in no time! Please, please, please? Please don't make me go alone, it's dark out there. Please?"

By the fourth please I couldn't stop laughing and I pulled my hand away from her and gently pushed her onto her backside so she fell in a heap of a dress and a smile. "Oh, all right! But I swear, Macy Ann, if we aren't back in two hours, you have dish duty for a month."

She pushed herself off the floor then and pulled my tired bones into a tremendous hug. "Oh, Cate, you're the best gal ever! I promise!" I couldn't do anything but keep laughing as I talked my body into motion and headed down the hall to my room to find an easy dress to toss on. As I passed Claire's room I heard her laugh and call out the word "sucker" to me loudly, and I knew she was right, even as I told her to kindly be quiet and trudged down the hallway. I'd surely regret my decision in the morning.

Ten minutes and a bit of lipstick later, we walked north down the sidewalk towards the next big USO dance. I hadn't even bothered with painting those lines down the back of my legs because I was too tired to care. I longed for the days before the war when hose were easy to get a hold of, and even easier still to put on.

It was the first day of November in 1944, and we were arm in arm enjoying the warm evening weather and discussing how cold it proba-bly was already back in Michigan, and then Iowa, where Macy grew up. Lord, Los Angeles had its perks in more ways than one, and mild winters were up there at the top of the list. Macy looked dashing and had thrown a simple wool pea coat over her dress. While I had touched up my makeup and tossed on a dress, I paled in comparison to my 'date for the evening.' Which, as far as I was concerned, was just fine, because I wasn't looking for any sort of attention anyway. My plan was to find the beverages, find a stool or a chair, and park it to watch Macy dance with her boys. My plan was to be a wallflower.

Of course, the best laid plans never really pan out how you hope. We entered the hall and the familiar noises hit my ears as the band roared loudly on the stage. Cigarette smoke filled my nostrils and the room, and I coughed a little in spite of the fact that I should have been used to it by now. We checked our coats at the coat room and then Macy led me to the bar where, as promised, she bought me a Pink Lady and got herself a Whiskey Sour. It seemed louder than usual, probably because I was so tired and everything is louder when you're tired, and though Macy was standing beside me I really couldn't hear a word she was saying.

She sipped her drink several times and then handed it to me just before motioning towards the dance floor. I nodded and smiled, and then my eyes searched for a perfect place to sip my own drink and hide out. The bar stools were taken, and it was pretty crowded anyway. I looked across the hall at the line of chairs butted up against to wall that were meant to give tired dancers a few moments reprieve or to give a couple a few moments privacy. I saw an empty chair towards the corner that looked perfect, but as I headed that way, with both drinks in hand, I noticed an extremely familiar face. I stopped a few yards short of the line of chairs and tried to figure out my next move without making eye contact. Maybe, I thought, maybe he hadn't noticed me. I averted my head the other way and made a beeline for the corner chair, and as I tried to make myself as inconspicuous as possible I couldn't help but wonder what on earth was he doing here.

I kept my head down and sipped furiously on my Pink Lady, letting the cream, gin, and lemon juice glide quickly down my throat. I had feared this happening, running into him, or someone like him, someone from those early days in Los Angeles. My attempts to be nonchalant and covert failed miserably, and I knew I'd never make a good spy or actor.

"Catherine?" I was looking at the ground when a handsome pair of shoes came into my line of sight. Oh, no. I wasn't going to be rude, but I wished he would have pretended not to see me.

"Hi," I managed weakly over the music. "It's been a long time."

"Yes, yes it has. Too long, in my opinion. How are you?" His voice was soft, yet deep and manly, and his tone put me at ease a little too fast for my liking.

"I'm well, actually." I realized what I must look like sitting there alone and holding two rather stiff drinks. So, I decided to go with just being funny. Funny was always safe. I shrugged my shoulders and nodded at the cocktails I was holding and said, "More than well, as you can see."

He laughed loudly which made me smile, and replied, "You always did have a great sense of humor." A woman next to me who was obviously uncomfortable with our loud exchange glared at us and got up to find another place to sit. I wasn't sure what she expected, you had to yell in order to be heard. He gestured at the empty chair beside me and asked, "May I?"

What could I say? No, I'm saving that for my friend who will be dancing non-stop for the next hour? No, I need a place to put my purse? I didn't want him to sit, but in some strange way, I also didn't want him to go away. "Of course, sure."

"So, Catherine, do you remember my name, or are introductions required?" He was playing now and it was adorable on him.

I chuckled and replied, "It's Cate now, actually. A lot has changed, but I still remember your name, Antonio."

"Ah, but not enough to remember that I go by Tony." His lips were soft and supple, not chapped at all like most of the army and navy boys I danced with. I couldn't take my eyes off of them.

"Right, right. Tony. So, Tony, what on earth is a guy like you doing at a USO dance? Aren't you afraid of being kicked around by all the military gentlemen for being unnecessary competition?"

He laughed a little bit and said, "Cate, I'm five foot four and I'm of Mexican descent, I'm always afraid of being kicked around." He paused, and then, nodding towards the dance floor, asked, "You see that gal over there in the yellow dress?"

"Yes," I said hesitantly, surprising myself by how much I hoped she wasn't his girlfriend. "Is she your date? Strange place for a date, don't you think?" I jested.

"Ha." He almost spit out the whiskey he was sipping, but caught himself and swallowed loudly instead. He leaned in like he going to tell me a secret, and all I could think of was how amazing he smelled. It was a mix of Skin Bracer and hair gel, and smelled divine. "No, no date," he said. "Well, I guess she's my date, but that's my sister. My mother doesn't allow her to come to these things by herself, even though she's twenty-two. So, my brothers and I take turns chaperoning."

"Brothers? You have a big family, then?" I actually didn't know much

142

about Tony. He'd been a neighbor on my old block and worked in a machine shop a few doors down from the store Jack and I had started. I realized then that, besides many daily pleasantries and a handful of small chats, I didn't actually know anything about him. And I found myself intrigued. For the first time since I'd met Jack in the foyer of my aunt's home, a man made my heart rate fluctuate a bit and my cheeks grow cherry with self-consciousness. I was more than surprised by my response, and I was pretty sure that it was attraction I felt and not the effects of the Pink Lady I had barely nursed.

"Well, there's four of us, if you consider that big. We all live in the area for the most part, which is both good and bad, I suppose. Family is such..."

"A blessing and a curse, I know." I finished his sentence and I think it caught us both a little bit off guard. I'd been speaking to him for less than five minutes and something felt like things were falling into place. It was strange and unsettling, but exciting too, and I couldn't take my eyes off of him. He looked extremely tan, though I knew it was his genetics and not the amount of time he spent in the sun that had made him that color, and his jet black hair was about three shades darker than his eyes, but Lord how his eyes shined in the low light of the dance hall. I swear his Mexican heritage never even occurred to me until he'd mentioned it, I just saw an incredibly handsome man.

We sat there looking at each other, each waiting for the other to make a comment or a do something, anything, to set something in motion. Finally he said, "Saw Jack the other day." There it was, the name I hadn't wanted to hear from this gorgeous man's lips. I closed my eyes and nodded, steeling myself for the worst.

I opened my eyes and sat up a bit straighter. I could be dignified about my soon-to-be ex-husband. I could handle this with the grace that was, in fact, my middle name. I could. But instead I blurted out, "How is the old cheat?" I said with a straight face. "I mean, how is he?" I laughed then to break the tension that I felt building between us, and knew it worked because I saw Tony's shoulders relax ever so slightly as he smiled at me.

"Ah, so that's what happened..."

"Oh, that and so much more, but I'll spare you the painful details." I'd spare myself from repeating them. It really didn't matter anyway, and if I spoke about it, it would just become real again, and I'd feel the pain of it.

"He went belly-up a few months back. Had to pack it up and head back east is what I heard." I sensed his happiness about delivering that message, and it made me like him even more.

"Hmm. That's too bad. Really." I was at least capable of compassion, if not composure.

"I'd heard you two had split, I mean, well, I'd heard, but I never got the same story twice." He was starting to get flustered, surely afraid he was saying the wrong things, but then he just sighed and looked me in the eye and said, "Honestly Catherine, I mean, Cate. I was just glad to hear you weren't with him any more."

I was surprised and I felt my eyebrows fly up. He was glad? An, "Oh. Glad?" was all I could manage.

"Yes, glad. And then I heard you left for Ohio or somewhere back east and I felt like my chance had slipped away." I couldn't breathe, and I couldn't help but wonder what was happening. It was one of those rare moments when you know that life was forever changing and you absolutely recognize that it's changing as it's happening.

"Your chance?" I wasn't usually this tongue-tied and I felt like all my feistiness and boldness had left me and dripped into my cocktail glass, melting into the liquor along with the sugar rim. Where were my words? "Your chance for what?" I shouted over the band, and as if they knew that I needed to hear him, the volume dropped significantly and we could almost talk in a normal voice.

He blushed ever so slightly, but looked me in the eye and said, "Why, to ask you on a date, of course. I was thrilled when Len Piper mentioned you were back in town, and I kept my eyes out for you, hoping I'd run into you somewhere, someday." His eyes searched mine, waiting for my reaction. I didn't know what to say. I had no idea he'd felt like that, and felt guilty even that I hadn't felt the same back then, which was crazy considering I'd been married at the time and, of course, I hadn't been looking at other men in that way.

I held his gaze, and then I felt my usual fearless self come back to me with every breath I took. I leaned over and set my drinks under the chair and then stood up before him. I saw a bit of fear flash across his face and I think he thought for a second that he thought I was going to walk away from him. His face relaxed a tad when I offered him my hand.

"Dance with me?"

Tony just sat there, stunned. This was not how things were done in

1944, and yet there I was, standing before a practical stranger, asking him to dance.

"Dance?" Now he really looked scared, and I wasn't sure what to make of it. I began to wonder if I had gone too far.

"Yes, you know. Swing, Lindy, Whip, Jive? Dance, Tony!" I was playing with him now and felt more and more like myself with every passing second. "What they are all doing out there on the dance floor." I gestured towards his sister and towards Macy, who was wrapped up in some unsuspecting sailor's arms.

"Cate, I don't, I..." His face dropped and he looked at the floor. He shyly looked up to meet my eyes, and he looked so handsome my heart nearly stopped. "Cate, sorry, I don't know how."

I almost laughed until I realized he was serious. "Really? Hmmm... Well, that's a problem."

"It is?" He was still looking up at me, those large dark eyes and his dark hair falling gently over his forehead making him seem more vulnerable than I'm sure he wanted to feel.

"Yes. I'm afraid so," I toyed. "But nothing a few dance lessons couldn't fix."

We both grinned then, and he stood up and took my hand and asked, "How about a walk instead? We can come back just in time to walk our dates home safely."

My smile said it all, and he gently led me towards the coat room as I discreetly caught Macy's eye on the dance floor, waved, and grinned. She smiled back and nodded. She knew I'd come back for her.

Tony and I walked for almost two hours, outside, in November, and though as the time passed the temperature dropped, neither of us seemed to notice the increasing chill. There were no lulls in the conversation, no awkward pauses, not even a moment where I felt less than comfortable. In an extremely strange way, it was as if I'd known him my whole life, though I'd spent maybe less than four hours ever actually speaking to him. I felt something I'd never felt with Jack. I felt home.

I think he felt the same because it wasn't the least bit odd or uncomfortable when he gently kissed me at the doorway to the Shriner's hall as Macy stood waiting for me just feet away, looking absolutely flabbergasted. He'd given me his phone number and address moments before, scrawled on a beverage napkin, and then just pulled me in so naturally and kissed me. I think I could have melted into that kiss and stayed there forever, were it not for the crowd milling outside on the sidewalk that was bumping into us.

He later told me that I was only the third gal he'd ever kissed and that he wasn't sure what had come over him except that he just knew he had to kiss me that night. He said he just couldn't leave me wondering about his intent, as if I could after such an amazing evening of conversation. I giggled like a schoolgirl as I recounted my night with Macy on the way home, and she kept laughing and saying, "I can't believe someone caught the eye of our Cate." She'd thought I'd sworn off men forever—perhaps, so had I.

I'd learned a lot about Tony in those first few hours, enough to know that I wanted to know more. Though he kept turning the conversation back to me, probing and interested in who I was, I managed to get him chatting about himself every now and then too. What little I'd learned was intriguing, and not at all what I'd expected for an employee of a locally owned machine shop.

Tony was a first-generation American, but still had strong roots in the Mexican desert. His parents had emigrated to America in 1912 to escape the devastating chaos of the Mexican revolution and, like many other Mexicans, they had found themselves in the Los Angeles area. They had come as educated people and found themselves working the land in agricultural jobs not unlike what my father had done. Tony's father pushed his family to do and be more, though, and he made sure that, above all else, his children received a good education. They traveled often between the United States and Mexico, with homes in both countries, but the children had set their roots in the California soil and had settled in to stay.

I was obviously new to the Los Angeles area and hadn't really been aware of the great influx of Mexican immigrants that had started a few years before my arrival. I'd heard comments before from some of my co-workers about how 'those immigrants' were multiplying ever so fast and how there had been no place for them to live. I had no idea that segregation wasn't just a Southern term, saved for the black and white folks of the Bible Belt. It was happening in Los Angeles as well, with much of the Mexican immigrant population being pushed into shoddy housing and even poorer working conditions. Tony was an American, to be sure, but his roots put him in a position of suspicion by others. That was, until they had a conversation with him, and realized he was more than just a farmer's son.

Tony, I learned quickly, had graduated with honors from UCLA in 1936 with a degree in Geological Engineering. He was as well-dressed as he was well-spoken, and though he was a small man in stature, he made a huge impact on those who met him. He was charismatic, but not in the showy way that Jack had been. He was more humble, and genuine and comfortable in his skin, and he had a magnetism about him that you just couldn't explain. You heard a little about him and just wanted to know more. He'd put himself through college and educated himself in the areas of business and machinery as well, and I could tell that his working in the machine shop was just a stepping stone for him and a gateway to something better. He was just meant for bigger things.

Three nights after our encounter at the USO dance we were sharing a drink at a local bar near his work. Again our chatter was seamless and easy and so comfortable that I didn't noticed how I'd slowly leaned into him over the course of our conversation and was close enough to lay my head on his shoulder if I wanted. He had noticed, though, and our second kiss was a moment I'll never forget. He looked at me gently as if he was memorizing my every cell, taking me in, making me his, and then he tenderly slid his hand over my jawline and wrapped his fingers behind my neck to delicately pull me into a kiss.

I'm not even sure how long that moment lasted, but it felt like forever, and I just remember thinking I didn't want it to end. When we finally parted lips, he quietly said with a soft breath that was sweet with bourbon, "Cate, what is happening here?"

It was all I could do to breathe and whisper back, "Something..." Something big.

Chapter Twenty

Lillie
Thursday, August 13, 1953
5:00 a.m.

Lillie slept restlessly while Elizabeth sat quietly next to her on the hard wooden stool in the eerily darkened room. So many moments had passed when she had wanted to wake Lillie to ask her things, to ensure she was still breathing. Occasionally she would murmur her name and wait in earnest for a sigh or mmm-hmmm from Lillie to belie her fear that Lillie had stopped breathing. At times her breaths were more audible, more labored, and more painful—the obvious result of a disturbed state of sleep. When Elizabeth couldn't hear them, and grew weary of calling her name and pestering her, she settled for keeping a light touch over Lillie's collarbone, feeling her chest rise and fall in slow gentle waves. Elizabeth wondered if, even in her sleep, Lillie ever really found the relief she was seeking, or if her physical and emotional pain were merely muted by her light sedated state.

Was Lillie dreaming? If she was, Elizabeth wondered what she dreamed about. Heaven? Her children? Her past? What in the world had she been through? Elizabeth felt her hunger for more details, a hunger she feared would go unsatisfied if Lillie died in her sleep.

While Elizabeth sat silently, her mind reeling with questions, Lillie did dream. Some were nightmares culminating in the labored breathing that Elizabeth outwardly noted. Some were sweet tidbits of memories of her family. Tender touches and laughter, childhood squeals, and melodious recollections of earlier happy times. In and out of memories, like a picture show of her life, she drifted from scene to scene without distinct segue. Lillie was so deeply entranced that she wasn't sure if she was dead or was still alive. Was this the heaven so many folks dream of, or simply still a dream? She bounced from one billowy memory to another and landed on one that brought back such a feeling of anxiety that she thought surely that she was quite possibly in hell. Her daughter Ada twisted and turned in her mind. Ada as an infant, Ada as a toddler, Ada as a six year old, bloodied and screaming, torn apart by a tragic accident, a moment in time that neither Lillie nor Ada had ever fully recovered from.

Ada was Lillie's middle daughter, and the only one, it seemed, that carried genes of pure unadulterated beauty. She was slightly smaller than the other girls and had sandy blonde hair that wrapped itself into ravishing, curling tendrils. Ada wore her hair short and stylish, though that wasn't her intent. Her eyes were crystal blue, the color of a robin's egg, and her face was full and rounded, giving her a healthy glow. A glow that somehow eluded her siblings. Her skin was the same fair tone as the rest of her family, but smoother, bordering on flawless, an amazing feat for one who only had the luxury of a bath once a week and lived in fields full of mud, dirt, bugs, and spiders. Ada was the only one whose face had been spared from carrying the hardness that was her life. She was simply stunning, and despite her hand-me-down and often torn clothing, she looked as though she had drifted off of a Hollywood movie set instead of from the middle-of-nowhere tobacco farm that she lived on.

Ada was made all the more beautiful by the contrast of her sister Nola. Nola was just eighteen months older than Ada, but as far from her beauty as she could get. Her face was thinner and had a haunting gauntness made worse by her patchy skin and well-formed smile lines that, even as a child, aged her face by decades. Nola's hair was dirt brown and straight as a whip, though wildly unruly with tangles. Her eyes were also blue, but muddy and sad and set deeply into her skull like a malnourished puppy's. The worst of it, the one thing that sealed her fate, was how her right eye turned wickedly inward towards the bridge of her nose while her left stared straight ahead; a trait made worse by Clay's neglect of it over the years, and his refusal to allow the doctor to attempt to correct it. Any one of her features alone were difficult enough, but the culmination of them led to one conclusion by many—Nola was surely the result of ignorant farm folk who had inbred one too many times, and although that wasn't true, it was a stigma that latched itself to her early in life and never let go.

Though their outer appearance was a shocking contrast, Ada and Nola never noticed the difference between them, and they often thought of themselves as twins who were simply born months apart. If Nola was teased, Ada quickly found herself by her sister's side, and the sneering would stop. If Ada found herself with the unwanted attentions of a man, Nola quickly found herself by her sister's side, and the lewd propositions would stop. They were like peas and carrots, both sweet and kind and essentially the same on the inside; except Nola's looks were hard and crunchy and slightly hard to swallow, while Ada's were as soft and as easy as they come.

Lillie's dream started in the way the others had, with a whiff of the memory fluttering in on a soft breeze. She smelled the heavy scent of bus fuel and blue star flowers and freshly turned dirt from the flower bed in the town square. She saw the grand old maples that speckled the lawn of the courthouse grounds, their limbs reaching towards the sky as if they could pluck down a cloud or two at will. She saw the leaf buds forming along the new thin offshoots, threatening to make a leaflet at anytime. She saw little ones on the sidewalks donning new shoes, fancy dresses, and hats to boot. She smelled ham, roasted lamb, rabbit pot pie, fried catfish, vegetables of all kinds that were either baked, steamed, roasted, or served raw. She smelled berry cobbler, apple pie, and jam cake. She smelled spring, and all its glorious hope of a fresh new season. Lastly, she saw the little church on the corner and the Easter celebration, which was the only reason they were in town at all that terrible day.

Lillie remembered looking at the church with the slightest bit of envy, a feeling that she didn't often give company to. All those people, free to come and go to services as they wished, made Lillie yearn to go even more. Lillie had loved going to church. She'd felt safe there, and welcome, and close to everything that was good and right in her world. She loved the hymnals and the way even the most stoic would sway when the rhythm of the song hit just right in their souls. She was smitten with the flow of words from the scriptures, even if they were just words in the old tongue that hardly made any sense to her. She loved how the preacher's deep voice boomed and echoed off of the small chapel walls and made her jump a little in her skin when he was especially poignant about a particular topic. She was particularly infatuated with how the light shining through the stained glass windows would cast colorful shadows on the parishioners sitting on the hard wooden benches, giving them blue or red skin tones, green hair, or purple blouses. She even loved the smell of the sanctuary, rustic and old, musty and stale, airless even, yet full of the breath of life.

She had gone regularly as a child, either with her family or with Mary and Josie. She had even wanted to be married in the tiny chapel where she felt so safe, but Clay had dismissed the idea as an "unnecessary cost," a phrase she would hear all too often in the decades following her marital union. He had attended with her once, the Sunday following their wedding at the courthouse, and then had never stepped over the threshold again.

So she attended alone in the beginning and had been happy to sit next to Josie and her husband Matthew and sing along with the old familiar songs, but that only lasted so long, as soon enough Clay caught on to the scent that it made Lillie happy. Then he quickly found some way to remedy her need for Sunday service. He said she ought not to be imposing on Josie and Matthew to come pick her up, or she had chores to do that couldn't wait until the afternoon, or he needed her help with this thing or another. All nonsense, all lies; and yet, as a young bride, Lillie hadn't been quick enough to figure out how to work around them. So she caved to his wishes and gave in to his desires.

While Lillie wasn't allowed to worship in the church for fear of angering Clay, she found other ways to celebrate the holidays that were important to her. Ways that Clay had a hard time arguing with, mostly because she made them center around him and his formidable appetite. If she made the heart of Easter about her best cut of ham and her famous blueberry cobbler, then Clay pretended not to notice that they were celebrating anything church related. If she served up steamed buttered carrots, mashed potatoes, and homemade bread, then Clay quickly forgot it was Easter. So though she couldn't attend church on Easter Sunday, she found ways to worship while cooking in her tiny kitchen with no running water and her old rickety wood-burning stove. She'd thank God for her provisions, no matter how slight, while she washed and prepared her vegetables, and she'd praise him silently for his sacrifice while she sacrificed her right to worship freely.

The Easter that Ada had her accident hadn't gone according to plan from the beginning. Lillie had tried her best to barter and trade for a good cut of meat, but had ended up with a large ham hock instead. The tough and gristly meat required a lot of patience for it to become palatable, so she'd settled on braising it and cooking it with greens, something she had ample amounts of that spring. She had collected all her needed items and found herself short of the flour she needed for her bread and for the crust on her cobbler. She had thought about asking to borrow some from Mrs. Adams, but while Mrs. Adams always gave her what she asked for, she did so with a chip on her shoulder, and Clay would often hear about it later from Mr. Adams. He'd talk about how Clay earned more than enough to provide for his family, and his wife needn't be bothering Mrs. Adams for staple items like flour or sugar.

So Lillie decided it wasn't worth the trouble, and she wouldn't dare ask any of her fellow sharecropping families because they had often less to spare than Lillie's family. She knew that most farm folks made the trek into town at least on Easter for service, and decided that if she could catch a ride on the back of someone's truck, then she would save herself and her husband a tongue lashing about borrowing.

Lillie let Clay know of her plans to go into town that morning, and while he grumbled about how he really had needed her to help him in the barn, his hunger for Lillie's cobbler won out over his distaste for her trip to town. At the last minute Ada and Nola had begged to tag along, and since Lillie's oldest child Connie could get the ham hock going easier without the girls underfoot, Lillie agreed to take them. It was a decision she regretted for years.

Chapter Twenty-One

Lillie
Franklin, Kentucky
Easter Sunday, 1944

Nola and Ada were typically fine companions, helpful and chatty, and pleasantly filled with laughter. Lillie loved their company and adored the way they secretly understood each other's nuances without need for explanations. It reminded her a lot of her and Josie.

That day, Lillie exchanged some potatoes for a ride in the back of the dust-covered truck that her closest neighbors, Karl and Ellen, owned. The weather was warm for early April, and the breeze made by the rickety black truck bumping down the rocky road was a welcome friend. As they made their way into town the girls were whispering and giggling about one thing or another—the anticipation of a large meal later in the day had fueled their energy levels to a ridiculous high. They scooted all over the truck bed, climbing over one another as if they each were boulders to be scaled and mountains to be triumphed. More than once Lillie had feared one of them would tumble right over the side. She rarely had to scold them, but after the third time of warning the girls to settle down a bit she began to regret her decision to let them tag along.

When they arrived in front of the general store, Karl stopped the truck and hung his arm outside of the window, rapping his knuckles on the side of the car door, telling Lillie and the girls to hop on out. The girls jumped like tree frogs over the side, while Lillie hoisted herself down to the end of the truck and let down the back hatch so she could slide herself to the ground. She came around to the driver's side while the girls skipped up and down the pavers in front of the store.

"Thanks, Karl. Sure do appreciate your kindness," Lillie had said.

"No problem, Lillie. We was short a few potatoes anyhow for supper tonight, so it worked out for all of us, I guess." Karl was a kind man, but he never gave out anything for nothing. He and Ellen sat in the cabin of the truck, dressed as nice as they could be, considering the choices in their closets. Lillie guessed they were headed to the church, one of the few time of the year that the two of them attended, but she wasn't going to be so nosy as to ask. "What time you think you fixin' to be ready to go back, Lillie?" Karl asked.

"Ah, I'll just be a right minute, but you just go on and do what you got to do, Karl, and we'll wait for you here," Lillie replied. She knew she was at Karl's mercy and she didn't want to anger him by being demanding. Seven miles back to her home on foot with two little ones and a bag of flour would be a fright more than she could handle this warm spring morning.

"Alright then. I'll see you in about an hour or so, Lillie. Well, depending on how long that there preacher goes on and on." Karl grinned his big wide smile and revealed his missing front tooth and another on the bottom. Ellen laughed at her husband's joke as Lillie watched them pull out into the traffic of the square and make a quick U-turn and then a left towards the chapel. She then turned her attention to her daughters, who were admiring the flowering weeds and spring foliage that grew alongside the store front.

"Come on, girls. Let's go get us some flour." Lillie opened the heavy door and heard the familiar sound of the jingle bell that hung at the top of the door frame to alert Mr. Roark that he had a customer. She shuffled her way up to the counter with Ada and Nola trailing closely behind, still whispering in each other's ears and letting an occasional giggle out. Lillie smiled at the sound of them conspiring about Lord knows what as she saw Billy Roark come around the corner.

"Why, if it isn't Lillie Woodard and her beautiful girls Nola and Ada. I sure do like your hair today, Miss Nola!" Billy hardly ever greeted anyone without paying out a compliment or two, along with a smile that could light up the whole store. Nola reached up and touched her short, mangled locks. She wasn't sure she'd even run a comb through them before they'd left the house, and the ride in the back of the truck couldn't have helped much either. Just shy of eight years, Nola squirmed under the attention, but suppressed a smile as she looked hard at the floor. Lillie thought her chin might well sink into her chest if Nola tried to look down any further.

"Hi there, Billy. Good to see you," Lillie said. "Hey Nola, what you got to say to Mr. Roark?" Lillie poked her daughter gently in the arm, prompting her to be gracious for the compliment.

"Thank you, Mr. Roark," Nola whispered, mostly to her belly. Mr. Roark leaned his long, thin body over the counter and patted Nola's head gently.

"It's good to see you girls! It's been a while."

"We don't get into town often, I guess. Clay don't like to drive much." Lillie tried to offer an explanation that he could sink his teeth into, but the truth was they didn't have much money to be buying anything anyway. Most of Lillie's "purchases" came from bartering and trading, and they grew as much of their own food as they could. No one was better at stretching a handful of items into two or three meals as Lillie was.

"Sure, sure. I understand. He must be real busy this time of year anyhow." Mr. Roark let it slide. He knew the truth. He'd heard how little the Adams family paid their sharecroppers, and how stingy Clay was with what they did earn. That's why he always let Lillie slide a bit on payment, or would accept less as a barter than he typically would. He also remembered the Lillie before Clay, the little girl who had found her place in the world in the sewing shop. He remembered how she would trail into the store on Mary Finn's coat tails, and how kind and helpful Lillie was even as a child. She had always had a special place in his heart, and even though Lillie had married poorly, she always would.

"So what can I get for you today, Lillie? Coffee? Sugar? Gum for the little ones?" Mr. Roark wiped the sweat from his bald head with his well-used handkerchief and then placed it back in the pocket of his work apron. The girls eyes lit up at the thought of gum, though they knew better than to react.

Lillie laughed. "I sure wish. Nah, just some flour today. But I ain't got no cash for you, Billy." She sat the canvas bag she'd held on her forearm up on the counter and opened it. She carefully took out two cartons and set them up on the counter beside her tattered bag. "I just got a couple dozen eggs if you'll have 'em."

Billy Roark didn't even blink, "Why, there's more than enough there to get you some flour AND sugar, Lillie!" Lillie grinned; she knew her old friend was looking out for her. "That is, of course, if you have a way to get it all home?" He looked down at Lillie's swollen belly and guessed she rightly had just a month to go before her baby came. She'd lost her Paul some four years ago, and he'd heard how devastated she had been. Even though her last child, the one that came last year, the one 'after Paul,' had fared okay, he didn't want her pushing herself too far with this one.

"Yes, we have a ride, and thank you so much." Lillie was floating on the inside. "The sugar would be wonderful, it's mighty kind of 'ya." Small gestures like Billy's always had a way of restoring her faith in people and reminding her that not everyone was as cold as her Clay. She reached out her hand towards Billy and he received it kindly with warmth, shaking it firmly as if they had just settled a large business transaction. Before he let her hand go he softened his grip and brought his other large hand in to engulf Lillie's small hand.

"Are you doing alright, Lillie? Do y'all need anything out there?" He'd heard the stories, he'd seen her kids, and he knew she had it bad. "Anything at all I can do for you? I know you've got to be missing the Finns and your ma and pa something fierce."

Lillie's knees nearly buckled. "Nah, Billy, really, I'm alright. I promise." Her eyes brimmed with tears at the mention of her family, and for a moment Lillie forgot herself. Uncomfortable quiet filled the large room, pushing itself into the corners until Lillie felt like she couldn't breathe. Finally, Nola's cough broke the silence that sat like an elephant on the counter between Billy and Lillie, and Lillie pulled her hand free of Billy's gentle embrace. She looked down at her girls, who were staring at her.

"Right, then," Billy said standing up a little taller, trying to make the awkwardness less obvious to the two little sets of eyes looking between Lillie and himself. "Who wants some lemonade and gum?"

"Billy, really, I haven't got any more to give 'ya, I…" Lillie wiped the tears from her eyes as she straightened herself up and smoothed her crumpled dress front over her taut skin.

"Nope, we's running a special today. It is Easter, after all! Free lemonade and gum to the tenth customers of the day. No questions asked." Billy grinned his old crazy grin, the one that Lillie remembered being so inviting to her as a young girl, that made her feel so welcome—the grin that made her feel she was just as important as the next folk.

"Well, girls?" Lillie looked down at her daughters, who could hardly contain their excitement. "I suppose you might be parched after that hot ride into town. Would y'all like some lemonade?"

"Oh, yes, Ma'am!" Nora and Ada squealed in succession and jumped up and down, bumping into one another and then their mama as well, who laughed as she protectively guarded her belly.

"I guess that's a yes then!" Billy said as he poured them each a glass and pushed them across the counter along with the large sack of flour and the smaller bag of sugar. "I'll carry these out for 'ya, Lillie, when your ride comes back." He found the basket on the tall bookshelves behind him that held the Dubble Bubble and grabbed three of the rectangular red, white, and blue pieces of gum. He handed them to Lillie and turned towards the girls. "Now your mama's in charge of when you get to have those, so you best be real good for her on the way home, eh?"

"Yes, Sir!" Nola and Ada said in between quick sips of their hand-squeezed, slightly sweet, but mostly sour lemonade that Billy's wife had made fresh that morning.

"Alright girls, let's get outside and outta Mr. Roark's hair." She turned to Billy and said, "Thank you so very much for your kindness. I'll bring these glasses back in after we're done. We'll just be out on that bench out front waiting for the Bloodsworths."

She scooted the girls out the door and threw a smile at Billy over her shoulder as he said to her, "Hope to see you again soon, Lillie, and you let me know if you need anything more." And he wondered if she knew how much he really meant it.

Lillie and the girls sat side by side on the small bench chewing their gum slowly, laughing together when one of them popped a big bubble and landed sticky pink stuff on their nose. They sipped lemonade and giggled about nothing, and everything, and for a moment or two they all forgot about the destitution they had to return to at home. Lillie prayed that morning on that bench that the church service would last just a wee bit longer; that the preacher would have just a few extra things to preach; that she would have just a few more magical moments with her daughters in the spring sunshine on the town square, sipping lemonade and blowing gum bubbles. It was the first time she was glad that she wasn't in the church with everybody else. She lovingly rubbed her belly and thought about the precious life that was growing inside her. She wondered if it would be another boy, like her Paul that she'd lost, or one more girl to add to the bunch. She tried not to think about the fact that this was the same bench that she'd met Clay in front of so many years ago, but then, if she hadn't met him, she'd never have had her five beautiful children, and another on the way.

As she laughed with Ada and Nola, she silently gave thanks for all of her tiny blessings, even in spite of the harshness that filled most of her days. She decided right then and there that the wooden bench outside of Billy's Roark's store was just as good as any bench inside the beautiful chapel down the road, and was a fine place for giving thanks. For the first time in months, Lillie felt alive and hopeful.

While Lillie enjoyed the warmth of the sun and the innocent company of her girls, Ada and Nola were growing restless. They'd long ago finished their lemonades and returned the glasses to Billy, and the gum in their mouths had become stale and tasteless. They'd taken to pulling it into long tendrils with their fingers, which lasted only as long as it took Lillie to notice them doing so. Church had indeed run long, and while Lillie could see some of the parishioners slowly drifting out of the chapel, she didn't see Karl and Ellen yet. She supposed they were enjoying fellowship with their neighbors, and didn't begrudge them time spent in the company of others. Farm life was often so isolating.

Nola and Ada took to making up games to pass the time, and eventually found themselves walking down the sidewalk while straddling the curb with one foot on and one foot off. They walked like ducks, one in front of the other, pretending to be like the soldiers they'd seen in the town square when their Uncle John's body had been brought back to town from Camp Wheeler three years prior. Occasionally, Nola would pop out with, "Left, left, left, right, left..." and Ada would fall quickly in step behind her older sister. Up and down the curbside Lillie watched as her girls pretended to be soldiers, arms straight and faces serious. Numerous cars, trucks and buses passed by while they waited, the larger vehicles creating a decent enough breeze to quench the unseasonal humid heat. Lillie lost herself in her daughters' play and giggled with a childish laugh when the sight of a butterfly abruptly stopped the game of marching soldier and turned it into a cat and mouse chase with the tiny, fluttering creature.

Ada was quicker than Nola, and had almost captured the little monarch when suddenly her laughter stopped. The toe of Ada's too big, hand-me-down shoe caught on the edge of one the uneven stone pavers, much like Lillie's had the day she'd met Clay, and sent Ada spilling forward towards the street. She tried to catch herself by pushing her thin arms out in front of her, but narrowly missed landing them on the curb. Instead her body propelled forward and she ended up toppling head over heels into the street in a delicate little heap.

"Ada!" Lillie was up fast on her feet as she saw her daughter's body piled on top of itself in the dirt. Ada lay there for a second and then popped her head up and grinned at her mama.

"I'm okay, Mama! Did you see me flip over?" Ada had said in wonderment of her talent. Lillie didn't have a chance to respond. The same moment that Ada was attempting to stand up and right herself again to get out of the street, the driver of a large blue Greyhound bus made a split-second mistake. Lillie couldn't even scream, it had happened so fast. One second she had felt a rush of relief that Ada was okay, and the next she saw the bus coming towards her daughter as if in slow motion. She could do nothing and she knew it. The driver was coming way too fast and was looking away down College Street at all of the Easter worshipers leaving the church. He'd swerved just a bit towards the curb with his distraction, and it was just enough for the bus and Ada to meet in a catastrophic collision.

Lillie heard the crunch of the metal against her child and the tiny muffled scream that didn't quite register in her brain. She smelled the burn of the bus brakes that had been hit many seconds too late. Ada. Her Ada. Nola was standing by herself at the side of the curb, silently crying, staring at her sister's bloody body. It was probably only seconds that passed as it sunk in what had just happened, but later it felt to Lillie like she'd stood staring at Ada for hours. Her trance was broken by Billy Roark who, amongst other townsfolk, had rushed past her to attend to Ada.

"Good Lord! Somebody grab Dr. Goodwin!" Billy yelled at no one in particular. He bent over Ada and checked for a pulse. "She's breathing!" Lillie was frozen, but felt the air exit her lungs in relief.

She grabbed Nola and pulled her close to her side as she watched Billy rip off his work apron. There was so much blood. Her tiny legs were awash in red, and her chest and beautiful face were splattered with it. He tried to figure out what needed to have pressure applied first, his years of service as a medic in the Great War kicking in as if it were last week and not almost thirty years prior. There was too much blood for a body that size, and Billy feared if she didn't get proper attention soon she wasn't going to make it. He saw the gore that had become of Ada's legs and decided the right was worse than the left. He wrapped his work apron as tight as he could around the top of her slight thigh and then took off his shirt and undershirt, tying them together to make another makeshift tourniquet for the other leg.

Billy was unaware of the crowd that had formed on the sidewalk behind Lillie, and of the bus driver who stood over them in speechless shock. Ada too was silent as Billy worked, and unresponsive altogether as he lifted her small body in his arms. The hospital was one block down to the south on Madison, and as he turned right down College Street he heard Doc Goodwin calling behind him, "I'm here, I'm coming!" Billy didn't stop, he just kept moving his long and lean sixty-three year old legs and sailed over the pavement until he hit the arched entryway of the hospital.

His voiced boomed and reverberated off the stone walls of the large bay room as he shouted loudly, "I need help here now!" Billy placed her up on the nearest empty bed and barely had time to get his arms out from underneath her before he was crowded out of the way by the nurses and a very breathless Dr. Goodwin. He slowly backed away as he watched the medical team go to work, poking Ada's small arms to make way for fluids and medications and cutting away her blood-soaked clothing to look at her injuries. "Mostly her legs," he heard himself say, "somehow her torso was spared."

"Never can be too sure," said Dr. Goodwin, who was a well-educated and well-practiced physician not far off from retirement. "She could be bleeding inside. We'll have to watch real careful for that, but I fear right now she needs surgery to get that right leg to stop bleeding so much."

Lillie entered the room terrified and gripping Nola's hand so tight that Nola thought she'd cry. She couldn't even see Ada for all the people surrounding her, and she wasn't sure she wanted to anyhow. She came up to Billy and placed her hand on his arms, which were crossed protectively in front of himself. It was only then that he became aware of his half-naked state and how his chest and arms bore the evidence of Ada's accident in sticky red streaks and splotches. "Lillie, I tried, I mean I hope I…"

"Thank you, Billy," Lillie said, interrupting him as she stared straight ahead at the conglomerate of people, blood, and bandages. "Thank you."

"Whose child is this?" Dr. Goodwin asked. Lillie froze. "I said, whose child is this?" he demanded as he turned towards the crowd of folks that were filling up the room behind Lillie and Billy.

Lillie took a step forward, dropping Nola's hand in the process, and said, "She's mine. That's my daughter, Ada."

"She needs surgery. Now. Any objections?" The doctor looked hard at Lillie.

"Whatever you have to do, Doctor. Please, just save her, please," Lillie responded with tears streaming down her face, and Dr. Goodwin's face softened.

"Of course, Ma'am. I'll do my best." He turned his back on her then and gave his attention back to his team. "Meet me in the operating room."

Hours later Lillie sat impatiently in a hard-backed chair in the small and stifling waiting room. Clay sat beside her, angry and silent. He had driven himself and the older three kids, Connie, Ben, and Joseph, into town once he had heard word from the Bloodsworths. A neighbor had agreed to watch her youngest. He'd said nothing to Lillie when he'd entered the room, but the look on his face told her all she needed to know. He blamed her. No matter what the actual story might be, he would blame her. The more time that audibly clicked by on the old round clock on the wall, the more sure Lillie became that Ada wouldn't be the only victim of this accident.

Finally, Dr. Goodwin came in and Clay jumped quickly to his feet. He towered over the old doctor by a good foot. The contrast between Clay's lanky but intimidating frame and the doctor's short and stout frame was quite apparent. Clay's whole presence screamed that he was going to be the one in control, no matter who entered the damn room. Dr. Goodwin, who barely made five foot four, looked up at Clay with a slight smile, attempting to break the tension.

"Lillie, Clay." Dr. Goodwin nodded towards them and stepped forward to shake Clay's hand. "She's alright. I got the bleeding to stop, and it looks like it was just her legs that were damaged. She might need more surgery in the future and some help learning to walk again, but she should be fine."

Lillie stood up slowly and walked towards Dr. Goodwin to embrace him. She was so grateful, so joyous that Ada was alive, that all she wanted to do was show her gratitude. Clay stopped her mid-step by flinging out his arm towards her chest. It hit her with a thud, and Lillie felt the pressure of it for minutes to come. She had been smiling just seconds before, so full of her appreciation that she had forgotten Clay was even there, but the moment she felt his forearm across her chest, her smile fell to floor with its own thud. She looked down at the cold tile under her feet and managed in her embarrassment to mutter, "Thank you, Dr. Goodwin."

"Sure, Lillie. You can see her in a bit." He picked her chin up with two fingers and looked her in the eye, "Let me know if you need anything." He turned his attention to Clay and narrowed his eyes a bit, giving him a cold hard stare which Clay did not return. "Sir," he'd said with a goodbye nod and with that he turned on his heel and left the waiting room.

Lillie sat by Ada's side for days, even amongst Clay's protests. At one point he even demanded that she come home, that the child could be watched over just fine by the nurses. Lillie had told Clay that he'd have to drag her out by her hair if he wanted her home that badly. She knew it would earn her no favors, but she figured she was already deep in the pig pen and a little more mud wasn't going to drown her. She wasn't leaving her child until she could see for herself that she'd be fine. When the moment came three days later that a pale and weakened Ada turned her head towards her mama and whispered, "Mama, I'm thirsty," Lillie knew that no matter the repercussions, she'd made the right decision.

Chapter Twenty-Two

Cate
Los Angeles, California
December 1944

I was technically still a married woman, and though it didn't bother Tony, it did bother me. Michigan was so antiquated in their thinking that they required a twelve month waiting period before they would grant a divorce. It was meant to give one time to pause and think about the consequences, but to me it just felt like a punishment. Being in Los Angeles at that time should have softened the blow of still having to remain Catherine Edens for few more months because most people didn't really care about such small details. For me, life was in the small details, and it bothered me terribly that I couldn't even change my name. It's probably why I pushed so hard to be called Cate from then on instead of Catherine. Some part of me was resigned to the fact that I just had to wait out the courts and deal with Jack still legally being my husband. There simply wasn't anything to be done about it. However, the more Tony courted me, the more anxious I became about it, and I found myself counting off the days on the calendar until I would be legally free.

I didn't let it stop me from spending all of the holidays meeting Tony's large extended family, and he was kind enough to leave out the part that I was legally someone else's wife. I suppose it should have bothered me that things were moving so fast with us, but it simply felt natural and right, so it didn't. It did strike me funny, though, that just one year before I had been sharing turkey and mashed potatoes with Jack, Len, and Betsy in a tiny apartment over a dilapidated store, and this year I was spending it in the company of my new beau and his largely Mexican family, eating tamales and sweet corn tomalito. What a difference a year makes, indeed.

Tony and I spent the Christmas holidays enjoying all the big city had to offer: Christmas shows and concerts, tree cutting and hot cocoa on the beach next to a bonfire. There was no snow to speak of, but it was the most festive Christmas season I'd ever had, although I'm sure it was the company I was keeping more than the lack of snow shovels that made it so. Between my work, my school, and the rest of my time spent with Tony, the new year crept up on me before I realized it, and with it came a bit of a surprise.

"Cate, are you nearly ready?" Tony was standing outside my bedroom door and was gently prodding me to hurry. I heard Claire's heels pass by him the hallway and she whispered "good luck" to him, though I wasn't quite sure why. I wasn't typically a slow dresser.

"Just a moment more. Promise!" I was having trouble with my hair. It had chosen the exact wrong night to decide to be unruly, and I couldn't quite get my curls to lay right. I'd chosen a slightly more elegant dress than I typically would have because Tony had made mention that he had somewhere special he wanted to take me. It was red, with three–quarter length sleeves and a square neckline. It was cinched tight at the waistline with a slim belt, and had a pleated skirt that hit the top of my knee. It had cost me a good chunk of my last paycheck, but when I had seen it in the shop window I had known that I had to own it for some reason. Something had told me tonight was the night, New Year's Eve, and a night out with Tony. I finally gave up on taming my curls and pinned my hair back with a flower instead. I slipped my feet in to the red high heels I had taken with me from my old apartment but had never worn, and as I put them on I thought: *Cheers to new beginnings.*

I opened the door expecting to find Tony anxiously standing there, but he'd been a gentleman as usual and given me a bit of space. I found him on the sofa, sitting on the edge of the cushion, wringing his hands together. He looked nervous and incredibly handsome, and I was instantly concerned that something was wrong. Then he looked up at me and his face softened at the sight of my dress and he said, "My Cate. Phenomenal..."

I curtsied playfully and said, "Oh, this old thing?" as he crossed the room and pulled me in for a kiss.

"Yes, indeed. It's terrible. You really ought to change." He played back, and I laughed as he added, "No, you're breathtaking. Really."

"Well, then, shall we?" I gestured to the door. "Wait, where are we going again?" I smiled, because he'd been adamant that it be a secret.

"Ah, nice try, Cate. No, no. Not telling. You'll just have to trust that

I'm not taking you out to some shanty…" He smiled then, and led me towards the door.

We exited our building, and I was so accustomed to walking everywhere I just stopped at the bottom of the staircase and waited to see if we were headed right or left. When Tony kept moving forward towards the street I hesitated and pulled back on his arm.

"What are you doing? We can't cross the street here, we'll get run over."

"Cate, I wouldn't dare even try. Besides, where we're going is too far to walk to, so I got us a car for the evening." He gestured towards a sleek black car with a pointed, slanted chrome front end and red rims. I'd never seen anything like it.

I laughed, knowing it was a joke. I didn't know much about cars, but I knew this one was expensive and there was no way that Tony had that kind of money, unless he was into something more than machinery.

"Very funny, love. Which bus stop do you want to head towards?" He always made me laugh, and so I giggled at the thought of the two of us in such a car.

"Cate, I'm serious." I stared blankly at him as he walked towards the car, produced a key from his pocket, and waved it in the air at me. "See, I even have a key." I stood speechless as he unlocked the passenger door and held it open for me like a high-class chauffeur. He gestured with his hand for me to have a seat.

"Tony, I… Where did you get this car? I mean, what is it even?" My mind was reeling. We'd never driven anywhere before to start with, and I certainly knew he couldn't afford the piece of artwork that was this automobile on his modest paycheck. I began to quickly wander down a road of distrust. How much did I really know about Tony, anyhow? It had only been a few months, after all. Maybe he wasn't who he seemed.

"This is a 1943 Fiat 2800 Berlina. Can you believe there's only maybe 600 of these classy gals out there and we've got one for the night?" When I didn't move he looked a little concerned. All I could think was is why exactly that he had his hands on one. "Cate, stop looking so shocked! I called in a favor from a friend. I just borrowed it for the evening."

"Some friend you've got, Tony…" I tried to pull my mind away from the path of suspicion that it kept heading down but I just couldn't understand who on earth would lend Tony this kind of car, or why we needed it in the first place.

Tony's grin had quickly faded into a worried frown, and he closed the car door and walked towards me, taking my hand. "Cate, what is it? I thought it would be fun, is all. I assure you, my means of getting the car are entirely legitimate. I promise, even."

I stood looking up at him in his immaculate tuxedo with his thick dark hair combed to one side, held there surely by a good amount of pomade. His cologne hit a breeze and made its way to my nose and was almost enough to convince me that I didn't care how he had gotten ahold of that car, that car that cost more than he and I could make together over the course of years. I hated that I felt like I did, so distrusting, but the truth is I had indeed sustained a few scars from Jack and his lies and antics over the years. It really shouldn't have surprised me that I was so suspicious, but it did.

"Cate." Tony gently took my face in his hands and looked me in the eye hard and deep until I couldn't look away for fear of losing it. "Listen, I know that you have no reason to trust a man after what Jack did to you, but you know me. I know it's only been two months, but you do know me. I wear my heart on my sleeve, and I'm more honest than even Abe Lincoln was. I'll explain it all later, but if you push it any further, you'll ruin the rest of the surprise."

As I listened to his words I knew he was right. I'd known it from the first time we'd really spoken at that USO dance. He was not Jack, and was as far from that kind of man as they came. I took a deep breath in and held his gaze, and all I saw there was love and adoration. This man loved me, though he'd never said it directly to me, and it made me realize that I felt exactly the same way.

"Okay," I finally said as I felt my shoulders relax.

"Okay?" He repeated as he started to smile. "So, you trust me then?"

I nodded and laughed and said, "Yes, Tony. I trust you," because the truth was that I did. I wasn't going to let my past turn me into someone who thought the worst of people, and I knew down deep that Tony would explain it all later and that it would indeed be a bona fide story. He led me gently to the car, where he again opened my door and assisted me in sitting down. I couldn't believe I was going to drive in downtown Los Angeles in such a ride, and I couldn't help but laugh as I thought about my aunt Rachel and if she could only see me now. It would probably be the second time in her life that she'd be speechless.

We toured the downtown area slowly, enjoying the car and each other's company along the way. I almost asked where we were headed a few times, but thought better of it and decided to just let go and enjoy the scenery instead. When we turned down Grand Avenue and pulled up in front of our destination, I was too shocked to say anything, but I heard a very nervous laugh escape my lips. He pulled into the circular drive and a valet came to collect the car and escort us out of it. As the valet opened Tony's door and a footman opened mine, I looked over at him and asked, "Tony, is this a joke? Are we really dining here?"

He smiled widely at me and said, "I never joke about dinner." He kissed my hand and promptly slid out of the car. He joined me on my side to help me out, and tucked my shaking hand under his arm as he started to escort me towards the enormous glass front doors. We took three steps when I stopped him.

"Wait," I said with more alarm than I intended.

"What is it, Cate? I promise you, this is all…" I cut him off. I wasn't worried about how he'd made the night happen anymore. I just wanted to breathe it all in.

"I just want to see it all for a moment, if that's okay. I've walked by before, but I've never been this close. It's exquisite!"

He looked at me tenderly and said, "Yes, she is," and I knew he wasn't just talking about the incredible architecture of the Los Angeles Biltmore Hotel, though to call her exquisite was an understatement. Her grand entry way was Romanesque in every aspect of the word, and the Italian-Spanish Renaissance style was both apparent and incredibly done. It was, indeed, a tribute to Los Angeles' Castilian heritage, and the grandeur of it was breathtaking. Six two-story-high pillars flanked the glass front doors and were capped by a stunning marble arch. I felt like I could have stood there all evening and still not have seen it all. Little did I know it was just the beginning.

We finally went inside after the doormen began to give us uncomfortable glances, and it was even more stunning than I could have imagined. It was like we had stepped back in time and were some place in southern Europe. Stone arches flanked each side of the massive lobby, and a small and simply carved marble fountain lay in the center of the room. The double staircase was the showpiece and was adorned with delicate bronze angels and was ornately detailed. On either side, the staircases led your eye up to the enormous and intricately detailed bronze doorway at the top of the landing, where an astrological clock clicked away the precious time.

Two large crystal chandeliers hung down from the impressive, exotic ceiling with large painted wooden beams and numerous gold accents. It was breathtaking and hard to take in all at once. My eyes darted everywhere, and though it was still heavily decorated with poinsettias from the recent Christmas celebrations, I hardly noticed. I had never seen anything like it in my life.

"Tony, what are we doing here?" I couldn't imagine he'd planned an overnight stay for us, first because it wasn't his style to be so forward, and second, because one night alone would have cost an entire month's rent payment.

"Well, do you remember reading in the paper how the hotel has opened up their second floor for military personnel to use while on leave?"

"Yes, that sounds familiar, though I can't imagine any floor of this hotel covered with cots and military men." It was a kind gesture that the Biltmore had done, providing tired men a place of glorious respite before they had to leave again and face the enemy.

"Well, it's true, and they ran an article a few weeks back about how they were going to host a fundraiser on New Years Eve so that they could continue to keep that option open for those here on leave. Let's just say that I..."

"Called in a favor?" I finished his sentence and grinned. "How come so many folks owe you favors, Tony?"

He laughed and shrugged and said, "Let's just say I always treat my customers right, and every now and again people remember your kindnesses." I nodded, and knew it was true. I later found out that one of the top managers of the Biltmore had used Tony's shop for machinery for a major project and Tony had apparently impressed him immensely. He'd told Tony that if he ever needed anything that Tony knew where he could find him. When Tony had called him to ask if there was any way he could get two tickets to the New Year's Eve Ball, the manager had said he'd do even better than that and had a car that Tony could borrow for the evening. I guess you can't underestimate excellent customer service, and Tony apparently had that to give each and every one of his customers.

I was still taking it all in and was feeling extremely nervous when I asked, "Tony, we aren't, um... Well, we aren't spending the night, are we?"

He laughed again and again kissed my hand and said, "Cate, I'd never be so presumptuous. Besides, I'm slightly more traditional than that."

His comment made me laugh, and I whispered in his ear, "Is that why you are out with a married woman?"

He grinned at me and said, "Precisely why!" I let him lead me to the ballroom then, and was so overcome by the hotel's grandeur that it felt a bit like a dream. Tapestries and artistic marvels were around every corner and in every nook and cranny. Nothing had been neglected, and I began to understand just how this establishment had drawn in the Oscars eight times over the last decade and a half. It felt like a movie set and I felt like a star as I strode through the hallways on Tony's arm. The only thing missing was my red carpet.

The Crystal Ballroom did not disappoint. I had read in the paper that the ceiling fresco mural was hand painted by a famous Italian artist who had once done work in both the White House and the Vatican. Once I saw it for myself, I believed it. The colors were astounding, and the scene was an imaginative mixture of mythical creatures as well as numerous gods, goddesses, and angels. It was incredibly romantic—and like nothing I'd ever laid eyes on.

I was so caught up in all that I almost pointed like a tourist at the incredible chandeliers as I said to Tony, "Look at those. They're massive!"

"I hear they are made of Austrian crystals and are over twelve feet wide." He grinned and shrugged when I looked at him incredulously. "What? I'm as cultured as the next guy!"

"Ah, love, maybe even more so." I pulled in closer to him and grinned from ear to ear as we moved through the ballroom to find our table. Tony held my chair for me as the waiter quickly approached us for drink orders. I typically liked to order my own drink, but I was so caught up in the fairy tale evening that I sat quietly as Tony discussed the wine selection with the young man in the spotless tuxedo.

We dined on canapé of anchovies, celery olives, crowned roast of lamb, potatoes a la hollandaise, asparagus tips, and Venetian ice cream. Some of it seemed terribly out of season and yet there it was on my plate, and it was delectable. Looking back, that night ranks right up there with one of the most memorable I've ever had, but not because of the hotel, nor the service, nor the food. It was the end-of-the-night surprise that Tony had planned that etched its way into my heart. When all the plates had been cleared and all desserts had been finished and all the wine had been sipped, that's when the evening became really interesting.

A large band flooded into the room in white tuxedos and bow ties. Dinner had been to the serenade of a small string quartet, which I thought was incredibly lovely, and I hadn't expected a band as well. I sipped my freshly poured champagne as the band warmed up and could sense Tony's anxiety beside me without even looking at him.

Are you alright, Tony?" I searched his face, which had suddenly gone incredibly pale.

"Yes, yes, I'm fine, Cate. Just fine." He tried to reassure me as the sound of a jazz piece filled the room. He was starting to make me nervous—and then it hit me what he was about to do. I was still married, and he was about to propose; and though I had no doubt about the man sitting next to me, I did have doubts about whether it was even legal to agree to an engagement. Though I tried to just breathe and sip from my crystal champagne glass, his nervousness was palpable and hard to ignore. One song, then two, then three went by and neither he nor I made a move. The fourth song cued up and was a Bing Crosby hit from earlier in the year called *I Love You*. Ten seconds into it, I heard Tony exhale loudly as he muttered, *Oh, thank God*, to himself as he got out of his chair.

He stood before me, wringing his hands at first, and then stopping himself and taking a deep breathe. "Cate," he said and then he cleared his voice and extended his hand out towards me. "Would you do me the incredible honor of…"

"No." I said immediately, trying to save him some embarrassment. I felt like I was in a daze, this just couldn't be happening. It wasn't the right time. I started scanning the room for an exit just in case we made a scene, but his response snapped me back to reality.

"No?" He frowned crossly and said, "Just like that? No?"

"Oh, Tony, it's just not the right time. I want to do things right with you and this just isn't, I mean I really can't…" I was visibly flustered and turning red, partly from all the alcohol and partly from the exchange we were having in front of the entire table.

"It's not the right time to dance?" He looked so confused, "Do you not like the band?"

A small smile played on his lips and then I was the one who was confused.

"Dance? You want to dance with me?" It was beginning to make sense, well sort of, considering he didn't know how to dance. "I thought, well…"

"You thought what?" He was toying with me, but as usual I recovered fast and gave him a smart reply.

"I thought you didn't know how to dance and I just didn't want you to embarrass yourself in front of all these people. That's all…"

He laughed then and said, "Oh, is that all?" and I sat there in my chair laughing just as hard as I nodded profusely. "Well, never you mind about my dancing ability. A man has to have some secrets."

"I suppose so!" He offered his hand again and finished the sentence he'd started moments before.

"Cate, would you do me the incredible honor of dancing with me… before this song ends?"

I immediately accepted his hand and said impishly, and with a bit of red still on my cheeks, "But of course." He led me to the dance floor and handled me with great care, and while I could tell he was new to it, his ballroom moves were spot on. As the song ended I lingered in his embrace for a few minutes and asked where on earth he'd learned to dance like that.

"Well, I had to do something to fill the nights that you have school. So, I signed myself up for dance lessons because I know just how much you love to dance."

"You did?" I was shocked that he'd put so much effort into doing something just to please me.

"Yes, well, I plan on dancing beside you for the rest of my life, so I figured I better look good doing it. Plus, I wouldn't ever want to stop you from doing something you love…" The lights from the chandelier played marvelously with his dark hair, and he looked more handsome than I'd ever seen him.

I couldn't help but smile, and said, "You really want me as your dance partner? I can be a little unruly at times. I might even step on your toes every now and again…"

His reply was simple and better than any ring he could have produced from his pocket. "Cate, I couldn't think of any one better to twirl through life with than you."

Chapter Twenty-Three

Lillie
Thursday, August 13, 1953
6:00 a.m.

Lillie woke up crying quietly and found Elizabeth quickly by her side.

"I'm thirsty," she said in a whisper. Her throat was dry, and she found it hard to swallow.

"Sure, Lillie, no problem." Elizabeth got up and poured Lillie some fresh cold water and helped her prop her chest up enough so she could safely take a few sips from the glass.

"Thank you. Boy. I feel right tired still. More tired than when I fell asleep, if that's possible." Lillie looked tired, like she'd been running, or working hard in the field. The truth was it had been her mind doing all the working while her body had rested, but the end result was the same. She was exhausted.

"I think your sleep was a bit restless, Lillie. What were you dreaming about?" Elizabeth knew her shift was over in a matter of an hour, and that she had things to do before the day crew arrived, but she pulled her seat in closer and leaned in towards Lillie.

Lillie thought for a moment about her dreams, and suddenly Ada's sweet face covered in blood and dirt came into her mind. "Ada."

"Who is Ada? One of your kids?" Elizabeth didn't know Lillie's children's names, or if they were boys or girls, much less how old they were. She realized just how little she knew about the woman before her, the woman whom she felt was now her friend.

"She's my fifth child, and a beautiful girl. She's sixteen now, but when she was six something pretty bad happened to her. I guess I was dreaming about that." Lillie's face was still, and her demeanor muted.

"Do you want to talk about it? I don't mind listening, Lillie, really I don't." Elizabeth tried not to sound too eager. It was obviously a painful story for Lillie, but one that Elizabeth still badly wanted to hear.

"I don't suppose it matters much now. What's done is done. I can tell you if you like, but it isn't a pretty story." Lillie laughed. "I guess I don't got many pretty stories anyhow."

Elizabeth smiled sympathetically. "So what happened to Ada?"

"Oh, where to start? I had gone to town to buy me some flour. It was Easter morning, you see, and Clay only let me make a fuss about it being Easter 'cause I done did up supper real nice for him. He likes him some of my cobbler, you know, but I had run outta flour a few days before…"

Lillie spun her story as she'd seen it in her dreams, as she remembered it in her deteriorating mind, as she felt it in her weary bones. She left nothing out, not the smells, nor the scenes, nor the way Clay had reacted. She shared it all with Elizabeth as if saying it out loud would absolve her of its burden after all those years.

Elizabeth sat silently listening, her hands folded in her lap, feeling her body tense at times and then relax with laughter at Lillie's description of things. She could almost see the two sweet girls popping bubbles with their gum and marching up and down the sidewalk like soldiers. She could smell the Easter food in the air and feel the sticky heat on her skin. She knew the very ward that Ada had been taken to and the operating room where Dr. Goodwin had fixed Ada's legs and saved her young life. She knew the waiting room where Lillie and Clay had waited for news of their daughter's fate, and where Lillie had learned of her fate with Clay because of it.

"Did she get better, Lillie? Did Ada walk again?" Elizabeth probed her further.

"Oh, she did. But it took a right good time." Lillie stopped talking and pictured her sweet-faced Ada as she was now; a beautiful young woman from the knees up. She pictured her distinctive limp and how Ada favored her left leg all the time, her right one still weak and rigid where the muscle had torn and the bone had snapped in several places. She remembered how in every photo that Ada was in she would turn the right side of her body away from the camera. How the skin was bumpy and the vessels shot like a purple spider web spreading all around her calf. In the heat of Kentucky summers, and in a place where girls still wore dresses most days, it was hard to hide her scars.

"Truth is, she never was fixed up right," Lillie said quietly.

"Oh, did Dr. Goodwin not do right by her, then?" Elizabeth was surprised. She'd never heard of shoddy work from the good Dr. Goodwin. "He's practically a legend round here, and when he retired and moved north to Lexington, folks mourned him for months, as if he'd died!"

"Nah, wasn't his fault, Elizabeth. He done saved her life that day, but he told us she would need more surgery. He was real honest about that the first day. It wasn't his fault, it was Clay's."

"How so?"

"Well, it took Ada a whole lot of months on crutches before she could walk on her own again. Almost a year, and to be quite honest we couldn't even afford the rickety wooden pair they gave us. Or the hospital bill, really. But Dr. Goodwin is such a nice right man, he said he'd chalk it up to a lesson learned for his nurses. See, the nursing school used to be right here in town until a couple years back. He figured it was good 'trauma training' or some such thing."

"I remember that. I was upset that I had to go up to Bowling Green to learn my skills when just the year before I could'a done it here in Franklin." Elizabeth sighed. "Well, that was mighty kind of the doctor, but why does Ada still have trouble, then?"

"Clay wouldn't let the doctor do any other work on her. He let me take her in once, about a month after she'd come home, but then he just flat out said no when I tried to set up more appointments, or talk about the other surgery she needed. I remember he said, 'Look, she be walking alright now with them crutches. Y'all just be looking for more attention.' But she wasn't walking alright, she had the worst sort of limp and a whole lot of pain most days. Terrible watching your child suffer and you can't get so much as an aspirin for her out of her daddy."

"Was it the money? Did Clay just not think you could afford it?" Elizabeth was pushing a boundary and she knew it—but she wanted to understand what kind of father would refuse his daughter the treatment she needed.

"Nah. I'd like to tell you that was why, but truth is he done sue that bus company and he got more than enough to cover what she needed. He got more than we was worth, more than we ever had." Lillie was ashamed. She knew how it sounded, and she was sure Elizabeth would think badly of her too for not fighting harder for Ada's legs. "He owed some money to a few folks here and there, and I heard he paid off whoever he owed, mostly 'cause they done heard about his getting money from the Southern Greyhound people. He didn't have much choice. But the rest of the money? I don't rightly know, but we sure ain't never seen none of it. He may still have it stashed somewhere, far as I know."

"That's horrible, Lillie. Poor Ada." Elizabeth was speechless. Her own father was a lot of things, but a miser he was not, at least when it came to taking care of his kin.

"Oh, she ain't the only one he did that to. My girl Nola done come out at birth with a bad eye. It turned real bad inward, you know? That could'a been fixed too, I heard, for not too much trouble either, but Clay wouldn't never let me take her down to Nashville where the eye doctor is. He'd just ramble about it not being necessary and how that's why God gave us two eyes, in case one went bad." Lillie shook her head, remembering all the times she'd brought it up and been shot down with a verbal lashing about how she didn't understand how money worked and how, if she'd had more boys, he could have earned a bit more from them working in the fields. How it was probably her fault that Nola's eye went in that way anyhow, 'cause none of his kin ever had bad eyes.

"Just last year she turned seventeen and got herself a ride down there for some eyeglasses." Lillie said. "I had taught her some of my sewing skills when she was younger and so she traded some work for little bits of cash here and there. She scraped up enough to get them herself. But I still don't think her eye will ever be completely right either."

Elizabeth was getting the picture now. She was understanding how Lillie had ended up in that bed at the age of forty-four. She suspected that Clay had much to do with it.

"Lillie? How long have you been sick?" Elizabeth asked her outright.

"Long time, girl, long time. More than likely right after Ada was born. I never did feel real good after that, and she was my first baby that came out so big. Nearly twelve pounds. My midwife Margaret done said I probably caught the sugar when I was carrying her and it just never went away. So fifteen years, I guess."

"Fifteen years? You've never had treatment for it, Lillie? Never seen a doctor for it until the last few months?" Elizabeth was completely dumbfounded. They were lucky to have the community hospital in town and good doctors like Dr. Baker and Dr. Hunter in attendance. With all they were learning about diabetes, there wasn't any real reason why Lillie ought to be lying there dying like she was. No acceptable reason why her kidneys were nearly completely shut down, why her eyesight was nearing blindness, why her feet and hands were numb and poorly perfused. Elizabeth had not understood, but she was beginning to.

"Oh, I saw Dr. Baker a few years back when I had my last baby, right here in this hospital matter of fact. Remember I told you how I lost Nathan at home? Well, since he was my second baby to come out still, Margaret refused to take care of me anymore. Something about it being too risky. She was scared for me, and of Clay too, I think, and rightly so, I guess. We was both scared."

"So you got care here in town? How'd you get Clay to let you do that?" Elizabeth could only imagine what a struggle that must have been.

"Well, with Margaret not wanting to get involved anymore, he didn't have much choice. He certainly wasn't gonna be the one to deliver my baby, and my girls, well, they was just too young for something so complicated. I didn't want Clay blaming them if something went wrong either. He never did take me in for my appointments, though. I got my boy Joseph to thank for that. He made some kind'a deal with the neighbors so he could borrow their car now and then, and he'd load me up and take me into town when Clay was out in the fields. Even the night my baby was born, it was Joe who'd brought me in. Clay couldn't even be bothered."

"Was your last baby okay? Any problems?" Elizabeth knew the child was alive at least, because she knew Lillie had seven kids total and she'd already heard about six of them so far.

"Oh, ya. He had me on that insulin, you know. The whole time I carried I was shooting that stuff into my tummy. It worked, I guess, because the last one was much smaller than the last four had been, just about ten pounds or so, and she came out all pink and screaming. Dr. Baker did a fine job, and nothing went wrong." Lillie remembered her last delivery with fondness. It was perhaps the last time she had felt true joy and completely whole.

"Why didn't you keep seeing him, Lillie? Dr. Baker, I mean. Surely he wanted you to."

"Course he did, and I told Clay that, but he just didn't see no reason why it was necessary now that the baby was out and fine. Joe kept taking me anyhow for a bit, paying for my visits with whatever he had in his pockets, but he ended up leaving for the army soon after that. It was good for him and bad for me, I guess. Honestly, I'm not sure what

176

difference it might'a made by then anyhow. I was in a right bad state pretty quickly."

"Wait a minute…" Elizabeth's face lit up suddenly with recognition. "Joe? Joey Woodard? Tall, right? And right handsome too?"

Lillie raised her eyebrows in surprise. "Ya, that's him. You know him, Elizabeth?"

"I went through high school with him, though he was a couple years behind me. Well, that is, when he went. He was absent a lot, if I remember correctly. A real quiet guy too, but gentle, and always really nice and cleaned up, even in his flannel and overalls. I think your other son, Ben, is it? I think he was in my class for a while, but then we never saw him again after the first year."

"Ya, those are my boys. Like night and day, those two. Ben took more his father's route and let Clay strong-arm him into working the farm instead of finishing school. Now he's working dairy farms just outside town and got himself a wife. Joe though, he has a quiet way about him, but he also wasn't as afraid to stand up to Clay as Ben was. Cost him quite a bit, I'm afraid."

"So Joe Woodard joined the army, huh? Wow. Never took him for that type of guy." Elizabeth sat in wonderment of her discovery. She knew more about Lillie than she'd thought, and the pieces were starting to come together quickly.

"Well, Elizabeth, I promise you it wasn't his love of guns and green uniforms that caught his eye. I just don't think my poor boy could take it anymore, and I don't blame him a bit. My Connie had done the same three years before, she done joined the Women's Army Corps, if you'll believe that! But when she left us, Joe took the brunt of Clay's anger about it." Lillie's face fell thinking about it, how she'd watched Clay take turns addressing his rage at her and the older kids.

"That must have been hard for you. To see him go after your oldest daughter had already done the same." Elizabeth felt Lillie's sadness cloak her like a wool pea coat, heavy and uncomfortable.

"It was hard. It was so hard to see him go. But, Elizabeth…" Lillie's eyes searched her friend's face, "it would have been harder to see him stay."

Lillie was ever so grateful that Connie and Joe had found a way out. Though it had made it worse for her when they had left, she took it with her head high, knowing it was the best she could hope for them at the time. They sought the protection of the government when their mother's meager attempts to shield them had failed. Even so, if Connie's leaving was shocking, then Joe's was devastating.

Lillie remembered how that whole scene had gone just two years before.

It was late August of 1952 and Joseph had turned eighteen, requiring him to sign up for Selective Service up north in Bowling Green. That was the closest office around, and it happened to be situated right next door to the army recruiting office, giving boys a chance to sign up on their own if they so chose. It was a tempting offer in an area dense with poor farmers' sons.

Joe ran full speed all the way into town the morning of his birthday to catch a bus to the big city. He was breathless and covered in sweat by the time he reached his destination, but he was so excited that he could have run for hours on his adrenaline alone. He had counted down the days for over a year, knowing his plan, just waiting until it was time.

He left early that morning, and for the first time he met little resistance from his father. Clay knew had no choice in the matter; the law said the boy had to sign up for Selective Service, so he had to let him go. However, Clay had sensed Joe's excitement, a snag that had almost foiled his plan. Joe had turned to leave the house and Clay had caught him around his bicep with a firm calloused hand as Joe walked by him.

"Boy, don't you go doing nuthin' stupid, you hear?" He was staring at Joe with biting eyes, eyes that conveyed his seriousness. Eyes that Joe could not meet.

"Yes, sir," was Joe's quiet response as he stared hard at a burly knot in the floorboard. Clay loosened his grip and Joe pulled his arm free and plowed through the door without a look back. He knew what he needed to do, and it would take more than firm grips, hard fists, and stern words to sway him. He was getting the hell out.

He caught the earliest bus that ran up to the city and arrived so early that he had to wait over an hour before the Selective Service office opened. He hastily signed his forms, only vaguely listening to the details of the document he was about to put his name on. He wasn't ever going to be drafted and he really didn't care what the paper or the kind middle-aged lady working behind the desk had to say to him. He would volunteer to go and choose his own destiny, and his heart felt light for the first time in years. He finished so quickly with his registration that he found himself waiting again, only this time on the small bench in between the army recruiting and the Selective Service offices. Joe felt himself break into an excited sweat at the vision of the army logo over the door frame.

A colorful advertisement hung in the lone narrow glass window, blocking most of the incoming light and making the tiny room appear cave-like and uninviting from the outside. The poster read, "The Army's Big 3!" across the top of the paper. Three pictures were displayed in a vertical linear fashion, enticing young men to sign the dotted line and join the army. Joe sat and contemplated each one. Number one was job training. Joe could choose from any of the jobs the army had available. He looked at the photo of a room filled with young men just like him leaning over complicated electronic devices and learning how they worked. Joe tried to picture himself there, amongst boys who didn't speak with a heavy southern drawl, and who hadn't grown up working in hot steamy tobacco fields. He wasn't sure farming was one of the hundred job selections he had to pick from, and the thought of something new and foreign to his skill set frightened him more than excited him, even if they would train him.

Number two boasted pictures of young men in the trenches of war, and stated that he could choose from any of the fast action branches of the combat soldiers. Joe could choose the infantry, artillery, or armor. Even this farm boy could be a hero, it told him. Joe already knew combat, though of a different kind. Fists instead of guns, words instead of bombs. It was number three of the Army's Big 3 advertisement that caught Joe's eye and made his heart race a bit. He could choose to travel. He could choose Europe, the Far East, or Asia. He could get so far away that the option of looking back would no longer be there. The six-letter word, "travel," clung to his retinas and made him smile without even trying. Yes, one of the Army's Big 3 would be his choice, and he knew exactly which one.

When the sergeant assigned to the little one-room office finally appeared, Joe jumped quickly off the bench but hung back a few feet, an attempt at being inconspicuous against the red brick building. The sergeant ignored him as he passed by, pretending not to see Joe, as if acknowledging the young country boy was beneath the high gloss on his freshly shined boots. Joe looked down at the cracks in the concrete and pushed around a weed that had popped up in between slabs with his work boot.

He tried hard not to appear as eager as he felt, but the anticipation of what he was about to do nearly bubbled from every pore in his forehead in the form of a nervous sweat. He snuck glances upward and watched as the young sergeant unlocked the glass door and let himself in, flipping the switch for the solitary light bulb hanging precariously overhead. Even in the light of late summer morning and the illumination from the naked bulb, Joe could tell that the room was still dark and dingy. It didn't deter him. He knew the army wasn't going to be a field full of roses, and if the state of the recruiter's office was any indication of the state of other army facilities, he was in for a rough ride. Then again, Joe also knew all about rough rides, and could probably show some of the other young recruits what survival was really all about.

Joe watched the sergeant as he set his brown lunch pail down on the oversized metal desk that was the signature green color of army fatigues. It was the only furniture in the room besides the big wooden desk chair that the sergeant had promptly sat himself in, and another, smaller, metal chair with a hard wooden seat and back. Behind the desk were three large beige filing cabinets, and it made Joe think about all the men's files that filled them. All the boys who were already living his dream. His eyes fell on a rickety stand to the left of the filing cabinet that was filled with powerful brochures meant for catching the attentions of apprehensive mothers and fathers. *We will take great care of your son*, they said. *We will make him a man! He will lead an amazing life with the army.* Joe realized he didn't even care if they were right. In so many ways he was already a man.

After a few moments of tempered lingering, Joe wiped the sweat from his brow with his well-used handkerchief and stuffed it deep in his back pocket. He finally felt the sergeant's eyes on him as his hand reached for the pull on the door. As he entered the tiny room, he saw the old lead paint peeling away from the walls, revealing several colors other than the light brown that currently adored the concrete. Spots of green and pink popped through occasionally and made Joe wonder what this old building had been used for prior to becoming a gateway for the army. The mild smell of mildew and bleach hit his nostrils, and he could picture the crisply ironed sergeant scrubbing away at years of neglect in an attempt to make due with what he was handed. Joe understood; he too had made due with what he'd been handed, until now, and the thought of the army sergeant doing the same helped him relax.

"Ya, boy. What can I do for you?" the sergeant asked, giving him a good once-over from his stringy hair to his clean but worn overalls and down to his dirty worn-down work boots. Joe felt like he was being sized up like a pig on slaughter day, and he only hoped he had the meat on his bones that the sergeant was looking for. The soldier wasn't but a few years senior to him and Joe knew it, but he could play the role of dumb farm boy if that's what it took.

Joe didn't waver for even a moment as he said, "You can get me on the next bus outta Kentucky. I don't much care what I do, just as long as it's far from here, sergeant."

"Well, ain't you an easy-to-please customer, boy? You know we are in the middle of a war, right? With Korea?" The Sergeant looked amused, and wasn't even trying to hide the smirk that was spreading across his face and filling in his juvenile dimples.

"Of course, Sergeant. I'm only asking you be fast about it, that's all I'm askin' for," Joe had replied, ignoring the sergeant's condescending tone. There wasn't anything the young serviceman could dish out that Joe's father couldn't top, and the only fear that he held in his heart that day was that he'd turn him away.

"You strong? You look strong," said the sergeant as he stood and took notice of the biceps that bulged under Joe's tattered work shirt. "Army's always looking for strong young men."

"Sir, I think that'd be me." Joe puffed out his chest a bit, playing the part, trying to get the role. *Lord let me get this role.*

The sergeant was silent for a few moments, holding Joe's gaze, trying to determine what he was worth, and if he was as serious as he seemed. Joe held fast, reminding himself to breathe. Eye to eye the two young men stood looking at one another, trying to figure each other out. Like lions in an open safari, they sized one another up. "Well then, boy," the sergeant said after a few moments, "I think I can help you." The sergeant put out his hand for Joe to shake, offering him more than a place in the army: offering him sanctuary.

It took all Joseph had not to hug the solid man in his khaki-colored uniform. His last beating from his father had left his ears ringing and his footing off balance for days, and Joe feared Clay would permanently maim him someday if he stayed. Clay couldn't throw a fist at the army, or tear a government contract to shreds with his loud harsh words like he did with his children and wife. He could do nothing about it at all, and that satisfied Joe more than anything. Joe shook the sergeant's hand and sat down on the wood-and-metal-framed chair next to the big desk. He found it hard to concentrate as the sergeant listed all the things Joe would need to do to complete his sign-up process. This paper, that form, this medical appointment. Joe hadn't really heard a word of it in his excitement. However, Joe's ears perked up when he zeroed in on one tiny piece of information that could stop him dead in his tracks.

"Wait, I'm sorry, sergeant, did you say you need my birth certificate?" Joe felt the blood rush from his face.

"Well, of course, boy. You think the army is just gonna accept your word that you're as old as you say you are? I need the original, but if you don't have it, your parents can take you down to the county courthouse in Franklin and request a duplicate be made. I can start all the rest, but without that paper, I can't really help you."

Joe's long, lean frame sunk with deflation in his chair. He loudly sighed as his mind race how to get around this obstacle. His father would never give his permission. He'd never just hand him over his birth certificate and send him on his way. Joe had no idea where he might keep it anyhow, even if Clay actually had the document. He righted himself in his chair and looked up at the expectant sergeant, who had temporarily stopped filling out the form in front of him.

"Is this going to be a problem, Joseph?" The sergeant froze with his pen mid-air, waiting for an answer.

"No, no not at all. I just have to go back down to Franklin to get it. I was just hoping to be getting outta here in the next few days is all, sergeant." Joe felt his sanctuary slipping through his fingers. He was so close he could taste it.

"Joseph. Joe, is it?" Joe nodded. "Nothing happens that fast with the army. Unless, of course, it's their idea, and then you can't move quick enough. I'll set you up a physical in a week. That ought to give you enough time to get what you need. After I get that paper and you get the okay from the doctor, I can find you a place for training pretty quickly. Just depends on what's open for you to do." The sergeant rose from his chair indicating it was time for Joe to go. He put his hand out towards Joe and said, "Bring me back that paper, Joseph Woodard, and then welcome to the army."

Joe stood on shaky legs and accepted the firm handshake as a promise. A promise of freedom. A promise at a chance for a normal life off the farm, away from his father, and on his own.

Joe was silent on the way back home. He sat in the back of the bus, looking longingly out the window for an answer to his dilemma. He searched the fields as they passed, looked at the large oaks out in the distance, and followed flocks of birds with his eyes, praying that maybe one of them could help him. That someone other than his parents knew where his birth certificate was.

He knew his mama had an inkling about what he had planned; she must have known that he would go too, after Connie left. Connie had been his rock, his protector, the cushion between himself and his father. It had gutted Connie to leave him and his siblings and mama. Joe understood, it was gutting him the same way now. He knew what she must have felt when she signed on that dotted line and joined the Women's Army Corps. She must have felt like it was the only answer, the only way she could survive, or she never would have done it. The thought of hurting his mother and leaving the little ones behind was the only thing that almost made Joe reconsider. Given the current problem, the only thing worse than leaving them was having to ask his mother to help him.

Joe sulked into the house just as the sun was descending on the horizon. His first stop hadn't been home. He'd gone straight from the bus stop to the courthouse. He took the steps in two leaps and flung the door open so fast that it had startled the guard. He approached the white-haired clerk with caution and she responded to his presence by removing her glasses and rubbing the bridge of nose with annoyance—as though the very fact that he was standing before her was enough to cause a migraine. She tossed her coke-bottle glasses on top of a stack of papers and looked at him with her permanent frown. She wouldn't budge on the rules anymore than a banker on interest rates.

"And how do I know you is who you say you is, boy? You got no identification on 'ya, and I ain't giving nobody nothing without having some proof." She waggled her finger at Joe while she spoke, reminding him of his teachers at primary school and making him feel small.

"Ma'am, I can't get no identification without my birth certificate." He was polite, hoping she'd cave, praying her rock-hard head would see how sincere and honest he was.

"Your ma and pa still alive?" she asked skeptically. Joe replied with a yes. "Well, good then, when you bring one'a them down here, I'll give you what you want." She waved him off and shooed him out of the room with a look that told him that arguing further would just end badly for him.

Joe left the courthouse feeling deflated, but not defeated. He just needed to think of a way to do this without alerting his father to his plans. He remembered how mad his father had been when he'd found out that Connie had signed up to go, and how much larger his anger had grown once he'd found out that Lillie had helped her. He'd never understood what Lillie had done to help Connie, but he understood it now. Lillie must have been the one to give Connie her birth certificate, and ultimately her blessing. He had been fourteen then, and strong, but not strong enough to stop what had happened.

Chapter Twenty-Four

Lillie
Franklin, Kentucky
March 1949

Connie's journey into the military had begun with as much nervousness as Joseph's. It was early April and Connie had just celebrated her eighteenth birthday, which had been in March of 1949. She'd waited a few days so as not to arouse her father's suspicions. She'd asked Lillie for her help, but the asking didn't come easy. Lillie had been planting the first of the year's garden items and, as usual, potatoes were the first things in the ground. She would follow the potatoes with her onions, lettuce, and radishes. Same thing every year, like clockwork. Connie was supposed to be sweeping the main room and kitchen, but she couldn't concentrate long enough to go over more than a few feet of flooring. The house was quiet for once, with the boys in the field, Nola and Ada at school, and the two youngest napping soundly in the next room after having played all morning in the sun. Connie tried to stay on task, knowing it would be impossible to finish her sweeping chore once her siblings started pouring into the house.

After a while she gave up and stood desperately at the window next to the fireplace, watching as her mother sat in the dirt in her dress and smock, scooting herself down the rows of hard earth. Every few minutes Lillie would dig a small hole, toss in a piece of a seed potato, and inch her way down the row in the dirt. She made small mounds over her potato pieces, and it made Connie smile when she patted each little mound three times for good growing luck.

Connie had tried to ask her mama the day before, but the words stuck in her throat—held there by a glue of guilt and fear. She and Lillie had been preparing the garden and she'd had the perfect opportunity to spit out what was on her mind, but Connie had choked on it every time she turned around. She'd sat silently beside her mother as they prepped the seed potatoes on the porch.

They cut and quartered each of Lillie's leftover potatoes, making sure no more than three eyes were present on any one piece. Then they placed the pieces eye side down in several dishes and poured lightly salted water over the top of them. They left them in the sun for the rest of the day and into the next afternoon, when the garden bed would be ready and the seed potatoes would hopefully be growing sprouts from the eyes.

Hours passed that morning, and Connie said nothing. She just kept watching her mama out of the corner of her eye, sneaking short glances, trying to determine if this was to be her moment. Every time she felt as though it might be, her mama would say something so benign like, "All done then with that. What's next, Connie?" and it would shatter Connie's resolve. Lillie, her mama, so unsuspecting, so sure her daughter would always be there to lean on. How on earth was she to do this?

Lillie and Connie turned their attentions next to pulling all the weeds that had tried to make a home in the rich soil, and with every pull of a dandelion or tug on a piece of crabgrass, Connie tried to formulate the words. It was on her mind the entire time she used the hoe to plow the soil, allowing it to be more receptive to water and root formation. They didn't have the big sturdy equipment that the Adams family used in their large home garden, and borrowing such items was again met with a lot of hostility from Mr. Adams. It wasn't worth the trouble most of the time, so Lillie just tried hard to keep her hand tools from rusting so she could get a lot of seasons' use out of them before they needed replacing. It was on the tip of Connie's tongue as she'd hauled wheelbarrow after wheelbarrow full of manure from over beside the barn.

She was relieved when their closest sharecropping family, the Burneses, came over to help. Lillie had helped them with their small garden just days before, and now Mrs. Burnes and her youngest son, Todd, came to return the favor. It was a reciprocal, yet unspoken, agreement that had gone on for years amongst farming families, and that, sadly, was a dying gesture. Many folks had started just focusing on their own troubles and home life, and stopped the tradition of banding together to get the work done faster. Lillie was grateful that Grace Burnes wasn't ready to let the practice of swapping labor die just yet.

Connie held her words close as she worked alongside Grace, Todd, and her mother, who were all helping to mix the manure into the tilled earth. She was grateful for the handkerchief that covered her nose and mouth, too, because it alleviated not only some of the stench from the fertile excrement, but also allowed her the freedom to remain silent.

Connie had almost blurted it out just before supper the night before, but Clay, Ben, and Joe had unexpectedly come up the dirt pathway to the house, home early from sowing the tobacco beds. Clay had been grumpy walking in, as he and the other sharecroppers were behind by a whole week and Mr. Adams was most displeased. So Connie held her tongue then, too, and prayed silently for God to tell her when the time might be right.

While she stood there, the house warm and silent except for the occasionally creak of the wooden beams underneath her feet as she shifted her weight, Connie got the sign she was looking for. Her eyes drifted from her mother's back to a line of old maples that formed an unofficial land boundary between the Adams' and Bloodsworths' farms. The trees were just on the other side of her family's garden, and far enough away that she couldn't quite make out their details. She couldn't really see whether or not new leaves were starting to sprout, or if spring would visit the trees late this year. From where she stood it looked as though a few of the tree tops were heavy with leaves, and she stared at them, trying to figure out what she was seeing. Then she saw it. Movement, fast and beautiful and synchronized. A flock of sparrows left its perch atop one maple and followed one another to the top of another, crowding its highest branches and giving the tree the appearance of having well plucked-over lower branches.

Connie watched group after group leave one tree and fly to another, and she began to wonder why the entire group seemed to move as one. Why not a single sparrow had fallen out of line, or ventured out on their own. Was there some unspoken agreement, some earthly vibration known only to sparrows, that told them when it was time to turn or fly or land? *No, perhaps not,* Connie thought. Perhaps there was simply one in the group strong enough, and willing enough, to take that first step off of the branch and in doing so find that the rest were willing to follow such courage.

That's when she knew she had her sign, and when it all came together in her mind. She and her mama and siblings had been like the sheep they were sheering two farms over; and like the birds crowding the tree tops; and like the cattle teeming and packed into the dairy barn. They acted as if they had no choice.

Truth set into Connie's bones as she watched Lillie carefully get to her knees and then push her heavy body to a tenuous stand. She wobbled her way towards the front porch, catching Connie's eye and smiling her kind smile while waving a bit to her eldest child. Connie came around to the front door and watched through the screen as Lillie cleaned the dirt off of her hands in the water bucket on the front porch. She carefully lathered up and made sure to get as much of the dirt out from under her nails as she could.

Connie almost stopped herself. She almost took the broom back up to go back to sweeping, but the image of the flock of birds flew through her mind until she could hear their tiny wings flap in her ears. *Now. I have to do it now.* If she didn't have the courage to be the lead bird for her family, they would always be at the mercy of Clay. So she closed her eyes, flapped her imaginary wings of courage in her mind, and took a flying leap off of the maple tree branch.

"Mama," Connie said through the screen door. Her eyes were hollow, pleading eyes, eyes that hadn't known sleep for days. "Please, do you know where my papers are?"

"Connie, honey, you don't really want to do this. Things will get better 'round here, we can try harder." Lillie was terrified. Connie was her rock, her partner in arms, and her oldest. Lillie depended on her, needed her, and couldn't imagine how she'd cope without her, but she was also the one person who'd endured Clay for almost as long as Lillie had. Deep down, Lillie understood. Deep down she wanted Connie to get out as much as Connie wanted to get out, but she wasn't letting her go without a good try.

"Mama. Please. You know that's not true. There ain't nothing you can say or do that's gonna change daddy. He's just getting worse. Short of shooting him, and that would just put you away in the jailhouse, we ain't never gonna be free of his mess." Connie spat the words at her mother in a most unusual tone. She felt the anger she had stuffed down deep and tidy rise like bile in her throat. She felt it coat her words with venom. It made her want to vomit.

"Connie! My word! What are you saying?" Lillie was shocked. Connie had never spoken to her in that manner or tone before. "Listen child, I heard from Ellen that we are on the brink of war again. She done heard it on the radio. Japan or Korea or some such country. That's no place for women." Lillie was desperate and conflicted. She knew Connie would be safe, that the army wouldn't send her daughter into battle, but Lillie was grasping for threads. She had to say something, *anything*, to change her mind. This just couldn't happen. She didn't think she'd survive it.

Connie looked at her mother's face, awash with anguish and pain, and she felt herself soften. Almost enough to change her mind. "Mama, we in a war here at home too. Only this one ain't got any hope of us being victorious." She walked up to her mother and took Lillie's small and calloused hands into her own. "Mama, I got to do this. I got to. You see how he looks at me, Mama. Mama…"

"Alright, alright," Lillie interrupted. She closed her eyes and exhaled as she pushed the image from her mind. Clay's salacious and inappropriate glances at Connie. His brushing so close to Connie's bosom and his hand precariously close to her hips. After Lillie's last baby, with her diabetes advancing rapidly, Lillie no longer interested Clay much in that way, and he'd turned his interest towards Connie. His own daughter. The thought of it made bile rise in her esophagus, and she felt her stomach turn on itself. Lillie swore she'd kill him if he ever really touched her, but that would leave her children without parents and she couldn't have that either.

Lillie went to her bedroom and rustled up the floorboard just beneath the bed. They didn't keep much in there, just the kids' birth certificates and their marriage certificate, all rolled up tight and held secure by some twine. Lillie felt the tears form at the edges of her eyes as she untwisted the knot and let the papers unroll in her hands. She found Connie's birth certificate and pulled it from the thin stack of papers. She replaced the floorboard as best she could so Clay wouldn't notice it had been disturbed, and she walked back out to the kitchen where Connie stood wringing her hands in anticipation. Lillie uncurled the document and smoothed it out against her chest and then she looked at it. The very paper that had brought her such joy to see when Connie was just a few months old now brought her great sorrow, and a small tear fell and landed on the form just below Connie's listed time of birth and just above her documented weight.

"Mama…" Connie reached out her hand towards Lillie. She could almost feel the rough paper on her fingertips, and could smell the freedom it would bring her. Like spring flowers unfurling on light airy breezes. That paper was her ticket to change.

Lillie wiped her eyes and handed Connie the paper, and then she pulled her beautiful daughter into a long embrace. Connie, whose kind, warm face was surrounded by magnificent and luscious brown locks, and whose big brown eyes told Lillie all she needed to know. She may have given birth to her some eighteen years before, but now she was giving her life, and it eased Lillie's pain and assured her she was doing the right thing, even though the right thing wasn't always easy.

Lillie anticipated Clay's anger once he found out. She urged Connie to quickly and quietly sign her contract and get her things in order. Lillie knew there was no hanging around after Clay knew.

The night, when Connie blurted it out over scraps of chicken and cornbread, Lillie found out just how right she was. Connie squirmed uneasily through most of the meal and picked at the food on her plate as she felt sweat start to form on her brow. She couldn't look at her mama and the kids. It might be enough to make her back down, and she needed to keep her mind in forward motion. All she could do was take a deep breath and know that this was a temporary moment. It wouldn't last forever, and then she'd be free.

"Papa," Connie finally said as her family was finishing the last of their food and the smaller ones were starting to fidget. "I got something to tell you..."

Clay's fork stopped mid-bite, and his eyes rose to meet her with a glare from across the table. Lillie looked up at Connie and then at Clay. She watched quietly as he forcefully shoved a piece of chicken into his mouth. In between chews he responded with, "Yeah, what's that?" He eyed her carefully, chewing his meat salaciously with a gaping mouth, daring her to continue.

Connie felt the air enter and exit her chest and then before she could change her mind she quickly said, "I joined the Women's Army Corps. I leave in two days for training. I'll be going to Fort Lee in New Jersey. I'll..."

Connie never got the rest of her sentence past her teeth. She was stopped short by Clay's fist as it slammed down with monumental force on the rickety and worn wooden table. The force of it shook the plates and tipped over several glasses, causing precious milk to seep through the cracks in the wood and soak the floorboards. Connie was out of her seat and had backed herself against the wall before she even realized she'd done so. She knew that look in her father's eyes, and she knew it well. Hell was about to rain down on their tiny ramshackle home, and even God wouldn't be fast enough to stop it.

Clay bored holes into Connie with his glare, and he slowly pushed his chair back and rose ceremoniously to his full six foot three. He towered over his family as the smaller ones ducked for cover in the lap of the older siblings. Lillie was out of her chair next, her face as pale as the taut white she wore around her plump waist. She watched helplessly as her husband's face filled with redness and his anger grew as fast as the weeds did against their front porch in spring.

"You. Did. What?" Clay spat each word across the room in Connie's direction, spittle dripping onto his near-empty plate as he spoke. Connie said nothing. She thought she'd been ready for this. She'd played this scene in her head over and over for days, reminding herself that it would be over quickly. That no matter what her father's reaction was, it would be over quickly. As she stood there with her tall, thin frame backed hard into the dirty wall, she forgot it all. All the practicing she'd done of what to say, or how to respond all left her. When she needed the weapon of her voice the most, it failed her, and she felt eleven again. Eleven, the age at which she first saw the true depth and capabilities of her father's rage. It had been after Clay had learned that his brother had died, and it seemed that that day, just as it did now, that a hurricane of fury had filled her father's eyes. It had just gotten worse from there.

Silence filled the room as Clay bored his hatred into Connie with a deadly stare. Lillie was frozen. She found the edge of the table with her hands to steady herself when she felt her body to start to quake. *Lord, what have I done?* She watched Connie's beautiful face turn sour, betrayed by fear. She looked around her wobbly dining table at her other children. They were also numb with panic and alarm. Ada and Nola huddled towards one another and leaned as closely into Ben as they could without actually moving from their seats. Ben's long arms reached around them both at a failed attempt at reassurance. The four year old had climbed quickly into Joe's lap when Clay's fist had slammed into the wood and had covered her eyes with her hands and buried her head so far into his shoulder that she saw nothing but darkness. Joe held her tightly but cautiously, fearing he'd need to move fast if Clay advanced on Connie or his mother. Even the baby, who had been cooing happily in the bassinet just moments before, was suddenly quiet. *Oh, Lord, what have I done?*

"I said," Clay's deep voice broke the silence that had clung to the curtains and covered the walls like a cloak. His words dripped poisonously to the floor. "You. Did. What?" Connie quivered as she looked at her father from across the table. She was grateful for the wide planks of wood of the table that spread between them. Grateful for some barrier, yet fearful with unease as to an exit route. She hadn't thought this through as much as she'd thought, and now she had put more than just herself in danger. Everything she thought she knew to be true about her decision fell apart before her eyes and landed in a mournful heap on her half-eaten cornbread. Suddenly none of it felt so right anymore.

She looked to her mother for help and found Lillie's face frozen with despair and anxiety. Then she caught Lillie's eye. In that moment something passed between mother and daughter that gave them both the strength they required to do what needed to be done. Some unspoken understanding traveled the short distance between them and settled with calm into both of their bones. Lillie nodded once at Connie, and faced her husband alone.

"I gave my okay. I did this, Clay, not Connie." Lillie stood there trembling. yet resolved to bear her daughter's burden if that's what it took. And though it wasn't true, Lillie said, "I'm the one who told her to sign up, it was my idea. I thought..."

Lillie didn't finished her sentence, because now she had Clay's full attention. He turned the full weight of his lofty frame away from Connie and towards her and hissed at her, "You thought? You." He stared at her with an abhorrent gaze, with eyes that melted her flesh and rocked her core. Lillie shuddered under the weight of it, but stood her ground. She would not beg him this time. She would not move.

Then it happened. Before Joe could move his sister from his lap, before Ben could get out of his chair and around the table, before Connie could make her way to her mother, before the little ones could hide under the table. Clay advanced so fast Lillie had no time to even throw her hands defensively in front of her face. Clay's large and calloused hand found the handle of the cast iron skillet on the stove top and he gripped it fast and hard. The skillet that was still warm. The skillet that still held the hot oil dripping from cooking his chicken. The skillet that had brought his family so many meals in the loving hands of his wife. The skillet his mother had given Lillie as a wedding present so many years prior.

Without a second thought, he flung his arm forward faster than a major league pitcher. He didn't flinch a muscle as the round black metal pan met with the side of Lillie's skull. The sound of it was deafening as metal met bone and Lillie's limp body slammed violently into the wood-burning stove, filling the tiny room with a second thump. The sound that Lillie made as she fell helplessly backwards as if in slow motion, landing in a heartbreaking jumble on the greasy kitchen rug, somehow broke the frozen tundra that their dining room had become and put the whole house in motion.

This time it was Clay who didn't see it coming. He didn't see his eldest son and eldest daughter fly around the table and lunge at him without a second thought. He didn't see or hear his younger children shrieking in horror at what he'd done. He didn't see his tiny daughters huddle at Ben's feet as Ben tried to break free from them and help his siblings. He didn't see the warm pool of blood that was quickly forming under Lillie's head. All he saw was the floorboard under his beet-red cheeks as he realized that he had just been knocked down. He saw a kitchen chair, his chair, in fact, broken and shattered and lying in pieces next to his abdomen. He felt searing pain across his upper back where Connie had slammed him with the chair, knocking him to the ground with such force that he would have put money on it that it had been one of his sons Ben or Joe who'd done it instead. Then he saw black as Joe's fist clocked him cold while he lay there, startled and in shock, on the stained and splintered floor.

Chapter Twenty-Five

Cate
Los Angeles, California
March 1945

Tony and I rang in the New Year of 1945 with class and style, and the rest of the year did not disappoint, either. We spent almost all of our free time together, and though it wasn't much, we made the most of every second. I spent a lot of time getting to know his family, who were all very kind to me, regardless of my background. Tony told them that he loved me, and that was enough for them. I never knew things could be so cut and dry. His parents were warm and kind, and his brothers and sisters were playful and loving, not unlike Tony himself. It was easy to see where he got it from. Though I'd been married to Jack for years, I had never felt that welcome or comfortable in his parents' home. I always rather felt as though they just thought I was some farmer's daughter who had gotten lucky with an upper-class businessman's son. It was different with Tony's family, and I felt myself slip into their charming ways without much resistance. I had never been happier.

My divorce papers came through in March, and Tony and I quietly celebrated over dinner at a local Italian restaurant that had quickly become a favorite of ours. We dipped and dunked our warm sliced focaccia into small ramekins of authentic Italian olive oil and sipped our wine while we waited for the chef's famous chicken carbonara. We were making small talk, really, trying not to make it seems to strange that I was on a date to celebrate the end of my marriage to Jack. Then Tony took it in a whole other direction.

"Cate?" Tony had a gentle and sympathetic look on his face. He knew I was feeling conflicted over been an official divorcée, even though I was thrilled to finally be free of Jack. "Are you happy?"

"Yes, of course," I said, because truly, I was. "It's just strange to think I am a divorced woman, even though it's obviously what I want. I guess I feel a little marked, if that makes sense." I wasn't ashamed, I just felt like people could tell just by looking at me.

"It's not like a scarlet letter anymore, Cate. Lots of folks get divorced, and you certainly had good reason." He took my hand and gave it a squeeze. "Besides, it obviously doesn't matter to me or anyone out here. Don't let it matter to you." His smile put me at ease, and I knew he was right.

"Yes, you're right, I suppose. Just feels odd to carry that title around. Well, and to still have his last name. I certainly don't feel like Mrs. Edens anymore."

Tony nodded in agreement. "So what do you think of marriage now?" he asked. He was nervous, and in the candlelight I could see his face start to turn a tad red.

I laughed. "Tony, it's not the institute of marriage that I oppose, just who I happened to be in that institution with! I just chose the wrong dancing partner, is all."

He smiled again and asked, "So, you would do it again?"

My heart rate sped up and I felt a flush hit my cheeks. I tried to tell myself it was the glass of chianti I'd been sipping, but I knew it was something more. I held his gaze as I thought about my answer. "Yes, of course. But it would have to be with someone more kind, and honest. Someone who will let me be me. Someone like…" My voice trailed off as I lost my words.

"Someone like me?" he asked simply. "Cate, would you marry someone like me?" Light beads of perspiration broke out on his forehead, but he held his gaze steady and looked me in the eye as he spoke.

"Tony, are you asking me something here, or are we just speaking in hypotheticals?" My breath quickened as he rose from his chair and pulled a ring box out of his pocket. I smiled widely as I watched Tony hike up the pant leg of his very distinguished suit so that he could fall to one knee in front of me.

He took my hand and said, "Cate, I'm asking if you will be my forever dance partner. I'm asking if you would do me the great privilege of being my wife." He popped open the jeweler's box to reveal the most amazing emerald-cut sapphire, flanked beautifully by two small diamonds. The sapphire is my birthstone, and I'd never owned one before.

I was speechless. It was like nothing I'd ever seen, and I reached out to touch it. "This is all so surreal. I mean I was just divorced a few moments ago, really, and now…"

Tony stayed where he was on his knee and gazed up at me as he said, "I know it seems like this is strange timing, but I just couldn't wait a moment longer." When I didn't say anything, he gently prompted me. "So..."

I threw myself into his arms and nearly toppled us both over in the process. The waiter laughed, and the woman seated next to us started to tear up. I felt as though I could have shouted to the world that yes, of course, I would marry him, but instead I saved my words just for him as I whispered in his ear, "Yes, of course... how soon is too soon?" Funny how you can go from one emotion to another without so much as skipping a beat.

We were married the following month. Contrary to his family's suspicions, the hurried date was not due in fact to my being pregnant. Tony had held that tradition close and we refrained from marital relations until we were in fact married, a provision I found both sweet and respectful. Though, to be honest, the promise of those relations pushed us both to move a little faster towards our nuptials.

Our wedding was more of a ceremony than a large church affair. I'd done the white dress and flowers ceremony before, and I just didn't feel like it was all necessary again. I knew, too, that a fancy wedding didn't necessarily translate into a wonderful marriage, and that what mattered most were the promises we made each other. The venue could have been anywhere, really, as long as it was Tony by my side. So we booked the courthouse for an afternoon, just after Easter, and exchanged our vows in front of his sweet family and our friends. Betsy Piper wept like a baby, and Claire and Macy cried a bit too, though I think the loss of a roommate was more moving to them than my promise of love to Tony.

I'd sent notice to my family, though I didn't expect they'd make it, given the distance and short notice, and honestly felt a little relieved because of it, though I missed having my parents there. My aunt Rachel sent a hideous antique mirror as a gift, which we found a home for in the bathroom of Tony's machine shop, and my folks sent along some money and a kind note wishing us well and saying how they'd like to meet Tony someday soon. Somehow that was enough for me.

The sentiments from Michigan were kinder than I'd expected, though I realized while reading the cards and notes from my kin that I really didn't care anymore what any of them thought. While it was nice to have their blessing, I realized I didn't really feel like I needed it. I had officially started over, and was as far removed from Kentucky and Michigan as was possible in my mind. There was no looking back for me, and all I wanted was to focus on was my future as Mrs. Tony Otera and whatever that would hold.

Tony was up front about children. He wanted them and he wanted quite a few, and though he was anxious to start trying he was more than happy to wait for me to finish my night school. It turned out he didn't have to wait too terribly long, because after the war ended in May the factory work all but ceased, and I lost my job on the line. It was wonderful news, actually, on two fronts. First, it allowed me more time to put towards my classes, so I finished a few months earlier than expected, which meant we could try for a family sooner. And second and more importantly, World War II was finally over, and our brave men could start to come home and rebuild again. It was a time for rebuilding for all of us, a healing of sorts, and a lifting of the clouds. Everything just seemed to fall into place.

Tony and I found a small apartment just after our wedding and quickly settled into married life. It was a third-story unit in west Los Angeles, just off Adams Street, in a neighborhood heady with Mexican influence. Tony's parents lived nearby, as did his brothers, and it was nice to feel surrounded by supportive family and to learn more about the culture from which Tony came. Our apartment was quaint and cozy and it instantly felt like home, though I think that had a great deal more to do with who I was sharing my home with than what the walls looked like.

By that summer I had managed to finish up my classes and I received my high school diploma, with an extra certificate in bookkeeping, though I wasn't sure what I'd do with it. Tony had been ever so proud of me, and acted as though it was as big of a deal as his having completed his bachelor's degree from UCLA so many years before. I think secretly, though, he was even more excited at the prospect of starting a family, and my having finished school freed up that possibility.

I would be lying to say that the thought of trying to conceive didn't bring back horrid memories. My last experience with it had dragged on for years, and though I'd learned it was Jack's troubles and not mine that were at the heart of it, I couldn't help but lend an ear to the nagging feeling I had that something still wasn't right. I wanted children desperately, had dreamed of them for years even, and was certainly ready to jump into that boat with Tony; but something just wasn't sitting well. I decided I couldn't do what I did last time. I could not sit at home, being the housewife, just waiting for the moment I'd become a lady in waiting. The thought of the long hours by myself during the day made me shudder, and after having tasted working life in the factory I wanted more for myself.

I found it quite easy to find work this time around, which was the most liberating feeling in the world. I knew I could support myself on my own laurels, should I need to, though I knew, being with Tony, I'd never have to. I found work briefly in a See's Candy factory on the assembly line, probably because it felt familiar to me from the work I'd done at the aviation plant, even though the end product was slightly sweeter than warplanes. For three months I wore a net on my hair and gloves on my hands while I picked misshapen pieces of caramels and chocolates off the line by hand. It was monotonous work, the kind where you clock in on a paper card, work on your feet for 8–10 hours watching candy fly by, and then clock out. There was no camaraderie like with Claire and Macy at the old plant, and it was hard for me to get as patriotic and excited about candy as I had about my work before.

After four months of the sickeningly sweet smell of candy and poor pay, I hung up my See's apron and moved on to the next chapter in my life. I wish I could tell you that it was my motherhood chapter, but it quickly became apparent that our attempts at starting a family would require a bit of patience.

Unfortunately, my patience on that topic had run out many years before. Though I tried not to focus on it, I'd be lying if I said I didn't think about it numerous times a day. I even attempted to mimic Tony's faith in the motto that whatever will be, will be, but as the months started to creep by without so much as a blip in my cycle I began to grow weary again, and the emotional fatigue of it started to set in faster than it had the first time.

I refused to allow it to tear Tony and me apart, though, and thank God, he was on the same page. We came first, always: it was our unspoken motto. When I'd start to get upset or obsessive about it, Tony would pull me in close and say, "We will be given the right children at the right time, my love... patience." I wanted to believe him, but he also hadn't lived through the nightmare of trying that I had with Jack. It's funny now to think back on his reassuring words at the time because they didn't soothe me as he had hoped, but now I fully understand just how right he was.

Tony made a point of steering me clear of complete obsession as much as possible. I found work as a switchboard operator once I left the See's factory job, and while it wasn't terribly challenging, the hours were wonderful and allowed me to make it home in the early afternoons to get dinner started before Tony came home from the shop. His machine shop had slowed down a tad with the end of war, and Tony and I found ourselves with a lot of free time over that summer and into the fall and early winter months. He was always so great about making plans for us on the weekends to get outside and explore—mostly for my benefit, I think, to keep my mind occupied with things other than a baby. We took long walks on the trails in the hills just outside Los Angeles, and he introduced me to all the local plant life and flowers. I'd grown up outside, and I think Tony knew that if he didn't get me back to my roots a little bit here and there, I would stifle under the stress of trying for children.

Of all the things we did together that year, perhaps some of my favorite happened on the beach. Even in the winter time, which isn't much to speak of in Los Angeles considering the winters I'd endured in Kentucky and Michigan, we were out by the water as much as possibly. One of our favorite things to do was to pack a picnic lunch and have a weenie roast down by the water. The beaches didn't have as many restrictions as they do today, so we were a little more free to enjoy such things. On some of our walks out, we'd gather small twigs and sticks and collect them in a box on our balcony at the apartment. Then, when we wanted to roast hot dogs on the beach, we'd simply take our box of tinder and start ourselves up a little bonfire.

It was on one of those late afternoon roasts in March of 1946 that I realized I might really have a problem. Tony had picked us a spot down by a rocky cove a bit off the beaten path, both because it was beautiful, and also because we wanted some privacy. I was relaxing as much as I could, given that my monthly menses had just started and I was tired and slightly crampy. It was a stabbing reminder that I still wasn't pregnant nearly eight months after we'd begun to try, and it was making me grumpy. Even the gentle lapping of the waves hitting the sand did little to soothe my irritability.

As I lay on the cotton blanket, I watched Tony gathering up more small twigs and things to feed our slow-growing fire, and suddenly a fire lit up inside me and I knew. I felt a sadness wash over me that I can't explain, and I knew that Tony and I needed to have a serious discussion that wasn't going to be easy. I waited until he came back to me and worked his magic on the open flames, and I tried to keep breathing as I watched the flames lick higher and higher, but it felt as though the nagging feeling I had was growing larger and larger along with the fire I was watching. Tony came and sat beside me as I lay on my side with my head in my hand. He patted my hip bone and caught the look on my face pretty quickly. He read me so easily, I didn't even have to prompt him.

"What is it, love? Are you really not feeling that well? We don't have to stay, I just thought the fresh air might do us some good."

I smiled at his thoughtfulness. "No, we've only just gotten here and you just built the fire. I'm okay." He looked at me quizzically so I added, "Really, I promise."

"Alright then, Cate." He snuggled in closer with his head near my face, and he closed his eyes against the bright sun and started to snooze. I watched his face for what seemed like forever, and the more I watched, the more sad I became until I found myself crying, and then sobbing. Tony immediately sat up and took my face in his hands.

"Cate, what is it?" He wiped away my tears but it only made them fall faster; and, for the first time in what seemed like forever, I just let it all go. Tony just held me and let me cry, because he knew I needed to. I think he needed me to as well. When I felt spent and as though I could cry no more, I finally decided to say what I needed to.

"Tony, what will you do if I can't have children?" I asked him quietly, not really wanting to know the answer, but needing to know it all the same.

"Cate, my love, it's only been a few months. You worry too much." He wasn't blowing me off, I really think he just wasn't concerned yet. I, on the other hand, had played that hand before, and denial had gotten me nowhere.

"It's been eight months. And nothing. And we weren't really not trying in the three months before that." I sighed and continued, "I've done all this before, Tony. Something isn't right here, and I think it's me. It's something with me."

"Why do you think that? I think we just need more time. It will happen, Cate." Tony looked concerned, and I wasn't sure if he was trying to convince himself or me at that point.

"Tony, I can't explain it to you, but I just have a bad nagging feeling that it's my fault. Well, my body's fault, anyway." I paused and asked again, "What will you do if I can't give you children? Would you leave me?"

Tony bolted upright and sat staring at me as though I'd grown a third head. "Now you are talking crazy. Never. I told you, you and I come first. Always." He sat pensively for a moment, as though the thought of never having kids had never crossed his mind. "I suppose, we'd adopt?"

"Adopt? You'd do that?" It was a thought that hadn't actually crossed my mind before. I assumed we'd either have our own, or none at all.

"Yes, of course! They'd still be ours, Cate." He frowned then and said, "But Cate, all this talk and you aren't even sure there's anything to be worried about. Although..."

"Although what?"

"Well, if you really feel like something is wrong, we can both go to the doctor's and just make sure." I couldn't have loved him more than in that moment. The moment where he would do anything to put me at ease, even if it meant subjecting himself to medical testing that he wasn't sure was even necessary.

"Could we? At least if I know what we are really dealing with then I can handle it. I mean, I know I must seem terribly impatient, but then again, I've..."

He interrupted, "You've done all this before, yes." He sighed heavily, and then nodded and said, "Anytime next week would be fine if the doctors can see us then. The shop's been pretty slow, so I'm sure I can get the time off."

I hugged him then so tightly, and we lay there on the beach watching the waves crashing upon each other and the sun reflecting on the water and sand. We both dozed off and on in the cool breeze and bountiful sunlight, and we held each other tightly, reassuring each other that we were there for whatever the journey brought us. Little did we know that we'd need every bit of that life raft to get us through the storm that was coming our way.

Chapter Twenty-Six

Los Angeles, California
April 1946

"What do you mean, two?" I was stunned and shocked, and suddenly couldn't feel my body. How was this happening?

"Well, Cate, it is unusual, I will say, but our tests are pretty conclusive." Doctor Monarch was sitting forward in his chair and leaning loosely on his elbows. It was an anxious pose, and I understood why. He wasn't at all sure of how I would take the news.

"So, two," Tony said flatly. I looked at Tony, who was looking between myself and the doctor and trying to make sense of it like I was. "How is that possible? I mean, how does that even work?"

"Well, there are all sorts of possible anomalies in life, Tony. I can't say I've seen this particular one before, and to be honest may never see it again, but it's true." He paused then, and studied my face. He had more news to share, and I held my breath as I waited for it.

Tony repeated himself, "Yes, but how does that work?" The engineer in him was flipping through mental files, twisting and twirling the few anatomy facts he knew in his head, trying to make sense of it.

Dr. Monarch sighed and said, "Well, the truth is, it doesn't. At least not in terms of reproductive ability. And there's a bit more, I'm afraid."

"More? There's more? Of course, there is." I blurted out what was on my mind because the shock of it had left me without a filter. "Go ahead, Dr. Monarch, I apologize, it's okay. Just lay it all out. We can handle it." Tony reached over and grabbed my hand. He was holding it so tightly my fingers were tingling in a matter of moments.

"So, Cate, Tony... Like I just said, Cate appears to have not one, but two uteri. I've seen oddly shaped ones before, even a few that roughly resembled a heart, but in your case, you have two small uteri. One is slightly larger than the other, but they are both smaller than they ought to be, the size of a child's, really, and they are attached to one another.

Almost like one normal sized uterus with a complete bifurcation down the center."

Tony's eyebrows were furrowed and his confusion showed on his face. "So can't she still carry a child in one of them? I mean, isn't it at least slightly possible?" Dr. Monarch face softened even more, and I could tell it was as hard for him as it was for us. I'm sure he felt like he was giving me a death sentence.

"No, Tony, for many reasons," he said. "First, I'm afraid the strain of a growing fetus would cause too much stress on the uterine muscle and would cause it to rupture. Neither one is of adequate size. Unfortunately a uterine rupture is not sustainable with the life of a child, or Cate's for that matter." He paused and then added, "But as I said, there's more, I'm afraid."

I nodded and gave him a weak smile. "Okay. It's okay." I couldn't stop nodding, and I wasn't sure who exactly I was reassuring.

"Well, even if the uterine wall could withstand such stretching, and I assure you I don't think that Cate's could, there isn't... well, there isn't an ovary on the left side."

Tony's face was unreadable. It was so distorted with confusion that I hardly recognized him. He was beginning to sweat and I felt him shaking slightly as he gripped my hand harder. "So, you are saying she has two uteri when she should have one, and she has one ovary when she should have two?"

"Yes, that's exactly what I'm saying. And the one ovary she has is actually, well, not exactly connected as it should be. The ovary is there, but the Fallopian tube is mangled, almost nonexistent, really. So Cate's eggs have no where to travel but into her abdomen." He looked at me then, because I think the pain on Tony's face was too much for him. "Cate, it explains why your periods are regular and why you were able to develop quite normally. You make all the right hormones, and I'd venture to say you've even got a normal amount of eggs in your ovary, but there just isn't any way for them to get where they need to go..."

I interrupted him and softly added, "And there isn't a home strong enough for them anyway, right?"

"No, I'm afraid not." He seemed out of words and a silence filled his tiny colonial-styled office. My eyes roved over his floor-to-ceiling book-cases, which were filled with medical indexes, popular novels, and the occasional history book. I took in his elegantly framed medical degree and undergraduate degree, and it was obvious to me that someone had spent a lot of money and thought in framing them. I was looking for something, anything to fill the void I felt in my mind. Dr. Monarch was a true east coaster, and a graduate from Harvard Medical School. He was the best in his field, which is why we were sent to him in the first place, and so I knew if he said it wasn't possible, then it really wasn't possible.

"Okay." It was all I could muster, and I said it to no one in particular.

"Okay? How is it okay, Cate? How?" Tony was staring at me with eyes brimming with tears. He was starting to come unraveled, and yet I suddenly felt completely calm about it. I had known, after all, that something wasn't right, and now I just knew for sure. Everything just seemed to make sense; and, in an odd way, I felt a little relieved to just have an answer. I could deal with the facts; it was the unknown that was more frightening to me.

"Tony..." I wiped a tear off of his cheek that had escaped his lashes, and said, "Whatever will be, will be, right? We will be given the right children at the right time, my love... patience." I smiled at him gently as my mind moved forward towards his talk about adoption.

"Those are my words, Cate. Not fair." He gave me a weak smile back and, though I could tell his heart was broken in some way, he nodded at me and said, "Yes, patience."

We thanked Dr. Monarch profusely for his hard work, and for giving us the answers that we needed in order to move on in our lives, and we headed out of his office towards the stairwell. Tony was gripping my hand like a vice and I couldn't feel my fingertips any longer, but I hesitated to say anything because I knew he needed to be holding my hand in order to make it out the door without losing it.

Finally I couldn't take the pain any longer, and so I stopped at the top of the stairwell and said, "Tony, can you let me go now?"

He turned on me then, his eyes furious and his face full of rage. I'd never seen him even slightly angry, much less full of fury, and it shook me to my bones. "Cate!" He'd said it loudly—shouted it, really—and it startled two women who were passing by. One glared at him and then gave me a sympathetic smile as if to say, "Men right?"

"Tony, what is it? I didn't mean to upset you so, I just..." He didn't let me finish, though.

"No, I will not let you go. Not now, nor ever. You will have to leave me first. I didn't marry you for your ability to make a baby. I married you because I love you and because no matter what comes our way, I want to spend the rest of my life with you." I tried to interrupt him, to stop him from making such a scene, but he just continued. "So, no! I will not let you go. I am sad for you, for us, but we will have children someday, I swear it. I will do whatever I can to make sure that happens, I will…"

"Tony!" I shouted at him then, and broke him out of his rant long enough that I was able to add, "I just want you to let go of my hand!" He looked down at my fingertips, which were now a funny shade of purple, and immediately let them go. I exhaled with relief and then started laughing as I rubbed my hand to increase the circulation to it. "I'm sorry, I'm so sorry," I said between my laughter. "I just couldn't feel my fingertips anymore, I needed you to let my *hand* go, is all…"

Tony started laughing then, and then he couldn't stop laughing. His deep bellows echoed off the concrete walls as we stood there at the top of the staircase, just having been told we would never have children of our own, laughing like a couple of school girls. I felt my tears fall and hit my new white sweater, and I laughed even harder. It was ridiculous and refreshing, and an insight into how Tony and I would handle most disasters in our lives. With a little bit of indignation followed by a whole lot of laughter.

When we calmed down and regained our composure, Tony pulled me into a hug. I held him tightly and whispered, "So, now what?"

He drew back to look at me and shrugged his shoulders. "Well, we adopt, of course."

"Really?" I said in disbelief. He'd meant what he'd offered at the beach. "That's really what you want?"

"I want children, and I want to raise them with you. So, yes, really." I kissed him then, hard, and passionately as if we were alone, and it was almost as good as our very first kiss a year and a half before. Almost.

Chapter Twenty-Seven

Lillie
Thursday, August 13, 1953
8:00 a.m.

Lillie lay quietly on her side in the same position Elizabeth had placed her just before she'd finished her shift. The clock on the wall read eight, and the smell of coffee wafting through the large room told Lillie that morning was indeed upon her. She closed her eyes, breathing in the rich aroma and wishing for a moment that she could have a cup of the comforting brown liquid that was often too expensive to be found on her shopping list. She pictured herself standing in her kitchen, her chubby fingers wrapped around her old cracked white mug, warm with fluid and cooled only slightly by a touch of cream. Lillie found herself smiling, thinking about all the quiet moments that she had had like that over the years, all the precious time she had to herself just before her house woke and the children stirred, just before her husband got up and ruined whatever day it happened to be.

Her smile began to fade, though, as she remembered how she had enjoyed those moments less and less over the last few years. She didn't use to mind the days that she had to re-brew her coffee grounds in order to pinch a penny here or there but, the last few months in particular, it had angered her. As she'd sip the secondhand liquid, weak and bitter from its rebirth, she'd felt ashamed, and then upset, and finally angry. She finally found herself angry at her circumstances for the first time in her life. Angry that she couldn't much feel the warmth of the coffee, whether fresh or not, because her hands were so numb they felt nothing at all. Angry that she couldn't much taste it anymore either, because her palate had become bland as of late and most things tasted all the same to her. Angry that it was her fault, yet not her fault. Angry that she'd let it come to this, where even her morning ritual had lost its sparkle, and that even the best part of her day was becoming unmanageable.

Towards the end of her days on the farm, the quiet of the morning had given her too much leeway to think about her two children who had left, her other two children she had lost, and how her body was betraying her with every passing day.

Lillie lay in the tidy hospital ward and thought about the very last time she'd made coffee, the very last time she'd thought she was still strong enough to fill the pot and lift it to the hot stove top. She recalled how she'd cried when the pot and its contents landed with a clatter and a splash at her feet. The feet that she could no longer feel, and the feet that she could, in fact, barely see, for the loss of her vision had become so great. She thought about how Clay had found her sitting helplessly on a kitchen chair rocking herself to and fro, trying to convince herself she was fine and that she was just tired. Clay had stood there silently for many moments, looking from Lillie to the mess in front of the stove and back again, and finally had given a snarled chuckle at the pathetic scene before him. Then he'd walked right out the door without a word and let the door slam on its rusty hinges as he'd made his way into the fields.

Lillie remembered how Nola had found her there moments later and had burst into tears, knowing deep down what it meant. Knowing that her mother was too far gone to save, and not knowing what to do about it. She remembered her tiny, eighteen-year-old daughter, with her coke-bottle glasses and short stringy hair, helping her up on her feet and practically dragging her back to her bed. She remembered having felt so tired and defeated that all she could do was close her eyes tightly and let Nola pull the covers up over her body and tuck them gently under her chin. Behind her eyelids, none of it had existed. Behind her eyelids she wasn't dying a slow death and she wasn't leaving seven children without a mother. Behind her eyelids she wasn't the feeble woman that she'd slowly morphed into over the years. She was just Lillie.

While she slept, she was just her joyful, soulful, healthy self, without fear or pain or anger. She let Nola put her to bed that day and had closed her eyes in defeat. Lillie had slept so hard and so long that even Clay didn't bother to disturb her. She vaguely recalled having heard talk from time to time of what should be done about her, and where she should be taken, but she'd shift a bit in the bed and shift a bit in her mind and return to the quiet calm that was her sleep. When she awoke the next day she felt slightly refreshed and almost ready to try again, but the decision had already been made. The plans had been laid out before her as if Clay were telling her what he'd like for dinner instead of that he'd chosen to no longer have her in his home, near his children, or in his heart. As if she were a piece of livestock who'd caught a virus and needed dealing with before she infected the whole lot of them.

Lillie was still thinking of those horrible moments when her day nurse came in with a chipper "hello" and proceeded to open the window panes one by one. As the light began to fill the room, Lillie began to wish for death. She welcomed it, even, with every chirp exhaled by a tiny bird, and every smell of blossoms on the late summer breeze. She told God in her head she was ready, she didn't care anymore, she was done. She no longer wanted to feel the pain of her body, and she no longer wanted to feel the pain of her heart. She was too tired to fight anymore, and she asked him urgently to take her soon. Then her nurse said something that made Lillie beg God's forgiveness and pray for a little more time.

"Lillie, I'm Ada Mae. I hear you have a daughter with the same name?" Lillie opened her eyes and stared up at the nurse with cautious eyes. She expected to see a judgmental face, a young face, a face who could never understand what she was going through. Instead she found the face of an older nurse with graying hair, knowing eyes and a kind, gentle smile. She smelled of something familiar, something sweet.

"Yes," Lillie replied in a whisper. Her Ada's face came into focus in her mind and she quickly added, "But she's just Ada. She's sixteen, and quite beautiful."

"I remember," the nurse said softly, toning down her perky demeanor. She could see the mention of Lillie's daughter had brought her patient pain, and she instantly regretted having mentioned it. Lillie lay still, not sure of what she'd just heard, or how this nurse knew her daughter. Then it hit her. "Do you remember me, Lillie?" Ada Mae asked in an unassuming manner. She knew perhaps that Lillie's mind had many holes where memories should be.

"I do." Lillie nodded slightly as thoughts flooded her brain like a picture book in fast forward. "You took care of my Ada some years back. When that bus hit her. When I thought she was gonna die and that my husband was gonna kill me right along with her, you took care of her. Many days, you did. Many, many days." Lillie's recall was flawless, the memory detailed like a fine piece of art in her mind.

"Yes, that was me. I wasn't sure you'd remember, you were so tired sitting by her side all that time." Ada Mae shifted her weight as she watched Lillie and tried to decide if she'd done the right thing by reminding her.

"Oh, I remember. I remember because you was so kind to me. Even though you knew we couldn't pay you a dime, you was still so kind. And you loved my Ada like she was your own girl. I remember that. Feeling like even if I wasn't there you'd'a done that. Taken good care of her, that is." Lillie exhaled, remembering those long days and nights by her daughter's side some ten years before. How exhausted she'd felt, how determined to stay she was, and how she'd promised God many things in the wee hours of the night if he'd just help Ada through. She'd promised him she'd take care of her, if only he'd give her back. He had held up his end of the bargain, but Lillie felt like it was way too late to try hold up hers.

"I remember your husband too. Conner, isn't it? No, Clay. He's a quiet man. I saw him a few times around town after that, but he never did acknowledge me." That was Clay all right. Quiet, and uninterested in the lives of others. A shell of a man, filled with the violence of a tornado on the inside. "Somehow, though, I never saw you again, Lillie."

Lillie felt her cheeks warm. "Didn't get out much..." Lillie mumbled with embarrassment. She wasn't let out much, was more like it. Especially after the incident with Ada. A prisoner almost, to the farm, to her two-bedroom shack and their few acres of land. A prisoner, later, to her disease, which stopped her from doing much of anything but what was necessary.

Then the older nurse said it, the thing that gave Lillie the will to push through a few more days. She said, "Is Clay still around? Is he gonna look after your kids while you're gone?" As if Lillie were on vacation and not lying there dying. As if Lillie would be back there someday, tending her children. "I know most men don't know their front from their back when it comes to raising kids. I hope he knows how to take care of girls."

Lillie's torso arched up and she leaned out of the bed before she even realized what was happening. She felt the vile warmth of stale water and crackers rise and exit her mouth as she vomited all over the white tile floor. She heaved and heaved at the thought of Clay with her children, a thought she'd been able to avoid for the most part by simply not thinking about it. By staying in the moment and not thinking about the future, a thing she knew well how to do. Now it was a thought she could no longer deny, and she had to fix it. Even if it were too late for Nola or Ada because they were all but grown, she had to fix it for her younger ones. And she made yet one more deal with God. "Two days," she whispered as liquid and bile dripped from her chin.

Lillie's nurse had flown fast into action, grabbing a bucket and towels as hurriedly as she could, and she didn't hear what Lillie had said. "Sorry, Lillie?" Ada Mae wiped her chin and placed a cool wet rag on her forehead. "I didn't catch what you said."

"Two days!" Lillie screamed it. Loud and unabashed came her yell from a place so deep within her that it echoed loudly off the walls and wandered down the stairwell to the other wards.

"Miss Lillie, I..." Ada Mae started to say but she was stopped mid-thought when Lillie grabbed forcefully at her arm and interrupted her.

"Ada, all's I need is two days. You got to give me that. Please, God. You got to give me that. I'll do good with them. Just two days, and I'll do what Little Red told me to do!" Lillie's eyes were so desperate and so woeful that Ada Mae quickly agreed to her request even though she had no idea what Lillie was talking about.

"Yes, Lillie, two days. You got it. Whatever you need, you got it." Ada Mae's voice was merciful as she watched Lillie's face relax. She still lay tenuously over the side of the mattress and above the collecting bucket. "Now let's get you lying back if your tummy is feeling like it's righted itself." Lillie nodded, and was grateful as Ada Mae gently helped her ease her back onto the bed. She settled into the pillow with her matted hair. She closed her eyes, sensing her promise was going to be fulfilled with answers brought to her in the darkness beneath her eyelids.

Lillie slept the greater part of the day, waking twice for short periods of time. Once she stayed awake only long enough to sip some tea and have a few bites of a soda cracker, which she found very dry and difficult to swallow. Her throat felt swollen and raw. The second time, Ada Mae had insisted she be bathed a bit, and Lillie was too exhausted to put up much of a fight about it, even though all she wanted to do was close her eyes. Lillie was tired, and trying her best to just to bide her time until Elizabeth came on again. Hours passed in silence, and Ada Mae worried that Lillie was slipping into a coma, that her body had finally succumbed to its fate. She worried Lillie wouldn't get two more hours, much less two more days; yet she'd seen many miracles in her many years as a nurse. She had always stood in awe of the mind's ability to overcome the body when it was important enough, and Ada Mae sensed whatever Lillie had on her mind was indeed so.

Just after supper time, Lillie was awoken by Elizabeth's soft hand as she lightly rubbed Lillie's arm. Lillie looked up at her new friend and gave her a small smile as she tried to shrug off her sleepiness. Lillie needed to wake up now and take advantage of this time with Elizabeth. She needed her, and she was finally going to take control of something in her life, even if it was on the last day of it.

"Hi there, Miss Lillie." Elizabeth smiled and said, "I hear you've been asleep all day. And I'm wondering," Elizabeth paused for dramatic effect, "if you've been dreaming about what I promised to bring you before I left this morning."

Lillie knitted her eyebrows in confusion and racked her brain. She'd dreamed a lot while she'd rested that day, and at some points was having a hard time telling if her dreams were real or just remnants of days past. "I'm sorry, Elizabeth, I don't remember..."

Elizabeth's face fell, though she tried her best to hide her disappointment. She'd been excited all afternoon about bringing her little treat to Miss Lillie, and had felt devilishly sly as she'd slipped it past her head nurse in her purse. She'd pictured Lillie waiting with baited breath for it all day, the anticipation of it making the hours long, but it seemed Lillie hadn't even given it another thought. She walked over to the counter top by the sink where she'd placed her bag and pulled out a bottle opener, followed by a glass bottle of Coca-Cola that was wet with sweat from meeting the warm evening air. She brought both towards Lillie's bed and got them close enough that she made sure Lillie could see them.

"Ah, Elizabeth. I forgot, but you remembered." Lillie's smile grew wider, showing Elizabeth the empty spaces in her mouth once again. Her grin grew as she watched Elizabeth pop the cap off with a flip of her wrist and insert a straw into the ice-cold bottle. She could hear the carbonation as the bubbles of her cola tinkered and popped inside the glass, and she could actually smell the sweetness of it. It was an amount of sugar that she hadn't been allowed in quite some time.

Elizabeth helped her to prop herself up so she was in a safe position to drink, and then she carefully handed her the bottle, wrapping the swollen fingers of both of her hands around each side. Lillie felt like a child, but not because Elizabeth had to help her. It just felt new and exciting to be holding her soda, and she anticipated with a giggle how it would burst on her tongue. Elizabeth helped her get the straw in her mouth, and Lillie pursed her lips around it and sucked in the sugary indulgence that she hadn't had in over two decades.

She sipped it slowly at first, and then faster as the flavor erupted on her tongue. It almost burned, she drank so fast, but she didn't care; and, like a child who forgets to take a breath, she finished it and let out the largest exhale Elizabeth had ever heard. Both she and Elizabeth started to laugh, slowly at first and then louder and louder until tears rolled down Elizabeth's face and Lillie's sides ached from the effort of it. As their laughter died down, Lillie looked up at Elizabeth and handed her the empty bottle and said, "Thank you, Elizabeth. So much. That was one of the kindest things you could'a done for me."

"You're welcome, Lillie." Elizabeth held the clear glass bottle in her hand and rubbed her thumb back and forth over the Coca-Cola label. She had had no idea that something so small could mean so much, but she sensed she had given Lillie more than just a drink. What she didn't know was that she had given Lillie a piece of her childhood, a moment of time before her life with Clay, when she had been quite happy. "I guess I ought to hide the evidence, eh?" Lillie grinned as she watched Elizabeth place the empty bottle and the opener back in her bag.

Elizabeth came back towards the bed and pulled up a stool. She knew she was running out of time and had perhaps even hastened Lillie's death with her carbonated delicacy. She dove in headfirst, forgetting herself and her white smock dress and her uniform cap. She brought up the first thing she thought of just to get Lillie talking again. "So, Lillie," she said. "I've been wondering a bit about what we were talking about last night. About Joey? How on earth did he talk Clay into letting him join the army? And your oldest daughter too, how did they do it? It just doesn't seem like Clay is the type to just let them walk away like that."

Lillie laughed and said, "No, you got that right!" Lillie shifted herself in bed, ready to tell Elizabeth whatever she wanted to know so that Elizabeth could see just what kind of man Clay Woodard was, though she was sure a picture was certainly starting to form in her mind. "Only reason they both got outta here is because they just didn't give him no choice."

"How do you mean?" Elizabeth sat with her legs crossed and leaned in towards Lillie's bed, propping her chin on her elbows; but she wasn't prepared for the story that began to unfold before her. Lillie started with how Connie had come to her with fear and worry in her eyes and had asked for her birth certificate. She told the tale of how Connie had told her father over their chicken and cornbread dinner, and Lillie closed her story with how she'd ended up in a bloody heap on her kitchen floor with a frying pan next to her head and a broken chair scattered across the room. Elizabeth was silent for a moment after Lillie had finished her story and then asked, "Were you okay? I mean, obviously you're still here, but my word, Lillie..."

"I guess I was out for some time after he hit me with my pan, and my children just kept checking my breaths while they cleaned me up a bit. I came to with a right headache and couldn't see straight for a while. Nothing too terrible, so I guess I was lucky." Lillie recalled how her head had felt like it would implode on itself, how the room spun round for days afterward, causing her to be sick to her stomach off and on, and how her vision was never quite the same again. The frying pan had hit so hard it was like it rewired certain things in her brain, and that's when she felt like the problems with her memory had really begun—then her diabetes took over from there.

"I'm not sure 'lucky' is the word I'd use. Lillie, why didn't he go to jail for that? Surely the sheriff would have taken him in." Elizabeth was sick thinking how he'd done that to Lillie and walked away scot-free. How was that possible?

"Nah, Elizabeth. We farming folk are real private like that. If you let the law look around your house once then they think they can always come back snooping. They try to find something to get you for." Elizabeth thought that it might have been a saving grace for Lillie and her kids if the sheriff had poked around more, but she kept the thought to herself. "Plus, that sure would'a pissed Mr. Adams off, and we didn't need no reason to make him any madder than he already was."

"So then, Connie obviously got to go. I mean I guess really, like you said, Clay really couldn't stop her by then, right?"

"Right. The day Connie left, though, Clay was nowhere to be found. He couldn't even get over himself long enough to say goodbye to her. He just went to work like it was any other day and never mentioned her again. Like he never had a girl named Connie.

"Connie was real sweet, though. When she got her first paycheck she started sending a little my way. I took up getting the mail everyday 'cause I knew she meant the money for me and the kids and not Clay. I was just real careful about how much I spent at once, and Clay didn't even seem to notice that there was a little more on the kids' plates at supper time, as long as his plate looked the same."

"She sounds really, nice. Your daughter Connie, that is," Elizabeth said. Lillie nodded and almost found herself in tears. If Connie knew now where her mother was she'd come screaming home to try to save her, and Lillie couldn't possibly have that.

"You know, I got me a granddaughter?" Lillie asked with her eyebrows raised, anticipating Elizabeth's surprise.

"You do? Whose is it?" Elizabeth was surprised. A grandmother at forty-four was fairly young, though not unheard of in a place where folks started their families as soon as they said "I do."

"Well now, Connie didn't just go and get her a job with the army. She done found herself a husband too. He's a real nice man, that Bill, and he sure loves his wife and girl. Maggie's her name. They named her Maggie. I couldn't really have asked for more for her. Connie deserves it, she grew up too fast in our house."

"Have you ever met her, Lillie? Your granddaughter?" Elizabeth said hopefully.

"Oh, yes, just once, though. Connie brought her baby home last year, and I was still good enough then to be able to hold her. She was so very small. My mama even came down from up north to see them and we had some pictures made then. At least Connie's baby will know what I looked like, someday." A quiet sadness settled on Lillie's face, and Elizabeth knew that look well by now. Lillie was getting tired, made more so by all the remembering she was doing. She had to keep her awake a while longer, and she had to keep her talking.

"That's really nice, Lillie. I'm sure Connie will tell her all about you." Elizabeth cleared her throat and startled Lillie, which helped to wake her up some. "Lillie, if it was that bad when Connie left, how on earth did Joe ever do the same?"

"You'd'a thought Clay would'a locked them all up after that, right? Well, Joe wasn't ever really close with Clay like my Ben was. And he wasn't all that afraid of him neither. Hard to fear someone you ain't got no respect for, see…"

"So that's why Ben never left? He got along with his father?" Elizabeth found it hard to believe that anyone could get along with Clay. Especially one of his children, whom he just seemed to neglect and abuse.

"I'm not sure 'got along with' is right. He had a healthy fear of him, and Ben didn't see what was so wrong with farming his whole life either. He just didn't really have no want to go nowhere, and so he learned to keep his head down and his mouth shut. Somewhere along the line he started believing his dad was right about some things, and he pulled away from the rest of us. Worst thing I could'a hoped for."

Ben was the one that Lillie prayed over the most. He was the oldest boy, and Clay's favorite. Clay spared him the torture he handed out to the others because he saw himself in Ben. Ben was bright, and saw early on that his opportunity for safety was in emulating his father. It was a brilliant form of protection in the beginning, but he played the role for so long that eventually it took hold and infiltrated his being. It wasn't much time before Ben's marrow began to rot away and he became a younger version of Clay. Just as strong, just as cutting, just as mean. This had pained Lillie as much as it pained her to watch her other children's suffering, most times even more. The difference was that she had failed to save him from himself, and that was a much harder pill to swallow. Of all her mistakes, her biggest one so far had been in failing Ben.

"Ben moved out some time ago. Got himself a wife and a job on a dairy farm across town. Sorry, I might'a told you that already. He'd see Clay every now and then in town and he'd come over about once a week with his wife for supper, but we never was too close. He was always real good to the younger kids when he came round. I think he hates me, though, almost as much as Clay does some days, although for different reasons. Can't say I blame him. I didn't do much to keep him safe from his daddy when he was younger, so he figured it out on his own. Just wish he'd found some other way..."

"Hmm. That's sad, Lillie. Really sad. Maybe having a wife of his own will calm him, you never know." Lillie stifled a smirk; she knew better than to believe a woman's love could change some men's hearts. "So how'd Joe get around Clay, then?"

"Well, after Joe knocked Clay out when he hit me with that frying pan, things got real bad between them. A few days later Joe got a walloping like he'd never seen before for something as small as not using the right tilling hoe in the field. They both knew it wasn't about the hoe. I think that's when Joe decided he'd do the same when his time came. He had three more years, but I think nothing would'a stopped Joe from leaving the same way Connie had."

"Well, Joe must have known Clay would be expecting it with him since they didn't get along. How did Joe get his birth certificate without telling Clay?"

"I got one for him." Lillie said matter of fact, like she'd forgotten what had happened the first time, when she'd helped Connie.

"You did? Wasn't that dangerous, Lillie? Weren't you worried Clay would kill you?" Elizabeth feared another painful story, and she held her breath.

"Ya, I guess so," Lillie replied. "It sure could'a been real bad."

Chapter Twenty-Eight

Lillie
Franklin, Kentucky
August 1952

Joe didn't sleep well the night he returned home from Bowling Green. He'd been quiet and pensive at supper and had picked at the fried chicken and green beans that were served, leftovers from the large mid-day dinner meal. Clay had noticed right away that Joe wasn't touching his food because Joe always ate up his mama's fried chicken as fast as it hit his plate, cold or not.

"What's up, boy? You sick or somethin'?" Clay's lips were coated with the grease from the chicken skin and he made no attempt to wipe it away as he ate.

"No, sir, just had a sandwich in town after the bus done drop me off." Joe tried not to look his father in the eye for fear of him figuring it out. "Not sick, sir, just tired." Joe was sick to his stomach, but for a whole other reason than a virus. He didn't know how to ask Lillie for help. He didn't know how to get the image of her lying on the floor after she'd helped Connie with a pool of blood under her head out of his mind.

"You sign up?" Clay spat through a snarled upper lip. Joe instantly felt himself start to sweat. He knew. Joe thought his father knew and he racked his brain trying to figure out what to say. Just as Joe started to form a lie in his mouth, Clay said, "Damn bullshit that government making you boys do that crap."

Joe replied with a quick, "Yes, Sir. I done registered." He hadn't lied yet. He had registered as he was supposed to.

Clay continued complaining as though he hadn't heard Joe. "They never do nothing for us, but they expect us to do for them if they tell us to. Goddamn slave owners, they is. A man works hard, real hard, and his thanks is that the boss man asks for more." Joe wasn't sure if Clay was still talking about his Selective Service Registration, or if he was now referring to the landowner, Mr. Adams. Clay tended to mush all his complaints together into one or two sentences, leaving most people unsure of what it was he was exactly complaining about.

"Clay," Lillie said, trying to change the topic before he got too worked up, "we are off to town tomorrow. I'm about plum outta sugar, and my flour is getting real low." Lillie had hidden her supplies earlier that afternoon, anticipating that she'd need an excuse to go into the square. She actually had enough flour for at least two more weeks.

"Already? Damn, woman. Seems like you just gone last week, and now you asking to go again?" Clay would say yes. The one thing he couldn't stand was to not have his meals as he liked them, and so it wasn't often that he'd deny Lillie access to getting what she needed to keep him properly fed at dinner, but he never made it easy. "I ain't got no money for you. What you got to trade?"

"I done some sewing for Mrs. Roark." It was a lie, and Joe knew it. Lillie hadn't been able to sew for over a year, with her hands hurting so bad and her fingertips so numb. He didn't know what his mama was up to, but he didn't like it. Good thing for Lillie, though, that Clay never paid her any mind, because he hadn't noticed the lack of cloth work over the last year. "And Billy—I mean—Mr. Roark, always let me put it on store credit if I need to."

"Don't you be owing nobody nothing. You make a trade, 'ya hear?" Clay glared at Lillie and pointed his fork at her as he spoke, making his point that Lillie wasn't to accept handouts from anyone incredibly clear. If Lillie had listened to Clay's rule about it, they'd have starved to death some time ago. "How you think you getting there?"

"Can Joe take me? In the Hudson?" Lillie's voice cracked a bit, and she quickly cleared her throat, trying to cover up her nervousness. Clay had inherited the car after his brother died some ten years before, and although it wasn't a smooth ride it was a reliable one; and even Clay couldn't turn down that kind of charity.

Clay looked from Lillie to Joe, who pushed his green beans from one side of his plate to the other and avoided Clay's eyes. Joe was trying to figure out what Lillie was doing and why she was dragging him into it. "Why you need Joe? He done got work to do."

Lillie righted herself in her chair and used the most confident voice she could muster. "Clay, I can't rightly carry those bags no more. I got to have some help, and Ada's got to be watching the little ones. I can't rightly take them with me." Every time she needed to go to town,

Lillie got the Spanish Inquisition from Clay. He didn't make it easy to get the staples she needed, even though most of it was to please him. "I'll be right quick about it. We'll go in the morning, and I'll be back in time to make your dinner. Joe won't be gone but an hour or so."

Clay eyed them suspiciously as he chewed a mouthful of cornbread. "Alright then, but don't you be draggin' yer heels. We got acres of plants to finish topping in the field, and we got to start pulling them suckers. Some of thems is big this year. I ain't got no help from Ben no more, he done taken up with them dairy folks over at Lynn Johnson. Says they pay him better. I just got Joe and Nola now, and I needs 'em to work!"

Joe cringed at the tobacco farming talk. He didn't think he could stand another minute in those lush green fields, doing mindless work under a hot and unrelenting sun. The more Clay talked about it, the more Joe knew he was doing the right thing. Joe's main reason for leaving may have been to get away from Clay, but he also wanted to leave the days of field work behind him.

"Pa, why you take all them flowers off'a the plants again? They're so pretty." Ada rarely spoke up at supper, and she suddenly had the attention of the whole table.

"What, you stupid?" Clay was quick to attack. "Pretty don't grow you a good plant, Ada. Pretty don't get you nothing but trouble, girl. Those blooms just suck all the water and life outta the rest of the plant and make the leaves smaller. You take off the bloom and you got yerself a mighty big leaf growing instead. You pick off those suckers too and you get you even bigger leaves." Clay used the word suckers to refer to the immature leaves that, like the flowers, also wicked away nutrients from the leaves. "You got to pick off the things that suck a thing dry before it's too late."

Clay wasn't talking about tobacco anymore, and his family knew it. Ada shrunk under his harsh words and chided herself silently for having said anything at all. Joe glared at his father, and Lillie looked at the food on her plate and lost her appetite. Day by day Clay confirmed how he felt about them, and it gave Lillie just the amount of determination she needed to go through with her plan.

Joe didn't sleep well that night at all. He tossed and turned, knowing his mother was up to something and not sure if it was something that would turn out good for him, or make life worse for all of them. He wondered if she just wanted to get him away from the farm to talk some sense into him. He had a weakness for his mama, and her tears would be hard to resist. He lay there in the dark room, which was lit only by the light of the ominous-looking moon, and wondered what tomorrow would bring. He wondered if his resolve would hold.

The next day Lillie gathered herself for her trip with a little trepidation. She knew in her heart she was doing the right thing, but she was having a hard time telling her shaking nerves that. She and Joe were both silent through her breakfast of eggs and biscuits. She'd look at him and he'd look away. He'd look at her and she'd find something else to gaze at. She didn't want to start crying, and she feared if she met his eyes she would do just that. She left the cleaning up to Ada, as Clay and Nola had left for the fields, and she and Joe climbed up into their twelve-year-old car.

The car started with a jerk and took off down the gravelly dirt road with a moan. Lillie's body ached with every bump it made, but she said nothing about it. A few yards down the road Joe said, "Mama, I..."

"No, Joe, not here. Let's just get out on the main road first." Paranoia had set in, and Lillie feared Clay could somehow hear them as they passed through the tobacco fields. She knew that it wasn't so, but she just wanted to wait until they hit the highway that would take them into town. She looked quietly out the window at the gently rolling hills of her homeland and took in all the various shades of green that graced the horizon. She smiled at the cows in the pasture that were grazing mindlessly and occasionally throwing out a moo for good measure. She thanked them silently for their precious milk that provided such wholesome food for her family like butter and cream.

Her smile widened as she passed pond after pond and saw all the young boys with their homemade fishing poles trying to catch elusive, feisty catfish and grass carp. Boy after boy, pond after pond, they'd stand there the same, shirtless and in overalls, barefoot and eager. They'd stand there sure they were gonna catch them something big to take home to make their daddy proud. Their mamas knew that this late in the day getting a bite was near impossible, but it kept the youngsters out from under their feet so they let them go anyhow.

Finally Lillie broke the silence and said, "You remember that day you and Ben was out fishing?"

Joe laughed. "Which day, Mama, there were quite a few, if I do recall."

Lillie laughed too. "Right. Well I'm talkin' about the time you and your brother snuck out real early in the morning and didn't come home until after supper. You remember? You must'a been seven or eight, and Ben was like nine or ten? Y'all spent half the day collecting them ugly catalpa worms in one of my canning jars and the other half of the day fishing every pond you could walk to. You remember, Joe?"

"Oh, yeah, Mama, I remember. It was May, and we was supposed to be helping daddy set the tobacco. But I told Ben that daddy would be much happier if we caught him some fish. I told him daddy couldn't possibly get mad at us if we fed him up real good!"

"And you could'a fed the whole county much as you two caught that day. It was like God gave you his own fishing pole and left you both to it. I must'a counted over twenty or so decent sized ones." Lillie laughed again and remembered her sons dragging a wheelbarrow full of fish up to her porch, both of them covered in dirt and sweat, grinning from ear to ear. "Ya, we had quite the fish fry the next day with all the neighbors, didn't we? Emma made her famous hush puppies, I made some bread, I think, and the Burneses brought coleslaw and baked beans. Even the Adams folk couldn't help themselves. I remember Mrs. Adams and Mrs. Bloodsworth wandering over with pies in their hands, their sorry husbands straggling behind them embarrassed to be eating with the sharecroppers, but letting their noses and the smell of delicious fried fish lead them over anyhow!" Lillie laughed a belly laugh and dabbed at her eyes as tiny tears of happiness formed in the corners. "Oh my, what a time that was, Joe!"

"Yup! It was a pretty good time, Mama." Joe said, laughing with Lillie. His smile started to fade, though, as they reached the Morgantown Road that would take them into town. "But I remember too how I couldn't sit down to eat, or Ben neither. Usually daddy spares Ben for some reason or another, but not that day. We both got the belt for leaving him alone in the field. Didn't matter that we fed us all for a week, he just couldn't stand the fact that his boys would disobey him like that."

"I know it. I remember the welts and the bruising days later. I remember that too, Joe." Lillie's smile fell to pieces as she realized even her favorite memories of her children were somehow tainted by Clay. "That's why I'm gonna help you. I can't give you your original, Joe. Your daddy done hide that from me along with everything else. But I'm gonna help you get a copy."

Joe nearly veered off the road. Had she said help him? So that's what this ride to town was all about. His mama couldn't stop Clay's abuse, but she could help him get himself out. "Mama, how did you know?"

"I just know, Joe. I don't blame you. Even Ben, who is so much like him, had to get away. He just didn't try to go as far. I know what you want to do and I know what you need to do it. Same thing Connie needed, only this time I got a plan."

Chapter Twenty-Nine

Lillie
Thursday, August 13, 1953
8:00 p.m.

Lillie asked Elizabeth to help her sit upright in bed, a position she hadn't been able to tolerate for some time. She was drained and sleepy, and needed a way to keep herself awake.

"So I took my boy Joe into town that day, and we went and bought us the stuff I had told Clay I needed. We used some of the cash Connie had mailed me. That only took a few minutes, with Joe's help. Then we left the car parked along the side of the store and crossed the street to the courthouse."

"Lillie, weren't you scared of what Clay might do when he found out?" Elizabeth was nervous, which she found slightly funny since she rationally knew she was listening to events that had already passed.

"'Course I was. But I figured it would only be bad *if* Clay found out, and I didn't have no reason to think he would. I had a plan, you see. I told my Joe that no matter what he heard me say in that there courthouse to the clerk, he just needed to play along. He was so nervous. All's the boy could do was agree and nod his head at me. He let me take the lead, and followed real close a few steps behind."

Lillie had approached the clerk with her biggest smile and her arms open wide as if to welcome her to her home. "Mrs. Hodges! How are you? It's been too long!" Joe was mortified, and confused as to how on earth his mother knew this uptight clerk in her well-polished high heels and meticulous tailored dress. His mama was going to make a fool of herself, and he felt his cheeks redden in anticipation.

The clerk looked up and squinted at Lillie. For a moment Lillie second-guessed herself. Maybe Cynthia Hodges wouldn't remember her after all—but then Mrs. Hodges felt carefully around the edge of her desk and located her glasses. She placed them on her face as she slowly stood up behind her small desk. Instead of ridiculing Lillie like Joe had thought she would, she broke into an equally large grin.

"Lilly Mae Garrett! My word, is that you?" She came around the desk, and Joe watched as the clerk scooped Lillie's face into her hands and stared for a moment. "Ah, of course it's you. I'd know those eyes anywhere, darling." She let Lillie's face go and grabbed her hands, giving them a squeeze, and Joe found himself wondering how they knew each other. County clerks did not spend much time in the same places as sharecroppers' wives. "Oh, goodness, pardon me, Lillie, it's Woodard then, isn't it?"

Lillie laughed and replied, "Oh, just for the last twenty-three years or so, but who's keeping track nowadays anyhow? Feels like it's been that long since I seen you! How are you, Mrs. Hodges?"

"Ah, Lillie, call me Cynthia. I'm getting too old for formalities, and they don't mean much anymore anyhow! I'm well child, well. Just getting more ripe by the day is all. I think the last I saw you was when the last of your family moved away and your mama and daddy were in town. Yes, yes, it was at that picnic in town, and I think you were pregnant with your third baby. I do remember a little girl and a little boy running round and round and your mama hollering at them to slow down." The clerk's face was soft with time and defined with fine lines that she carried regally. She always had been a classy lady.

"Well, that was some time ago, I guess, 'cause this here's my third baby. This is Joseph." Lillie motioned to Joe to come forward a bit and shake Cynthia's hand; and while he hesitated for a second, he knew the more polite he was, the quicker he would get what he needed. He hoped she didn't recognize him from yesterday. He wondered if he should mention his being there just a day before and then decided against it. His mama said to play along. Then again, the clerk was the one who told him to bring his mama back with him. He opened his mouth to say something about his attempt yesterday and then stopped before he ever let go of a sound. Her glasses. She couldn't see without her glasses, and she had taken them off when he'd approached her desk yesterday. She had no idea it had been him.

Joe settled on saying, "Nice to meet you, Mrs. Hodges."

"You too, Joseph. You know, I've known your mama since she was little? Well, a young lady, anyhow. She used to work over yonder with Mary Finn in her sewing shop. Your mama is one of the finest seamstresses I ever did see. Everybody wanted their dresses done by

Lillie Mae Garrett!" Joe looked at his mother with surprise. He knew she had sewn some in her day and had been working a job when she'd met his daddy, but he had no idea that she was as good as Mrs. Hodges alluded to.

"Well, everyone except Mrs. Prink, perhaps!" Lillie laughed, remembering old Mrs. Prink and her particular tastes. Mary Finn had called her the sorriest soul she'd ever known and had told Lillie that people like her needed some extra loving because they just never could love themselves.

"Ha! That old crazy bat? She died some years back. Still as rich as a movie star and all alone with no one to leave her inheritance to. Worked out well for the city, which collected all her assets. Only time she ever gave back to the town other than when she handed out rude comments!" Cynthia laughed a good-natured laugh as she remembered the woman who had given Lillie and every other person in the town a difficult time.

Lillie's eyebrows popped up in surprise. "And all this time I thought it was just me!"

"Nah, sad one she was. Anyhow, you sure was missed when you quit working with Mary. I was happy for you that you got married and all, but sad to hear you gave up your craft so fast and moved out of town. And then when Mary passed it was a sadder day still."

Lillie gave Cynthia a small smile. The memory of Mary's death was still fresh and raw, even twenty years later. She'd felt like she'd lost her own mother in some ways when Mary died. The cancer had ravaged her body so fast that it shocked everyone in town. When James Finn had to close up the shop because his girls just weren't interested in carrying on their mama's dream, it had felt like Mary had died all over again, like a little bit of Lillie had died too. A few years later, James Finn had made the decision to leave the farm in the capable hands of Josie and her husband Matthew. He had moved north to Ohio, looking for work in the big city of Cincinnati and looking for a new start in life in a home that wasn't haunted with memories of his Mary. Josie and Matthew had quickly found farm life to be more than they could handle, and living in Mary's house had turned out to be more than Josie's heart could take. They'd made the move to Cincinnati like Josie's daddy James had, and only came back once a year to visit Lillie and some other relatives who had stayed. Lillie had cried like a baby the day she'd had to say goodbye. "Yup," Lillie said, "those was some hard times."

"And the rest of the Finns left a few years later, right? Well, anyway, we haven't had a decent seamstress since!" Cynthia caught the sadness in Lillie's voice and said, "So, old friend. What can I do for you?"

Lillie cleared her throat and tried to put on her courage like an old coat. It was there somewhere, she just had to make it fit over her shoulders again. "Well, it's actually kind of a funny story…" Lillie looked at Joe as if to say, *Here we go, fingers crossed.* "My husband Clay asked me to put some things away for safekeeping some years ago. Like our marriage certificate and the kids' birth certificates and such. He told me to hide it real good so no one else might find it." Lillie paused and took a deep breath. She licked her lips and told herself that lying for the sake of her children was okay. "Well, the thing is, I did!"

"You hid them real good?" Cynthia was skeptical, but she played along. If Lillie was up to something, she supposed it was for a good reason.

"Oh, so good in fact," Lillie laughed nervously, "that I can't find them! I had dug a hole in the yard some years ago and had them all inside an old tin, 'ya know? And anyhow, I figured I'd always remember where I'd buried them, but fact is memory doesn't hold all that well as you get older…"

"You got that right, child!" Cynthia laughed. "I can't remember where I put my glasses most days, but then I can't see to find them. I think my husband thinks it's a sport now, and he just laughs while he watches me pat every surface of the house looking for them!"

This made Joe laugh too, and the three of them stood there for a moment letting Lillie's story settle. Finally, Lillie said, "So, many, many holes in my yard later, and I just can't find the darn thing! I'd ask Clay to help me, but he'd be right mad if he knew I'd lost them."

Cynthia's face became serious. She remembered Clay too, from when Lillie and he were first married. He'd been quiet then, and sort of shy, but always polite. Then she remembered him too from the time he showed up in the courthouse to sue the Greyhound bus company over Ada's accident. He hadn't been quiet or shy or polite. He'd been rude, and abrasive, and he'd scared her as she'd tried to explain the court procedure to him. She knew exactly what Lillie meant when she said that Clay would be right mad.

"Goodness, Lillie. That's quite a pickle," Cynthia said. Lillie stood before her old client with pleading eyes, trying to maintain her composure. "Tell you what, if you got an hour I can make you some copies."

"Right here?" Lillie wasn't sure how that was possible.

"Sure. Since this is the courthouse for the whole county, the state gave us a machine called a xerographic copier. We just call it the old Model A. She's slow, but she gets the job done!" Cynthia loved this new technology, and she always felt important when she talked about the capabilities of their small county courthouse. It didn't hurt that the mayor was kin to the governor either, and had cut him a deal on the machine.

"Thank you, Cynthia." Lillie held back tears. "That would be wonderful."

Cynthia Hodges took Lillie's hand and said, "I may not be able to sew a button on a shirt like you can, but I make a darn good copy. And I don't see no reason to tell Clay. None at all..."

A tear slide silently down Lillie's face as she gave her old friend's hand a tiny squeeze.

"So, Lillie," Elizabeth asked quizzically. "How did you get around Clay finding out it was you who got him a copy?"

"Well, it wasn't hard as I thought. Clay's not too up on documents and such and what's required to get something printed. When he started blaming me again, Joe just told him that he went to the courthouse himself and got him a copy made. Clay was so mad by then anyhow that I'm not sure it much mattered to him how Joe had done it, he only cared that he *had* done it." Lillie was tired from telling Elizabeth her story. Her eyes felt heavy, and she found herself sliding down in the bed.

"How did Clay find out? I mean, I'm sure Joe was smarter than to tell him over dinner, given what happened with Connie." Elizabeth at least hoped Joe had been smarter.

"Well, I told Joe he needed to get his things all ready, just like I had told Connie. 'Be ready,' I'd said, 'and then you could be thinking about telling your daddy.' Turns out Joe had other ideas. I guess Mr. Adams owed Joe some money for some odds-and-ends type jobs that Joe done for him. He only paid Joe, though, when Joe asked for the money."

"Mr. Adams sounds mighty penny pinching," Elizabeth said.

"You have no idea." Lillie closed her eyes and was glad her tale was almost finished. She needed to rest. "Anyhow, Joe went right up to Mr.

Adams with his daddy standing not but twenty feet away and told him he done joined the army and was leaving and could he please have his money he owed him."

"He did not! Why that's a right smart place as any to do it, I guess." Elizabeth was so enthralled in the story she didn't notice how tired Lillie was getting; how droopy her eyelids were; or how relaxed her body had become.

"Well, it certainly saved him a walloping, that's for sure. Clay couldn't say a damn thing about it. Joe said Clay just stood there getting all mad in the face and gripping his collecting bucket full of tobacco blooms and spitting into the dirt every few seconds. He knew he couldn't make a scene in front of the Adams folk or the other share-croppers."

"But what about when Joe got home? Didn't he let him have it then?" Elizabeth was nervous to hear what Clay had done to Joe, because surely he'd done something.

"Nah, Clay had a different plan in mind." Lillie wiggled down further in the bed, and for the first time she felt the open sore on her backside as she did so. She winced a bit, but decided she could tolerate it for a little while instead of stopping her story and asking Elizabeth to turn her. "Joe came right home after that and finished packing his bags. He knew he'd have to be ready to leave real quick if Clay started anything. He was real quiet, and we was all nervous as heck."

"So what did Clay do to him, Lillie?" Elizabeth asked impatiently.

"Well, nothing." Lillie said matter-of-factly, as if that were a normal occurrence for Clay to behave as such.

"Nothing? He really did nothing?" Elizabeth sighed. "I guess I don't understand."

"Oh, child, you will in just a second. I ain't done just yet." Lillie smiled at Elizabeth, her new friend, who seemed to care an awful lot about a family she'd never really met. "Well now, Clay didn't come in from the field till just when we was finishing up supper, which he hardly ever did, so we all figured we was all in for it real bad. But he came in and didn't say nothing to nobody. He just sat down in front of his plate of cold food and ate real quiet-like. None of us moved a muscle or batted a lash, even though we was done by then. We just sat there eyeing each other, trying to figure out what Clay was up to."

"Oh, Lillie, that must've been nerve-racking. I'm nervous just waiting to hear what happened." Elizabeth was leaning forward so far on her chair that Lillie feared she might fall onto her.

"It was frightful, to tell the truth. To see Clay so calm, it was almost scarier than seeing him all red and mad. Anyway, he took his last bite of whatever I'd made that night and he set his eyes on my Joe and all's I could think was, *Oh my, here it comes.*"

"What did he say, Lillie?" Elizabeth wrung her hands together, waiting to hear what fate Joe would meet.

"Well, he asked him when he was leaving, and Joe told him he needed to be in Bowling Green in the morning. And then Clay said the damnedest thing. He said to Joe, 'I guess I ought to just take you up there then. Be ready to go by six o'clock tomorrow morning and I'll give you a ride.' Just like that. That's all he said about it." Lillie remembered being absolutely astonished. Clay had never done anything like that for any of his kids; in fact, he often did the opposite and made it downright difficult for them to get something they needed.

"Wow." Elizabeth sat there silently for a moment taking it in, but inside she was still pensive. She sensed there was more to the story, and she was right. "So he just offered to take him up there, huh? Just like that? Without giving him any trouble?"

"Well, for a long time I thought so. They took off the next morning after we all said our goodbyes to him, and Clay didn't come home until it was time for dinner around noon. I figured he got him up there and then went straight to the field, which he did, but I had no idea what had happened on the ride until Joe wrote me some months later and told me what his daddy had done."

"I knew it sounded too good," Elizabeth said. She looked at Lillie's face and realized how tired she was getting. "Oh goodness, Lillie, I'm so sorry, do you need to rest? I've completely forgotten myself. We can finish later, if you want."

"Nah, nah, I'm almost done here, Elizabeth, and then I'll rest after that." Lillie shifted a little and felt relief on her sore. She could go on for a few more minutes, but with every second her eyelids felt more and more like sandbags, and she struggled to keep them open. She felt slightly panicked by how tired she felt, and wasn't all too confident about being able to do what she needed to do with Elizabeth.

"Alright then, Lillie, but if you need to rest you just say so."

"Right then, so Joe told me his daddy drove him out to the Bowling Green Road and headed north like he needed him to. The Adams farm is just west of Salmons, 'ya know. Kind'a one half dozen or the other whether Salmons or Franklin is closer to shop in, I guess. We is off Vantrease Road and that runs right into Morgantown Road if you just go out a bit. We just take that right on in until it hits North Main Street in town. Every now and again I could only catch a ride into Salmons instead of Franklin for shopping." Lillie stopped for a minute and took a deep breathe.

Her mind was veering off course and she knew it, but somehow she couldn't pull herself back to whatever she had been talking about. So she continued to babble a bit and said, "That was always weird for me. Ain't nobody know me there in Salmons like they do in Franklin. Ain't nobody remember me from when I was little and had it good. That part was kind'a nice 'cause they didn't look at me like they felt sorry for what I'd become. They figured I was always just a farmer's wife and didn't know no better. They all know Clay, though, in Salmons, and sometimes they act like they as scared of me as they are of him until I treat them real nice and they see. They see I'm not like my husband."

As Lillie digressed, Elizabeth just listened. She was getting a picture now of where Lillie lived. She had only been out that way a few times when she herself had traveled up to Bowling Green, and she remembered thinking how far out all those farming families really were. How long it must take them to get into town to do anything at all. She understood now how Lillie hadn't really had a choice about getting medical help without Clay's consent. Lillie didn't drive, and it was way too far to walk for a healthy person, much less someone in Lillie's condition. Plus, Elizabeth saw how she didn't have the money anyhow, even probably with what Connie sent home.

"So, Lillie, what happened on the way up there?" Elizabeth tried to steer Lillie back on course as Lillie's mind began to wander.

"What's that? Oh, right, well Clay was stone cold quiet as he drove, and he took him up the road a few miles. Then, just before they hit the street that turns off so you go to Woodbum, Clay pulled the car over to the side of the road. Joe said he wasn't quite sure what to make of it, so he just sat there as his daddy got out of the car. He watched Clay open the trunk and take out his bag and he watched Clay put it down in the dirt alongside the weeds and grass. Joe said he figured out real fast what was happening, and he opened his own car door to get out and just stood there looking at Clay while he waited to hear what he was gonna say."

"And what did he say, Lillie?" Elizabeth's eyes were big and her eyebrows were knitted together. She couldn't believe what she was hearing.

"He said something like 'Boy, if you think you's is old enough to be a man and join the army, then you can find your own way there.' And then he left my Joe standing there as he turned the car around and came back to the farm. He parked somewhere else so I wouldn't know what he'd done, and he went to the fields to work his day."

"He just left him there? In August? With nothing?" Elizabeth was flabbergasted. "Did he at least wish him luck, or say goodbye? I mean, he knew Joe would probably go to war, right? He had to have known it might be the last time he'd see him. And he didn't say anything?"

"Nah. He just did the same thing to Joe that he done to me when he brought me here. Guess he didn't see no reason for saying goodbye." Lillie knew now just what Joe had to have felt that day because she had felt the same as he'd driven off the month before without so much as a word to her. Disposable. Her family was disposable to Clay, and if they weren't doing something to suit his needs anymore then he needed to be rid of them. He was picking off the suckers.

"I just can't believe a father could do that to his son. Unbelievable, Lillie." Elizabeth's frame sank into her chair. She felt deflated, and heartbroken for Joe.

"Yes, it is, I guess, 'cept you don't know Clay." Elizabeth nodded, but she felt like she was starting to know him. Then Lillie added softly as she closed her eyes to sleep, "It was the last hit Clay could give Joe and get away with."

Chapter Thirty

Cate
Los Angeles, California
Summer 1946

Life got terribly interesting after our meeting with Dr. Monarch, and led us down pathways I never expected. The initial relief I had felt in the doctor's office about just finally having an answer was quick to fade, and the reality of our situation hit home hard. For so long I had imagined what a child of mine would look like. Would she have my hair and skin tone, or would he favor his father? Would he like baseball like his dad, or would she be interested in dancing like her mom? What would our little ones be like? Laying those thoughts and images to rest took more energy than I'd expected, and I found myself in quite a state of grief.

Tony, however, wasted absolutely no time in searching out information about local adoption avenues. He hadn't spent all the years I had imagining what pregnancy and childbirth would be like. He hadn't tried to picture what traits he might pass down to his son or daughter. He hadn't really let his mind go to those places, so, for him, it was easier to end that chapter and move onto the next. Not easy, just easier. Three months later, while he was gathering all the necessary documents and information, I was still grieving over the loss of what I felt was my right as a woman to bear children. It was especially difficult, I think, because I came from such a long line of fertile women, and none of my sisters had had any difficulty in that department. In fact, their only problem was that perhaps they had too many children. I didn't cry much outwardly, but inside I felt as though something had died.

Tony did his best to cheer me up and try to keep me moving forward. He took me out for dinners, twirled me around at any dance party he could find, and introduced me to a few new cocktails. I just kept moving right along with him to wherever it was that he took me because I knew that if I stopped I might fall apart, and I really didn't want to do that. I brooded in silence most days, trying to reassure Tony how excited I was to be pursuing the adoption option; but, to be honest, I couldn't have cared less at that point.

Things turned around, though, eventually, as they typically do after some time passes. My sadness lifted, and I began to enjoy the outings more and more. I tried to replace the images of my own children with those of another child, one not born to me, but mine all the same. I purposely tried to imagine what that child would look like, and after a while the image didn't disturb me so much. In fact, I found it rather exciting. One night over dinner at home something clicked.

"Mmmm. Delicious, Cate. Best pork chops I've ever had." Tony wiped his mouth with a napkin and stretched back in his chair, tugging at his belt line uncomfortably. "My only complaint is that I ate too much!"

"Hmmm. Now that isn't my fault, I'm not the one who put the second chop on your plate. I believe that was you, darling." I smiled at him from across the table.

"You look well, Cate. I mean better than you have in a while. Are you feeling better?" Tony had been ever so patient with me, and even though he didn't fully understand my grief, he gave me the space I needed to just sit with it. He never rushed me through anything I was feeling, and it was one of the many reasons I loved him.

"I do feel better. Less sad, I think." I paused, and leaned back in my chair thoughtfully. "You know, it just struck me today that I've spent all this time grieving over the loss of children I never had, and really I ought to turn that around."

"Turn it around?" Tony looked at me quizzically.

"Yes, turn it around. Instead of focusing on what I can never have, I need to focus on the new things yet to come—what I will have in my life instead." I felt calm, and things were finally making sense in my mind.

"Don't cry over spilled milk, you mean?" Tony grinned. "Sorry, my mother's favorite saying. Only she'd say: *No llores sobre la leche derramada.*

I chuckled, but added, "Well sort of, I guess, except that saying always implies that you are crying over nothing. Losing my chance to have our own children isn't nothing…" I knew he didn't mean it that way, but I just wanted to be clear.

"I didn't mean…" He looked stricken, like he'd slapped me or something.

"No, I know. I know what you meant. I just meant more that I shouldn't cry over what I've lost anymore because I need to focus on what I've gained. I mean, we have a real chance to help a child here, and then to become parents at the same time. Now that, that's really something to be excited about."

Tony stood up then and came to my side of the table. He pulled me up into his arms and said, "Now there's the Cate I know. You're amazing."

It was fall by then, and we'd researched which adoption agencies were the best to work with and what exactly the process entailed. We knew we'd need to save a bit more money before submitting an application, in order to afford the fees, so both Tony and I threw ourselves into our work in order to put a little more away each month. I didn't love my job as a switchboard operator like I had loved my work at the plant, but it paid decently, and again, the hours were such that I was free by the afternoon.

The owner of the machine shop where Tony worked, Mr. Diaz, was a longtime friend of Tony's family, but he was aging rapidly and his failing eyesight was making it hard to keep up with the demands of the office work. As Tony said, Mr. Diaz was getting so old that he couldn't stay awake past noon anymore and spent most of his time napping on his desktop. Tony had mentioned to him that I'd gotten my certificate in bookkeeping and might be able to help him out. I think poor Mr. Diaz was tired enough that he conceded and accepted my help. So most of the evenings in the fall of 1946 were spent sorting through years of poorly managed paperwork and records. I had my work cut out for me, but the challenge of it was just what I needed at the time.

By December Tony and I felt like we'd saved enough money that we could submit our application to the adoption agency. We decided to start with the Los Angeles County Department of Adoptions, as they seemed to have the greatest resources and ability to interact with other private agencies. I think the day we decided to go was almost as exciting as our wedding day, and in some ways was even more so. We were beginning our journey towards parenthood and were ready to embrace it with open arms. We were even open to what type of child we might get. Girl or boy, young, slightly older, or infant, it didn't really matter to us. We were a little surprised, and disappointed, to find that we needed an appointment to even submit our paperwork in the first place, but we were lucky and were able to schedule one for the next week.

That weekend waiting was as nerve-racking as it got. Would whoever it was that interviewed us like us? Would they think we were fit parents? We had steady jobs for sure and a roof over our heads, but we weren't living the high life. Would what we had to offer be enough? As it turned out, Tony and I worried about all the wrong things, and the woman who interviewed us was less interested in who we were and more interested in what we were.

We arrived early, dressed to the nines, and sat nervously, waiting for Mrs. Brown to finish what sounded like a very upsetting phone call. She sounded frazzled and angry, and Tony and I couldn't help but look at each other and think the same thing.

"I hope she has a chance to relax before she sees us. She sounds rather riled up." I was so nervous my crossed legs were bouncing up and down faster than a rubber bouncy ball in a box.

Tony put his hand on my knee to steady me and said, "It'll be lovely, Cate. Really. We have a lot to offer." His weak smile told me just how nervous he was himself, though I thought it sweet he tried to comfort me.

A few agency workers passed by, and both did a second take as they went. Then one gal walked past, looked at us and I could have sworn she said, "Fat chance," or something to that effect. I looked at Tony, but he hadn't even noticed. He was too busy studying the pattern that the marble floor tiles made. Fat chance? What did that mean? Surely I was imagining it. We were dressed just as nicely—if not more so—than any of the gals who'd walked past, and yet I felt like I was suddenly the bottom of the barrel. I found it so odd that I almost said something to Tony about it, but just as I opened my mouth, Mrs. Brown opened her door. She looked exhausted and weary, and as we stood to introduce ourselves I could feel her taking us in with her eyes and the response I saw on her face was not what I expected. She looked horrified.

Her disheveled appearance had nothing on the state of her tiny office. Papers and file folders covered every surface except for a one-foot square bit of her desk on which I imagined she scribbled her notes every now and again. I immediately began to question whether we'd come to the right agency. How on earth did a child's file, much less a child, ever make it out of that kind of mess? She motioned towards two leather backed chairs opposite her desk and nervously perched on the edge of her own chair.

"So," she started rather slowly. "What exactly is it that I can do for you?" I found her wording odd, as if she wasn't sure exactly what her agency was about. And she hadn't bothered to introduce herself.

Tony and I looked at each other, and I nodded at him to go ahead and speak for us. "Well, I'm Tony Otera, and this is my wife, Cate." I smiled at her, and she nodded briefly and then turned her attention back to Tony. Tony lifted up the packet of papers we'd brought with us and said, "And we've come to submit our paperwork. To start the process. Towards, uh, adoption." He smiled then, widely, the word adoption playing on his lips.

She stared at him and said nothing at first, and then slowly and carefully delivered her message. "I see, Mr. Otera, was it? Well, I'm afraid perhaps that we have a misunderstanding."

Tony's smile faded quickly as he looked from Mrs. Brown to me. I shrugged an 'I don't know what she means' at him and said, "I'm sorry, is this not how it's done? We came by last week and your secretary said we'd need an appointment. Is there some other process? We're very new at this."

"No, no. This is indeed the process, but you'll have to forgive my secretary." She paused, trying how best to deliver the blow. "I'm afraid, she may not be aware of certain... well, rules that we have in place."

"Rules?" Tony was sensing her seriousness, and I could feel his tension even a few feet away. "What sort of rules?"

"Mr. Otera, may I ask you, what is your background?" Her face took on a tired, placid appearance, and it made me even more anxious. Somewhere along the line, she had stopped caring about her job.

"My background. Well, yes. I was born in Los Angeles, attended UCLA where I got my degree in geological engineering, and now I work in a machine shop in Inglewood. I have it all right here in my paperwork." He again lifted the papers as if to say, 'aren't you going to look at them?'

Mrs. Brown pursed her lips and replied, "Perhaps I misstated my question. What is your ethnic background?"

"I'm American." Tony was dead faced and getting angry. He suddenly knew exactly what the rules were about, whereas I hadn't quite caught on yet.

She gave him a small smile and said, "Cute. Yes, American, indeed. But you are of Mexican descent, no?" A small gasp escaped my lips, and I suddenly felt my heart race. She couldn't be serious.

"Yes," said Tony. "My parents were immigrants from Mexico, but I was born here. And I'm not exactly sure what that has to do with anything that we are trying to achieve here."

"Well, sir, given the difficulties we've had in the past with certain ethnic groups, the county has seen fit to place certain restrictions on who may adopt from our institutions."

Tony's face was completely red and he took a few breaths to steady himself. "Are you referring to the Zoot Suit Riots, Mrs. Brown? From three years ago? I assure you, I am not of that kind of crowd, and neither is my family."

In 1943, tensions between the Hispanic community and white American service members in Los Angeles had grown to such proportions that a series of riots had ensued. The servicemen, for various reasons, found major fault with the Mexican population because the Mexicans had decidedly ignored issued rationing requirements and donned extravagant attire. The style the men wore became known as a Zoot suit, and to the servicemen it was a slap in the face, and they considered the making and wearing of the suits extremely unpatriotic. It was wartime, after all, and making such items and wearing them was a mockery of all the sacrifices that everyone else held dear. We had noticed the tension around the city a few times, but honestly Tony had such a way about him that you just didn't see his ethnicity, you just saw him.

"Mr. Otera, no one is accusing you of being part of any kind of crowd, but as you well know, things in this city have been terribly tense between Mexican-Americans and, well, the rest of the city."

"Right. The rest of the city. Funny, I've never really felt that until just now, and I've lived here my whole life." He held her gaze, steady and confident, and I saw her take a second to regroup before she continued.

"Yes, well, unfortunately, the County Adoption Agency sees things differently. Last year a new rule came down clearly stating that we are not to, under any circumstances, allow the submission of paperwork for biracial couples. It's a terribly rough world out there, and to subject a child to that sort of environment from the get-go is just..." She stopped herself and tried to backtrack. "Oh, I don't mean your environment, it's just that folks can be so judgmental."

"Indeed they can, Mrs. Brown. Biracial, you said? I didn't realize

Cate and I were of different races. Yes, judgmental is a correct assessment." We sat in silence then, each waiting for the other to make a move, until I finally decided to pipe up.

"So, that's it then? You can't, or won't help us?" I leaned forward towards her without even realizing it. I was beginning to feel panicked and desperate. She said nothing and just shook her head.

I turned to Tony shaking and stood up to go. "Tony, we'll find somewhere else. We will. And I doubt these people will ever find one of their children a better home than we can provide." I took his hand and pulled him out of the chair, because I was sure that, if we stayed a moment longer, he would leap across the desk and throttle the disheveled Mrs. Brown.

We started to walk away when she threw one last dart our way. "Good luck," she said tiredly. "Almost all of the private agencies out there have the same policies in place. Solidarity, you know."

That's when I felt the nausea kick in, and I barely made it to the curb before I lost what little lunch I'd managed to eat before coming. Tony rubbed my back as I retched, and when I finally was able to stand upright, I looked at him, tears streaming down my face, my mascara in a blackened mess on my cheekbones, and asked softly, "Now what?"

He placed his hand on my face and wiped away at my rouge make-up while gently pulling me into his arms where he whispered, "Now, we have faith."

Chapter Thirty-One

Cate
Los Angeles, California
July 1947

I've always believed in God, but I wouldn't say I'm a fanatic about it. As in, I figure someone created the world and likely watches over us, but we control our own destiny. Tony had a stronger faith, rooted in Catholicism, and a strong belief that we had to trust in God and the universe to provide. He basically believed that God has plans for each of us, so when things don't go right we have to have faith that there's a reason. We had two conflicting views on the way in which life works, and one word hung in the air between us. Faith. What did that even mean?

I would soon find out. Not because I wanted to, per se, but more because I needed to. Without some form of faith, I'm not sure I would have made it through the months—and years, really—that followed our infamous "interview" with Mrs. Brown.

We walked away feeling so deflated and beaten down that day, but soon Tony replaced that with anger, and rightfully so. He refused to take Mrs. Brown's word that all agencies had the same policy, so he dragged me and our packet of paperwork all over Los Angeles and its surrounding cities, searching for someone who would speak to us. We had a few places who were willing to look it over, but in the end we received the same reply. Biracial marriages were not a good choice to place a child. I felt like screaming at them. I'd known hundreds of white men in my lifetime and not one of them could hold a candle to my husband, and yet, no one seemed to care. He was Mexican-American and I was white. Period. End of story.

After a year of trying to get someone to listen to no avail, we had the discussion that both of us hoped we'd never have to have.

"Cate," Tony said quietly. "Are we done?" We were lying together on the couch listening to Ralph Edwards on Truth or Consequences on the radio. I had my head in Tony's lap, and he was sipping a bit of whiskey with his feet up on our coffee table.

I didn't move. I knew what he was asking and I didn't want to be done, but we really had hit the pavement hard and still had come up short. "Do you want to be done?" I asked as my voice cracked a bit.

"No, Cate. I don't. I still have faith that God will provide. I know you struggle with that, but for me, I just know it to be true." He sighed a long, tired sigh, the kind you hear from old men in rocking chairs on front porches just before they fall asleep. Tony was exhausted. "But I feel like this is the end of this road. At least for now."

I sat up and looked at him, and was surprised at how much the past year had aged him. Tiny lines danced around his eyes that hadn't been there before, and the beginnings of salt and pepper flirted with his hairline. We were sacrificing ourselves for the idea of having a family—and then something suddenly struck me. We already were a family.

"Can we be enough? I mean, if it's just you and me for the rest of our lives, is that enough for you?" I held my breath, because as much as I didn't want to stop trying, I also was slowly killing myself with the stress of it all. We needed a break, and soon.

He looked at me deeply and lovingly and whispered, "Always, Cate. You've always been enough."

He filed our package of paperwork away in the back of our closet the next day, but it took many more years before he and I were able to file away the hope we had held onto for so long. Still Tony would sometimes randomly say, "Someday. Someday, Cate, God's going to really show you what faith is." I envied his conviction.

I did have faith in one thing, though, and that was in Tony. His work at the shop was unrivaled; and, if the truth be told, Tony was the shop. He was the one who built the relationships with the customers, innovated and invented to form new products, and marketed the store. So, I wasn't terribly surprised when he came home one day with an idea.

"You know what you and I need, Cate?" He was sheepishly grinning, and I knew he was up to something instantly.

"Oh, Lord. What? What is it you and I need?" I was frying up eggs for dinner, an old standby of mine when my zest for cooking ran away from me. Breakfast for dinner, something I still enjoy.

"An adventure." He grinned widely then, and swatted my backside playfully. "Eh? Right?"

"An adventure? Like an outing, or are you thinking a vacation? We do have that money we had saved for the adoption fees..." We had saved a lot, but neither Tony nor I had dared mentioned using it before now, just in case, I think. Spending it meant we really were done trying.

"No, nothing like that. But... it would involve a bit of our savings." He was trying to stay relaxed, but I could tell he was nervous.

I kissed him gently and felt him soften a little. "Go on..."

"Well, Mr. Diaz is not well, as you know, and his oldest son came into the shop today to tell me that it's likely a matter of months. Prostate cancer, apparently." His face fell a bit when he thought of his kindhearted boss.

"I had no idea. I knew he was sick but... Why didn't he say something?" I was sad to hear the news. Mr. Diaz was probably one of the nicest men I'd ever met.

"Pride." I nodded, and Tony continued, "Anyway, it would appear that none of Mr. Diaz's sons have any interest in the company, so they'd like to sell."

"So we'll be out of jobs? And you want an adventure? I'm confused..." I rubbed my eyes out of tiredness. I'd been working so much for Mr. Diaz that I had quit my work as a switchboard operator months before. That shop was our whole livelihood. All I could think was that the old saying is true. *Don't put all your eggs in one basket.* Of course, I always liked to add: *and if you do, don't trip!*

"The shop is the adventure, Cate!" He was grinning again from ear to ear, and I could tell he really wanted this.

"How so? Do you want to buy it, Tony?" I already knew the answer, but I asked anyway.

"Mr. Diaz's son said that he'd make me a fair offer. There are so many things I could do with it if it were ours, and you know the profit margin on the place, we'd triple our salaries! And you're practically running the back of the house anyway. We could really do this Cate. If, well, if you want to."

I pulled the eggs out of the frying pan and flopped them onto the plate next to the buttered toast and bacon. I turned towards Tony, spatula in hand and shook it at him. "Well now, you better make this work, or you'll need to plan an adventure to hide from me!"

The next month Tony and I gave birth to our first baby when Triumph Products was born, and we couldn't have been prouder. Tony named it Triumph because he felt triumphant over the discrimination we had felt over the last year. He said that no matter what the color of his skin was, he would prove he could be a successful business owner, and that Mrs. Brown and everyone else who'd shut the door on our previous dream could take that to the bank. I let him have his moments of feather fluffing. He deserved them.

I continued to handle the bookkeeping, though my duties began to grow as our business started to take off. I helped create and distribute a lot of marketing products too, like pens, notepads, fliers, and mailings. We threw ourselves into the shop like we would have thrown ourselves into parenting. Tony expanded the business so much that we were able to—and quite frankly needed to—hire more employees. He was the brains of the shop, working side by side with engineers who brought in blueprints and plans. He'd offer a tweak here and a change there, and each customer walked out with exactly what they needed and wanted, and then they referred us to their friends.

While Tony handled special order items himself, the bread and butter of the shop were the nuts, bolts, and screws that Tony himself designed and manufactured. Mr. Diaz had already invested in the large machinery that was required to fashion things like the top parts of fireplace tools from steel or copper rods. Tony's imagination really was without limit, and while it doesn't sound like terribly exciting work, there was a huge market for small parts. Tony learned very quickly how to tap that market, and was the sole distributor for a lot of parts for some big name Los Angeles companies. In all honesty, although it was pretty fun to see Triumph Products on the side of a marketing ballpoint pen, we didn't really even need the promotional material. Tony's hard work and quality products sold themselves, and our growth under his guidance was incredible.

Tony was determined to raise 'his baby' up right and to be as successful as possible. By the end of 1947 we were clearing fifty thousand dollars a year in profit, which by today's equivalent is more than triumphant, it is astounding. You might think that with that kind of money coming in, and with more employees at hand doing the nitty-gritty stuff, that Tony and I would use some of that money for a new house or a vacation somewhere together. But Tony had other things on his mind. Bigger things. Shinier things. In early 1948 Tony approached me about an idea that he and his brother Hector had concocted, and when I heard what the idea was I nearly choked on my coffee. I think my response was something to the effect of "You want to do *what* exactly?"

Chapter Thirty-Two

Cate
Los Angeles and Feather River Canyon, California
January 1948

If Triumph Products was our first child, then gold mining was our second. Yes, gold, as in *There's gold in them there hills*. Tony's education had been in geological engineering, though he'd never actually worked in that field and had essentially become an expert machinist instead. Even so, he had studied nature extensively, mostly for the purposes of being able to survey the land and what hazards it might present when man wished to build upon it. He would often say, "To interpret a landform is like trying to quantify God's artwork. Difficult at best, but fascinating." He was used to getting his hands dirty and he loved to be outdoors, and by that point in our marriage, so did I.

Tony's younger brother, Hector, had never gone to college, but would often help out in the shop in between his other odd jobs. We saw a lot of Hector and his wife, Julia, over those years, as well as the rest of Tony's family, but we were probably closest to the two of them. So, it didn't surprise either Julia nor I when the brothers started scheming. I just never imagined it would be about panning for gold.

"You want to do *what* exactly?" I had been sipping coffee and reading a book on a Saturday morning. We'd settled into such a routine at work that I should have known Tony would get an itch for something new.

"Gold, Cate! I know it sounds crazy, insane even a little bit, but my buddy Jacob from college did it last spring and summer and said he came away with his pockets full. Okay, he made enough to put a down payment on a house." Tony's face was lit up like it was Christmas morning and he'd gotten that red shiny wagon he'd always wanted.

"We have enough for a down payment on a house, Tony. And I thought you liked where we live. So, that's not really what it's about." I frowned a bit. We knew nothing about gold prospecting, and even less about where to do it.

"No, it's about adventure, Cate! And just think about spending the summer doing something fun and outdoors! You can't tell me you love being in that office all day."

"We do fun things outside all the time. Just last weekend we had that weenie roast on the beach with the Pipers and your sister." I wasn't going to make this easy for him. I sort of liked our routine lives for once, and I wasn't really in need of an adventure.

"Weenie roast? You're comparing the chance to spend time in one of the most beautiful canyons on earth to a weenie roast?" Now he was frowning. I'm sure he hadn't expected any sort of resistance from me, as I was usually pretty congenial about most of his ideas. He hadn't thought he'd have to work that hard to convince me this time.

"Okay, so you've already thought about where you'd like to pan for gold. Care to enlighten your wife?" I put my book down and crossed my arms in front of my chest. I felt a little bit left out of the decision-making process, and it made me uncomfortable and a tad cranky.

"Feather River Canyon. It's amazing, and so incredibly beautiful in the summer and…" He stopped when he saw the horror on my face. "What?"

"Tony, Feather River? As in the Feather River that is north of Sacramento? As in the Feather River that takes eight hours to get to?" We had talked about camping there once, but had decided it was too far to go for a weekend trip; and now he was talking about making that trip numerous times in one summer.

"Yes, Cate. Jacob says it is the place to be. I know it sounds far, but that's part of the fun of it, don't you think?"

"Tony, we don't even own a car!" It was true; we walked or caught buses most of the time because everything we wanted or need to do was relatively close, and parking was always such a problem in downtown Los Angeles.

"Well, that's the other part of the adventure. What do you say we buy a car?" He smiled at me and I shoved my hands further into my armpits and tightened their hold. "Okay, I can see you aren't happy." He came and sat beside me, and I avoided looking at him.

"Cate, my love, it's just a thought. It sounded like fun and a way for us to get away and be outdoors this summer. I just, well, after the last few years, I mean…" He sighed, trying to make his point, and I felt myself soften. "I just thought we could use a bit of sunshine, is all."

We sat in silence for a few minutes before I decided to speak. "So, who would be involved in this adventure? Because I'm not up for living in a tent for four or five months, and you can't be away from the shop for that long anyway."

"Well," he said rather sheepishly. "Hector and his friend Roberto are willing to do most of the dirty work if you and I can do most of the funding for supplies and such. We'd split the earnings fairly. We'd need some equipment, though, and a car, of course. We have the money to do it…"

"You've thought a lot about this, then?" I looked at him like he'd kept a secret from me.

"Not the details really, just the idea. I figure, who better to help with the details than my lovely wife? You're better with that stuff anyway." A grin played on his lips as he spoke.

"Flattery will get you nowhere, Mr. Otera." I was starting to warm up to the idea, but I need to really mull over what it would mean for our lives before I conceded. "Well, let me look at the finances and what we would really be talking about here. Can I think about it?"

Tony smiled and then kissed my cheek, and I responded by playfully pushing him away. "No way, mister, no trying to sweeten the deal. I said I'd think about it!"

He stood up then, and smiled and said, "Fair enough. I'm going to head into the shop for a bit to work on a rush order. I'll be back in a couple of hours, and then maybe we can go out tonight instead of you cooking." He knew he'd have to butter me up, and I was willing to take whatever pampering he was offering even if I knew that I'd likely say yes in the end.

Contrary to my sensible side I did agree, but only for a few months, and then, if it wasn't terribly successful, we would bow out. We had to wait until April before the ground really thawed and the rivers were flowing well again. I learned an awful lot about panning for gold pretty quickly, and it started with the fact that we would need more than just a pan. I set up the logistics for Hector and Roberto as far as what they would need to survive up there with nothing but small towns nearby, and no one at all near the panning sites. Though I thought he'd exaggerated a tad, when Tony had spoken about Feather River Canyon, he really did mean a canyon, which made everything that much more challenging.

Feather River is the main tributary off of the Sacramento River and runs northeast of it, just north of Sacramento. It has four main forks that join together at Lake Oroville. There wasn't much up that way city-wise once you went north of Yuba City, and the small town of Oroville itself was just that, a small town. I knew we were going to have to plan well so that Hector and Roberto were safe and well fed, though their main concerns seemed to be about having the right equipment to get rich fast. It was like trying to tame a bunch of excited little boys and get them to see that they really did need to slow down before making a turn. Thank goodness I had Hector's wife Julia on my side. Between the two of us we were able to convince them that they would need more than just a few matches and a sleeping bag if they were going to make it much longer than a few days.

We got slightly lucky in that Tony's friend Jacob decided to bow out this year, citing his ailing mother, but I suspected it was more a story of an unwilling wife. The only good that came from that was that he had a lot of the miner's equipment that we needed, and he had also built a temporary shelter that, as far as he knew, was still standing. I was hopeful that the winter had been kind to it, because I just didn't see how a simple campsite was going to be adequate for the guys and for us as well when we came up. I wasn't a princess, but sleeping on the ground didn't sound terribly fun for more than a time or two.

Tony and Hector found the established site a little less appealing because, I think, they wanted to branch out and explore on their own. They wanted to take that gamble and see if they could choose wisely. Julia and I were insistent that a shelter was the wisest choice and that the boys could always take day trips here and there and try out different areas. Jacob's old site was located just inside the start of the canyon on the North Fork tributary. North Fork is about 100 miles long and flows down through Lake Almanor through the Sierra Nevadas and eventually meets Lake Oroville. It was somewhere along the southern part of North Fork that Hector and Roberto were going to set up shop.

We spent a good deal of the rest of the winter planning, and the boys read up on as much as they could about the process. Jacob was kind enough to come over a few times and go over the equipment, not because it was complicated, but because I think he was just really excited about it. In the meantime Julia and I started collecting appropriate clothing, sleeping bags, blankets, food supplies, fishing gear, and other various camping gear. Jacob had apparently liked to live off the land, but knowing our guys, they much preferred a few conveniences, and so did I. It was mountainous terrain, and again fairly solitary, so I knew there was no walking three miles to the store for eggs. I was so meticulous because I knew that we'd be up there with them most weekends, helping them and bringing them supplies.

I wasn't wrong about that. In the beginning Tony said we needed to go up every weekend, just until they got on their feet a bit. The truth is we went up every single weekend, save one or two, all that spring and all throughout the summer, until the fall set in. We worked hard during the week, making sure our mainstay income was well tended to, and then we packed up mid-day on Friday and head up in our new car. As promised, and needed really, we'd purchased a Pontiac Streamliner. It was big enough to haul us and the supplies, and occasionally Julia when she got homesick for her husband.

I'm really not complaining about all the traveling because, honestly, that summer was the most fun that Tony and I had ever had. It was a ton of effort, but so enjoyable that it just didn't seem like it was work. Tony had been right; it had been just what we needed to reset.

I'll never forget the first time we drove up to the site to set Hector and Roberto up for the season. When we passed Sacramento, the excitement we all felt in the car was almost unbearable. We were really going to be gold prospectors, just like during the gold rush of the late 1800s. As we drove north on State Route 70 and passed through Oroville, we could hardly contain ourselves. Lake Oroville was a spectacular site, even from a distance, and the more we drove the more convinced we were that this is what heaven must look like.

Unfortunately, the site Jacob had chosen was a tad tricky to get to; but then, it had also led him to some great finds the year before, so we were willing to trek it as needed. Thank goodness there were small dirt paths that allowed us to drive fairly close to the site, but it was still a half of a mile trek from where we could park to where the shelter was, and we were in a canyon for sure. Jacob and his pals had beaten down a fairly decent foot path, but at least a quarter mile of our hike to the site was literally down the side of a mountain.

I probably would have cared a bit more about the difficult hike up and down, but the first time I stood at the bottom with the river flowing gently by us and looked up at the canyon walls and blue sky and felt the warmth of the sun on my face, I knew we'd done the right thing. It was enchanting, and magical almost. I just couldn't imagine that God could have made a prettier place than that.

When I say canyon, I'm sure images of rock walls are quick to creep up, but the walls of this canyon were covered in lush greenery and teeming with wildlife. Pine trees, fir trees, and madrones covered most of the landscape. I'd never heard of much less seen a madrone tree before, and just like everything else that summer, it fascinated me. Its bark is a distinctive light red, almost orange color, and it almost looks paper-thin. It's unique in that the bark peels back and reveals a silky-smooth green bark underneath, the color of peas. The stunning nature of the bark plays second fiddle to its beautiful evergreen leaves and the small white bell-shaped flowers it sprouts in the spring. It trades its flowers for small red berries in the fall. Nature's art is what I call them. I'm sure it was just another tree to some folk, but I was absolutely mesmerized by them.

There was definitely something about that summer that I can only describe as life changing. I'm sure the thought of working a forty-hour week and then packing up the car and driving eight hours to a camp site that you have to hike to down the side of a mountain to reach doesn't sound like much fun, but anyone who has worked really hard at something they love will understand. It made us feel alive and connected, both to each other and the amazing earth that we lived on. I felt Tony's passion for the outdoors, and it seeped into my bones with every largemouth bass or channel catfish that we caught for our supper, and with every spring turkey that Tony shot down during a hunt. We brought supplies every week, but we also learned how to live off the land as much as possible.

It was probably the one time in my adult life that I completely understood where my pop had come from all those years. While he grew tired and weary of farm life as he grew older, he had loved it as a young man. He always said it made him feel alive, cultivating something from nothing with just his hands and a few small tools. He always said it made him grateful, and though I didn't understand it then, I do now. I always thought he was a bit of a fool to say he was grateful for our dirt floors and meager existence, but spending those months in the canyon with Tony and the rest of our small group brought me to a different conclusion. If you can see that everything you really need to live is already provided for you, then everything else is just gravy. Some say that the fresh air of the mountains clears your head, but for me, I think it cleared my soul, and helped me peacefully lay my past to rest.

By the end of the summer we'd come to believe that Jacob had either lied about how much gold he'd found or he'd been a much better prospector than we were. Each day Hector and Roberto would scout out a spot that they felt good about for digging and would set up the wooden sluices in the river. Tony himself had designed and made the boxes at the shop, and was quite proud of what he considered a unique design. They always reminded me of the washboards my mother used to use for scrubbing our clothing—up and down the board, in and out of the water until the stench and dirt from the field were mostly gone. The sluices had a flanged end called the flare, and flowed into a long fifty-inch rippled tray. They'd place the flare of the sluice box about four inches higher than the end of it, and the river water would flow over it, acting as a natural filter. That's all a sluice is, really, a natural washing machine for the dirt you feed it. The rippled tray collected all the fine particles of gold that might be in the dirt.

Gold mining may sound fairly exotic, but it really is fairly simple, and even I did my fair share. We'd take turns rotating who did what, but my favorite part was feeding the sluice. First, though, we had to decide where to dig from, and it was any man's guess as to what area potentially held the jackpot. Hector always dug out of the river behind large rocks and in crevices, and Roberto and Tony preferred to dig in the soft dirt walls of the river bed. Regardless of which they chose, all the dirt got shoveled into a wooden box tray with a screen bottom, basically a sifter, so that only the smaller particles would go through the screen and into the bucket underneath. Then one of us would sit and gently feed a handful of dirt at a time through the flare of the sluice and then let the magic of the river do its work. The sluice sifted and sorted even more, and we hoped that it was catching all of our gold particles and flakes.

Once that bit was done and we'd let the dirt wash a bit in the sluice, we'd dump what we had collected into a bucket and start the panning process. Panning was my least favorite, but it gave Tony a big thrill. He'd sit and swish the pan around, handful after handful, waiting and hoping that all of our work would start to accumulate in the ridges of the gold pan. I only disliked it because more times than not, no gold ever showed up, and it left me feeling disappointed. Running the sluice was a lot more calming, but it was probably because I generally perched myself on a rock and had my toes or feet in the water the whole time. If that's not tranquility, I'm not sure what is.

Now I'm not saying that we didn't find any gold, because we did find some, but it was basically only enough to cover what expenses we'd accrued over the five months that we gave it a whirl. Tony and I were out maybe a few hundred dollars, but in the end, the perspective it gave us was worth so much more than anything that the dirt river bed ever could. Children or not, we were going to be okay, as long as we saw our lives as one big adventure.

At the end of August, we were all together around the campfire at the mining site. Though we didn't always, Tony and I had brought some wine and whiskey up with us along with some store-bought steaks that we'd kept cool in a small portable ice box. We both sort of knew that we probably weren't going to be coming back again and that our days of panning for gold were drawing to a close, so we decided we'd go out with a bang. I sat next to him snuggled under his arm, watching the smoke billow upwards towards the sky, and I let out a huge sigh.

"You alright, Cate?" Hector was asking as he looked a bit concerned. We'd all really bonded over the summer, and I think he took to me like an older brother, feeling a bit protective.

"Oh, yes." I was alright, even more so. "It's just that I spent so much time these last few years wondering how on earth I was ever gonna live without having children in my life. I guess I just couldn't picture it."

An uncomfortable silence filled the campsite, and Julia avoided my eyes while Roberto and Hector stared deeply into the fire. I had called out the white elephant in the room, and no one knew what to say about it. I started to wish that I hadn't said anything, but I knew why I had. These people were my family, and I know they had been worried about me for some time now. Tony broke the silence and asked me, "So you can picture it now?" I nodded at him and he added, "And what does it look like?"

"It looks like this, I guess, and that's not so bad. I'd still love to raise kids, but the truth is, the rest of life is enough also. You all are enough, and I am grateful. For each of you. Truly." I felt my eyes start to well up and dabbed at my eyelashes, willing the tears to stop.

Hector spoke next and surprised me by saying, "I know you really want to be a mother, Cate, but, well…" He looked down at Julia cautiously, and she nodded a bit and smiled at him before he continued. "Would you perhaps settle for being a godmother instead?"

I let his words sink in, and then my eyes went immediately to Julia's tiny abdominal bulge that had had me wondering a few weeks earlier. I immediately felt sadness wash over me, but just as the sluice washed away the unnecessary debris from the good stuff, I let it flow away, and all I felt was happiness for them.

"Really?" I said in a bit of a shrill. "I'd be honored!" I looked at Tony, who was grinning broadly at his brother, and I realized he had already known.

He puffed out his chest and said, "Yes, I knew. And I'm to be the godfather. So you see, we are parents of sorts after all!"

I almost fell into the fire I got up so fast, and I threw my arms around Julia and Hector at the same time. Julia started crying and held on to me for dear life. When she finally calmed, she pulled back and looked at me seriously and said, "I hope it's okay. We were afraid to upset you."

I pulled her into a hug and whispered to her, "It's more than okay, it's wonderful."

She looked at me then, studying my face, and said, "You know, for us, being godparents is more than just an honorary role. It means if something were to happen to us, you will step up and take our children as your own." I nodded that I understood, and then she added, "Even if they turn out to be brats!" We both laughed, then, as the brothers poured everyone a congratulatory shot of whiskey. And when Hector and Julia welcomed their daughter some seven months later and I held her for the first time, I thought to myself that I could never love a child more, and would of course raise her as my own in a heartbeat should that need arise. Because that's indeed what godmothers do.

Chapter Thirty-Three

Cate
Los Angeles, California
Spring 1949

Though I wouldn't have thought it possible, we became even closer to Hector and Julia after that summer. Tony's parents, his sister Violetta, and his other brother, Juan, were also a big part of our lives, but not like Hector and Julia. Juan had joined the navy during the war and had liked it so much he stayed. He was stationed out of San Diego so we saw him when his ship was docked, but often he was out to sea. Tony's sister Violetta was a bit of a wild one, and had little desire to settle down or marry, much to the dismay of her mother. She worked really hard at her job at a department store and never asked anyone for a handout, and Tony and I supported her choice to just be who she was. That was one of the things I loved most about Tony's family. There really was unconditional acceptance.

We were the first ones that Hector called after their daughter Josefina was born on March 11, 1949, and we were the first ones at the hospital to see her and hold her. Julia looked exhausted, but incredibly beautiful, as she lay on her side with Josefina tucked in close by in her pink swaddle blanket. I approached the bed slowly, shaking a little. I was extremely nervous, though I wasn't sure why. I felt in my bones that this little one would change my life somehow.

"Oh, Julia, love, she's beautiful." I whispered. Julia pulled the blanket back away from Josefina's face and smiled tiredly.

"Thank you, Cate. I'll take your word for it because I'm so tired I can hardly see straight." Tony was hugging Hector and grinning widely as he congratulated him.

"Was it as horrible as they say?" I knitted my eyebrows. Some of the ladies who'd attended the baby shower for Julia had decided that sharing their birth stories might help Julia to feel more prepared, but really all it had done was horrify her, and she'd burst into tears the moment they had all left. I'd done my best to reassure her that everyone has a different experience and her birth might not be so bad, but coming from me I'm not sure it did much to lighten her load.

"Oh, no, not really." She smiled weakly. "I mean, it wasn't fun, if that's what you are asking, and I don't want to do it again anytime soon, but it wasn't that horrible. I just haven't slept in days. My back was hurting so, and then of course my water broke just as we were crawling into bed last night." Her eyelids drooped a bit, and I could see her body relaxing into the bed.

"Have you fed her yet?" I was hoping to hold her, but I didn't want to cause Julia any more stress.

"Yes, just finished before you came. They say she has to go to the nursery soon. They don't let you keep them in your room, though at this point I'm so tired I don't really mind..." Dark circles surrounded her eyes, and she closed them again softly and started to doze. Her face usually looked so young, and suddenly she looked ten years older. I guess that's what kids do to you, only I didn't think it happened that fast.

"Julia, may I hold her, then? I'll just sit right here with her quietly so you can rest. I'll be ever so careful." I tried to keep my enthusiasm at a low; I didn't want to seem overly eager, but I was coming apart at the seams wanting to touch the baby.

Julia's eyes slowly fluttered open as she responded, "Oh, of course! That would be lovely, Cate, she'd like that, I'm sure." She gently pushed Josefina towards me, and I picked her up like she was made of china and cradled her in my arms. It was the most amazing and surreal feeling, and I couldn't imagine a better sensation in the world. I shooed Tony and Hector out of the room, as their excitement and volume level had incrementally increased over the last few minutes. I motioned at them and then towards Julia, who by that point had already fallen asleep. Hector crept up and kissed Julia's forehead and then my cheek, and then he and Tony left the room and quietly closed the door behind them.

I sat down in the wooden rocking chair next to Julia's bed and looked down at my goddaughter with fascination and reverence. She was ever so perfect, and I couldn't help but to think how wrong I had been about Feather River being God's artwork. Josefina was his finest masterpiece, and I wasn't sure he could ever top her. Her thick black hair fell over her peacefully closed eyes, and she breathed so quietly that I found myself placing my hand on her chest to make sure it was still rising and falling. I realized what a gift she was, not just to Hector and Julia, but to Tony and me as well. Surprisingly, I didn't feel one bit of jealousy or resentment that Julia and Hector had been so blessed because, though we were not able to have children of our own, God had provided anyway. Faith indeed, just as Tony had said.

We saw less and less of our friends over the next few years and more and more of Tony's family. His parents still owned their original home in Mexico, and they had one in Los Angeles on 24th Street as well. Tony's grandmother still lived in the one in Mexico and had been rather ill lately, so his parents decided to go back to Mexico for a while to tend to her. With his folks gone, Juan off at sea, and Violetta exploring all the dance joints and bars in Los Angeles, that left Hector, Julia, Tony, and me as the family. Tony had always been about family, and our title of godparents just solidified that sense of devotion even more. Friends came and went; but, for Tony, family was family. I'm pretty sure Josefina was the most spoiled child in all of California, because she really had two sets of parents who doted on her day and night.

Julia and Hector moved into Tony's parents' home after they left for Mexico, and we ended up spending most of our days after work and on weekends at the 24th Street house. It became like a second home for us, and we all felt quite comfortable there. I could see why Tony's parents had liked it, with its four bedrooms and large backyard where citrus trees and an avocado tree grew. I always thought to myself that if Tony and I ever decided to buy a home I'd want a lemon tree and an avocado tree planted on the very first day we moved in.

More than the trees even, the front yard boasted several gardenia bushes, and one day Tony had cut a few of the blooms for me and had taken them home. He put them in a small crystal vase on my bedside stand, and they were my very first gardenias ever. They quickly became my favorite flower. Every time those bushes bloomed I would find the same sweet gesture in a vase next to my bed, and every time I see a gardenia I think of Tony. So many memories were created like that in that house, and even though we didn't live there at the time, it was the first place that really felt completely like home.

Hector had opened his own shop in between calling it quits at Feather River and Josefina's birth. I think he knew he'd need steady income and he, like Tony, was a bit of an entrepreneur. He named his shop Water Solutions, and they had large machines from Acme Gridley that made land irrigation products like valve fittings made of brass. It wasn't quite as successful as Triumph Products, but it provided them a good income for their growing family, and it was work that Hector enjoyed. The two brothers often sat and formulated ideas and business plans while Julia and I fussed over Josefina and discussed how well she was growing and developing. It was quite contrasting conversation.

"Peas she likes, but not so much carrots." Julia laughed freely as she watched her daughter roll back and forth on the blanket in the middle of the family room floor.

"Now, see, I would expect the opposite! Who likes peas anyway, silly girl?" I playfully patted Josefina's bottom as she rolled closer to me. She was a plump baby, and she made me finally understand why people always want to pinch a cute baby. From the kitchen table on the other side of the room we could hear Tony and Hector's discussion, and it made both Julia and me roll our eyes.

"Turquoise! The desert is loaded with it, apparently." Tony was talking animatedly about a new adventure that Jacob had mentioned to him. We didn't catch all of the words, as Tony was speaking quickly and sometimes would switch over to Spanish but, regardless, Hector did not meet Tony's enthusiasm with his own.

"The desert, Tony? Who is going to man the camp? I can't anymore." Hector looked crestfallen, like he wanted to be excited too, but just couldn't quite muster the energy it required.

"We hire people, then, Hector. This could be a huge amount of money for us!" I knew Tony, and he was wound up about the idea, though he hadn't really thought it through. He'd mentioned it to me the night before, and I had shot him down immediately and then given Julia a heads-up so she wouldn't lose her mind when she heard him talk about it. He hadn't been happy with me and had insisted that Hector would be on board, and though I suspected differently, I kept my mouth shut.

"Tony, I love you, brother, but…" he stopped and looked over at Julia, Josefina, and me as we tried to pretend that we weren't listening to their conversation. "Listen, Feather River was fantastic, and I'm so glad we took the opportunity to do that, but our lives are different now. We have the baby and all, and well, I just, I…" His voice trailed off, and I could tell it was hard for him to turn Tony down. He looked up to him, and disappointing Tony was the last thing he ever wanted to do.

But Tony made it easy on him, and though I saw his face fall, I knew he understood and also agreed. "It's okay, brother, it was just an idea. And you're right, you belong here—so does your money." He patted Hector's hand, telling him he would lay the idea to rest, and they changed the subject to the current baseball season that was coming to a close soon.

We truly did feel happy, and mostly fulfilled, though a small part of me wanted to take Josefina home with us at the end of the day. It just felt wrong to be without her for too long, and it left me feeling a little empty. She filled something in me that I just couldn't explain.

It was the fall of 1949 by then; I was thirty-one, and Tony and I had been married about three and a half years. I couldn't even picture what my life had been like before him because he and his family were my whole world. I still kept in touch with some of my siblings and, of course, my mom and pop, but after several attempts at trying to get them to come out to visit, I gave up. None of my family had met Tony, and it made my heart a bit sad. One afternoon, out of the blue, I asked Tony to do something I'd never thought I would. I asked him if we could go back to see my family.

"To Michigan? In the winter?" Tony frowned a bit, but if I knew him he was thinking about it for sure.

"Well, it's still fall, and we have another month or so before it starts getting really cold." Fall was beautiful in Michigan as the leaves turned and the air cooled slightly. It reminded me of hot apple cider and pumpkin pie, leaf piles, and cool night air. It was second only to a Kentucky spring when everything jumped back to life for me, and things got a chance to start over.

"Hmmm. What brought this about, Cate? I thought you never wanted to go back."

"To live, no, but to visit, perhaps. More so, I want my parents to meet you. I know we aren't terribly close, but it's still important to me for some reason, and I've tried to get them here but my mother has such problems with migraines and my pop just started a job with the VA. Do you not want to meet them?" I suddenly felt like maybe it was a bad idea. Bringing my biracial marriage to Michigan wasn't the safest thing I could think of doing.

Tony came over and hugged me. "Ah, but of course, Cate. I'd love to meet your parents and family. You have sisters and cousins there too, yes?"

I nodded, "Yes, some. Most are scattered through the south, but it's really my mom and pop I'd most like you to meet. I want them to know you like I do, to put their speculations to rest."

"Their speculations, huh? And what about your aunt Rachel?" He looked nervous. He'd heard my stories, and I'm sure being politely ostracized wasn't at the top of his to do list.

"What about her? My folks don't live with her anymore, so we wouldn't even have to see her. Mom and Pop moved in with my gran on the other side of town, my mom's mother. Apparently she's not doing well, like your grandmother. She's in her seventies, I believe."

Tony sighed and gave me a wry smile. "When do you want to go, then? Soon? You tell me, and I'll arrange the travel." He'd never understood my family and how we could all be spread so far apart. To him, family lived close so they could help one another get through life, and my parents seeming lack of interest in their children's lives baffled him. For me, it was just the way it was, and seemed fairly normal. My folks had seven children, and I knew it was probably difficult just to keep up with everyone.

"I love you, Tony. Thank you. I think we should go this month before the roads start to ice. I think if we went during the winter, your west coast skin might freeze to death." I laughed and he agreed.

"Probably so, my love." I could tell Tony was uncomfortable, but only because he'd always imagined meeting my family on a visit in Los Angeles, on our turf, and not on Michigan soil. "But for you, I'd buy a parka."

We both laughed then at the image of Tony in a parka, and I started to feel excited about our trip. Something inside me needed it and felt like it was the right thing to do. Maybe the only way I could completely let go of my past was to face it again and see how it made me feel. I just hoped and prayed I wasn't wrong.

Chapter Thirty-Four

Cate
Hazel Park, Michigan
October 1949

Over the next few days, Tony's adventurous side kicked in as he started planning our trip. He decided that the Greyhound bus line or a train was probably the best way to manage, unless we wanted to drive the whole way ourselves. I pushed for us driving so that if we needed to leave quickly we could; plus we could stop and see a few things along the way. I figured that way we could salvage the trip in the case Michigan ended up being a disaster. I think all the road trips up to Feather River had soured Tony on hitting the road for long stretches for a while, but he agreed to it anyway, mostly because I think he wanted to make me comfortable.

It took us over five days to travel the 2,300 miles to Michigan. It was a long haul, but we tried to make it as fun as possible. The road took us through Nevada, Utah, and Colorado. After that we wound through the mid-western states of Nebraska, Iowa, Illinois, and a bit of Indiana before we crossed over the state line into Michigan. We made very few plans as to where we were going to stay, and we stopped when we found a town interesting enough to dabble in for a few hours. If we saw a sign that said "World's biggest ball of yarn" or anything unique like that, we stopped. We got out frequently to take in the scenery of the mountains, or to breathe in the fresh country air of the the midlands—well, once we got past the farms and such. It was no five-star resort vacation, but it was a trip I will always remember, because that was Tony for you. His sense of adventure didn't end with mining for gold in some hidden canyon; he made everything as exciting as a backyard childhood escapade.

We stopped a few hours just outside of Detroit to get a bite to eat, but also, I think, to gather ourselves for what we might end up walking into when we arrived. My folks had sounded excited when they heard we were coming, and they knew that Tony wasn't exactly white, but I feared their faces might betray what they truly felt when they actually met him, and I didn't want Tony's feelings hurt. We found a HoJo's restaurant that served up typical fare like burgers and fries and diner food, but they were best known for their signature orange rooftop and for the twenty-eight different flavors of ice cream they served up. I was always a sucker for a great cone, so it was an easy choice. We'd just had our coffee poured by a middle-aged lady named May who had fine hair and a dirty apron when I decided to come clean with Tony.

"So, you know I told you a lot about my past, right?" Surprisingly, I wasn't nervous at all about what I was about to share. I just really needed him to understand what it was he was about to face.

"Yes, of course. But it doesn't really matter, Cate. You aren't your past." He smiled at me as he reached for the cream and sugar. He liked two dashes of cream and one sugar in his coffee, no more, no less.

"No, of course not. That's not what I meant. I just want you to understand that my folks are much different than yours. They are good people, but they don't understand how diverse the world is like you and I do. They've been somewhat shielded from it, I suppose."

"Well, Cate, I didn't expect that Roseville, Michigan or Kentucky are anything like Los Angeles, if that's what you're concerned about." He furrowed his brow in confusion. "Are they prejudiced?"

"No, it's not that. I may be way off base here, but you just need to understand where my folks came from before you judge them."

"It sounds like I'm the one to be judged here, Cate, not the other way around..." He looked worried then, and I'm sure he was picturing a mob waiting to greet us at my folks' front door with pitch forks and fire sticks yelling "Go back to Mexico!" even though he had never lived there.

"You know what I meant, Tony." He just shrugged at me and raised his eyebrows, signaling me to continue. "Well, if I was poor growing up, then my pop was flat broke. My pop was born in 1887 and my mom in 1891, both born in Kentucky up near Logan County. My pop's daddy, my grandpop, was born a full-blown red-head, if you'll believe that, and my granny is actually full-blooded Shawnee. Her father fought along side Union troops during the Civil War, and when it was over he moved his family to Kentucky from Ohio where some other Shawnee had settled. Well, life changed for them there, and my granny was put into the local school system to learn to read and write."

"Wow, I'm sure that was a shock for her." Tony was listening intently to my story.

"Well, I'm sure. It was there in school that she met my grandpop. She is a bit of a headstrong woman and set in her ways, but quiet too, and not loud in her stubbornness. She simply digs her heels in about something and waits for my grandpop to fold. And he always does. I suppose it is sweet that he just wants her happy, but it made everyone a tad afraid of her, and terrified about confronting her. She was never very warm with us growing up, and we always had to be silent at her home. I never really felt as though I knew her all that well, even though I saw her all the time. My grandpop was the opposite in every way, and we were more than thrilled every time he'd come around, and we never could figure out what he'd seen in her. Something about her being so obstinate attracted his kind soul for some reason. Thank goodness my pop took after his daddy instead of his mother, personality-wise."

"So, you're telling me you are a quarter Shawnee?" He looked incredulously at me.

"I never thought about it like that, but yes, I suppose so." He looked horrified, and I panicked. "Is that a problem, Tony?"

He suddenly laughed and put me at ease as he said, "No, not at all! I'll just have to remember to hide the hatchets if I ever upset you!"

I started laughing and said, "The only thing I've ever chopped with a hatchet is firewood, my love."

He was on a roll at that point, and said, "But I bet it came naturally to you!" I swatted at him then.

"My granny did not hack people to death. Talk about pigeonholing…" I couldn't help but smile at the thought of my tiny granny yielding a hatchet and running through the backwoods at the enemy. She was so tiny she could barely handle the fireplace poker. "They still live in northern Kentucky, by the way. I don't think she'd ever move."

"I had no idea you were part Indian. So there's some color under all that pale skin after all. Just makes me afraid there's more secrets you've been hiding." He sat back, relaxed, like he was watching a movie and couldn't wait to see the next scene. All he needed was to kick up his feet and ask me to pass the popcorn. "You have any unsavory characters in your family? People I ought to avoid, perhaps? I mean besides your aunt Rachel…" He laughed at his own joke, and peered at me suspiciously.

"We did have slave owners in the family. Does that make you want to run?" I was playing with him now, though what I said had some truth to it.

"Oh, really?" He raised his eyebrows at me. "Wasn't that deemed illegal back in 1865 or so with old honest Abe's Emancipation Proclamation?"

"Very funny, Tony. I meant we had slave owners in the family. My mom apparently came from some wealth, though by the time she was born her father had let the riches dwindle a bit. I guess his parents, my great-grandparents, were mid-level land owners back then and owned a small plantation where they had some fifty or so slaves that worked their tobacco and cotton fields. I'm not sure if you know your history, but when the Civil War first started, Kentucky was a neutral state and refused to pick a side. They thought they could be mediators for the Union and the Confederacy, which was nice in theory, but harder to execute in reality. I forget exactly what happened, but I believe the South decided to ignore Kentucky's neutral position and invaded and set up some forts. Kentucky wasn't too keen on that, and obviously it eventually joined the Union. To my family's credit, I heard stories that my great-grandfather was one of the few slave owners who freed his slaves of his own volition instead of taking up with the Confederacy as many others did, and many of his former slaves fought in the great battles helping the Union win. He even gave most of his land over to the cause, and lost a good bit of his money in the process."

Tony was mesmerized. "Wow, Cate. You do have a sordid past. And here I was worried that you were a divorced woman." He laughed, and then added, "I'm joking, of course!"

"It is quite a colorful foundation, I guess. Not everyone can say they have a slave owner and an Indian in their bloodline!"

I knew it sounded exciting, but the truth was, my family was from Kentucky and had been there for more years than I could count. My mom had told me once that her family line could be traced all the way back to the Revolutionary War, which made my family some of the original Americans. That had always made me ridiculously proud.

"So, Cate, what are you trying to tell me here? I haven't heard anything that makes me want to run yet." He looked at me expectantly.

"Well, really I just want you to see that my family at its core are simple farm folk, really. Both lines from as far back as anyone can remember made a living working the land in Kentucky. They aren't terribly—" I paused, searching for the right word, and the best I could come up with was "—cultured. They aren't cultured."

"Cate, do you think my family is any different?" He studied my face, trying to figure out what I was so worried about, and to be honest, I wasn't even sure.

"Your family is full of adventure, Tony, and your father, he knows so much about the world. Sometimes I think he has an encyclopedia for a brain." Tony's dad was one of those people that you could ask just about anything and he'd know something about it. It got to be a game sometimes, to try to find a topic that his father knew nothing about, but we found that if you asked him something he didn't know, he would go and research it, and by the next day be able to spout off a full-page report on the subject. It was pretty amazing.

"Yes, but it wasn't always that way. They came to America to try to find a different and better life for themselves. The same reason, I imagine, that your folks moved out of Kentucky to Michigan, and why you came back to California. The only way my folks could do that was by being adventurous and by being open to new things. It was a habit that just sort of took seed and grew in all of us. My roots, though not as interesting, aren't altogether different from yours."

"Oh, but they are, Tony. Your family is very different from mine." I could see it, why couldn't he? Then I realized it wasn't that he couldn't see it, he just didn't care. It didn't matter to him.

"Cate, no matter who they are, it doesn't change who you have become. I will love them because they are a part of you, my love, part of your story. It doesn't matter where that story began. And it seems to me, with such historical folks in our family, your bloodline and parents are more cultured than you give them credit for."

"You really feel that way? I just wanted to lower your expectations is all, so you aren't disappointed."

"I have no expectations, love. To be honest, your stories put me at ease a bit." He looked more relaxed than I had seen him the whole trip, and he smiled at me from across the table.

"They did? How?" I wasn't sure how telling him that I was really just a small-town kid who barely owned a pair of shoes growing up and that my parents were as simple as simple came could put him at ease.

"Well, I figure if your granny is a dark-skinned gal, born of an entirely different culture and place, and they love and accept her, then why wouldn't they love and accept me too?"

I was shocked. I had honestly never even given it a thought. We had never discussed my granny's past because she was just my granny, and my pop's mother. It hadn't mattered. And now Tony was my husband and their son-in-law, and I knew he was right. I had been so caught up in being judged by adoption agency after adoption agency, by people who didn't know us at all, that I began to worry that the people who did know me would do the same. My logic wasn't sound, but that's what it boiled down to. I was afraid they would reject him, and in doing so would shut the door on me forever, just like the agencies had done.

"You know what, Tony, you're right." I felt myself relax a bit, and I started to imagine a different meeting with my parents, one that didn't involve tears or pitchforks or closed doors. They wouldn't care once they got to know him. What was there not to love?

Tony and my pop hit it off immediately, something I had not expected. My pop had changed since I'd last seen him, and was more relaxed and rested. He'd gotten a job with Veteran's Affairs doing some administrative-type work, and he told us that working with the Veterans had really opened his eyes to a lot in the world. I suspected it was the helping others that had him feeling so inspired, but regardless I was just happy to see him happy.

I had never seen my pop talk as much as he did with Tony over the week that we came to visit. It hadn't even started out with the awkwardness that often accompanies new introductions. They just seemed to like one another comfortably from the start. I really couldn't have asked for anything more. It wasn't quite as comfortable with my mom and Tony, but then I had never been completely comfortable with her either. She seemed a tad more alive, though, than in previous years, but there was still something empty about her eyes.

I couldn't believe that after all the years that had passed since my little brother Samuel's death it still affected her so, but my gran said she still spoke of him often and was still filled with a lot of sorrow over her loss. I guess some things you just really never get over, no matter how much you want to. It filled me with fear that I'd never really find my own peace over the loss of being a mother. I didn't want to just survive my loss as my mom had. I wanted to overcome it.

It was good to see my mom, though, regardless, and my gran too. I spent a lot of time at my gran's bedside just listening to her stories and asking questions about life in another era. I'd been running from my past so long that I'd forgotten my history, and those were two very different things. My mom sometimes sat with us, but often she lay down to rest instead. I learned that her migraines had become increasingly worse over the years, and her doctors couldn't seem to get a handle on it, so she spent a lot of time sleeping.

My sister, Lina, came up from Ohio to visit midweek and brought a few of her children along with her, so we got a chance to catch up a bit. It made me realize how much I missed having her and my other siblings around, although I really hadn't been around most of them since I was much younger. I had hoped to see more of my siblings, but I learned through Lina and my mom that some of them weren't doing so well in their own lives and couldn't possibly get a way for a few days. I felt a tad helpless hearing their stories because, from the sounds of it, there was nothing anyone could really do to help any of them. Or so I thought.

My mom shocked me one morning by telling me they were likely going to be taking in my niece Diana on a permanent basis. My older sister, Vera, who lived in Russellville, Kentucky, had had a run of bad luck ever since she'd gotten pregnant with Diana, and now the bad luck was becoming Diana's inheritance. Vera had gotten involved with a local boy just before the war and found herself in a family way, but in the end was without the family man. It turned out the young man actually already had a wife and three other children just two towns over, and Vera had been left devastated, alone, humiliated, and pregnant. That was in late 1942, and just after that the man was drafted into the army and never returned from his overseas tour. He never met my niece Diana, and this second devastation was a blow my sister had never really recovered from. I knew she'd moved up to Michigan for a bit after the baby was born so that my mom could give her a hand, but the living situation had been a trying one at my aunt Rachel's home. After Vera had taken Diana back down to Kentucky for a visit, she decided to stay there. It seemed Vera had met another man, this one unmarried, and eventually she had moved to Russellville after accepting a marriage proposal from her newfound gentleman.

Unfortunately for Diana, her mother's new husband didn't take well to being a father, even after several years had passed, and Vera was so love-struck she refused to see it. Over the last few years things had apparently grown increasingly tense, and it had become clear that there had been a line drawn in the sand between Vera's husband and her daughter. Vera was being made to choose sides, and she had chosen her husband instead of her own blood. Diana, who was almost eight, had been emotionally neglected by her mother and oftentimes verbally abused by her stepfather, and she had definitely been left hanging in the balance.

I felt ashamed that I hadn't known about any of it, but then Vera and I had never really been close, and my parents were quick to defend her. She was a fragmented person, held together by paperclips and scotch tape, and I was the opposite, put together with mortar and superglue, and we had rarely seen the world the same way. I loved my sister, but couldn't understand how she could choose a man over her own flesh. There Tony and I were, absolutely crushed that we would never have what she had, and there she was, giving it up freely for a two-bit man. It made me wonder if Vera would consider allowing Tony and me to raise her.

"Mom, don't you think raising another child might be a bit too much for you and pop at this point? I mean, with your headaches and all?" We were sitting on my gran's back porch, enjoying one of the last sunny days of the fall season while sipping my mother's muddy coffee. It was syrupy at best, and required three sugars and a lot of cream just to ease it down your throat.

"What else are we to do, Catherine? Your sister is not like you." She looked tired, though she'd slept twelve hours last night and then taken a late morning nap, and I wondered what sort of drugs the doctors had her on for her migraines.

"What do you mean by that?" It wasn't like my mom to comment on my siblings to me, and I'd been shocked at all that she'd even told me Vera's whole story.

"She's not strong like you. She's like a china set that breaks easily and you, well, you're more made of cast iron." I didn't know how to respond. It was the closest my mom had ever come to complimenting me.

"I'm not always strong, Mom. I have my moments too." I studied my mom's face, and she raised her eyes to hold my gaze. She was searching for a safe place to lay her words.

"Catherine, perhaps I've not said it enough, or maybe ever, but I am proud of you." She paused, and my breath caught in my throat. "You've made mistakes, there's no doubt about that, but you've always managed to stand up straight through it all and hold your head high while you correct them. Your other siblings aren't like that. They make mistakes and seem to stay stuck to them. They act as though they have no choice in the matter. You, though, you make good choices."

I felt my eyes start to swell with tears, and I swallowed, trying to hold them back. It was the most honest moment my mother and I had ever had. She was being the mom I had always longed for. The mom who saw me. I could imagine now what she was like before Samuel had died, just as my sisters and brother had described. She had been loving and encouraging and engaged, and I finally got a glimpse of that other woman.

"Catherine, Tony is a good man. Your pop and I like him very much, and your gran too." She smiled gently at me. "You two will make lovely parents some day."

I felt a wave of nausea crash over me. I hadn't told my parents our bit of news, and I think my mom out of respect had just stopped asking about when she'd get grandchildren out of me.

"Mom, I have something to tell you, actually..." She held up her hand then, and gave me a sympathetic look.

"I already know, Catherine. Lina told me. Don't be cross with her, she was worried you'd be so devastated you wouldn't recover from it, but I told her that wasn't possible. Not my Catherine. She will rise above."

Tears slipped through my eyelashes and ran down my face. "But why did you just say that then? Knowing we can't have children?"

"Because I know what you are thinking. You are wondering why, if Vera doesn't want to raise Diana, why can't you have her. Am I wrong?" She raised her eyebrows expectantly at me, waiting for an answer. I shook my head no, because she wasn't wrong. It was the first thing that crossed my mind when my mom told me that she and my pop would be taking her in soon.

"Catherine, it crossed my mind too, and your pop's." She was struggling to find the right words, and she broke my gaze and looked past me to the oak trees behind me that were already losing their orange and yellow leaves.

"Mom, we could ask Vera, couldn't we? I mean, it couldn't hurt to ask. I know Diana's older and doesn't know us well, but with time we could..." I was starting to get worked up, and my mom did something out of character and raised her voice above mine to stop me.

"Catherine, stop. We already tried." Her face fell as she told me.

"You did?" I instantly felt the sting of it. "Well, what did she say?" I sat up a bit taller, bracing myself for what was surely bad news.

"She simply refused. She said she'd let us have her, but that was it. No one else, not even you. I'm so sorry. She was quite adamant, and Diana's situation is so dire we really just need to get her here as soon as possible. We just aren't in a position to bargain with her."

"Is it because of Tony?" I felt the slight of the word *biracial* again, and was crushed that it applied even in my own family.

"No, dear girl. No. She doesn't even know enough to know about Tony's racial background. It's about her. Like I said, she isn't like you. Giving her daughter to us is one thing, she can handle that. Giving her daughter to you, her one successful sister, is like voluntarily putting her hand in a vat of hot liquid: it hurts too much, and she just doesn't see the point."

"Does she know we can't have our own?" I practically choked out the words, and they burned my throat as they left my mouth.

"She knows. But honestly, it wouldn't make a bit of difference even if you could. She's a broken person, Catherine, and when china breaks it never goes back together the same way. The seams are always a tad weak, and the pieces never fit together again just right." I sat silently, looking down at my hands. It was my worst nightmare. A child needed parents, a child who was of my own family, and we still couldn't have her. I was flattened yet again by my inability to be a mother.

Then my mom did something she had only done a handful of times in my life. She got up and pulled me into an embrace and let me cry as she soothed my hair. When I quieted after a few moments, she pulled back and took my face in her hands.

"I said you'd be great parents someday because I believe you will be. Have a little faith, Catherine. You are strong enough to believe."

I wasn't so sure anymore about my strength. I could feel a hole ripping through me, and I started feeling as though I could never possibly fix it. I looked into my mom's eyes and suddenly I understood her own hollow place, and it absolutely terrified me.

Chapter Thirty-Five

Lillie
Thursday, August 13, 1953
11:00 p.m.

Lillie slept for hours, soundly this time. Elizabeth didn't have to wonder if Lillie was still breathing because she heard her snoring all the way down into the stairwell. She went about her nightly duties as planned, and passed some time by helping out with a cranky infant in the pediatric ward for an hour or so. She checked in on Lillie every now and then and was slightly disappointed to find her still asleep. Elizabeth prayed she hadn't brought on more trouble than it was worth with her little soda pop gift. Rose and Elizabeth checked off another chore as they folded more towels together by the light of the sad naked bulb in the laundry area. Even Rose, who was not the least bit intuitive, picked up on Elizabeth's anxiety about Lillie.

"How's she doing?" Rose inquired shyly. She was hesitant to step on Elizabeth's toes given their disagreement the night before, so she tread lightly with her words.

"Hmm?" Elizabeth was so distracted thinking about Clay and Joe and the rest of Lillie's family that she only half-heard Rose's question.

"Lillie, how is Lillie doing? I heard from Ada Mae that the doctors think it'll be real soon."

Elizabeth snapped to at Rose's comment and looked at her friend with knitted eyebrows. She wanted to argue with her, to correct her and tell her, what did she know? But deep down, Elizabeth knew Rose and Ada Mae were probably right. Soon Lillie would go into a coma-like state from which she wouldn't awaken, and she would slowly slip away.

"Elizabeth, I'm sorry, I..." Rose felt terrible. She could sense the pain in Elizabeth's chest and could see the hurt in her eyes.

"No, no, Rose. You are right. It's gonna happen soon. It's just so sad, is all. If you could just hear some of her stories and what she's lived through..." Elizabeth stopped herself as she mulled over what to say next. They were Lillie's stories to tell, and not hers. She had been privileged enough to have Lillie share them, and she wouldn't do Lillie the dishonor of gossiping about her as she lay dying two floors above them. "Anyhow, you're right. Probably the next day or so. But then, it's weird, Rose, she sat up in bed today and talked to me for a long time. She hasn't had the strength to do that for weeks! It's like she caught some second wind. Amazing how good she looks, actually..."

"Oh, no, don't you do that." Rose had seen this so many times. Family members of the dying seeing their loved one suddenly get better and becoming hopeful that somehow, through some miracle, they might be spared the death that was just looming over them. And then watching their hearts break when a rapid decline followed and death knocked at the door with hungry hands. "Elizabeth, honey... you know folks do that sometimes."

"Do what?" Elizabeth knew. She knew just what Rose was talking about. She had seen it too. But she wanted to believe that maybe this really was a turning point for Lillie, that maybe her body was going to pull it together. That maybe it wasn't too late after all.

"It's her rally, Elizabeth. I know that you know that. It's what they do. It's what the dying do, girl. It's like they have to feel normal just one last time, or finish just one last thing before they can let go." Rose approached her friend and grabbed her suddenly into an embrace. "I know you know, Elizabeth. Just help her finish whatever it is she thinks is left undone, and then you got to help her let go."

Elizabeth hugged her childhood friend tightly and felt the tears well up. A small sob escaped her lips, and she whispered to Rose and to herself, "Okay. I can do that." Could she do that?

Rose released Elizabeth, but continued to hold her hands. "You want to do something for Lillie besides fluff her pillows and make her comfortable? You find a way to help her let go."

Elizabeth nodded, knowing Rose was right. She let go of Rose's hands and wiped her eyes with the back of her hands, sniffling and trying to regain her composure.

"Come on, then, let's get you some tissues." Rose said, leading Elizabeth to the ladies room, where she helped Elizabeth wipe the mascara from underneath her lashes and assisted her with pulling herself together.

An hour later Elizabeth found herself sitting in the dark, listening quietly to the sounds of Lillie's heavy breaths. She wondered if perhaps Lillie had already slipped off to a permanent sleep and the snoring was just an indicator of how deeply she had gone. She watched Lillie's chest rise and fall and thought about all the babies that had probably drifted off to sleep on that bosom, and how many babies had drifted off to God in the same place.

Some people say that you can tell a lot about a person's life by the state of their face, and Elizabeth thought that to be fairly true. Most people carried their burdens right there for all the world to see with wrinkles, frown lines, and scars, even as they tried to hide it all inside. But Lillie's face was deceiving. Even within days of her death, her face seemed calm, and beautiful. For Lillie, it was her body that told her tale instead. A mother's breast, stretched out, droopy, and well-used. Worn and tired legs and hands, blue and purple, gnarled and numb, starved for what they needed by a body that failed them. Her backside, riddled with the worst of her visible wounds from a war that started so long ago in her own home. Lillie's face gave nothing away about her life with Clay, but her body told all her secrets.

Lillie startled Elizabeth when she suddenly opened her eyes from a dead sleep and called out her name. Elizabeth jumped up to her side at the sound of it and said quickly, with reassurance, "Yes, Lillie, I'm still here."

"Ah…" Lillie felt relief. She had made it through her nap and was still alive. She still had some time, then. She opened her mouth to speak and felt an incredible rawness in the back of her throat that she hadn't felt before. She needed water, and then she needed to act fast. Lillie knew she was playing on borrowed time. "Water?" she managed to squeak out, and Elizabeth immediately filled a glass for her and helped her to sit up enough to sip through a straw. She guzzled it down, drowning out the sweet taste in her mouth that the soda had left. Finally she felt like she had the strength to do what she needed to do. She cleared her throat and squared out her body so she had the best angle she could to face Elizabeth directly. "Did I ever tell you about my wedding, Elizabeth?"

Elizabeth stopped and looked quizzically at her. It wasn't what she had expected to hear. "Uh, no, Lillie, you haven't. You said you were married in the courthouse, right?"

"Have a seat, Elizabeth, I got some talking to do." It was the first time Lillie had ever been directive with her, and though it surprised her, it didn't bother Elizabeth a bit. She felt relieved, actually, that Lillie had so much to say, especially since she had so much she wanted to know. "And get you a comfortable one and not that old doc's stool..." Elizabeth laughed at Lillie's orders and crossed the room to pull the heavy, handmade rocking chair up to Lillie's bedside. The loudness of the heavy wood on the tile made Lillie cringe.

Once Elizabeth got herself settled, she said, "Okay, Lillie, I'm ready."

"Right. Well, we was married real quick-like after I met Clay. I ran into him in town for the first time just before spring in 1929. I had just turned twenty, and I was working for Mary in her sewing shop. Well, I was working alone, really, because Mary kept falling ill that year and wasn't in the shop too much. Anyway, Josie had just gotten married the fall before. She's my best friend, 'ya know, and Mary's daughter, and I guess I was a fright lonely, looking back." Lillie paused, thinking about that time in her life when everything had been so simple. When she'd questioned nothing and expected even less.

"So when did you get married, then? I mean, you said right quick..." Elizabeth could tell Lillie wanted to share her stories, but she also knew she was going to have to keep her engaged and on track. She could see Lillie's mind wander off in between sentences, almost like she was watching a movie and then telling Elizabeth what she was seeing. Elizabeth didn't want her getting so lost in the scenery that Lillie forgot to keep telling her story.

"We was married June first of that same year. Just about three months after I met Clay. And no, I wasn't pregnant, if you's wondering..." Lillie grinned, her gap-toothed smile hinting at a little mischief.

"Nah, I wasn't, I..." but Elizabeth was wondering, and she caught Lillie's grin and laughed. "Okay, you got me. So why so fast then, Lillie?"

"Like I said, I was real lonely-like, with Josie hitched and her mama all laid up. Then my family decided in May that they was gonna move come summertime into town. My pa was real tired of working farms. He got his self a job, doing something with the water company. It was an easy choice, really, seeing how my daddy was getting older and it was closer for the younger kids to get into school everyday. They found themselves a real nice house near downtown Franklin and settled in for a few years there. I think he worked for the city of Franklin for about seven or eight years. They eventually moved up to Michigan somewhere to do the same kind of work, but for a bigger city. The

Finns were real happy-like for my folks, they didn't hold no grudges or nothing."

"That was really nice of them. To not be bitter at them."

"Well, I think my daddy maybe saw a life for me and Clay there. A chance to move on without leaving Mr. Finn in the lurch see. Fact, I think that's why Clay asked me to marry him so fast, too. I used to think it was sweet, 'ya know. That he loved me so much that he just couldn't wait to make me his wife, but now I just see that like everything else, what Clay wants, Clay gets, and he ain't none too shy nor patient about getting it."

"What do you mean? Why would Clay ask you to marry him because of the Finns?" Elizabeth didn't see the connection right away.

"Clay always looking out for himself first, Elizabeth. By marrying me, he not only got himself a wife, but he got himself a wife who was working for one of the kindest and most generous farmers around. Clay ain't no fool. He knew Mary Finn was sick, and the first time he met my daddy he learned that my folks were thinking about moving into town. He knew James Finn would need all the help he could get. He saw the right perfect scene for himself. Me and him, sharecropping with the Finns, taking home good money and living in my parent's old house."

"Oh, I see." Elizabeth frowned. "That's terrible, Lillie."

"Oh, I didn't see it that way at the time. I just saw me and Clay there growing us a family, and as happy as my ma and pa had been. I didn't see I was just a way to get more money for Clay. How could I have? I was in love."

"So you really loved him, Lillie? You didn't see none of his meanness then? Not even a little?" Elizabeth was curious. She didn't see how Lillie didn't have any clue at all about who Clay was. Surely there must of been something about him that gave her a hint of the real Clay.

"He wasn't always that mean. Besides, when you are wooing a girl, you say all the right things, right? When you're trying to get what you want, you act however it takes to get it. That was what Clay was good at. I guess, thinking about it now, there were probably a few things that should'a bothered me, but it wasn't like they was big enough to not marry him."

"Like what, Lillie?" Elizabeth wasn't just thinking about Clay anymore. She had a sinking feeling in the pit of her stomach. She was thinking about the boy who was trying to woo her, trying to sweep her and her daddy off of their feet.

"Well, like when we'd be out in town. He'd be real sweet to me, but folks seemed real scared of him. I thought it was just 'cause he was so tall and strong. Turns out it was probably 'cause they done had a run in with him some other day. And how he'd say real nice things to me, but then be real short and snappy when folks didn't get him what he wanted fasted enough. Or how nothing was quite good enough, he always had something to complain about. I just didn't see it at the time. I just didn't see it 'cause it wasn't directed at me. Not then, anyhow..." Lillie found herself frowning like Elizabeth had been for the past few minutes. Lillie was kicking herself silently as she said her words to Elizabeth. She couldn't believe she had been so blind. Elizabeth sat silently next to her with the same sentiment, but was feeling grateful that the veil was lifting a few inches every time Lillie told another story about her Clay.

Lillie had wanted to be married in the church. She'd thought about it many times, and had felt even more sure about it after watching Josie and Matthew say their vows before the hand-carved altar at the Presbyterian chapel. She wanted to make sure God knew she was going to make good on her promises, and something about just saying some words to a judge didn't feel right to her. But Clay had said he didn't want to wait long enough to do what a church wedding required. Getting married outside of the courthouse required blood tests, and those required more money and six weeks for results, neither of which appealed to Clay. That was the first time he shot Lillie down without remorse, and the first time that Lillie had gone along with whatever Clay wanted. It was the first time she'd given away a little piece of herself, and she didn't even know it.

Lillie didn't get the venue she'd wanted, but she had the dress of her dreams. It had been crisp white and not a shade darker, like newly fallen snow, unmarred by time or people. She had pure intent, and to Lillie, that was the only color that said just that. Lillie was a larger girl, even back then, before all the butter biscuits and marmalade had made a permanent home on her thighs and abdomen. She knew she'd never find a dress off the rack to fit her short stature and roundness, and she knew she could do a garment more justice than anything factory-made anyhow. So she gently turned down Josie's offer to take her to Nashville to buy her a gown as a wedding gift and started plotting her own plans to make her dress instead.

Lillie's first thought was how she'd love Mary's input. All those years as her apprentice had left her very skilled, but also very used to needing validation from Mary about her work. Lillie lacked only confidence in herself and nothing more, and though Mary had told her time and time again how wonderful Lillie's designs were and how quality her work was, Lillie could never really tell herself that. Lillie had a reverse curse of the young, Mary would say.

"Most young folk run round her with all their peacock feathers out, strutting and a-telling people how skilled they are when really they don't have much to show but some razzle-dazzle pretty colors. Then they get older and their colors fade, but their feathers are stronger, and deep down they really are something to be looked at. But you, Lillie, you got real talent and yet you got no strut, walking round town like you are invisible, like your insides are as brown as your hair. You need to show your feathers now and then, Lillie, because yours have *real* color. You got to believe that you are worth something, Lillie, because if you don't, nobody else will either."

Lillie lay in the dark thinking about Mary's words and about how right she had been. Lillie could see all the good things in others and none of it in herself. She didn't have clue what it meant to strut.

"Lillie," Elizabeth's words broke into Lillie's thoughts like a jackhammer, and Lillie jumped. "What did your dress look like?"

"Oh, Elizabeth, it was beautiful." Lillie smiled widely, showing Elizabeth a little of her feathers and finally giving herself credit for something. "I did an amazing job of it."

"You made your own dress?" Elizabeth raised her eyebrows in surprise, but then gently let them fall into place as she remembered Lillie's sewing past. "Ah yes, that makes sense. I thought your friend Mary might'a had a hand in it."

"Well, she did a little bit, I guess." Lillie's grin softened as she thought about the day she'd gone to Mary to tell her about Clay and to ask her about her dress. Clay had only just asked her in May and started pushing her to choose a date in early June almost as soon as he'd proposed. Lillie knew if she was going to be married in a wedding dress, she would need to get working on it right away. She still had her regular customers and work to tend to, so her dress would be an after-hours affair. She had some ideas, and headed to the Finn's house to see Mary about them as usual.

The Finn home had always been a safe haven for Lillie. A place of complete acceptance and a strange calm, even though it was rarely quiet with all the Finn kids running around. Lillie would feel it before she ever turned a doorknob to enter and would carry it away with her for hours after leaving. That house was filled with love. It was quite elaborate for a farm home, like a house you might see in the heart of town, near the square. It was the same canary yellow that the sharecroppers' homes were painted, a favorite color of Mary's. Lillie loved how the Finn home was so elegantly simple at its core. It was actually just a big square on the inside and was built as functionally as possible. Not a detail had been left out as far as making the home easy to run went, and that had been all James in the design. He wanted life to be effortless for his wife and kids inside their home because he knew outside of it he had no control over the chaos of the world. At least inside of the house he could make his family feel secure.

Though the core of the house was simply designed, the outside was highly decorative. Long wooden planks framed out the house and ran horizontally all the way around, and the molding around each window was painted a crisp white, providing a nice contrast to the yellow, but with neither color competing for your eye. A large covered porch graced two sides of the house, and the roof line of the porch broke the facade of the house into two distinct stories. The porch roof was held up by short fluted columns, placed every ten feet or so, that met solidly built bases of brick work. Classic three-foot white balusters framed out the porch in between the brick bases and white columns, and were topped by simple white hand railing. Over the front door the simple porch line was disrupted by a large gabled roof. The gable was adorned with alternating styles of finishing shingles because Mary hadn't been able to make up her mind between the octagonal and diamond-shaped shingles, and James hadn't wanted to make her choose. He had instead installed both shapes and chosen to alternate them two lines at a time. From far away, the two shapes were indistinguishable, but to Lillie it was what gave the home so much character and complexity. To Lillie, it was James and Mary in a nutshell, and the kind of harmonious matrimony of two styles that she hoped to find with Clay.

A very large picture window adorned the front of the house and let brilliant light into the sitting area long into the afternoon. It was in that room that Lillie had waited while Mary's nurse finished her bath on the day Lillie had come to see her about her dress. Lillie stood, looking out to the porch, taking in James' handiwork and then breathing in the genius simplicity of it all. She instantly felt safe again, and although Lillie didn't know it at the time, it was one of the last times she'd ever feel that way.

"Lillie?" Peggy, the nurse, interrupted Lillie's thoughts as she invited her back to see Mary. "She's in a right bad state today, dear. So do be quick about it."

Lillie ignored her rude tone and climbed the staircase to the upper level. She hesitated outside Mary's bedroom door, her hand hovering over the round doorknob. She hadn't been sure if it was right of her to seek out Mary's approval of her dress... no, of her marriage plans. Mary knew her better than most, almost better than Josie, even, and if anyone could guide her she knew it would be Mary. Lillie turned the knob gently in her hand, feeling the door latch let go gently of its resting place and eased the door open quietly.

Her eyes adjusted quickly to the darkened room where she found Mary resting peacefully in her wood-framed bed, covered by several quilts. It struck Lillie as funny, considering how warm the room was, and then it struck Lillie as serious. Why was Mary so cold? She cautiously approached her bed and sat herself on the floor next to it. Lillie leaned her body into the mattress and placed her head near Mary's arm. She reached up under the covers and held Mary's hand as she slept, and Lillie wept quietly into her own shoulder.

The two women stayed like that for over an hour. Mary, in her tightly made bed, tucked in nicely, and Lillie on the dusty floorboards, sitting in an awkward sideways manner. The nurse had surprisingly been kind enough not to interrupt, and so lay the teacher and student, the young and old, the landowner and sharecropper's daughter. Mary, the master of true living, hand in hand with Lillie, the naive and complex young woman who took life as it came and accepted all that was handed to her, both good and bad, without blinking an eye. It was an odd pairing for sure, and yet somehow it all made sense. Mary's eyes finally fluttered open and quietly rested on the back of Lillie's head.

"Lillie? Is that you?" Her voice was weak, and her breaths slow and shallow. Her cancer had won the battle over Mary's will, and her body was slowly and quietly shutting down.

Lillie sat up and then stood up. "Yes, Mary, it's me. I hope it's okay I came to see you..."

"Good Lord, child, always." Mary smiled her big beautiful grin, and though it had lost some of its shimmer of the past few months, Lillie could see she was still there. "You come to tell me something?"

Lillie chuckled. "Josie told you already?" Lillie should have known, Josie couldn't keep a secret longer than a second or two.

"Well, you know my Josie. She was never known for lips of steel." Mary looked at Lillie with love and said, "Don't be cross with her, she was just excited for you. She said you seem real happy, Lillie."

"I am. I am, Mary." And Lillie was happy, and hopeful. As she looked around Mary's bedroom, she hoped she and Clay would share a room like that someday, one filled with memories, and babies, and love. She hope she and Clay would build a house just as sturdy, just as beautiful as James and Mary had. She was happy indeed. Lillie forgot all about her dress, the whole reason she had come in the first place, and instead she surprised herself and said, "Mary, I'm real happy, but I'm scared too. What if I'm not what he wants? I mean, what if I'm not who he thinks I am?"

"Lillie, child. Who else are you going to be? You can only be who you are, and Clay will be who he is. You can't change him, and he can't change you, unless you want him to. No matter what, you got to be you, through and through. That's what makes a good marriage, Lillie. Folks being real with each other and accepting each other." Mary paused, and thought for a second. "That, and remembering what I told you about seeing people."

"You mean how most folks just want to be seen?" Lillie thought back on their days in the sewing shop together and all the small chats they'd had. The chats that at the time had meant nothing, and in the end had meant everything.

"Yes, Lillie. You just work real hard at really seeing Clay, and making sure he knows you see him. You're good at that, Lillie. You work real hard at loving him through his rough parts, and even through the parts you may not like, 'cause those are there, child, somewhere. We've all got them. You do that and just be your beautiful self and I'm not sure how you can lose in it."

Those words carried Lillie through many rough days and hard moments. It was the last time Mary had imparted her wisdom on Lillie and the first time Mary had been wrong. Lillie had lost everything.

Chapter Thirty-Six

Lillie
Thursday, August 13, 1953
Close to midnight

Lillie finished describing her dress to Elizabeth with more enthusiasm than she had felt in a long time. Elizabeth soaked up every word, imagining Lillie in her glory, on one of the most precious days of her life. It made Elizabeth smile to think of her like that, all young and healthy and hopeful. She wondered where it all started going wrong for her.

"Lillie," Elizabeth said, when Lillie had finished telling her the story of her hurried wedding day and her handmade dress, "What happened to Clay? I mean, when did you start noticing him change?"

"Well, it was real gradual-like, Elizabeth. There wasn't any one moment that turned him ugly, but I guess a string of events over time. Funny thing is, I saw his ugly earlier than when all his bad behavior started, and I loved him anyway." Lillie sighed. "A curse and a gift."

"What do you mean?" Elizabeth asked. "You mean like all the little signs you had before your wedding?"

"No, it run deeper than that in me." Lillie thought about how to explain herself to Elizabeth, which was an odd feat for sure, considering that Lillie hadn't quite understood it about herself until recently. "Mary always told me I had such a gift, my mama did too. Both of them said they saw it in me from when I was little. I never did see it as a gift. It just was how I was."

"What is your gift, Lillie?" Elizabeth could have guessed it, but she wanted to hear it from Lillie.

"Well, I used to think I learned it from Mary, but truth is, it's just how God made me for some reason. I'm strugglin' with how to explain it to you 'cause I don't rightly understand it myself some days." Lillie paused and gathered her thoughts while Elizabeth waited patiently. "It's like if I see something real simple like a tomato, and it's all covered in dirt and has some rotted spots on it, 'ya know, from a critter or a mold or something. You might pick it up and throw it out, right? Before you even look at it closer."

"Probably so, Lillie. There are other tomatoes to be had," Elizabeth said matter of fact.

"See, that's how I sees it different. I'd right pick that tomato off the vine, same as the others, and put it in my basket, same as the others. It was still a beautiful thing to me. I'd wash it the same and dry it the same. I'd see its ugly parts, but to me it didn't mean the core was rotten, it just meant it had a few rough patches that could be dealt with. So I'd just cut it open and cut out the ugly in it and use the rest that was good."

"Is that how you see people, Lillie?" Elizabeth suddenly understood. Lillie simply saw things for what they were, both beautiful and ugly, both spectacular and appalling, and she didn't attach extraneous meaning to any of it. It was as if the core of every cell of Lillie's body screamed for balance, and when there wasn't balance to be found she always, mostly unknowingly, found a way to create it. That was simply the only way she could survive.

"Ya, that's right. We all got our ugly parts, but that don't mean we're worthless. There's good in everybody; and when you understand the ugly, it's not so scary or intimidating." Elizabeth knew she was talking about Clay now.

"So that's how you put up with him, Lillie? That's what made you stay all that time?"

"I'm not sayin' that's all that made me stay. There are lots of reasons for that, Elizabeth, but I'm saying I guess I saw Clay for Clay. I saw who he was, really saw, and I loved him anyway. I loved him through his ugly."

"But, Lillie, he didn't deserve it." Elizabeth was bewildered, and tried to imagine loving someone like that. "He was so cruel to you!"

"Well, that's where I went astray, I guess, Elizabeth. That's where I messed up real bad." Lillie sighed, and she felt tears sting her eyes. "I didn't get the part that you can love somebody and not let them mistreat 'ya. I didn't understand that just 'cause you see and accept someone for what they is doesn't mean that you gotta keep them around. I mean, a rotten tomato is still a tomato but it don't mean it's any good to anyone if the rotten bits are so many that they've taken over. Some of 'em belong with the compost, and there ain't nothing to be done about it."

"So is that how you put up with Clay like that for so long without losing yourself?" Elizabeth felt like she finally had answers to what she'd been wondering from the first day she'd met Lillie some weeks ago.

"No, Elizabeth, I think I done lost myself alright. Look at where I am. I'm dying alone, while my kids are in his care. I'm beginning to think I done lost my mind."

"I don't think you've lost your mind, Lillie. You're still in there, even if things look a little different now." Elizabeth didn't really know what else to say. She could feel Lillie's remorse hanging in the air.

Lillie too was at a loss for words. The only thing she was sure of was that she couldn't let go just yet. She still hadn't done what she told Little Red she would do, and until that time she would feel her shame covering her like a warm wool blanket on a hot summer night.

Elizabeth let Lillie rest after their chat about her wedding, and though Lillie tried to sleep, she found it difficult to relax. She thought of her wedding day again in vivid detail. She'd carried white daisies wrapped tightly around the base with some leftover ribbon she'd found in the shop. They were simple and pretty, and weren't boastful or overly elegant. They fit Lillie perfectly and took none of the attention away from her dress. She remembered how surprised Judge Hammond had been when he'd seen her in formal wedding garb. Most of the folks who married at the courthouse were farmers, or kin of farmers, who didn't have a dime to spare for the marriage license, much less a dress. And then there was Lillie, dressed to the nines and shining like a church bride. Clay had borrowed a suit from his cousin who, as it turned out, was decidedly many inches shorter than Clay and much larger in the chest. Lillie had offered to alter it, but Clay had shrugged her off, saying it was good enough for such a short affair. Lillie had felt differently about her dress. Even if the clock ticked and the wedding was over in the blink of an eye, she wanted her dress to be amazing. She wanted it to be timeless.

She kept it simple as well, but it fit her like a glove, which was no easy feat given her stoutness and the fact that she'd had to enlist Josie's help to pin it. Mary had insisted that Lillie use some of the silk fabric that she'd saved from Josie's dress and had given Lillie free reign on anything else she might find in the shop. Lillie decided on a tasteful ankle-length skirt and a simple, non-plunging V-shaped neckline. It was essentially sleeveless, though she'd gently capped the shoulders with the delicate wisps of lace that seems to float and flirt with her upper arms. She kept the rest of the dress plain, but tediously hand stitched together small pieces of leftover lace, the result of which was a stunning four-inch-wide belt of sorts that Lillie pulled around her middle and just under her plentiful bosom. She made it long enough so that it could be tied into a large bow in the back so that it would gently hug her voluptuous hips.

It was the one time that Lillie could recall Clay being speechless. When she pulled up in front of the courthouse in Josie's truck and got out on Josie's borrowed strapped shoes, she had looked up to find Clay standing on the walkway of the courthouse simply staring. In the moments just before they took their turn before the judge, Clay had taken her hand and squeezed it and said, to no one in particular, "You're beautiful." He'd always complimented her, but had never told her she was beautiful until then. She held onto those two small words for a very long time because she felt like she had finally been seen.

As the story goes, that didn't last too long, and Lillie often said it was as if his love for her had developed cataracts over time, making it difficult at first to see her and, in the end, damn near impossible. In the very end, he was so blinded by his rage that he couldn't see anyone anymore, much less his ailing and fragile wife.

"Hey, Elizabeth?" The room was much darker than it had been just moments before, but Lillie was starting to lose track of time. She cleared her throat when she'd heard no answer and tried again. "Elizabeth?"

She heard footsteps then from around the screen, and she closed her eyes as she waited for Elizabeth to come to her bedside.

"Miss Lillie, do you need something?" It was the nurse with the husky voice, the one who smoked Lucky Strikes and smelled heavily of perfume. It almost made Lillie gag.

She looked up at the older nurse and asked, "Where's Elizabeth?" Lillie felt panic setting in. Had she dozed off through her whole shift? Had she missed one of her last chances? She still had much to say, and she felt nauseated for a whole different reason than the scent of cigarettes mixed with perfume.

"She's just on a break, Miss Lillie. She'll be back real soon. Don't you worry none. Let me get you some water." The nurse poured her a fresh glass and then turned around and helped Lillie into a semi-sitting position. Lillie winced with discomfort at every move. She suddenly felt every open sore and raw spot, every tender joint and swollen tissue, and she lost her breath with the position change.

"You alright, Miss Lillie? You need some pain medication?" The nurse frowned in concern and wondered why Elizabeth hadn't medicated Lillie to the point of near sedation, given her state.

"Nah, thank you." Lillie didn't want to be any drowsier than her failing kidneys made her feel already. "I'm just a little sore, is all. Too much dancing in my dreams last night." She smiled half-heartedly, which made the older nurse smile.

"Alright then, Lillie, take in some water if you can, and I'll let Elizabeth know you're up and asking for her when I see her." The nurse didn't baby her, and she appreciated that. She left Lillie to sip the straw on her own, and Lillie savored every drip of the cool liquid as it hit the back of her tender throat. She wondered how much longer her body would hang on, how many more hours she had to do what she had promised. Then she began to formulate her plan. Her eyes roamed the darkened room searching for an answer, and they landed on the bedside table. It had a small drawer underneath where Lillie had seen nurses stash paper and fountain pens. It dawned on her what she needed to do, and she realized she needed to act fast before Elizabeth came back in the room. She reached out her arm and set the cup down on the edge of the bedside table, freeing herself for her mission.

Lillie could barely move on her own anymore, and after not having eaten for days she barely even had the energy to maintain the sitting position that she found herself in. But Lillie had spent the last year practicing mind over matter, focusing on the task at hand and not the pain or discomfort of her body. She could do this, no doubt, she just had to convince her muscles of the same. All she needed to do was push her body up to a full sitting position and then swing her legs over the side of the bed. From there she felt like she could lean forward enough to reach the side table and open the drawer. She took just a second to think about it because if she thought about it too long, she'd convince herself it was impossible. She wiggled herself up on her elbows and then wrists and pushed her backside up further in the bed. She felt the bedsore Elizabeth had been talking about and it felt as though her tailbone were ripping into a thousand tiny pieces, but she moved anyway as her breath caught in her throat with the pain.

Lillie wiggled and tugged at her legs, pulling and pushing them towards the side of the bed until she felt them fall one by one down the edge and dangle gently against the bedsheets. She took another deep breath and pushed herself up to a sitting position. Her world tilted and twirled and her vision doubled and blackened. She hadn't sat up like that in so long that her mind had no idea how to handle it. She closed her eyes, waiting patiently for her body to adjust, and she breathed in and out slowly, willing herself to finish what she had started. She was almost there.

When the room stopped spinning and her head cleared, Lillie gripped the sheet tightly with one hand and reached for the drawer pull with the other. She knew that one small mistake would land her on the floor and in a heap of trouble. She cautiously reached forward towards her goal and finally, after a few precarious moments, felt the metal knob of the drawer under her fingers. She tugged gently at the wooden drawer and let out a huge sigh of relief as it opened.

She had just enough room left to lean a bit further and feel around inside the drawer for what she was looking for. Her fingertips were numb and she had to concentrate hard to distinguish between one object and another, but when she finally felt what it was she was after she gripped the items tightly and fell back into the bed in a glorious heap. She laughed in spite of her pain and took a few seconds to catch her breath before she attempted to right herself in the bed. In a last push, she pulled her legs back up the side and tucked them under the sheets. They were so numb that she had to look down to make she had them fully under the sheets, the way they had been when Elizabeth had left her.

Lillie didn't take much time reveling in her success. She knew Elizabeth would be back any moment, so she immediately got to work. She gripped the pen in her gnarled hand and squinted her eyes as best she could in order to see that what she was writing was legible. She wrote a few simple lines on the piece of paper she'd grabbed from the drawer. When she was done she managed to toss the pen back into the drawer and got to work folding her note in half and then in half again and then in half again until it was small enough to fit in her palm. Just as she completed her last crease she heard footsteps coming. She quickly tucked the note under her covers and laid her head back. She was sweating profusely from her efforts and was slightly short of breath, but she felt triumphant. She closed her eyes, regaining her balance, and silently applauded herself. She had done it, she'd written down what she couldn't bear to say out loud, and all there was left to do now was to set the scene in motion.

Elizabeth entered the room quietly on light feet and was slightly confused by what she found. Lillie was breathing heavily and was moist with perspiration. She was positioned awkwardly in the bed, and the drawer to the bedside table hung precariously open. Lillie was quiet, with her eyes closed, but Elizabeth got the feeling that she wasn't really resting as soundly as it appeared. She looked at the bedside table and then at Lillie with wonder, but then shook her head as she decided it was impossible. Lillie couldn't possibly have had the strength. Hillary, the nurse that covered for her while she took her break, must have left it open. Elizabeth gently closed the drawer and took a closer look at Lillie.

"Lillie? You okay?" She gently rubbed Lillie's forearm as she spoke.

Lillie's eyes flung open, and she smiled in spite of herself. "Yup. I'm good."

Lillie looked at Elizabeth with a little excitement and a little trepidation. She decided that she had to tell her the whole story, but she just didn't know where to begin. She watched Elizabeth as she tidied the work station in the room. Lillie wasn't sure how to begin saying what she needed to say. "Elizabeth?" Lillie said cautiously.

Elizabeth looked up from the stack of linens she was counting. She caught the nervousness in Lillie's voice, and it piqued her curiosity. "Yes, Lillie? Is there something I can get you?"

"You got to do that right now? I wanted to tell you some things..." Lillie looked at the open cabinet and the stocking that Elizabeth had to do. She didn't want her in trouble, but what she had to say finally trumped all rules as far as she could tell.

Elizabeth didn't even hesitate. She quickly closed the door to the linen cabinet and approached the bed, pulling the doctor's stool with her. She sat close to the bed and gave Lillie an anxious look. "I'm all ears, Lillie."

Lillie sighed gratefully, and knew that God had given her Elizabeth as a last gift. A consolation prize for a lifetime full of woeful moments. "What I got to tell you, well, it ain't pretty."

"Life's not always pretty, Lillie. Look where I work, I know that. It's okay, whatever you've got to say is okay."

"I want to make you see Clay. I know you done got a feeling like you don't want to, but I need you to." Lillie knitted her brows, conveying her seriousness.

Elizabeth was confused. It wasn't what she expected to hear, but the one thing she had learned about Lillie over the last few days was that she didn't waste words. If she thought it was important enough to say, then it was probably important enough to listen to. "Okay, Lillie, go on…"

Lillie sighed with relief that Elizabeth was receptive, but her foggy head was making it hard to discern where exactly to begin. "Well, now, I can't rightly tell you just when he done turned bad. It wasn't any one moment or the next. Just one moment piled up on the next, I think, 'fore he couldn't breathe no more and bits of him died."

"Hmm," was all Elizabeth said, but inwardly she said: *I know what you mean, Lillie, how life just piles it on day after day and you feel like you are slowly suffocating.*

"Well now, most folks got a safety net when life gets like that, and if they's smart they take it when it's offered. I guess I tried to be that for Clay for a long time, but he just done use it against me instead, to tie me up, and tangle things." Lillie thought about the first time she she'd seen his rage, and how terrifying it had been to her as a young woman. "So I guess I started seeing changes in him just about a year after we was married. Now I ain't saying he was ever really lovey-dovey to start, that's just not Clay. But he was kinder and more patient, at least with me, anyhow."

"Did something happen, Lillie?" Elizabeth held her breath in anticipation.

"Well, nothing big just then, but a series of tiny things. My folks done moved into town in July, and they hadn't even loaded the first of their things in the truck before Clay was on the Finn's doorstep asking about a job. That was in late June of 1929. My daddy had been kind enough to vouch for him and sow the seed in Mr. Finn's mind, and with Mary gettin' worse, Mr. Finn took all the help he could get." Lillie thought back to the day that Clay had told her they could stay in Lillie's childhood home. He had been so elated, so awash with relief and excitement, and Lillie felt like she couldn't have loved him more. She was going to raise her family on the same worn hardwood floors and in the same cozy rooms that her mother had, and she felt as though she'd won the big prize at the fair.

"So anyhow, we moved Clay into my folks' old place and tried to make it our home. Clay worked real hard for Mr. Finn. Clay and Mr. Finn weren't real friendly like my daddy and Mr. Finn was, but they worked well together, and Mr. Finn done pay him more than his fair share for his work. Tell you the truth, I'm not real sure how much Mr. Finn paid attention to anyway. Mary got worse real fast over that summer. She had the cancer, of the breast they think, and it was just a-growing everywhere it could in her body."

"Oh, Lillie, how awful." Elizabeth had seen it many times, life coming to an end way too soon due to an unseen invader.

"It was hard, but I was glad to still be so close by, to be able to help her through it." Lillie thought about the days she'd spent doing for Mary what Elizabeth was now doing for her. Bathing her, listening, sitting at her bedside. "Ya, it was hard alright, but I wouldn't take a moment of it back for something easier."

"Did it take real long?" Elizabeth asked softly.

"No. By late August she had withered down to nothing, and she slipped away in September. Next to losing my babies, it was the hardest day of my life." Her sorrow was palpable even some two decades later. With hollow and weepy eyes Lillie remembered the sight of her friend and mentor lying still in her bed. Lillie sniffled quietly and continued. "But Josie and I got each other through, and Clay and Mr. Finn just threw themselves into working the harvest. Wasn't nothing else to do, really. They buried her on a Sunday and were busy working the next day in the fields. If you gonna cry about it, you might as well water them crops with your tears. No room for wasting anything, I guess."

Elizabeth held back own tears and sat quietly for a moment. Finally, she said, "I don't remember the Finn name when I grew up."

"Nah, you wouldn't. Mr. Finn done complete the season and then he couldn't take no more of being in that house without Mary. He had built it for them, 'ya know, and without her, it just didn't make no sense. So he decided to move up with his sisters to Louisville, up north yonder." Lillie paused and then added, "No one blamed him, we all felt her loss pretty big."

"What happened to Josie?" Elizabeth wondered out loud about Lillie's only real friend.

"Well, she and Matthew gave it a whirl at running the farm, but it didn't last too long 'fore they realized they was in over their heads. Mary and James left some big shoes to fill, and though Josie and Matthew tried, they just didn't have the same kind'a working relationship with folks as Mr. Finn had. Folks didn't trust Matthew like they had Mr. Finn, and they didn't work as hard for him. 'Cept Clay. The one good thing I can say for Clay is that he always worked real hard in the field." A hint of sadness touched her voice as Lillie recalled how quickly her "ideal" life on the Finn farm had come to an end. How everything had slipped away in a season or two. How she'd gone from being surrounded by family and friends who loved her to being alone with Clay, who tried to love her in his own way, but who had lost the fight with devil not long after their vows.

"So how long did you all live there, then? In your folks' old house, I mean?"

"Well, Josie and Matthew gave it just a few months before they figured they just couldn't do it. I think Josie just knew she didn't want to, but also that her husband wasn't cut from the same stock as her daddy. So anyhow, they put the farm and houses up for sale the next spring, and some big shot came down from up north and swooped it up pretty quick."

"They got lucky, then? I heard of farms sitting for sale for years and rotting away in the mean time."

"They got out just in time, before the depression done hit us hard here. Lucky don't really begin to describe it for them." Lillie held no jealousy about it, but had been tremendously sad to see the Finns leave, especially after her folks had moved into town the summer before and Mary had died. She remembered the day she suddenly almost found Clay and herself homeless. The day Josie had come knocking on her door to tell her the farm had sold. The day she first saw Clay's rage.

He broke her mama's jewelry box that day, the one she left with Lillie as a small wedding present. It was tiny and round and simple, much like Lillie, and was the prettiest item she owned. The value likely didn't exceed that of a few gallons of milk, but Lillie had loved it. It had been hers, and it made her think of her mama when she opened it each night to place her wedding band in it just before bed. She remembered standing timidly in the doorway of the bedroom that had been her parents' room for such a long time as she told Clay the bad news.

She watched quietly as Clay removed his socks and work trousers. He'd teetered on the edge of the bed, his long frame leaning over as he snagged the top of his dirt-encrusted socks between his fingers and yanked them unceremoniously off of his blistered feet. She watched him as he rubbed at his soles and picked at some dried skin on the side of his little toe, the result of a hard-earned callous. Clay had been so tired that day that it was as if he was in his own world, and he was certainly unaware of his young wife watching him from the threshold of the small room.

He stood up and unhooked the shoulder straps of his overalls, letting them slide down his back and allowing the bib to flap forward over his slight abdomen. He let loose the buttons on one side of his hip, and with no fleshy meat to hold them up the trousers came to an abrupt halt on the dusty wooden floor. As he stood there in his dust-covered white t-shirt and his faded boxer shorts and nothing more, Lillie felt compelled to tell him. Later she would wonder if she'd picked that moment because she'd known he couldn't rightly go running out the front door hollering at Josie and Matthew in nothing but his underthings, or if she chose that moment because he'd looked so tired and vulnerable and incapable of anger. Why ever she'd picked it, she'd underestimated his ability to spew his indignation in a half-naked state.

"So what did Clay do when he found out? I'm sure he wasn't happy!" Elizabeth broke into Lillie's thoughts once again as Lillie realized she'd let her mind drift back and had forgotten to take Elizabeth with her. She looked over at Elizabeth, who was perched on the edge of her seat with her eyebrows knitted tightly together as she tried to picture Clay's face, red with outrage and agitation.

Lillie chuckled. Not happy wasn't the half of what Clay had been. Furious, livid, and irate came to mind. "No, he was not happy at all, Elizabeth. He was every word opposite of that, and I think if his breath could'a done the speaking for him he would'a been shootin' bullets and fire outta his mouth, Lord help him. Well, actually, at first he didn't do nothing." Lillie remembered it more clearly as she spoke.

"What do you mean? He just stood there and didn't say anything?"

"Exactly that. He had his back to me at the time, see. He'd been undressing after a long hot day, and he was real tired. So tired I thought he might not have the energy to even be that upset about it. Boy, was I ever wrong. Ya, he just stood there. In his shirt and undershorts standing real tall-like and real still, and I wasn't even sure he'd heard me. So I remember I says to him, 'Clay, did 'ya hear me? Jos and Matthew done got themselves a buyer. We might have to be moving soon...' And he still didn't move none, even though I knows he heard me that time." Lillie shivered, remembering what came next.

"You alright, Lillie?" Lillie had gone pale and shook gently as if she were chilled. Her breath quickened as the memories flashed through her mind, and she struggled to control her body.

"I'm alright, I'm alright." Lillie slowly eased her breathing and continued. "I've seen Clay rage so many times, Elizabeth, but it ain't nothing like the first time I saw it. It was the most frightening thing I ever done seen. He stood there and then slowly lowered his head so his chin was restin' real nice on his chest, and then it's like his whole body filled up with something dark and devilish and he started gettin' real shaky-like. And then I saw him ball up his fists into tight little wads. I was real frightened he might hit me then, that he might blame me somehow."

Elizabeth sucked in a breath and realized that she'd been sitting there almost as tense, with her own fists balled up into tight little wads. The thought of Clay hurting Lillie sickened her, and yet Lillie's whole reason for being in the state she was in was because Clay had hurt her. Over and over and over. "So, he hit you then?" Elizabeth whispered it as if saying it too loudly would make it too real.

"Nah, not that time. Fact, he never hit me until several years later. He just exploded with words. He was cussin' and swearin' some things I ain't never heard before. My daddy had always said that that was the devil's talk and we shouldn't never have no reason to be using them kind'a words. Well, Clay's folks ain't never believed in that, I guess, because Clay sure knew a whole lot of them words! Then he went and took it out on my things. He whipped around real quick, with the eyes of a beast, I swear, and looked right at me. But I know he didn't see me, he just saw red, that's all he saw. He flung himself at my dresser top and chucked all my things clear across the room. They hit the wall and landed in a big old mess of a heap on the floor."

"Oh goodness, Lillie!" Elizabeth felt her eyebrows come together in a furrow.

"Ya, it was something to be seen. He just brushed past me in the doorway real hard and went sulking on the back porch awhile. All in his knickers and work shirt, if you can imagine that!" Lillie smiled a little at the memory of her long, lean, and young husband pouting like a child and practically naked on their back stoop. It had frightened her at the time, but today it sort of made her laugh to think of it.

"So, Lillie, why did that memory upset you so much a few minutes ago, then? I thought you was gonna tell me he did something awful to you," Elizabeth said, her voice giving away her confusion.

"Didn't he though, Elizabeth? I'd never seen him like that before. I thought at that point I'd had me a solid man. A little odd at times, but hard-working, and solid. I thought I had me a man more like my own daddy." Lillie understood Elizabeth's bafflement at her visceral response to the memory. After all, Clay hadn't physically hurt her.

She shifted a bit to look at Elizabeth and searched her friend's face for a clue how to explain it. "Elizabeth, he might not have left me all bruised up and he might not have shattered my arm, but he shattered my world. In that second he broke my heart. It's like thinking you is wearing a diamond and finding out it's just a fake and knowing that you got to find a way to love it anyway."

Lillie sighed, and then it occurred to her exactly how to explain it. "I remember sitting on the floor next to my dresser looking at all my scattered things, some of my only things, really, and my eye catching my mama's trinket box. She gave it to me on my wedding day to hold my wedding band when I couldn't be wearing it. 'To hold our love,' she'd said." Lillie smiled fondly over her mother's words. "Anyhow, I saw her box lying there with the hinge all broken and the top all cracked in two, and I started sobbing. See, I felt all cracked in two also, cause I'd always thought that box was made of real mother-of-pearl and it turns out it was just fake. They call it f-f-f—something starting with an f?"

"Faux, it was faux mother-of-pearl? Yes, some of it can look so real." Elizabeth had a few trinket boxes like that as well, items she'd been given on her birthday or at Christmas time. She knew just the material Lillie spoke of. "You thought it was real until then?"

Lillie laughed. "I know it sounds dumb and I know I probably knew it wasn't real, but I wanted it to be, so I made it real in my mind." Elizabeth nodded. She was starting to get the picture. "Turns out it was made of plastic! Pearlized plastic! Imagine that!" Lillie laughed louder at her young eye that had seen what it had wanted to see.

Elizabeth spoke over Lillie's laughter and said, "Ah, Lillie, I'm sure it was upsetting having your mama's box all broken like that."

"No, Elizabeth, it wasn't so much that, although it did upset me for awhile. Things is just things in the end. What upset me so was realizing that Clay was like that box."

"What do you mean? He was broken and fake?"

"No, he wasn't fake, he was who he always had been. I just wanted him to be a real man like my daddy so much that I didn't see that he simply wasn't. Until he broke for the first time, I just didn't know what kind of man I actually had, and by then, well, it was too late to do anything about."

"Why's that, Lillie? Why couldn't you have left?" Elizabeth's confusion was palpable and was slowly churning and turning into an anger over Lillie's inaction. Lillie should have left him right when she'd seen him for who he really was. She should have moved along with Josie and Matthew, or gone into town with her parents. She should have done something. That's what Elizabeth would have done. Lillie lay silently until Elizabeth prompted her with a clipped tone. "Seriously, Lillie, why didn't you leave him?"

"Because, Elizabeth," Lillie sighed and closed her eyes. She whispered the next few words just before she dozed off into a restless sleep, "Because I was three months late. I was pregnant, Elizabeth, and ain't no way Clay would'a let me leave with his child."

Elizabeth sat eerily still, taking in how Lillie's situation had started. So innocent, and sweet even, in the beginning, if even slightly naive. She imagined how Lillie felt stuck at that point. Even if she'd been brave enough to leave, Clay would have followed, he would have found her and he would have made her life even more of a living hell. He'd have taken her down anyway, perhaps in a different manner, but he would have found a way, and he'd have taken her family down with her. She pictured angry knocking on Lillie's parents door, and endless stalking in the town square, or the church, or anywhere Lillie may have ended up. A scary picture of Clay was starting to form in Elizabeth's mind, and even she felt slightly frightened by this man. A man she had never met, but who had, in an odd way, brought this intriguing woman into her life.

"Lillie…" Elizabeth was quieter than the indignation she had felt just moments before. Lillie's eyes remained closed, sealed shut by an emotional roller coaster of a day—and a failing body. Elizabeth stood up and closed her eyes, taking several deep breaths, taking in the mixture of smells that melded together to remind her of not only where she was, but also of what was really happening. Bleach, mixed with salty sweat, humidity mixed with the air from the circulating fan, her own lotion mixed with… mixed with death.

Elizabeth's breath quickened as she opened her eyes to look at Lillie. She frantically began sniffing the air as if she was trying to discern what was cooking in the kitchen. And then she caught a strong whiff of it as the fan clicked its way towards her and pushed the odor on its breeze. How had she not noticed it before? It was so distinct and so familiar that finally Elizabeth couldn't deny it. It smelled like cold hotcakes with maple syrup and an odd added fishy odor. It was horrific and familiar. It was the smell of impending death.

Chapter Thirty-Seven

Cate
Los Angeles, California
September 1950

Almost a year had passed since our visit to Michigan, and it had been relatively uneventful. We doted on Josefina, promoted the store, took weekend trips here and there to see something new, and all in all just settled into our lives in Los Angeles. We were blessed to again become godparents when Julia and Hector welcomed their second daughter, Carisa, just sixteen months after Josefina's first birthday. She was an easy baby with a mild temperament, and although the girls were close in age, she didn't seem to add any chaos to Hector and Julia's lives. It was as if she had been there from day one.

Our time with the girls helped us both to heal some from our own loss, and we thought about being parents less and less, though it never really went away. I made a very conscious effort to fill up the void I felt before it had a chance to grow and rip me open, yet I found it difficult and exhausting work. One day all those years of heartache just came to a head.

"You've got a letter, Cate. From your mom," Tony called down the hall from the front door as he took off his shoes. It was early September again, and we'd had a terribly hot summer—which was a little unusual for Los Angeles—and it seemed to want to linger into the fall. Tony came into the bedroom where I had been ironing a few things and wiped small beads of sweat from his forehead.

I was drenched, and thought I might be slightly insane to be ironing in this kind of weather, but it needed doing. "I swear, Tony, if next summer is anything like this one was we need to get some sort of a cooler."

"It's just a few months a year, Cate, not really that bad. Now Mexico, that's a hot summer." His shirt was moist around the collar and under his arms, and there he stood pretending it wasn't that hot. It irritated me.

I absentmindedly said, "Yes, and that's why we live here and not there." I finished a crease in Tony's black work trousers and moved on to one of my shirts.

Tony waved the letter in front of me. "Did you hear me earlier? Your mom wrote you. Unusual, isn't it? She usually just calls."

I was grumpy and hot, and I snapped, "Well, people do still write letters, you know. Doesn't mean anything is wrong." He raised his eyebrows in surprise; I rarely snapped at him. "Sorry, I'm just tired, and want to finish this before my make-up melts off."

He sat down on the edge of the bed and then pushed himself back towards the headboard until he was half lying down and half sitting up. "Do you want me to read it to you?" He slid his finger under the envelope flap and started to open it.

I sighed, "Sure. Better yet, you read it and give me the gist of it. I'll read it in full later."

"Hmm. You are tired, aren't you?" I ignored him. I didn't want to read the letter because I already knew what it said. So I continued ironing in silence as Tony read to himself. The only sound that filled the room was when he turned the paper over and then refolded it once he was done, shoving it loudly back into the envelope. The crinkling of it made my spine crawl, and I almost burned a hole in my blouse.

Tony lay there for a few minutes, not saying anything, until I couldn't stand it anymore.

"Well, aren't you going to tell me what she wrote?" I looked at him and noticed how red his face was. He was a cross between looking mad and thoroughly defeated. "Hey, you okay?"

"It just doesn't seem fair, Cate." He sighed angrily, and then continued. "How is it that a couple like your folks who are in their sixties can be awarded full custody of a young child and we can't even get our names on a list? Like we have the plague or something."

I stopped working then, pushed the ironing board towards the wall, and carefully unplugged the iron. I sat on the edge of the bed and looked out the window at the palm trees that lined our busy street. Even they seemed to be begging for mercy from the heat, and they were a tropical plant. They looked as saggy as Tony and I felt.

"Tony, it isn't fair. It won't ever be, but Diana is where she is supposed to be. And perhaps, though they are older, she is just what my parents need to feel alive again."

"But they already got to have children, Cate, and now they have another. And what do we have? A machine shop and a tiny apartment? Two beautiful goddaughters who, at the end of the day, aren't truly ours?" It was rare for Tony to feel so wronged. He usually blew most stuff off as meant to be and was always telling me to keep the faith. But with the passing years we were both feeling the strain of it. We were hitting our mid-thirties, and most of our friends who had children were deep in the depths of elementary school life. They were done birthing babies and were working on just raising them.

There was always such a conflict in our lives. We were ever so grateful for all we had: our things, our fortunate and successful business, our loving family, our goddaughters. Beyond that I knew Tony was my family, my only forever bond, and most days I did feel like he and I were enough. That if no one else entered our lives for the rest of our lives, we would both die knowing we lived a happy life. And then there were days when our gratefulness was shallow. Days like today, when the injustice of it all sliced through us once again and tore at the edges of what held us together. I was so confused sitting there that day, feeling like we'd been slapped in the face by fate yet again. Did I allow myself my anger and jump into the pity party that Tony was trying to pull me into, or did I stand up and refuse to join him?

I stood up carefully and slowly faced him. "We can't keep doing this. I'm done."

Tony looked panic-stricken. "Done? What does that mean?" He sat up a little straighter and leaned towards me.

"It means for years now we've held on to the hope and belief that we will be parents. I feel like some days we walk around each and every corner just expecting to run into our future kids. And every opportunity or child that we hear about that might need a good home we get excited about, and then we fall down with disappointment when it doesn't work out. You keep saying to have faith, but what I have is hope, and while it sounds like a good thing to have, it's slowly tearing me apart."

"Cate, I... I'm sorry. I just really want to believe..." Tony's eyes were wet with tears for maybe the fourth or fifth time in our marriage.

"Believe. Yes, my mom said the same thing. I believe we were meant to have an amazing life together, I'm just not so sure anymore that it includes having children. I feel like we keep waiting and holding back because our life will really start when we get our kids. Well, I don't want to do that anymore. I want to live now, like this is all there is. I want some peace at night. I need to let go."

"I thought we were living, Cate. I thought, well, all of our trips and adventures and time with Hector and Julia and the girls… was that not living to you? I mean, what I just said before, I was just feeling mad, we have so much. We are living, aren't we?" He looked absolutely crushed, as though I'd told him our lives were a sham.

I sat down beside him then and took his hands in mine. "Yes, love, of course we are, but only just. We've let these phantom children hang over us like a rain cloud for far too long. It's time to clear the air, is all. It's time we truly had some sunlight on our faces." I paused, and searched his eyes. All I saw was pain, and it felt terrible that I was the one inflicting it with my words.

"Tony, can you let go with me? For me, and us? If it is meant to be then it is meant to be, but we can't keep waiting around like our lives depend on this one thing."

A tear slid down Tony's cheek. "You're right, Cate. Of course. We need to move forward." He nodded slowly, letting it all sink in.

"You don't have to give up your faith, Tony. Just have faith that whatever comes our way is just as it should be, whether we understand it or not. We just need to put our best foot forward every day, and the rest is really out of our hands."

"When did you become so spiritual, Mrs. Otera?" He gave me a small smile, and I felt my Tony coming back to me.

"I'm not, per se. I've just come to realize that there is so much out of our control, and that trying to control it by worrying or whatnot just eats you up inside." I thought about that for a minute and then added, "And I never want to have that hollow empty look in my eyes like my mom has. Ever."

Tony kissed me then passionately and we spent the afternoon sweating and cuddling on our bed. We talked about nothing and everything, and sometimes we just lay there quietly, feeling each other breathe. By the end of the day I think we both felt a little lighter somehow, and for reasons other than the five pounds of water we'd lost due to the heat. We were letting go together, hand in hand, and it felt like just what we needed.

Chapter Thirty-Eight

Cate
Los Angeles, California
Early Summer 1951

"You know what we need?" Tony looked sharp sitting at our small dining table one morning in early June. I was frying up a couple of eggs before we both headed into the shop. Tony really liked his eggs, and though I was pretty tired of cooking the same thing every morning, he asked me for so little most days that I didn't have the heart to refuse him.

"What's that? No, no, wait... you think we need another adventure?" I laughed, only half joking. Any time Tony started out with *You know what we need?* he was up to something bigger than a walk on the beach.

His face fell a little. "How did you know?"

I came over and sat in his lap as he pretended that it bothered him that I was crinkling his work pants. I adjusted my pleated skirt so it fell evenly over my knees and coyly looked at him. "Because, Tony, I know you. What are you up to?"

"Well, first, you're burning my eggs, love..." I looked over at the frying pan to check and then jumped up when I noticed he was right, then flipped the eggs, rolling my eyes at him as I did so.

"You can cook them yourself next time if you don't like how I do it." I smiled sweetly at him. He made a face back at me. It was our playground banter that kept things fresh every day and made me so fond of my husband.

"No need to get all crazy, Cate. You haven't heard my idea yet." He was pouting at me, and I had a sinking feeling this *was* way bigger than a walk on the beach.

"I got a letter from my father. Well, Hector did, but it was to both of us. He has a business venture he's interested in, and would like our help."

"Like our help? How? Monetarily? Because Mexico is quite the commute, my love. And I can't do the weekend drives again like we did with Feather River. Hermosillo is, what? A twelve hour drive at best?"

"Yes, it is far, and yes to helping out with money, but…" He hesitated, and cleared his throat before continuing. "But it's going to require a great deal more than that, I'm afraid, and it's even more of a drive than Hermosillo. My dad is interested in purchasing a lead mine in Naranjo, Sinaloa."

"Where? And what? Lead?" Not what I expected at all. "Why lead?"

"It's down the coast a tad from my parents, and a bit more, well, inland. Cate, Mexico has been going through a transformation of sorts over the last couple of decades, as I'm sure you've heard my dad talk about. It seems everybody is moving away from farming and agriculture towards more industrial-type business. And there's a lot of growth in the cities, and it means a lot of construction."

"They need lead for that?" I was confused. Lead was in our gasoline. Lead was used in paint products. I wasn't seeing the connection.

"Well, it's used in building materials and soldering for pipes and such. Plus, where's there's lead there are usually other usable materials, and the government is investing in these type of things. They want the economy to keep heading up. They are heavily tariffing imports of most things and encouraging communities to become self-sufficient. As crazy as it sounds, it's actually a good time to own a mine in Mexico."

"It sounds dangerous and remote. No, it sounds like it's a good time to run for the hills." I plopped his eggs on a plate and brought it over to the table in an absentminded fashion. My head suddenly felt foggy, and I couldn't believe we were discussing another big endeavor already. I thought that Feather River had gotten it out of Tony's system, but I should have know that all it did was whet his appetite for mining.

"It does sound dangerous, but the good thing is it's already an established mine with known profits. Not huge, but the potential is there if it was managed better." He pushed his eggs around with his fork, lost in thought. "We wouldn't have to go right away. We have some time to get ready, but maybe it would be a nice fresh start for us."

"We need a fresh start?" It had been months since I'd had my meltdown in the September heat, and I'd felt refreshed ever since. I felt like I could breathe again for the first time in a long time, and I rarely found myself looking at other people with their kids and thinking that

I wished that was me. I didn't feel like I needed a fresh start. I felt like I'd had one already.

"Well, no. I mean, maybe." He put his fork down, and I could see he was so intent on our conversation that he was losing his appetite.

As I stood there watching my husband, I realized that he may have let go of the idea of our own children those many months ago, but it had left him with a void to fill. It was a void I couldn't fill for him, no matter how much I wanted to, and I could see the only thing that would heal this hard-working man of mine was more really good hard work. The kind of hard work where you sweat all day, wishing the day were over but loving it all the same, and collapse into your bed at night from exhaustion, only to get back up and do it all over again with a smile. That's the kind of thing Tony needed to fill his empty space. The shop was pretty much on autopilot, and most days he was so bored that he made work for himself just to keep busy.

"When?" I couldn't quite concede just yet to the idea.

Tony's face perked up a little bit as he looked at me and he raised his eyebrows. "Really?"

"No, I just said 'when'… Just like Feather River, I need more information, Tony. That's how I operate. You base a decision on what feels right, and I base it on facts and a little bit of what feels right. That's just me, and I think you know that. So you figure out the who and what and why of it, throw out some numbers, and then we can discuss it."

"You know most men just come home and tell their wives how it is. You? I have to fight for it." He smiled lovingly at me without a trace of malice in his voice.

"Well, I'm not most women. You know that too." I paused, then added, "And most men don't uproot their families to northern California to pan for gold or drag them down to Mexico to mine for lead. Most men buy a house and get a job and never move." I was smiling, and playfully crossed my arms over my chest and leaned back into the counter. It was my best *I'm still in control* pose.

"Well, I'm not most men. And I suspect you knew that the day you married me."

"Yes, yes I did. And I suspect you knew just who you were getting when you married me," I toyed back.

"Two peas in a pod, I guess." He smiled mischievously and added, "Kind of like lead mines and Mexico." I guffawed at his comment and took a tea towel off the counter, balled it up, and threw it towards him as he laughed and pretended to dodge my incoming projectile.

"Dear Lord, Tony! I said I'd think about it!" But I couldn't help but join in his laughter.

I have to give Tony credit. He knew that selling this idea to me was going to take some work, and he did his best to be persuasive. He put together a business plan of sorts and researched the success of some other mines in Mexico in order to show me it would be worth my while. The truth was that the minute I realized there was a void in Tony that needing filling, I had already decided that we would probably go, but I still wanted him to make sure it was a safe decision. We would have to live down in Mexico, after all, and it would mean time away from his brother and the girls. I had grown used to seeing Josefina and Carisa almost daily, and it would be a difficult thing to give up. Not to mention my sister-like relationship with Julia, which, over the course of the last few years, had been a lifeline. But Tony was my immediate family, and as much as we loved our goddaughters I realized we couldn't build our lives around them and they couldn't build theirs around us. We just had to do what was right for us for now.

By October a chill was finally settling in the air, and I had gone ahead and agreed to investing some of our money into the Mexico lead mine project—but I hadn't fully committed to the idea of living down there. The middle of the desert, which was fairly hot all year long, didn't sound like a good enough reason to leave Los Angeles and our lives just yet. Tony was patient, and was happy I was willing to at least invest funds. I think he felt as though, if we had our money in it, then I might be more convinced that we should be down there making sure we got a good return on our investment. My husband was nothing if not smart, and I, indeed, felt more and more of an interest in seeing what was going on in Mexico.

I ran down the stairs one early November afternoon to grab the mail and found an unexpected package. It was crumpled and dusty, and I could barely make out who it was from. I licked my thumb and ran it over the return address, and my heart skipped a beat. Tony's dad had promised us photos of the mining area so we could get a better sense of where it was we might eventually move, and the pictures had finally arrived. He was an incredibly kind man, albeit a tad overly so. I think he wanted Tony and me to come down and be a part of the mine so badly that he tried to soften the blow for us early on. He'd told us we'd be comfortable, much more so than how we'd lived up at Feather

River, and that there was a house on the mine's property that had a swimming pool. He'd left a few minor details out, and the first images of it were not exactly exciting. In fact, I think "horrifying" was more the word I'd use.

"Oh my heavens, Tony." I stood in the front doorway of our apartment with my mouth hanging wide open.

Tony came from the bedroom into the living room. "Cate, close the door behind you, love, the cold air from the stairwell is getting in." He stopped talking when he saw my face and he realized what I must have in my hands.

"Is that them?" His face lit up, and he was clearly excited by getting a first glimpse at our investment. He'd talked my ear off for weeks about the ins and outs of lead mining and had been impatient to see what our money had purchased.

"Yes, but Tony..." I couldn't even speak I was so confused. "Tony, these photos, are they, well, are they of our lead mine?" I held them out to him and stood frozen in the threshold with the door agape. Small breezes kept catching the edge of my blouse, causing it to flirt with my waistline and allowing my slip to peek out.

Tony approached me cautiously and took the pile of photos from me. He pulled me into the apartment gently by taking my hand and closed the door behind me by kicking it with his heel. He stood next to me, flipping through the ten shots that his dad had developed and mailed. He kept flipping through them until pure exasperation hit his face and he collapsed into the couch.

"I don't understand, Cate. He told me it was already an operational mine! I promise! I hope you know I would never have gotten us in if I knew." He suddenly perked up and sat on the edge of the couch. He leaned forward and said, "Wait! Cate, these must have been taken a long time ago. These must be old photos."

"No, Tony, look at the date printed on the side. They were taken last month, or at least developed last month." I had already looked, and Oct '50 was clearly printed on the borders of all of the pictures.

"I can't believe my father would do that! There must be some mistake, Cate." With his eyebrows furrowed and lips pursed into a bit of a scowl, his face revealed a feeling of betrayal and confusion.

"No wonder he hasn't called. There are no lines out there. Heck, there's nothing out there. I don't even see an outhouse." I picked up a photo of what looked to be a half-built house. It was brick and had several window openings built in already, but no roof, and certainly no plumbing. "I mean, I lived better in Kentucky when I was just a farm kid. At least we had well water. And a roof."

"Is there a note?" Tony's voice was flat, and I could tell he was disappointed beyond belief.

I pulled open the dusty envelope again and coughed because of the cloud of dust it sent up my nose and mouth. Stuck to the side there was a note, and I carefully pulled it out. It was written in Spanish and clearly written with the intent that Tony would read it and not me. I was starting to seethe. It was so unlike his father, and all I could feel was hoodwinked.

"Here, I can't read this. My Spanish isn't that good yet." I had been learning Spanish from Tony and Hector slowly, but I spoke and understood it better than I was able to read and write it. I handed him the paper and he sat very still, reading the note while still perched on the edge of the couch. It was a short note, but it seemed like it took him forever to read. When he was done, he sighed heavily and looked at me with a bit of relief in his eyes.

"Ah, well. That explains that." I could tell he was trying to figure out how to translate his father's mistakes into language that his angry wife could grasp.

"Do I even want to know? No way I'm living there, Tony. It doesn't even have a roof." I was fixated on the no roof thing and I'd taken my *Cate's mad and not really interested in what you have to say* pose, which generally meant that I tucked my arms tight across my chest, steeling myself for the worst.

"He basically says the original mine was in pretty bad shape. The land around it was over-mined and caused a few sections to collapse. Whoever built it wasn't necessarily the best geological engineer, apparently. The house in the pictures has a good foundation and there's already a pool built. Not filled, but built. He says the equipment at the original site was in decent shape, but that they could certainly use my help or Hector's to really get it running smoothly. He says he's got ten workers who are great at manual labor, but not so great at figuring out how to build a new mine."

"So, basically, he is starting from scratch." I paused, and thought about what it really meant. "And he needs you, because without you, there's no lead mine."

"Yes, but the bones of it all are there. I could go down and survey and make a plan and just check in every now and then. I could do a lot of it from here and then just check on progress. I could..." I started ignoring him then and walked out of the room and into our bedroom, where I flopped down most unladylike and buried my face in a pillow.

A few minutes later I could hear Tony's light-footed steps on the hallway vinyl. Then I could smell his cologne, which for some odd reason always reminded me of Feather River because it smelled earthy and airy at the same time. Today, though, it just made me mad. I felt the bed sink down as he sat on the end of the it, and I tried to just steady myself and breathe. I could feel a ray of sun hitting my back and I could feel Tony's eyes on me. Both felt warm, yet I was chilled to the bone.

"Cate, what is it? Is it really that bad?" His voice was soft and velvety, and if I wasn't so mad at him I might have found it sexy.

"No roof, Tony. No. Roof." It was muffled as I spoke into my pillow, but I think he got the picture. I sure had.

"Cate, you know there will be a roof. So it's not about that." He waited for an answer, and when one didn't come he asked again. "What is it, Cate?"

I flipped over slowly and stared at the ceiling, trying to sort out in my head why I was feeling so mad; and then I suddenly just knew. I propped myself up on my elbow and looked at Tony. "It means you are going by yourself. If we are going to recover any sort of money on this deal, then you are going alone."

"Yes. It would mean that. At least for a small amount of time. Just until the house there is finished." He sighed heavily, and his shoulders dropped as he added, "Or, we walk away."

I was shocked. "You would do that?" It was all we had talked about the last three months. We had planned together and gotten things set at the shop so that everything would go smoothly in our absence. We had started to dream again together, and although I had thought that we still had an option to decide about the mine, I realized we had decided many weeks before, as we felt our hearts really starting to heal completely.

"I would. If that is what you need." He wouldn't look at me, and kept playing with the edge of the bedding with his foot.

We sat in silence for many, many moments as I let his words slide over me and under me and into me. He would give up his latest dream if I said I needed him to.

"No." I said quietly. "We can do this. We can find a way." I was solid in my answer because I knew it was the right one.

"Really? Cate, I promise I'll get that house and pool up and running first thing so you can join me. I promise. We might not have running water out there, but we can do pretty good with a well. It's not ideal, but you know it can be done. Just give me a month or two and I'll have you by my side again."

"That's all I really ever want, Tony, to be where you are. So, if it's here, or Mexico, it makes no difference, I suppose." I curled up next to my husband and hugged him from behind.

Tony pleaded with Hector and Julia for their help, and while it was unusual, I joined in to try to persuade them. Julia and I could handle the shops for a bit, I said. They practically ran themselves anyway, and with the two of us working together we could cover it. I was practically over at their house every day anyway helping with the girls, so Julia would be well taken care of. Tony promised all of us it would be no more than two months. He needed Hector's machinery expertise because he felt like that's where he was stronger. Though he felt confident in his engineering knowledge, it had been a while since he'd put it into practice, so he wanted Hector's input there too. Tony pleaded with Hector that this was their big chance to put all that knowledge to work. Tony's pull over Hector was strong this time, and I think after two babies and a couple years of working the store, Hector needed the adventure of it too.

Tony and Hector left two weeks after the photos arrived, just before Thanksgiving. It wasn't the best timing in the world, but Julia and I made due and put together as good a feast as any with the rest of the family who were around. It was the first time I'd ever been away from Tony, and on a holiday to boot, and I realized I never wanted to be that far away again. There was nothing at all to fill that void, no matter how much I tried—and I didn't want to try, anyway. The ache of it made me love him even more.

We all agreed it would be best if the house and mine were in close proximity to each other so that meals would be easy to prepare and serve. If someone needed a break from the underground once the mining started, they'd have a place of revival. It made more sense for security, too. We'd always be close to the work site at night, so wanderers wouldn't get any ideas about stealing the ore that we'd worked hard to bring up.

So, Tony surveyed the land around the half-built house, and was pleased to find a downhill grade that he felt would work rather nicely for the mine site. It was literally yards away from the house. It meant that once I was there I would never be far from his side. The thought of that alone got me through the long weeks of him being away over the holidays.

True to his word, he pushed hard for a finished house and a working well before anything else. To his delight he found he had a willing crew that worked as hard as he'd been promised. The house was finished in a matter of three weeks, and though it was more of a primitive dwelling than a house, it was enough shelter that we would be comfortable. It was brick-framed, with a wood-beamed roof that was then covered with sheets of corrugated tin. The windows weren't windows in terms of glass and screens. They were more like large openings strategically placed to allow the best breeze through and keep the inside cooler than the outside. It was Tony's version of a cooling unit, and it worked so well I wish he had had some input in the design of our apartment as well. There were large wooden window coverings that hinged at the top, and we could prop them up and open during the day and still get some privacy at night.

Tony also built out a large porch that was made from roughly cut wooden beams and covered thatch-style to keep it cool. I found in the months to come that I spent most of my time on that porch, preparing food or cleaning clothes, and it reminded me of both of my grandmothers and my mother, who seemed to have lived on their porches in the summer time back in Kentucky. Once I was in Mexico I understood it better. No matter how great a ventilation system Tony had put in, when it was over a hundred degrees outside, the best place to be was under the covering of the porch with a cold rag on the back of your neck.

The well went in shortly after the house was done, and I traded places with Hector just after the new year. While I knew I would miss Julia's sweet company, and of course her girls, I was excited to go. Hector had done a heck of a job fixing up the large motor that would be the heart of the mine. Even though he hadn't invested in it like we had, we promised him a fair share of the first bit of earnings from it. He was terribly humble and professed that it wasn't necessary, but I suspect he was thrilled with the prospect of taking home a large sum in the future to his girls, and was grateful to be repaid for his time away from home.

I had never been to Mexico before my move down there, though I'd heard lots of stories. To say I was nervous as I prepared to go is an understatement. When I say move, I really mean move. We knew this was to be a permanent situation at least for a year or more, and it required a lot of tying up of loose ends and the packing up of our lives. We decided to give up our apartment, seeing that we wouldn't be there for such a long time, yet it was still incredibly hard to see all of our things in boxes that were labeled "kitchen" or "living room." I managed to sell a lot of our furniture, and I had quite a haul that I hoped to bring down to Mexico with me. That still left a lot of boxes with no home. Hector and Julia once again opened their doors to us—or at least our things—and stored our boxes in their overly crowded garage without question. It was just how his family was.

Tony came back up to Los Angeles with a truck to bring me down. As we loaded the last of our things onto it and locked our apartment door for the last time, we were both a little bit choked up. It was the only place we had ever lived together, and we had had so many hopes and dreams for our lives in that little place. We had dreamed of bringing home babies there and raising them until the walls closed in and got too small. It turned out our world was too small instead. As the lock caught in the door jam for the last time with a loud click, he looked at me and I looked at him, and he said, "Well, that's it then. Done."

"Yes, done." We both knew what we meant.

"On to something new, then?" He held out his hand to me just as he had done the first night we'd chatted at the USO dance, and I gladly placed my hand in his yet again.

"Yes, of course. Let's dance." We held each other's hands tightly as we walked down the flight of stairs to the idling truck that waited at the curb to whisk us off on our next adventure.

Chapter Thirty-Nine

Lillie
Friday, August 14, 1953
6:00 a.m.

Elizabeth gathered her things as the clock ticked closer to the end of her shift. Lillie had fallen into a deep, coma-like sleep, and Elizabeth feared the worst. She feared it was her final sleep, a sleep well earned, no doubt, but a sleep that was coming slightly too soon. She felt unsettled and uneasy, as though the few stories she'd heard of Clay were merely the tip of a very large iceberg. An iceberg that, like the captain of the Titanic, she might never see. An iceberg that had already shattered Lillie's world, and that Elizabeth feared had more damage to do if it was not properly recognized.

Within minutes of the shift change, she could hear the rustle of fresh nurses and the gurgling of freshly brewing coffee on the floors below her. She was exhausted, and it was all she could do to hold herself up on the wall in the corner of Lillie's room. She hadn't drawn the curtains, nor done her last set of vitals. She hadn't freshened Lillie's water, nor tidied her area. She'd simply let Lillie sleep, hoping and praying against all that was natural that Lillie would live through one more day.

Elizabeth started when she felt a light brush on the side of her arm. She looked up to see Ada Mae with a soft, kind smile on her face and a sympathetic and understanding gaze in her eyes. She smelled of soap and lavender, and the mixture of her warm look and her inviting scent reminded Elizabeth of her late mother. She felt the emotions of the past few days release themselves though her tear ducts and brim on her eyelashes, and though she tried desperately to wipe the tears away before Ada Mae noticed, the older nurse caught her hand and gave it a knowing squeeze.

"It's okay, Elizabeth," Ada Mae said with such authority that Elizabeth stopped short and looked up at her.

"I'm sorry, I just, I... I'm not sure what's come over me." Elizabeth was at a loss for words, something that rarely happened to her. But then, she rarely cried at work either.

"Elizabeth, come." Ada Mae took Elizabeth by her elbow and led her gently towards the stairwell. She guided Elizabeth towards the courtyard, smiling politely at her passing coworkers and nodding towards the early morning visitors who'd come to see the few children who occupied the pediatric ward on the floor below. Elizabeth saw none of them clearly. They were all merely shadows in the background. She didn't smell the coffee brewing anymore, and didn't notice the scent of the scrambled eggs, bacon, and hotcakes being made in the kitchen that wafted down the corridor and found its way through the dusty vents. She vaguely saw her feet as they followed Ada Mae may out of the back door and into the small courtyard that lay between the main building and the annex. Even as she found herself sitting beside Ada Mae on the cracked wooden bench that had been dedicated to some mayor or another, she couldn't remember how she'd gotten there.

Ada Mae handed her some tissues and sat quietly as Elizabeth attempted to regain her composure. The spot on the bench was shady and cool as the morning sun started to rise up over the eastern part of the building. She could hear the whistle and chirp of the cardinals in the large maples and oaks that towered overhead. It was rhythmic and loud, like an alarm clock trying to awaken her from her sorrow. She steadied her breaths to their high-pitched cadence and soon found her eyes dry and the world around her coming into focus. She sniffled slightly and shifted uncomfortably on the bench as she realized what a scene she'd just made. Her grief turned to embarrassment as she looked over quietly at Ada Mae, who sat stoically with her hands folded in her lap. She was quiet, her face and shoulders relaxed, as she sat next to Elizabeth without judgment.

In that moment Elizabeth couldn't have appreciated anyone more. She hadn't negated her feelings, shushed her sobs, or told her how to feel. Ada Mae had simply gracefully taken Elizabeth's hand, led her to a safe place, and allowed her to feel what she was feeling. It was the greatest gift of validation that anyone had given Elizabeth in a long time. A gift that Elizabeth knew Ada Mae extended to others daily. She had seen her in her work with patients and families; she had witnessed so many moments of Ada Mae's quiet presence, and yet she had never been the recipient until now.

"Do you want to talk about it?" Ada Mae's stern voice broke the silence.

Elizabeth sniffled, wiping delicately at her nose. "I'm not sure, I just..." Elizabeth never really talked with anyone except for Rose. She rarely gossiped or shared information that wasn't hers to share. "I'm not sure it's proper if I..."

Ada Mae cut her off coldly. "If you what? Talk about a patient?" Ada Mae wiggled slightly on the bench, an uncomfortable shuffle, an awkward movement. "Well now, I usually would agree with you. I know some of these gals round here make sport of chatting about who is in here for what and who is from what kind of family and whatnot. Ain't right, if ya ask me, but then again, nobody really ever does that."

Elizabeth looked up at Ada Mae, and a small smile started to form on her lips. She started to laugh a little bit, thinking about how her coworkers were worse than a bunch of hens at feeding time. Cluck, cluck, peck, peck, peck. No one was safe from being talked about once they got going. Elizabeth had just learned to tune them out, and she suspected Ada Mae had learned to do the same. "Can you imagine, Ada Mae?" Elizabeth laughed out loud. She straightened herself up into a most arrogant pose and looked down her nose at Ada Mae and said, "Pardon me, do you mind if I pretend I've got life all figured out so I can talk down about just about everybody I ever met?"

Ada Mae laughed a hearty laugh and added, "Never mind that my own daddy is a farmer or a limestone miner. I'm a nurse, and that surely makes me better than all y'all needing care here."

Elizabeth's laughter rang out and hit the sides of the building with such force that it made her laugh even harder.

"That just about sums it up!" Elizabeth said once her and Ada Mae's laughter had died down a bit.

Both women sat side by side, wiping at the tiny tears that had found their eyes from their outbursts. Finally Ada Mae said, "You know, Elizabeth, I kind of know Lillie—and her husband Clay, too. I met her before, some years back."

Elizabeth's smile froze as she turned towards Ada Mae. "You have? When? I mean, where?" Elizabeth's mind raced with the possibilities. Ada Mae was around Lillie's age; maybe she knew her as a child. Maybe she knew Clay.

"I had just started working here when her daughter Ada got hit by a bus. Lord, she must'a been six or seven at the time. It was probably about ten years ago, I guess. Anyway, I took care of that little girl for days and days. They wasn't sure she'd make it at first, she'd lost so much blood..."

"Oh my gosh!" Elizabeth surprised herself with her outburst. "Her stories are true! Lillie's stories are true! Well, what am I saying, of course they are. I just, I mean, I've only heard things from her and from a few folks in town who knew her years ago, and I guess I'd sort of hoped that they weren't true."

Ada Mae knitted her eyebrows in confusion. "You hoped she'd made it all up?"

Elizabeth sighed. "No, I knew she wasn't telling tales, but the things she's told me about Clay so far—I guess I was hoping she was exaggerating..."

Ada Mae snorted. "Not likely. He's not a real nice guy, and that's being kind, to say the least." Ada Mae went quiet for a few moments, pondering what to say, and then a tiny smile played on her lips as she looked at Elizabeth. "I can tell you a bit more, if you want. Long as you don't think me a clucking hen like the rest of them."

"Oh goodness, no. I mean, yes, please tell me whatever you know, and no, of course I won't think you a gossip. I just need to know, Ada Mae. I need to know her. I can't tell you why, but I do."

Ada Mae shifted uncomfortably. "Well, alright then. Like I said, I was just new to town here, came down because my husband got himself work at the courthouse. Worked out real well that this hospital was here and needing help. We ain't got no kids, see; wanted 'em, but the Lord didn't see fit to give us none. So I just worked a lot, worked real hard and gave my patients most of my attention. I just felt like I ought to be taking care of someone, I guess, if I wasn't gonna have no kids of my own. So I volunteered for all the pediatric patients. I needed them, I guess. Those kids got me through some real dark days."

"I suspect you saw them through some real dark days too, Ada Mae," Elizabeth said gently.

Ada Mae sniffled and dabbed fiercely at her eyes with her handkerchief. After all those years of waiting and wanting a child, she never did have one; and even now, years later, it still stung.

"Anyhow, enough about me." Ada Mae sat up tall and continued. "I had seen Lillie around town a lot before Ada's accident. She was always real nice, saying hi to folks and all. Always had some of her brood with her. And everyone seemed to know her, so I was assuming she'd grown up around here, though I never did ask no one. Didn't like gossiping even back then. Lord, look at me now, running my mouth like she's my business."

"It's okay, Ada Mae. I don't think Lillie would mind. I think she wants me to know her story. She needs me to, for some reason."

"Well, alright then. Still don't feel right." Ada Mae sighed and continued. "Anyhow, turns out Lillie'd moved here when she was just a youngin', and she used to work at with a local seamstress, though I can't recall her name..."

"Mary. Mary Finn." Elizabeth whispered it. It had all been true.

"I never did know her. I think she'd passed long before I ever came round. No one ever did revive that little shop of hers, it just sat there empty-like." She paused, shifting her thoughts to Lillie's daughter. "Well, I was on duty the day her Ada got hit by that bus, and I was there every day after taking care of her. I just felt bonded to that girl, can't tell you why, but I just couldn't leave her lying there getting handed from one nurse to the next. Don't get me wrong, I went home to bed each night, but I didn't sleep much. I felt like my head and heart were still on the peds ward. Still with little Ada." Ada Mae thought about the young girl from her past, her moon-round face and blonde curly tendrils. "Much like how you feel about Lillie, I suspect. I can still see her in my mind like it wasn't but last week, that little girl. And her mama, Lillie, well, she never left her side."

Ada Mae's mind was engrossed now, thinking back to those volatile days of not knowing if the young girl was going to walk again, or, for that matter, if she'd even wake. She'd seen some gruesome accidents in her time with adults, as farm life offered ample opportunity for injuries and mistakes. But she hadn't seen anything like that with a child before little Ada. Her leg had been so mangled she remembered thinking it looked a bit like road kill mixed with the roots of an old tree. Not something anyone should ever think about a six year old's leg. She remembered almost having to have Clay removed by the police for the scene he made at Ada Mae's bedside about four days after she was struck. "But that husband of Lillie's, Clay... He wasn't here but a couple of minutes, and even then it was just to make trouble for Lillie. He was more concerned that his household was in chaos without Lillie home than with how little Ada was doing."

"Hmm." It was all Elizabeth could manage. Her thoughts were racing, and she held onto every word that slipped through Ada Mae's

312

lips.

"I can still remember him threatening Lillie, and I can still see Lillie flinching at his words, yet holding her ground. Clay had indeed threatened her. 'Woman,' he said, 'she don't need you here, she done got these here women treating her like a princess or something. She done be taken care of. You best be gettin' your backside home by tonight, or I promise you, you see my wrath like you done never see!'"

Elizabeth shuddered. What did that mean? Or even more, what did he do when she did come home? Ada Mae continued, her voice fierce now, her anger rising like it was happening all over again. "He came 'round three or four times, and by the last time, he'd all but come undone. Fire in his eyes and spittin' nails at her with his words. He was so red in the face I thought he might just do in his heart right there, God willing. Only way we got him to leave and stop coming was by tellin' him we'd warned the police about him and that if he came around threatening Lillie and disrupting Ada's treatment again, he'd find himself in jail. Apparently he and the sheriff weren't on real good terms from his younger days, so that got him moving along real fast. He never did step foot in the hospital again. Not even when Lillie had her last baby here a few years ago." Elizabeth remembered that story, too; how she'd done it all alone.

Elizabeth breathed deeply, and then asked Ada Mae, "How long was she there? How long did you take care of Ada?"

"Well, I can't rightly remember, exactly. Couple of weeks, maybe? I tell you what though, Ada should'a stayed longer. A lot longer, but apparently, from what I heard anyway, Clay turned his attention to the head nurse, threatening he'd sue them all for keeping Ada without reason to try to get more money outta him. The hospital knew they couldn't pay the bill anyway, and so they let her go home, on a borrowed pair of crutches that were the wrong size. Poor child, that one. They never did have her leg fixed right, from what I heard…"

"No, I know. Lillie said Clay sued the bus company, but she didn' t know how much he got. He surely didn't pay back the hospital or use it to fix Ada's leg, and Lillie could only give a good guess at what he' d spent the cash on." Elizabeth remembered all Lillie had said. "Do you think he made good on his promises? Do you think he hurt her badly after Ada finally came home?"

Ada Mae sighed, "I will tell you this, and maybe she told you already. Lillie was pregnant at the time. Very, very pregnant, though I think 'cause she's such a large woman, most people didn't think much about it. Anyhow, I heard, and I can't confirm this, Elizabeth, but I heard Lillie lost that baby about a week after she got home with Ada."

Elizabeth was silent, reeling from the impact of what she'd just heard. Baby Nathan. The second son Lillie had lost. The baby that Lillie had rocked and cried hysterically for just weeks before. "Are you saying it was Clay's fault? Lillie said he was a big baby, that her diabetes was probably what went wrong with him."

"Well, that might be so, but rumor went round that she lost that baby due in part to Clay using Miss Lillie's abdomen as a punching bag. Payback for her not coming home when he said so."

Elizabeth felt the wind leave her lungs, as though she herself had been punched in the gut, and her head spun from the thought of it. "Why? Why did people think that?"

"Well, her midwife, Margaret, said..." Ada Mae stopped and shook her head, her hands covering her face in embarrassment. "Lord listen to me go, I'm just as bad as those clucking hens. I guess I been listening as much as they been talking all these years. I shouldn't be..."

Elizabeth interrupted, "Wait, you know her midwife? Who was it?" Elizabeth knew all the midwives in town, as most of them rotated through the hospital to train up or help out now and then, and the laboring mothers were some of Elizabeth's favorite patients to tend to. When Ada Mae didn't answer right away, she demanded in her sternest voice, "Who was her midwife, Ada Mae!"

Ada Mae startled at Elizabeth's commanding tone. "Margaret. Margaret Nevels. Did you know her?"

Elizabeth knitted her eyebrows, thinking hard, running through her mind's card catalog of folks she knew. She'd thought she'd known just about every midwife in town, but was finding out day by day how little she really knew about anything. "No, I've never heard of her before. She live around here?"

"Nah, she used to, but I heard she done passed last year. Her heart or somethin'. Don't suppose you'd'a known her anyhow. She didn't wander much into the hospital. She preferred to do her work out in the fields, working mostly for the country mothers, farmers' wives, sharecroppers' wives, and the like. Women like Lillie. She delivered every one of Lillie's babes except her last one. The good doc here tended to that one 'cause of her losing those boys."

"Mmm hmmm." Elizabeth was lost in thought. She wanted to know every last detail about Lillie, and she was quickly realizing how impossible a task that would be, given the time Lillie had left. "So... why did Margaret think Clay had something to do with losing Nathan? Lillie said he had been a really big baby. That they'd had to break his collar bone to get him out. She said it had been her sugars..."

"Well, that might well be part of it, Elizabeth. Again, I'm not saying that any of that gave that little one a good chance at life, but I remember hearing how Margaret had found all these bruises on Lillie's belly when she'd come to tend that birth. How Lillie had played it off about how clumsy she'd been in the weeks before, being so tired and all 'cause of Ada. How much bleeding Lillie said she'd had in the week before she delivered. I remember real well how distraught Margaret was about Lillie losing that boy, but I remember even better how adamant she was that something more than just Lillie's diabetes had caused his death."

"He punished her," Elizabeth whispered definitively. Clay had punished Lillie, and she'd paid the ultimate price. Her mind reeled. She'd imagined a push or a shove here and there, harsh words and a devil-like fury. She knew about the frying pan incident before Connie had left. But never did she imagine he'd be so cruel as to beat up his pregnant wife for wanting to stay by her daughter's side. With downcast eyes and a brokenhearted feeling, Elizabeth said, "Funny, I've been wondering why Lillie never stood up to Clay. Why she let him bully her over and over. Why she never tried to leave. They say hell hath no fury like a women scorned, but in this case, I think hell hath no fury like Clay when Lillie stepped out of his lines."

Ada Mae sat quietly, her hands resting gently in her lap, her face pensive and disturbed. Finally, she turned to Elizabeth and said, "Where was she to go, Elizabeth? Her family had left, she didn't drive, and she was a housewife on a tobacco farm. She has seven kids all in all. Where was she to go?"

Elizabeth's eyebrows arched in surprise. "You know all that?"

"I spent a lot of time with Miss Lillie those weeks that Ada was with us. We spent a whole lot of time talking. I understand how you feel so connected to her, why you like her so much. I understand more than you think..."

Elizabeth sighed, feeling defeated. "It just makes her seem so helpless, so incredibly weak and pathetic. And she isn't. I just don't understand, she isn't any of those things."

"No, she's not, but she's also just a woman, who tried to do the best she could, given the life she found herself in."

"Yes, I know she did. I mean, I can tell how she just kept moving forward with her head high until she just couldn't any longer. But I guess I wonder why she never asked her folks for help. Why didn't they come help her?"

Ada Mae smiled softly and placed her hand on top of Elizabeth's, patting gently. "Elizabeth, you assume a lot."

"Pardon me?" Elizabeth was surprised at Ada Mae's directness.

"You assume everyone thinks like you." Ada Mae paused, and then said softly, "And you assume her family knew."

Elizabeth was stunned. How could they not? How could Lillie have been through so much without one person in her family having known? "Surely she told someone."

"Elizabeth, I'm telling you this from my own past now." Ada Mae's eyes glazed over as she spoke. "My daddy was a beater too, and I grew up on a farm a lot like Lillie. I got more scars and injuries than you can imagine, and ain't most of it visible. My mama was a lot like Lillie. It seems like she should'a chosen differently, gotten out, found us a new life, but truth is... well, truth is, that ain't the way things work down here. Lillie, like my mama, thought she'd found a solid man, a hard-working man who could provide. And maybe she did, but ain't nobody really know what happens behind folks' closed doors. Why they do what they do, and why they ain't leave when it gets bad? Only they really knows." Ada Mae paused, and then added, "These was real rough times, in a real rough place, in a real hard life. Ya, the women are real hardy, they can handle a lot, but they at the mercy of so much that's outta their hands. Some of them find themselves at the mercy of their men, and they don't see a way out, so they stay."

"And they do the best they can..." Elizabeth understood all too well.

Chapter Forty

Cate
Naranjo, Sinaloa
January 1952

I'd never been more grateful for my upbringing than I was the year that we lived beside our mine in Mexico. We were in the middle of nowhere, a two-hour drive from the Gulf of California, and at least an hour to the town of Los Mochis. We were seventeen hours south of Los Angeles and four hours north of Mazatlán, Mexico, as far from the coastal living of both of those cities as was possible. Its remoteness was all too familiar. It was all hard labor and long days, and we had very little to work with. It was, again, a scene I knew well.

The problem wasn't that things weren't available. The problem was that the mine was located fifteen miles from the nearest town in the middle of the desert. There was no real road to speak of, though we'd managed to make one of sorts from all of our traveling back and forth to the small grocery shop and farmer's market that the closest town of Naranjo, Sinaloa, had. It wasn't much more than a stop on the Pacific Southern Railway, and a home to those who raised cattle and crops like sorghum, corn, wheat, and soybeans in the vast and ample desert. Without that railway, I'm not sure how the town would have survived.

Most of the workers lived in the town and would travel daily to and from the mine site by piling into a big work truck. Sometimes I could send a list of things we'd need with one of them and a few extra *pesos* to make it worth their while, and they would do a bit of shopping for me. The men were generally good about bringing their own food from home, but I still liked to provide small treats where I could. Of course, I also had to feed myself, Tony, Tony's father, and his cousin, who all typically slept on site. Tony's parents had temporarily moved to Naranjo because the five-hour drive to their home in Hermosillo on weekends had become too large a burden. Truth be told, the real reason was that Tony's mom refused to sleep near the mine for fear that the ground would collapse as she dreamed. Some nights, when I swore I could feel the ground shake, I thought she was on to something.

Though it was a destitute situation for sure, I did have a few more luxuries than my mother had had when she was raising me. Tony tapped into the mine's energy source, and we were able to keep a small icebox for meats and cheese and things. Unfortunately, there was no running water, so an outhouse was the only bathroom solution we could really come up with. It had been tried and true throughout history, Tony had said, and I had replied that history must not have been able to smell anything.

The water well was a godsend, as it had been in my youth, and provided us water for drinking and cooking, as well as for filling the swimming pool and the smaller pool that we used during the mining process. I alternated between the work pants I had worn during my aviation plant days and simple cotton dresses because they were the coolest options. While Tony's mom ventured out a few days here and there to help me, I was in charge of domestic duties, and I still handled the bookkeeping when necessary.

It was there, on the porch, by Tony's mom's side, that I learned to make tamales, mole sauce, and *caldo de mariscos*, a seafood soup of sorts. Fish and beef were the easiest to come by, given the nearby cattle ranches and the proximity of the Gulf of California, so I learned a lot of different ways to prepare the same staples so that no one went hungry and food kept its appeal. The whole situation again gave me an appreciation for how my mother had helped us all survive out in the tobacco fields under similar circumstances. It was, just as I had suspected, and just as Tony had hoped, hard work. Definitely the kind where sleep was not hard to find, and where mornings came too soon.

The first few months we were still doing a lot of construction, and so we obviously saw very little in the way of profits. Those were our days of faith, something that was coming easier to me as time passed. We had to believe that all of that back-breaking labor and those mind-numbing engineering calculations would end up being worth it, because when the sun beats down on you at a hundred and ten degrees, you better believe that what you're doing is worth it. Otherwise it's way too easy to quit. For me, the light in Tony's eyes was what made it worth it.

Tony was thrilled with building his plans. I watched him pour over, and literally sweat over, his initial plans on how and where to build the shaft for hours, if not days, only to ball them up and start all over again. He wanted so badly to do it right and to keep his men safe while they were underground that it probably took a month or so more than it should have. The men didn't mind, though; it was work, and Tony was pleasant with them, unlike some of the other bosses they'd had on mining sites in the past. They were also extremely grateful that Tony was more concerned with their safety than his profits, an idea so foreign to many of them that they almost didn't believe it.

The men, in turn, would sometimes bring their wives along for the day to help me prepare food, or just to give me company. It was their way of giving back to Tony, I think, though they never said that. One of the wives, named Marta, was trying to hone her English just as I was trying to hone my Spanish, and I think she came out some days for that reason alone, but I never minded. She was sweet company, and gave me gentle and helpful cooking tips that I desperately wanted and needed. I embraced my domestic goddess status because I knew it was what was needed and that Tony appreciated every little thing I did for him. I'd been in the business world so much in the past years that getting back to the basics of filling a day with housework and cooking was a bit of an adjustment. Tony very much saw my work there as just as important as what he was doing, and that made my tinkering on the porch a whole lot more enjoyable.

I think the height of my complete domestication came with an unexpected delivery just five months after we'd settled in. Marta had come out with her husband, Carlos, and was helping me tend to the very small garden that I had just started. I felt sort of bad, because Marta was pregnant and fairly well along by then, though she didn't have any solid idea when she was actually due. "Oh, around July, maybe?" was the best she could come up with. She looked ready to burst and it was only May by then, but who was I to judge? I'd obviously never been pregnant. She was such a jovial soul, and if I hadn't known she was pregnant I never would have guessed, as she never ever complained about anything. This was true too of the day she went into labor, which was the very same day she spent squatting in my garden. I was so oblivious, I thought nothing of it, and figured that it was probably the most comfortable position for her to be digging in the dirt. I never questioned why she didn't just sit, but now I know it's because she was contracting all day and that her squatting made the contractions a little more comfortable. We were so busy that I hadn't noticed her bouts of deep breaths and bouncing on her legs until the late afternoon, and by the time I noticed and figured out what was happening I had also figured out it was probably too late to get her back to the town midwife.

When she finally admitted to herself that she was in fact in labor, she stood up straight and slowly waddled towards me, catching my eye as she came my way. I dropped the shovel I had in my hand when I saw the single tear roll down her cheek, and immediately understood what was about to happen. All I could ask her in my broken Spanish was, "Is it time?" All she could do was nod, and then a strong contraction knocked the air out of her, causing her to grip my arm and lean into me. I called out for the other women on the site as I gently guided her back towards the house. Tony's mother had come that day, and I was ever so grateful for her knowledge and calm because I was feeling anything but knowledgeable or calm. One woman gathered sheets and towels and blankets as another sought out Marta's husband, Carlos, at the mine, and then brought clean water from the well. Being the youngest of my siblings I'd never attended a birth before, and Julia had been rather private about hers with the girls. Yet, it seemed, everyone was looking to me to actually help Marta.

Tony's mom walked me through it, really, while I tried my best to walk Marta through each contraction. Marta seemed to naturally know what to do, and was much calmer than I'm sure I would have been. I imagine now that she had probably witnessed many births in the town and knew just what to expect. It was likely the same reason she hadn't panicked in the garden as her contractions mounted. She simply knew what needed to be done, and did it.

I don't remember many of the women's names from those days; they all seem to blend together in one conglomerate of a person, but I remember Marta's well. I strongly suspect that she remembers mine. After it was all said and done, after I had witnessed the beautiful ability of her body to give another person life, after I had laid her wet and squealing daughter on her chest for the first time and gently dried her off, Marta had looked at me and said, "Cate."

With tears on my lashes, I responded with a "Yes?"

She shook her head and looked at the baby and said, "No. *Su nombre es Cate.* Her name, it's Cate." She paused and misread my shock for confusion or disapproval. " *¿Está bien?* Okay, Miss Cate?" She looked from her daughter to me, with the most innocent and pure love I'd ever seen. As she grinned widely I knew I couldn't do anything but nod emphatically with joy, and I broke into a huge smile myself. I already had two goddaughters, and now I had a namesake as well. I felt incredibly blessed in that moment. Although I knew I would never be able to experience giving birth as Marta had just done, she and God had allowed me to experience it anyway, in my own way, of course. I never again felt cheated or robbed of the glorious joy of delivering a baby, because I already had.

Months later, when the mine was finally constructed, the shaft had been dug, and the wooden structures and mechanical pieces were all in place, we all celebrated like we'd just built a second White House. Not a lick of ore had been mined and yet we were all still giddy with excitement, Tony so much so that he paid for a rather large feast for everyone who'd had anything to do with it. More than the food, more than the company, this one gesture pulled a small group of men in together tightly and made them all Tony's loyal employees. His royal highness was grinning wildly from ear to ear, and I knew then that even if we never mined a lick of lead, we'd been successful in coming there. Tony was whole again.

That was a thought I held on to quite a bit over the coming year as, despite our best efforts, the land yielded only small amounts of lead and zinc. The men grew weary and tired, yet felt secure in the fact that Tony was still paying them a fair wage. I, on the other hand, watched cautiously and then nervously as our savings started to really dwindle. We had more going out then we were bringing in, and the news I kept getting from our shop in Inglewood was shockingly similar. It wasn't on autopilot like we'd thought after all. Without Tony's touch and innovations, his customers had started looking elsewhere to fill their needs. We were bleeding heavily on both fronts, and yet Tony seemed to want to hear none of it. I think he wanted the mine, his creation and his baby, to succeed so badly that he couldn't picture a scenario where it didn't.

I hung in there and clung to whatever small profits we could find. Tony wouldn't leave even with news of the shop failing because he was convinced that once they hit the jackpot, that would cover it all. I hung in there with him, out of love for sure, but also out of the knowledge that Tony and I no longer had a home in Los Angeles. We'd essentially given it all up for a chance with the mine, and had taken a huge gamble. Tony apparently wanted to roll the dice as long as he possibly could;

and, as we had no home to go back to, I stayed along for the delusional ride.

A little over a year later, in the late winter of 1953, I got a phone call that brought us back to reality faster than I had ever wanted. Ricardo, one of the men who worked just under Tony, had made a run into town for a few things. He returned in an extreme hurry. I watched as his work truck hauled it across the desert at an alarming rate and almost tipped a time or two. He was streaming dust as the truck flew, and it swerved erratically in his haste. Ricardo stomped on the brakes just in front of where I was standing, and I might have been frightened except that I was covering my mouth and coughing incessantly because of the dirt he'd just unsettled. He seemed to fly out of the truck and then grabbed me by upper arms, speaking incredibly loud and fast to me in Spanish. That's when he scared the wits out of me.

He was frantic and pointing towards the town, and I wasn't sure if he was trying to tell me something was wrong with Tony's mom or if something bad had happened in town. My Spanish was infinitely better than when I'd first come down, but at the rate he was clipping I couldn't catch anything thing except telephone. I never could have anticipated what he was actually telling me. I reached up and grabbed his elbows. "Ricardo, slow down. Slow down." I repeated it in Spanish and tried to get him to look at me directly. His eyes were roaming wildly over the mine, and I could tell he was looking for Tony.

I finally shook free of his nervous hold and grabbed his face. "Ricardo, *lentamente*. What is it?"

After he took a few breaths he gathered himself and did his best to explain his message. When I finally got what he was saying, he had to catch me because I nearly lost my mind and almost passed out right there in the dirt.

"¡*Ayúdame*! ¡*Ayúdame*!" He was yelling now for help, but it sounded distant, like I was in some other place watching him try to hold me up. "Mr. Tony, Mr. Tony!" He gently placed me on the ground, but kept my head in his lap. "*Señora Cate. Por favor, Señora Cate.*"

I didn't pass completely out, but the moments that followed were a bit of a blur. I remember Tony coming and picking me up and carrying me to the bed. I remember cool cloths on my forehead and small sips of water. I remember the nausea and the overwhelming smell of bile. I remember the whispering as Ricardo repeated to Tony in the corner of the room what he'd told me just minutes before.

I remember Tony's dead silence. It was that silence that brought me out of my funk, and I was shaking when I sat up and called Tony over.

"Tony, I have to go. I have to. Those girls. They need me." I was whispering towards the end because I still couldn't fully comprehend what had happened. Tony came and sat beside me on the bed. He still hadn't said anything.

"Yes, we must go." He paused as his mind surely reeled. "But I can't shut the mine down that fast, Cate. It'll take me a couple of days. I really can't even think right now…"

"I'm not waiting a couple of days. I'm going, and then you can come when you can." I knew he understood that's the way it had to be, but I wasn't sure how he'd survive even the few days I'd be gone with the news we'd just received. I could tell he was devastated, and I myself was too shattered to really take in anybody else's feelings, even Tony's.

"Yes, yes, of course, Cate. Of course." We took just a moment to sit in each other's embrace and cry, and then I heard Tony's sweet soft prayers escape into the hot afternoon air. When he stopped praying and said amen, we both flew into action. I was pulling out a bag and throwing in my essentials, he was yelling orders to his guys about what he needed them to do to get me back to Los Angeles quickly. We were eleven hundred miles from Los Angeles, but if driving all night was what it meant to get there then that's what I was going to do. In less than an hour I was on the road, and when I left Tony all he could whisper was, "Kiss my nieces for me and tell them I'm coming for them soon."

That truck ride back to Los Angeles was the longest and most agonizing time of my life. I only let the driver stop three times to use the facilities, get gas, and to grab a quick meal. I felt like I was wasting time, and just kept picturing Josefina and Carisa's sweet baby faces. I sat there mulling over the words I'd heard Ricardo say to me.

Ricardo's wife, Sofia, worked at the little general store and often ran the register, swept the floors, and answered the phone while taking messages for the ninety-nine percent of the townsfolk who didn't own a telephone. Violetta, Tony's sister, had called the store's phone line. She was crying violently and speaking so fast that it had taken Sofia a few moments to understand who Violetta was and who she was looking for. Sofia would sometimes come out to the mines to help me and had picked up a little bit of English, but was by no means fluent. Violetta, who had spent little to no time in Mexico, had the Spanish fluency of a five year old. Compounding the chaos was the crackling phone line that spit and whistled incessantly like a fireworks show. In the days to come I could hear the conversation over and over in my head as if it were I and not Sofia who had answered the phone that day.

Crackle. Pop. Sizzle. Hiss.

"Hello? Hello?" Violetta sobbed uncontrollably. "Hello? ¿*Hola*? Is anyone there?"

"*Sí. Sí. Hola. ¿Quién es?*" Who is this, Sofia had asked over and over, until Violetta had finally managed to spit out her name and explain that she needed to get a message through to Tony Otera. "*Ah, sí. Conozco a Sr. Otera y a Miss Cate.*"—I know them, Sofia had responded sounding concerned. "¿*Qué pasa?* What is wrong?" The phone line crackled loudly in her ear, and she winced as she tried to hear Violetta's response.

Violetta had calmed down enough to try to put words together in Spanish. "*Hubo un terrible accidente automovilístico,*" The phone line snapped violently and crackled again as she continued to try to explain between English and Spanish. She finally finished with, "The injuries were very bad. Uh, *lesiones malas.*"

Sofia quickly understood why Violetta had been so upset. "¿*Fueron gravemente heridos?*" The phone line hissed again as Violetta said something that Sofia didn't hear. "*Perdón,* I'm sorry. You say *muerto?* Mr. Tony's *hermano* is dead?" She held her breath, waiting for the answer.

Another snap of the line and a sputter followed until Sofia distinctly heard Violetta reply, "*Muerto,*" and then the line abruptly disconnected.

What made its way to me via Ricardo was that there had been some sort of accident and it had somehow involved Hector and Julia, but not the girls. I just couldn't imagine such a scenario, as Julia was rarely without her daughters. All Ricardo kept saying was *Muerto, Muerto.* Dead, dead. Every time I replayed it in my head I had to fight to not pass out or throw up. I couldn't believe it. Tony's mother had taken the news so poorly that she started having chest pains, and Tony's father refused to leave her side. I think they were just both too heartbroken to move.

All I could think the whole time was about how we were the girls' godparents, and that meant we were now, in the absence of Julia and Hector, their parents. I had prayed for and wanted children of our own to raise for so long, but not like this. This was not at all anything I had ever imagined. These were my godchildren—not my children—and I didn't want to become their mother this way. The pit in my stomach just grew and grew. I silently prayed over and over for God to give Julia and Hector back. Those little girls needed their parents to raise them, not Tony and me. It was a strange thing, because the one thing I'd longed for for forever was being handed to me in full, but I didn't want anything to do with the way the package was wrapped.

When we reached Los Angeles, the streets couldn't pass fast enough. I practically jumped out of the car before it was completely stopped and made a beeline for the hidden key under the mat. It was almost morning and the house was still dark, which would normally be typical, but under the circumstances it felt a little eerie. I entered the house expecting to find Violetta asleep on the couch or Juan standing guard over my nieces, but instead what I found as I went from room to room was no one. The house was empty, and Josefina and Carisa were gone. I was confused, and wasn't sure what to do. I just started making phone calls. First Violetta's, then Juan's, then some of our mutual friends who had no idea what I was talking about. I had just sat down on the couch when I saw a car pull up and recognized it as Hector's car; only Hector obviously wasn't driving it, Juan was. The girls were in the back seat. I steadied myself as I opened the door for them, not knowing what to say or do, really.

The girls saw me and started running as fast as their tiny legs would allow. I heard a small "Aunt Cate, Aunt Cate" from Josefina, who was just three, and as petite as petite got. She plowed into me, and I picked her up and held her tight to my chest like she would be ripped from me at any moment. She buried her head in my neck, and I held back my tears for fear of falling apart in front of them. On the inside I was crumbling like a dry mud cake. I still wasn't sure how this could be happening, and seeing the girls made it even more surreal. Carisa was just a few months shy of turning two, and she took just a tad longer to get to me. When she finally reached me she just kept calling me "Cat, Cat." It was her name for me, no matter how many times her parents had corrected her and told her it was Cate. Seven months prior they had come down to Mexico to visit. I was astounded at how much they'd both grown since then, and that they'd both remembered me so well.

I consciously avoided Juan's eyes. If I looked at them, I knew I'd have to face the truth. If I looked at them, it would all become too real.

We stood there for many moments with the girls thoroughly wrapped around me and me making absolutely no effort to pry them off. They were like a warm blanket in the middle of a freeze, and all I could do was pull them a tad closer. Finally, Juan cleared his throat to get my attention. When I looked up at him, I could tell just how exhausted he was.

"Where were you guys? We drove all night and no one was here." I was still a little confused, and also avoiding the obvious.

"We were at the hospital." He paused when I looked at him quizzically. "The girls refused to leave, so we let them just sleep in the chairs in the waiting room. It seemed like the right thing at the time. Now I'm not so sure..."

"Sure, of course." I patted Josefina's back and then soothed down Carisa's unruly hair with my palm. "But why were you still at the hospital? I'm sorry, I'm just so confused. We heard that they were well, you know..."

Now Juan looked puzzled, and it struck me suddenly how much he looked like Tony. I'd never noticed before. The only difference was his closely-cropped hair and dark tan, both courtesy of the U.S. Navy.

"I'm sorry, Cate, what do you mean?" His eyebrows were so tightly knitted together that they started to morph into one large eyebrow. I kept my focus on that so I wouldn't cry.

"Well, we were told they were in an accident and were, well... that they didn't make it, Juan. Have they not been moved to the mortuary?" I whispered it although Josefina was but a few inches away from my face. I assumed that at three she was too young to know what that word meant.

Juan's face went white and he gasped. "Who told you that? Is that what my mother and father think? Oh my goodness. Violetta! I knew I should have called down there instead of her."

I perked up at his indignant tone. Maybe we'd gotten bad information after all. Maybe my silent pleas for the last eighteen hours hadn't gone unheard. "So, they are still alive then?" As I said it, I was begging God for it to be true, promising him I would never lose my faith again if he would just relent and make it so.

"Heavens, yes, Cate! I'm so sorry that's the message you got. I was surprised to see you here when I pulled up. Now it all makes sense. Violetta's Spanish is not so good, my folks kind of gave up on trying to teach her after a while and said she just spoke a teenager's version.

She must have mixed up some words when she called down to get a message to my parents and you all. Unbelievable!"

I nearly dropped Josefina out of relief, but caught her on my hip when she squealed. We later heard from Violetta that she had said, "*No muerto*" but all that had made it through the poor connection was *muerto*. I was reeling from the news. I knew that it still had to be pretty serious if they were still in the hospital. "Juan, what happened? How bad is it?"

"Well, we aren't sure of the full story. Apparently a longtime customer gave Hector tickets to see a play just outside of west Los Angeles. He was really excited about it and wanted to take Julia, of course. They asked Violetta to watch the kids, and she agreed because it was so rare for Julia to trust anyone with the care of the girls—well, besides you and Tony. Anyway, it looks like they got sideswiped by a large cargo-type truck, and it caused their car to flip several times. It went over the guardrail and rolled down an embankment off the freeway. Hector was pinned inside, and Julia had been thrown through the windshield. I imagine it was a pretty bad scene." He sighed, thoroughly exhausted from being up all night, I'm sure, and also from having to say those words out loud.

"Oh, my, Lord." I could picture the bloody scene that had probably occurred. It made me shudder, and I immediately felt nauseated. "Are they going to be okay?"

"I hope so, Cate. Julia is not awake yet, and to be honest it's probably for the best. Her little body took a good beating. They are keeping Hector sedated because every time he wakes he screams in pain. I guess he has several broken bones. Mind you, they wouldn't let us see them, though, so I'm telling you this second hand."

"They are alive, though. I just can't believe it. I thought they'd…" I couldn't finish my sentence because it was too painful to recall how I had felt the whole ride up to California. I squeezed the girls gently, and then realized that they probably needed to eat, be bathed, and put down for a nap. The need for normalcy kicked in, as did my protective instincts. I snapped myself back to reality in a matter of seconds. These girls still had their parents, thank God, but they needed me right now. I was going to be the one to see them through this tragedy, and I was more than willing to fill that role for as long as need be. I was ever so grateful that it wouldn't be long-term for their sakes. I couldn't do anything to help Hector or Julia heal, but I hoped that by caring for their daughters I could make it possible for them to rest easier and get better faster.

I called down to the town in Mexico as fast as I could to alleviate Tony and his parents' pain; to give them the right story of what happened. However, Tony never got the message I relayed. It turned out the mine could run itself without Tony there, and he decided to leave just hours after I had. He drove the entire way up like I had, thinking his brother and Julia were dead. I'm sure his journey felt just as long and as sorrowful as mine had been.

I washed the girls and fed them a late breakfast, or early lunch of sorts. I had just finished reading them *Pussy Cats and Puppy Dogs,* a longtime favorite of theirs, when I heard a car pull up in the drive. I took a peek out the window and discovered it was our car, and watched with disbelief as Tony quickly removed himself from the front seat and practically ran for the front door. He was obviously feeling the same panic and impatience at getting here that I had felt my whole ride up. I quickly kissed the girls' foreheads and closed the door and met my husband in the entryway. He looked and smelled terrible, and I couldn't get to him fast enough. He began sobbing in my arms as I quickly found myself repeating: "It's okay, it's alright, Tony, it'll be okay."

He pulled back from me and let out a sorrowful sigh as he quietly said, "It'll never be okay, my brother... and Julia..."

I touched him gently and took his hand, and through my own tears managed to say to him, "Tony, they're alive. They made it. They're going to be okay."

The look on his face was what I imagined mine had looked like just hours before when Juan had corrected me on the story. Confusion, perplexity, relief, and disbelief.

"What? How? I don't understand, Cate..." He wiped at the tears on his cheeks with the back of his hand, and I watched as his shoulders slumped in sheer exhaustion. He must not have stopped the whole way up except to refill the tank, and now his own tank was on empty. I quickly told Tony what Juan had told me, and, after a few choice words, he collapsed on Hector and Julia's couch and didn't move. He threw his arm over his eyes as if to shut out the world.

I scooted his legs over to the side and sat beside him, holding his other hand. Then I said what had been on my mind since Ricardo had frantically approached me in front of the house in Mexico.

"You know, Tony, there was a point in my life when I thought I would do anything, give anything, to have the chance to have children to raise. I wanted it at all costs, really, and I even pleaded with God most nights that there had to be some way." Tony put his arm down and looked at me with the same sadness and relief that I was feeling. "But the whole way up here, all I could think was *no*, this isn't right. Not at all costs, because these are not our children. Give them back their parents."

"Funny, I thought the same thing. Well, that and that we were lucky to have had them all." He stopped and wrinkled his brow and added, "We are so lucky, Cate, and so very blessed." I nodded at him and started to cry.

I pulled myself together long enough to make us both a bite to eat. We quickly realized we were both so exhausted that we needed a nap as much as the girls had. I called and checked in with the nurses at the hospital, and after finding out that both Hector and Julia were in guarded but stable condition, I suggested to Tony that we both get a little rest before the girls woke up. That way we could drive ourselves safely to the hospital in the evening to see them. Neither of us felt right about sleeping on Hector and Julia's bed, so we tucked in side by side on the narrow couch and slept like rocks for over two hours. And while I lay there side by side with my husband. I had the strangest dream I'd ever had, and have never had one like it since.

I dreamed of little girls, two of them, who were related to me, but who weren't Josefina and Carisa. And they weren't just any little girls, they were my daughters. They were beautiful, with curly, unruly hair, not unlike my own, and they were lively, yet had a haunting sadness to their eyes. They were covered in dirt from head to toe. But the strangest part of it was that neither one of them had any shoes. All I kept saying in my dream was: *Why don't my girls have any shoes?*

Chapter Forty-One

Lillie
August 14, 1953
6:30 a.m.

Lillie awoke again hours after telling Elizabeth about her wedding and the early years. She found that Elizabeth was at her side, waiting, even though her shift was almost over. She just couldn't seem to ready herself to leave.

"Hey there, Lillie, how are you feeling?" Elizabeth leaned in and placed a gentle hand on Lillie's shoulder.

Lillie stared back at her blankly, trying to discern who she was, exactly, and where she was, exactly. She stared past Elizabeth's head at the light that was starting to come in through the window. As the sun started to rise, she saw shades of orange and red and yellow dancing like lightning up and across the wall towards the ceiling and covering her bed. She felt as though she could touch it, grab it, and pull it towards her. Her hands weakly lifted from the top of the bed as she picked and grabbed at the light show before her. She wanted to be bathed in its warmth—the oranges, the reds, the yellows. She felt so cold.

Elizabeth stepped back and watched as Lillie picked at the air, persistently trying to grasp something. Something that wasn't there. Lillie's eyes were hollow and vacant and fixated on the ceiling. It was as if Elizabeth wasn't even in the room. Lillie didn't seem frightened or upset. Quite the contrary, she appeared as calm and serene as Elizabeth had ever seen her. Elizabeth quietly found herself a seat next to the bed and watched as Lillie continued to grab, and she couldn't help but wonder what it was she saw. Her eyes wandered down Lillie's broken body, and she tried to take it all in. She tried to accept what was happening.

Lillie's rotund abdomen, Lillie's swollen feet and fingers, Lillie's discolored legs, Lillie's pale face and sunken eyes. Lillie's eyes. Not the eyes Elizabeth had spoken to just hours before. These were eyes that had journeyed elsewhere; that were seeing what the normal eye could not see. Eyes of those who pass. Twenty minutes went by in this manner, with Lillie busily working to catch some unseen entity and Elizabeth studying Lillie's body. It felt like hours to Elizabeth, who was at a loss for what to do. She wasn't sure if she was hoping that this was it for Lillie, that this was the start of her passage home, or if she was praying for a miracle.

Finally, Lillie laid her arms down and exhaled loudly, ending it with a satisfied "hmmm." She lay with her eyes closed, breathing deeply and calmly, like she was capturing the scent of warm apple pie or freshly baked cornbread. Elizabeth watched her chest rise and fall, scared to look away. Frightened that if she did, it would mean the end. After a few very long minutes, Lillie's eyes fluttered open and her head rolled towards where Elizabeth was perched. "Hi," was all she managed with a raspy voice heavy with phlegm and thick with mucus. She tried to clear her throat, and it threw her into a coughing fit that turned her face purple and caused Elizabeth to start to panic.

"Lillie? Take a deep breath, Lillie. You got this. It's okay…" Elizabeth was standing over her now and looking down as Lillie struggled to eventually even out her coughing fit and breathe with more ease. Lillie cleared her throat, and asked for some water as she regained herself.

Finally, Lillie blurted out, "You seen that light show, Elizabeth? What a summer storm we must'a had!"

"I must have missed it, Lillie."

"Shame. Shame. Most beautiful thing I ever saw. Lights of every shade of red and yellow and orange dancing on the ceiling, down them walls there. Never seen nothing like it in my life! It was like you could grab it and wrap yourself in it, and nothing would hurt you ever again."

"Hmmm. Sounds amazing, Lillie. Now I'm really sorry I missed it." Elizabeth was suddenly exhausted.

"Elizabeth?" Lillie caught Elizabeth's eye and held a long and steady gaze. A loving gaze, but one that meant business.

"Yes, Lillie?"

"I've got to be going real soon." Her voice didn't waver, nor crack, her eyes didn't brim with tears; she just called out the pink elephant in the room and laid it on Elizabeth's lap for inspection.

"I know, Lillie." Elizabeth held Lillie's steady gaze, but shifted uncomfortably. "I know that."

"I got to tell you one more story. One that might not make much sense right now, but you need to hear it it."

For the first time Elizabeth wasn't sure she had the strength for another of Lillie's stories. She was weary, frightened, and sad, but something in the way Lillie said what she said caught her attention. This was to be her final story. The last time she'd ever share a bit of herself with anyone, and that thought made Elizabeth sit up a little bit straighter in her chair.

"Okay, Lillie. I'm listening." Lillie reached out for Elizabeth's hand and held it tightly as she started to speak.

"I know you wondering why I stayed with Clay all them years. I think I done try to help you see. I think you wondering what happened to Clay, too, to change him from his self to the varmint he become now. And I know you's wondering how I can forgive him after all he done to me."

"Lillie, I… it's not for me to judge, I…"

Lillie interrupted. "But you wondering anyhow. And I can't rightly blame you. I been wondering the same lately. Mostly as I been trying to explain it to you, I been trying to explain it to myself. It didn't happen overnight. It was a real gradual-like thing. I just missed the early signs is all, missed 'em, ignored 'em, loved him anyway."

"I know, Lillie, that's what makes you who you are."

"Well, I see him now. Too little too late, I know, but I see him and I need you to see him too. It's real important."

"Okay, Lillie, I'm listening." Elizabeth felt anxious. She wasn't sure she wanted to hear what Lillie had to say, even though she knew deep down she needed to.

"Where to start…" Lillie sighed loudly and tried to shake off the foggy feeling that was starting to set in over her head.

"So I already told you we got married on the first of June of 1929. Later that month, my folks done move into town like I says. An old friend of my mother's was a teacher in town, and her husband worked for the water company. He helped my daddy find a job, and they didn't take no time at all to decide to take it. Worked out real nice, as Clay done move into my house with me. I think I done told you that part already. Anyway, that first year was a good one, actually. I felt real happy-like about my life. Even with losing Mary that September, I felt real happy. Like she was helping make it that way for me." Lillie paused, trying to remember what she'd already told Elizabeth, not wanting to repeat herself.

She continued with, "Clay worked real hard for Mr. Finn and then for Matthew after Mr. Finn done leave town. Took real pride in his self about that, and most folks took notice of it real quick. He might not have won no personality contests, but he sure did work his self hard. Might have been why he took it so bad when Josie and Matthew made up their minds to sell the Finn farm. He felt like he'd wasted his time, been robbed of what was due him."

"I guess I can see that. What did he do after the Finns sold their farm? Did you stay on with the new family who bought it?"

"For a few months we did. But it didn't work out none too good. Josie and Matthew moved away in fall of 1930, so Clay didn't have no chance to really show the new owners, the Hadens, what he was made of. Most of the fall harvest was done by then, and winter was setting in. My belly was growing right quick with my first, my Connie, and I suppose we just looked like a couple of no-good squatters to Mr. Haden. He was from outta town, see, and he didn't know no better. He didn't know how hard Clay would'a worked for him. He brought some sharecropping families with him and gave us notice right before Christmas."

"Oh, my goodness, Lillie! What on earth did you do? Where did you go in the middle of winter?"

"Well, at first I thought we was gonna have to live with my folks in town, but then Clay put his foot down and said he'd rather die. And Clay wasn't sure what he would do for work in town anyway, as he had always been a tobacco farmer. He didn't know nothing different, didn't own a suit or have no other trade. He just farmed tobacco all his life."

"Who did he work for before you got married? I don't remember you saying." Elizabeth remembered her having mentioned that before.

"He worked for the Adams farm for many years before I met him. So, I guess he felt he had to go back, that it was really our only choice. And Clay wasn't none too happy about it. And Mr. Adams wasn't none too forgiving about him having left in the first place. Fact, I think I remember Mr. Adams slammed the door in Clay's face when he first saw him standing on his porch step in January."

"So, how'd Clay get him to take him back?"

"He done what Clay does best, and that's set his mind to it. It took a whole lot of groveling, and finally he drug me out there with him so Mr. Adams could see my swollen belly. That might'a hit something soft in Mrs. Adams, if there is such a spot, because Mr. Adams agreed to take him back—but with a few things changed. They gave us the smallest of the sharecroppers' houses, the one the closest to the Adams house, so there wasn't much privacy, and they saddled him with a cut in what he was making before. We was pretty desperate to have a home and to have work for Clay, and Mr. Adams was pretty desperate to make sure Clay knew he was gonna pay for leaving in the first place for something better. Match made in hell, I suppose."

"I guess you were lucky to have a place at all at that time."

"I guess that's how we tried to see it too. Kept hearing reports of folks outta work all over the place, but I guess Mr. Adams done have faith that President Hoover was gonna fix it right quick. What did we all know? Yeah, we was lucky indeed."

"So, is that the same house you still live in, Lillie?"

Lillie laughed softly, "No, I suppose it's the house my family done live in, since I live here now. But I'll be going to a better home soon." Lillie's words hung in the air between herself and Elizabeth. The brutal cold hard truth, like the day Lillie and Clay had carried the boxes that held their few possessions into their new homestead. The home that lay just an acre or two away from Mr. Adams' front doorstep. The home that had seen twenty-three years pass in Clay and Lillie's life—the birth of nine children—and many cold winters in between. Elizabeth could feel how Lillie's life, like the truth she just spoke, was savagely frigid.

Silence swayed in the warm summer breezes that snuck in under the slightly cracked windows, and Lillie's mind began to wander. "Anyhow, where was I?" Lillie felt confused, but she was as determined as Clay had been all those years ago to finish the deal, no matter what she had to pay to do so.

"You moved into your new house off of the Adams' farm. So that was January of '31?"

Lillie knitted her eyebrows. "Yes, must'a been, 'cause my Connie was born in March that year. Took her three whole days of labor 'fore she decided to show up, and she was late every day since. Only the Women's Army Corp was the thing to straighten her out on telling time." Lillie laughed a little, thinking about all the times that Connie had been late to this or that. How it could take that girl twice as long to milk a cow as her siblings, or chop up wood for the fireplace, or even make a simple cornbread pudding, for that matter. It was just how she was. The only thing she ever did right on time was sign up for the military, and Lillie knew just why she hadn't dragged her heels on that one.

"A year and a half after my Connie, my Ben came along. Quiet Ben, like his daddy in a lot of ways, 'cept I suspect it was more a way of surviving than who he really is. Guess he figured if he was Clay's little buddy then he'd be off his radar, and well, maybe that boy's smarter than we gives him credit for, 'cause Clay done mostly leave him alone. He into dairy farming now, he done had enough of tobacco farming, I guess."

"I think you might'a mentioned that." Elizabeth was quiet, listening and waiting for the real turning point in the conversation.

"Joe came along a couple years later, then Nola two years after that, and then Ada two years after her. We was happy then, I think, as happy as you can be, given what the country done went through. We didn't have much to start, so what was a little bit less? Least we could grow us some food. Them folks in the cities didn't have that option. We sharecroppers all just banded together-like to help each other. There was no fences between us folks back then, Elizabeth. We just did what needed doing, helped each other out, and tried to make the best of it where we could. Those folks in the big cities were hocking apples for five cents a piece just to try to make some money for food. Least we could grow us some here and just eat 'em."

"I was born right after President Roosevelt took office. Can't say I remember much of those early years, I just remember mama being real careful-like with what we had."

Lillie laughed. "Well, I was the queen of rationing at my house. Can't say it pleased nobody too often, but it needed to be done, so I done it. 'Course, Clay never seemed to suffer. He always did take his fair share first. Anyhow, those was the best years, Elizabeth. The happiest, I guess, even though we was the poorest we'd ever been. We really was mostly okay. Clay worked real hard and I loved on my babies and kept us fed and clothed as best I could, and Clay and I got along alright. We did alright."

"You didn't see none of his meanness then?"

"I didn't say that. It was there, but it was in little bursts. A bit at a time, manageable. Like he rationed his anger then like I rationed my potatoes. I think it mostly started the day Josie and Matthew told us they'd sold their farm, and it just grew from there. Like a snowball running downhill, picking up speed and snow as it goes. Sure, little bits and pieces broke off now and then, and he'd rage about this or that, but he kept his anger all balled up and hidden, mostly."

"When did it get bad, Lillie?" Elizabeth could see now how they had slowly built a life together; how the little things, the tiny moments of anger could be forgiven; how Lillie didn't seem to have a choice but to keep seeing the Clay she wanted and needed to see.

"Well, like I said, it was building, see... over time. The Adams folks aren't the most generous or nice kind of people you ever met. Mr. Adams worked Clay real hard-like and never told him how good a job he did. He worked Clay like we owed him some debt, like he was gonna punish him long as he could for Clay having left before."

"So he just grew resentful."

"Yes, I suppose that's what it was. A little fire got lit the day Josie told us their news, and Mr. Adams threw kindling on it every day since. While I tried to make the most of it, see the best in people, be happy, Clay went the other way. He done let it eat at him. Where I saw enough, he saw not enough. He just never was real happy with anything."

"So what turned it bad, Lillie? Did something happen in particular, or did he just get meaner over time?" Elizabeth asked again.

Lillie sighed as she felt her eyelids start to droop. She was tired, and thinking about how Clay had changed over the years made her sad, and then even more tired. But she pushed forward, like she'd always done. "Well, it was one unfortunate thing after the other, I guess. It started when we lost our baby boy, Paul, in 1941. It was a real rough year. The Nazi folks overseas was starting up the war, invading everybody here and there, and it was real scary-like. We wasn't real sure if they was gonna try and make our boys go if we joined the war. By boys, I mean Clay. I wasn't sure how we'd make it without him or Mr. Adams, but thank the Lord it never was an issue."

"I know a lot of farmers who were exempt from being drafted because their farming was considered so important to the country. I guess it was a good time to be a farmer."

"Yes, maybe so. Whatever the reason, we sure was glad he didn't go. I'm not sure I'd have made it without him." Lillie paused a moment, and Elizabeth thought how ironic Lillie's statement was. Lillie sure wasn't making it now. Maybe it would have been better if he'd gone to war. At least she might have had a chance.

"Anyway, after we lost Paul something tore open in Clay. I think something died in me and something came alive in Clay. Like the fire that had been lit finally really ignited, and he blamed me. He blamed me for it all, for some reason. And I just kept forgiving him and trying to see, really see, him, the real him. I knew he was in there somewhere. I wish I could tell you I found him, but I'm not sure I did. But I never did stop looking."

They sat there silently for a few moments before Elizabeth finally prompted and asked, "So Paul died, and his anger grew?"

"It started with little outbursts over my cooking; or the way I'd baked a jam cake; or the way I'd hung the sheets to dry on the line out back. Didn't matter what, really, he'd just pick at my seams, trying to get me to fall apart. It got worse after his brother died, though, and then after Nathan passed, well… even having our two other children couldn't help heal him. He just never was the same."

"Clay had a brother who died? Wait, you mentioned that before, I think."

"Yes, his only brother, actually, though he has a sister, too, who lives in Nashville somewhere. His mama done struggled having kids. His brother, Wesley, lived not but a few miles from us. If Clay got all the meanness in him, then Wesley got all the kind. He was a good man."

"How did he die, Lillie? In the war?" Elizabeth looked down at Lillie's face. "Oh, you look exhausted, Lillie. You should rest some."

Lillie's eyes were barely open and her breathing had slowly become labored as she'd spoken. Her skin had taken on an array of colors, and Elizabeth felt ashamed that she hadn't been more attentive to her medical needs. "Lillie, really, you should rest some. You can tell me more later."

Lillie's eyes fluttered open, and she gave Elizabeth a small smile, one that pulled at Elizabeth's heart and brought tears to her lashes. "Thank you, Elizabeth, for listening. For seeing me." Lillie closed her eyes and drifted off into a deep sleep, her breathing slowing as Elizabeth tried to convince herself that Lillie hadn't just said her goodbyes.

"We'll talk later, Lillie. You can tell me that last story then. Okay?" Elizabeth spoke again to the silence room, "Please? Later?" Then the smell of death washed over her again as she collapsed into the chair beside Lillie's bed and sobbed.

Chapter Forty-Two

Cate
Los Angeles, California
Spring 1953

The months ahead flew by fast for me, and I often wonder how I managed to get through them in one piece. I'd been through a lot in my life, but the sudden responsibility for taking care of two little girls, plus tending to their parents as they healed, was a culture shock beyond anything I had ever expected. I'd always thought that I had been so involved in their lives when we lived over on Adams Street. I had always felt like I understood what all it took to raise little people. But that was when I could go home at night to my own bed and sleep a solid eight hours and not have to worry about the things that are required by small children, like grocery shopping, bedtimes, baths, playtime, and, well, things that those who have children understand. When Hector and Julia were well enough to be released, but not well enough to be on their own, things got even more hectic. I had never worked harder in my life.

I never returned to Mexico, and somehow when I left I sort of knew that would be the case. I had made many friends there in town and had gotten along great with the crew. It made me sad that I wouldn't get a proper goodbye, but I also knew that I was just where I needed to be. Tony had it a bit harder, though, and really couldn't stay in Los Angeles for long. He'd taken a little over a week and had sat by Hector's bed for many hours, watching as they turned him and heavily medicated him, but he knew in the back of his mind that he couldn't stay. He had to either close up the mine or get back to it, even as his heart was pulling him in a whole other direction. He wanted to stay with me.

It was probably for the best that he didn't stay and that he sent his mother up to help instead. We women of the Otera family tended to have the stronger stomachs, and it turned out we'd need them. Sparing all the really gory stuff, Hector had sustained a severe concussion and multiple bone fractures. The worst was a tibial fracture that had broken through the skin and had required surgery and a device that encircled his leg with pins and screws entering his skin. It wasn't pretty, and with his dominant hand and arm in a cast, he was fairly well unable to care for himself in any manner. He was essentially the third toddler in the house, needing bathing, feeding, and help walking, not to mention a bit of wound care. Just about the only thing he didn't need help with was his emotional state. He was like a rock, and inspired us all with his good nature and positive attitude. Secretly, though, I think he liked being doted on just a tad.

Julia, on the other hand, was quite the opposite. Physically she was fine, though I wouldn't say completely so. Her head had taken the brunt force of the impact, and after many precarious days where terms like "swelling of the brain" and "ischemic event" were tossed around by her doctors, she eventually walked out of the hospital with a few bumps and bruises and some temporary stroke-like symptoms. They didn't feel temporary to her, though, and her emotional state was extremely unstable. When she couldn't recall a simple word like "sugar" or "milk," she'd get so frustrated she'd slam her fist on the table. And when she couldn't remember her daughter's name once, she'd sobbed like she was dying. It was heart-wrenching to watch my friend and sister falling apart. I knew, though, that if anyone could piece herself back together it would be Julia. She just needed some stronger glue, and that glue was what I was sure I could provide.

In the same way I taught Josefina and Carisa their alphabet, I taught their mother how to remember things a bit easier. We labeled simple things that she kept forgetting, like the toaster or sink, so she wouldn't feel so frustrated trying to recall them. There were notes stuck to just about everything in the beginning, and when she felt like she no longer needed the reminder she would remove the note and throw it away. It took a good five to six months before they were all gone, and even then she would hesitate over certain words and names for items. I was in awe of her determination, but it came at a cost. I could tell she was in a severe depression, though in those days it wasn't something one openly talked about. Every now and then she'd open up and say something to give me an idea of what was going on inside her head.

"Cate?" She was sitting at her kitchen table in a yellow floral house dress and shuffling her coffee cup back and forth in between her hands. It was a habit she'd gotten into the past few weeks, and it reminded me of a nervous tick of sorts.

I was folding towels a few feet away on her couch, and the girls were coloring on the floor. It was a rare moment where they weren't in perpetual motion, and it was nice. "Yes, Julia? Do you need something?"

She smiled softly at me. "No." She spoke in short sentences, mostly because, I think, the effort of forming longer ones wore her out. We were assured she would regain her former abilities eventually, but that it would take some time. I didn't respond, and just waited patiently for her to find her words. When she did, it wasn't anything I expected. "Do you think I can do that?"

I raised my eyebrows and looked down at the lavender towel I had just folded. "What? You want to do the laundry?"

She shook her head at me, clearly frustrated that she hadn't gotten her question across correctly. "No." She sighed. "Can I take care of my girls? Ever?"

I suddenly completely understood. "Are you worried that you'll never be able to care for them again, Julia? Is that what your sadness is about?"

She nodded, and I watched as her eyes filled with tears and she choked back a sob. It was becoming an all too familiar scene with a woman who used to rarely ever cry, and it was unnerving. I put the towel down and glanced at the girls, who were watching us both with strong interest. "It's okay, girls, your mommy is just tired. She had a busy morning. Josefina, love, can you take your sister into the bedroom to play? I'll be there shortly." She nodded at me, but ran to her mother and kissed her cheek softly before taking her toddler sister by the hand and leading her down the hallway. It broke my heart.

I sat down across from Julia and took her hands in my lap and held them tightly to keep her attention. "Julia, listen. Nobody does this job better than you. I promise you, you will be back at it soon. The doctor said it will just take some time, is all. You had a good bruise on your brain, it takes time to heal that sort of thing."

A tear escaped her lashes and rolled down her face and off of her chin. "You're a good mother, Cate."

I stopped breathing for a moment, and I closed my eyes. They were words I had longed to hear, but now I just wanted her to take them back. "You are their mother, Julia. Not me. They know that. They need you just as much as you need them, and I have complete faith that soon you will be the one folding their laundry, tucking them in bed, and pulling your hair out when they fight." She looked away from me, and I gently pulled her face back towards me so she was looking in my eyes. "Hey. You. You are their mother. You're going to get there again. Just have a little faith."

The moment the word "faith" escaped my lips I realized what an important concept it was. Julia had lost hers somewhere along the way, and she was a mess. I was finding mine, and had never felt stronger. As I sat there encouraging Julia and trying to build her back up, I realized I did have faith, and not far from that faith was the dream-like image that kept creeping into my days of my shoeless daughters that I had yet to meet.

Julia did get better, though it took some time, of course, but she eventually fully recovered. Hector mended up nicely as well, and was anxious to get back to his work and his shop, which had somehow managed to stay afloat. While they were both picking up the pieces from the life-shattering accident, Tony and my businesses were falling apart. It wasn't anyone's fault, really. While we were in Mexico we knew the machine shop was struggling without Tony at the helm, but there wasn't much we could do about it. We had invested so much in the lead mine that he had to stay and keep it operational until we at least broke even, and even that idea was looking a little bleak.

I had moved into Hector and Julia's house for obvious reasons, and now that they had both mostly gotten back to normal, I realized that I had no place to go. I had been there almost six months by then, and had seen Tony only four times. Each time he had made the long drive up to visit, and each time we discussed what we were going to do. With the mining slowing down and the machine shop essentially going under, it didn't make sense for me to go back to Mexico, but we also couldn't afford our own apartment anymore. We were in a weird sort of place where we felt stuck and we couldn't move forward. On his last visit we'd had a little heart-to-heart.

It was summer again, and I wasn't sure where all the days and months were going, but lately they seemed to be leaving us behind. "Tony, I think it's time we sell the machine shop and salvage what's left of it. I've done the math and looked at the records. We're on a steady decline, and we either need to sell or we need to figure something out to get business going again." Tony sighed and propped his feet up on the coffee table. Hector and Julia had taken the girls to the park, mostly to try to reestablish some family time again, but also to give Tony and me some space since we had so little time together. He clasped his hands behind his head and leaned back like he was resting on a beach somewhere, but he didn't look relaxed. He just looked tired.

"My heart's not in it anymore, Cate. And even if it was, I'm not sure I have the time to revitalize the place." He paused, thinking carefully about his choice. "You're right, we need to sell."

"We could talk to Hector about absorbing some of the company and equipment. Maybe we could be part owner in his shop for a while until we figure it out."

"You mean like business partners?" Tony didn't seem sure, which surprised me because they were so close.

"Well, yes, sort of. Why do you sound like you think that wouldn't work?" I was perplexed, because on paper it made a whole lot of sense.

"It's his shop, Cate." He said it like that should explain everything.

"Yes, of course. It is, and it still would be. We'd just have a share in it." I really didn't understand.

"Cate, it's like inviting yourself to dinner. Can you see it like that?" I suddenly got it, it was a territorial thing. Hector's shop was Hector's and Tony's was Tony's, and never the two shall mix. Tony considered it rude to ask for a part of what his brother had built, and I assume he would have felt the same had someone asked to join him in his shop. Apparently family was family, but brotherly bonds had rules.

"Besides," he said, "I've already talked him into two adventures that didn't pan out so well. I'm not sure why he would trust me again." He frowned, surely thinking about Feather River and the lead mine.

"Well, what do you want to do, Tony? The mine is all but dead in the water, love, and I know you know that. We have to have some income."

"We offer them help." He sounded so exhausted, almost too tired to explain himself, but I pushed him in that direction anyway.

"I'm sorry, I thought that's what I've been doing all these months. I practically ran both shops as best I could, plus I cared for their children and both of them as well. What more are you wanting to offer?" I was suddenly feeling mad and resentful. I had given everything, and now Tony was making me feel like I was their guest. They still had a thriving business and a home. We were down to practically nothing.

"Sorry, no, I didn't mean it like that." He sat up a little bit straighter as he sensed my anger rising. "You've done an amazing job, Cate, more than anyone ever expected of you, but they don't owe us anything, my love."

"Well, of course not." I snapped. I hadn't done any of it expecting anything in return. I'd done it out of love, but I also didn't want to be homeless. All the months of separation and caregiving had caught up with me, and I felt utterly and suddenly bone-tired. Not to mention that my temper was short.

"Cate, don't be upset." He pulled me down beside him on the couch. "We aren't destitute yet. We still have some assets."

"Yes, but you want to offer to help them more? I can't do any more, Tony, and if I try I feel like you and I will crumble. I just can't let that happen."

"All I meant was we sell the shop and shut down the mine, which will take a bit of patience for sure, but is manageable in a few months' time. Then we ask Hector if I can help out in his shop. Be his employee for a while until I figure something out. He won't say no, in fact I think he needs my help, but won't ask for it because our shop is in such dire straights."

"Isn't that what I just suggested?" I was miffed, and getting more irritable by the moment.

"No, you suggested I become his business partner, and cut in on his dance. I won't do that, but I would work for him. I'm not so prideful that I can't do that in order to support us." I didn't know what to say because I had lost rational control of my thoughts. Just a year before, our lives had made sense, we were thriving and happy, though covered in Mexican dirt and sweat. We had a sense of purpose. Now I just felt like a fall leaf flapping in the wind.

"Where will we live, Tony? I mean, we gave up the apartment, and we certainly can't afford another one right now."

"Here." He said it matter of fact like he knew something I didn't.

"Tony, this is Hector and Julia's home." I felt my anger slip away, but it was being replaced by desperation as I began to realize the situation we were in. I had been so busy caring for Hector's family that I'd—no, we'd—let our own family of two fall apart. It was disconcerting for sure.

"No, this is my parent's home, remember? And they aren't planning on coming back anytime soon, even after we close the mine. They are happy in Mexico." He looked at me sternly and then said, "This is everyone's home now."

"What? Does Hector know that?" I was so nervous that what had been a happy arrangement would soon become tense that I couldn't see the blessing in it all.

"He's always known that. My father told him straight-up that all of his children were welcome here if they needed a place to live. It's why no one blinked when you moved in completely."

"No one blinked because I was the help." I scowled at him. Why were we on such different pages about everything today?

"Just like you didn't blink about helping them. They didn't even think twice about this. We're family, Cate. You are their family."

"Well, I didn't know the Oteras had so many unspoken family codes." I was starting to calm down a bit, but things were still so chaotic in my mind. We sat there together silently, side by side, just holding hands, and I still couldn't make heads or tails of my feelings. Finally, a thought floated in again that made my confusion all make sense. A thought about two little girls with no shoes, and I realized two things. First, I was feeling so unglued because I was just certain that those girls, whoever they were, had some part in our future, and with the way things were looking I just didn't see how that could really be so. And second, I realized I had never told Tony about my dream. Six months had passed since I'd had it, and I'd thought about it every day in some shape or form, and still I'd never mentioned it Tony. It made me realize how far apart we'd grown, because I used to tell him everything.

"Tony, did I tell you about a dream I had a few months back?" It was time to start moving forward. Some of our dreams had died, but I knew more were left to be fulfilled, and it started with getting back on the same page with my husband before we ended up in different chapters entirely.

"No, you didn't, Cate." He looked at me quizzically, sensing my excitement about it, and he leaned in closer to listen. I loved that about him. No matter what I had to say, he wanted to hear it.

I told him how real it had felt and I set the scene for him as best I could, knowing that one can never really convey exactly how a dream felt or played out. I tried, though, to give him every detail, decoding everything I could remember about it, giving him, I hoped, the same feeling of warmth and love that I had felt towards the girls in my dream. I told him of their crooked, gentle smiles and their haunting, knowing eyes. I told him of their worn dresses a few sizes too small and of the cloud of dust that seemed to surround them both, though neither seemed to notice. And lastly, I told him of their feet.

"And they had no shoes, Tony. Not just because they'd taken them off, but because they had none."

Tony sat there in silence, taking it all in. He usually would make some sort of comment about my dreams, typically something funny or poignant. But he sat there saying nothing. After a few awkward moments where I considered that my husband must think I sounded insane, I prompted him, "Tony?"

He seemed to be in a trance-like state, staring at his own shoes, taking in the leather and the workmanship that had gone into making them. My voice snapped him out of it. "Hmmmm."

"What are you thinking?" I was afraid to ask, but I had to know. I had put so much energy into remembering this dream I just knew there was something to it, but now I was considering whether or not I was crazy.

"I had a similar dream, Cate. About two girls." He looked at me with tears in his eyes.

"What?" My voice cracked. I couldn't believe it. "When?"

"I don't know, a few months ago. It had seemed so real, but then, don't most dreams? I guess I just discounted it. Well, honestly, I sort of thought it was about Josefina and Carisa because they are our goddaughters."

"What else do you remember, Tony?" My inner self was holding her breath.

"Well, I remember feeling like a father figure to them, but I couldn't see their faces like you did. But I did see..." He paused, and looked at me expectantly. "Cate, I did see their feet, for some reason. And I remember thinking to myself, *Why is it that they have no shoes*?"

Chapter Forty-Three

Lillie
Friday, August 14, 1953
4:00 p.m.

Lillie drifted further and further into the dark. Most of her life she'd been slightly frightened by the inkiness of night, but this kind of darkness comforted and welcomed her. She felt her body loosen muscle by muscle, as it hadn't done in many months, and she felt her back ease into the bed gently, pleasantly even. Her mind swirled around the last bit of conversation she'd had with Elizabeth about Clay's brother, Wesley. It was about the day his body had come home from Camp Wheeler in Georgia. It had been May 19, 1942, and it had been the day her Clay had died too.

The days before Wesley's body had arrived home in Franklin flooded back in crystal clear images, like she was watching it happen all over again. Clay's mama Essie had come over unannounced in the middle of the day from the west side of town. Lillie had known instantly that something was terribly wrong. Essie still lived way over on Harris School Road, where they'd moved when she had come to Franklin as a newlywed many, many years before. It had been her family's land for generations, and a place where one of the first county schools had been located in the mid-1800s. It had been Clay's childhood stomping grounds.

At first Lillie had thought something had happened to Clay, but then she realized that didn't make much sense. Mr. Adams, not Essie, would have come running if it had been Clay. Lillie had stood there staring at Clay's mother's face, a face that was typically cold as steel—a face that was now crumbled in grief and torment. It was the only time Lillie ever saw that Essie Woodard had a heart. She knew right away it must have been something really bad to have broken it. She'd known grief for sure, as she'd been widowed some fourteen years prior when her husband, John Earl, had been just forty-eight years old. He'd died in his sleep. Nobody had ever known just why, but after knowing Essie all those years, Lillie had always guessed it had been the stress that his wife had laid on him his whole life. His heart just couldn't take anymore. Though now, looking at her wrinkled and weathered skin and her sorrowful eyes, Lillie wondered if maybe losing John Earl so young hadn't been the thing that had hardened Essie so. Perhaps she'd been lighter before, kinder, and loving. Perhaps Lillie knew nothing about it after all.

"Lillie, where's Clay?" Essie finally managed to say the small words that came out in a whisper.

"In the field, I suppose. It finally done rain and the soil's real moist, so they's setting the tobacco plants. What's happened, Mrs. Woodard? What is it?" Lillie wiped her wet hands on her apron and reached out to lead the old woman into her tiny kitchen. For the first time ever Essie Woodard didn't rebuff Lillie's kindness, and she allowed herself to be led to one of the wobbly wooden chairs that surrounded the long oak table. She collapsed into it and started to sob. Lillie hadn't know what to make of it, nor what to do. This typically frigid woman was melting before her, and she wasn't sure what to do about it. In the end she gave her the space to do what she needed to do and set about putting hot water on for coffee.

She pulled two of her best plates down from the lower cupboard, two that didn't have chips or cracks, and brought them over to the table. Lillie kept herself as busy as she could while giving Essie the time she needed to collect herself. She uncovered the jam cake she'd made just that morning, the one she'd hoped to surprise Clay with. She'd used the last of her blackberry jam that she had canned last year, and she'd even topped it with caramel icing, a real treat indeed. She sliced into it without a second thought, serving herself and Mrs. Woodard each a hearty slice, even though she knew neither woman would likely touch much of it. After she finished percolating the coffee, she poured it into her cobalt blue enamelware mugs, hand-me-downs from Mrs. Adams, who had replaced hers with ceramic-type mugs that had been hand painted and custom-made.

After some time, Essie looked at Lillie and said, "Wesley's been killed."

Lillie gasped and then paused a moment, letting Essie's words sink in, and then said, "Oh, my word, how? He ain't even over in the war, Mrs. Woodard. He's in Georgia! How's he been killed?" Lillie sat in a state of shock and confusion.

Essie started to cry again and then caught herself. She wiped at her eyes, picked up her coffee mug, took a sip, and tried to get a hold of her emotions. "He done work a desk job. Personnel or some such thing. Them Camp Wheeler folks done see fit to keep him stateside, for which I was most grateful at the time. If I'd have known, though, what would happen, that he might'a been safer in Europe, I'd'a said send him."

"Essie, I don't know that that's true... I done heard some horrid stuff about our boys over there..." Essie interrupted her before Lillie could finish her thought.

"No matter, army done kill my boy anyhow. His desk was behind this partition wall, real thin-like, see. And the room he worked in was right next to the arsenal..." Essie stopped, and Lillie couldn't imagine where she was going with all this. "Some dumb boy done accidentally fire off a shot in that arsenal and it passed through that wall like it was paper. It passed through my Wesley's head, like it was paper." Essie erupted in sobs, and Lillie sat dumbfounded. It was such a random thing, Wesley working at a desk and being killed like that.

Lillie said nothing; she just reached over and held Essie's hands as she cried. Finally, she straightened up and looked Lillie in the eyes. "Sergeant Ream done come tell me. He say he went right away, that he didn't even feel it. That it was like he'd just felled asleep. He said that he was a good soldier, my boy. That everyone liked him, that he work real hard."

"I'm sure he was. I'm sure." Lillie paused. "How can I help you, Mrs. Woodard? What is it I can do?"

Essie looked at her daughter-in-law as if seeing her for the first time, and said, "You got you a good heart, Lillie. My Clay don't rightly deserve you."

Lillie was shocked. "Essie, I, I mean, Mrs. Woodard..."

"You want to help? You tell my Clay for me. I'm not sure I got me the strength to do it. You do that for me, Lillie? Please, I just, I can't..."

Lillie felt her body go limp. Of course she would do it, but the picture of Clay as he heard the news had started to formulate in her mind, and it made her shudder—a bone-shaking kind of shudder that broke her out in goosebumps and drained the color from her face. "Yes, Mrs. Woodard. I'll do that."

Essie Woodard disappeared as suddenly as she'd arrived, and left Lillie to deal with Clay alone. She told him shortly after he came in from the field, all covered in mud and sweat, and exhausted from a long day of setting the plants. She told him in private, on the rickety front porch that whined and mewled as Clay paced back and forth, listening to her. She watched his color drain, and she watched him finally stop and hold steady to the porch post so he didn't fall to the ground. Finally, she watched as Clay silently wandered off of their land and into the field, walking aimlessly into the early evening.

To her surprise, he never said much about it. He never raged at God, or screamed, or threw fists around about it. He just quietly and quickly shut down. Whatever humanity had been there, whatever heart he had had left after losing Paul, well, it flew away like the gunshot that had flown through the partition wall and killed his brother.

Folks say a person can't change overnight, but Lillie knew different. She saw it happen. She knew there had been a little fire raging in Clay for a while: about his isolated childhood; about losing his daddy so young; about losing work with the Finns; about tobacco farming in general; about working for the Adamses. But losing his brother was like throwing gasoline on it. He had exploded inside, and he had nothing left to give but shrapnel.

Essie Woodard made it through Wesley's funeral without too much of a fuss. The old stubborn lady was back, and she wasn't going to show anybody her pain again. She died not but four months later, silently and alone, from a heart attack, the doctor had said. But Lillie knew it was from a broken heart. The day of the funeral, though, Essie sat silently beside a mute Clay as Wesley's body was given up to God in prayer. Like any son of Franklin who was lost during military service, Wesley was given full honors. The entire town gathered on the lawn of the courthouse as his coffin made its way down Main Street, from the Methodist church where the service had been held, towards Green Lawn Cemetery, where his body would be laid to rest later that afternoon.

Lillie had never seen anything like it. Folks from all parts of the countryside had made it into town to reverently honor Wesley. Lillie's eyes wandered from storefront to storefront, where she noticed that not just one, but all of the shops and businesses on the square had been closed for the day, and that not just one, but every single shade had been drawn. Inside the church was the same. Soldiers from Fort Wheeler had paid the fare themselves to come attend services, and those who hadn't been able to come had sent floral emblems, notes, and letters, all of which paid homage to the esteem in which Sergeant Wesley Woodard had been held by his brothers-in-arms. It would be one of the first of many funeral processions for young soldiers that Franklin would see over the next decade as the war over in Europe heated up.

It moved something in Lillie. Seeing all that touched her in a way she had a hard time describing. Though she'd spent very little time with him, she'd felt a kindred spirit in Wesley. A man who'd overcome what his brother Clay could not. A man who hadn't let his life circumstances change who he wanted to be. A man who woke up every morning with virtue on his mind and a jovial smile on his lips. Clay had let it all kill him over the years, and Wesley had let it make him stronger.

As Lillie watched the military guard fold the flag that had lain on Wesley's casket with precision and hand it to a stoic and silent Essie Woodard, Lillie said a prayer. She promised God she would be more like Wesley, and not like Clay. That she'd let her losses and her failures strengthen her. That no matter what happened to her, she would always find a way to see the light in things, to love unconditionally, and to forgive. While her prayer took hold and held fast, Lillie looked at her husband. She looked at Clay and she knew that she would need that prayer daily, because Clay had slipped away and replaced himself with the worst kind of version of himself. She looked at Clay and knew he'd just died too.

Chapter Forty-Four

Lillie
Friday, August 14, 1953
7:00 p.m.

Elizabeth approached the hospital with her head down and a foggy feeling she couldn't seem to shake. She'd expected to go home and collapse after having had such an emotional night and morning, but sleep had been difficult to find. She'd wrestled with her sheets, her pillows, and her racing mind. Somewhere around noon she'd drifted into a light shut-eye and dreamed of Lillie standing on the edge of a burning tobacco field, waving goodbye to her with a peaceful smile on her lips as her worn house dress flapped in the wind, dancing playfully on her ample hips. It was both a comforting and disturbing dream that left Elizabeth in a cold sweat and shivering in the middle of a hot August day. She'd slept very little after that.

She staggered tiredly over the white hexagonal penny tile that covered the annex's entryway and slowly climbed the few stone steps that led her up and under the double limestone archway. She made her way down the short hallway that led to the staircase in the middle of the main floor and gingerly began her climb up to the third floor. She wasn't sure if she wanted to see what she'd find when she reached the top, but the intense need to know propelled her forward, heavy footstep by heavy footstep. She reached her very last stair and stood there for a moment, her eyes shut and her hand gripping the railing tightly, steeling herself for what she might see. A deep breath filled her lungs as she steadied herself and rounded the corner onto Lillie's ward with more bravery than she felt.

The odor that had lingered timidly in the air that morning when Elizabeth had left was now formidable and saturated every corner of the room. It was unmistakable, and as Elizabeth's eyes drew first towards the catheter bag filled only with a small amount of blood and then towards Lillie's heaving chest, she knew. Her ears filled with sounds of Lillie's laborious breathing, the resonance of her body struggling to find oxygen permeating the room. Lillie lay with her eyes closed, an oxygen mask fitted tightly to her face, though for all the good it was doing it may has well have lain on the floor. Her skin was both yellow and pale, and each rattling breath shook her heavy chest, making it seem as though Lillie were awake and consciously moving her own body.

Elizabeth approached the bed slowly and gently placed her hand on top of Lillie's. It was cool to the touch and startled Elizabeth, though she wasn't quite sure why. Her nail beds were a bluish purple, reminiscent of a Kentucky sunset after a rainstorm, and her arms were a mottled mishmash of yellows and reds. It was the color palette of the dying.

"Lillie," Elizabeth whispered as she gave Lillie's hand a slight squeeze. "Lillie, it's Elizabeth. I'm here, I'm back." Elizabeth stood there motionless, afraid to move, afraid to say more for the fear that she really wouldn't get a further response. She found herself saying, "Lillie, Lillie, come back. Come back, please, I'm not done. I need to know more. I..."

She heard footsteps approach her from behind, but knew she needn't turn around to find out who it was. Ada Mae's voice broke the tension as she softly said, "She slipped into a coma, Elizabeth."

Elizabeth felt her breath leave her in one swift motion, and her knees became weak with anguish. She reached for the edge of the bed to steady herself and softly asked, "When?"

"Just an hour ago." Ada Mae shifted her feet uncomfortably. "There was no time to call on you. Elizabeth, there is nothing to be done here. It's just her time."

Elizabeth's arms broke out in goosebumps as her eyes began to fill with tears. "I'm not ready for this." Elizabeth felt devastated and shocked, and then surprised that she felt so. She'd known from the first day she'd laid eyes on Lillie's withered body that this was where Lillie's path was leading; and yet, when the moment had actually arrived, it was filling her with a fear she'd never experienced. A sense of panic she hadn't anticipated.

"Elizabeth," Ada Mae said softly, "Lillie left you something."

Elizabeth's eyes shot up towards Ada Mae's face. Lillie had nothing, so how had she left her anything? Elizabeth couldn't move; she felt frozen to the floor. Finally, she managed a weak, "She did?"

"It's a note. I found it, actually. In her bed, tucked in her hand." Ada

Mae reached into the pocket on the front of her nursing uniform and pulled out a small piece of wrinkled, folded paper. She held it out on her palm towards Elizabeth and waited for her to take it.

Elizabeth just stared at it, shaking with unease and a sense of foreboding. Then she reached out and took Lillie's last words from Ada Mae's hand. She unfolded the paper and gasped. Her knees nearly buckled, and Ada Mae helped her find a chair. She stared at Lillie's chicken-scratch words as if she could change them if she looked at them long enough.

"You okay, Elizabeth?" Ada Mae stood in front of Elizabeth with a furrowed brow.

"Yes, I… Did you read this, Ada Mae?" Elizabeth went pale. She didn't know what to do.

"No, it said your name on it so I just tucked it in my pocket. Everything alright?" Ada Mae took a step towards Elizabeth to comfort her, but was startled as Elizabeth quickly clamored out of the chair and away from her.

"No, don't… I can't stay, I can't do this." She turned and ran down the staircase with tears streaming down her face. She stopped short at the bottom and leaned heavily into the baluster. She uncrumpled the note and stared again at Lillie's words. Words that she knew would change her life. Words she knew would change the course of everything, and not just for her. She watched her tears fall onto the paper and the ink start to smudge. She was still standing there, trying to gather herself, when she heard Ada Mae's footsteps coming down the staircase. Ada Mae stopped at the landing, the evening sky turning purple and orange in the large window behind her.

"Elizabeth?" Ada Mae's face had softened, and Elizabeth looked up and met her friend's eyes. "It's time. She's going now."

Elizabeth stood frozen to the floor. She looked from the paper to Ada Mae and back to the paper again. She closed her eyes and took a deep breath in. She smelled lavender, and tobacco—and change. She smelled Lillie, and she knew what she had to do.

"Elizabeth, are you coming, then?" Ada Mae's voice was softer, waiting for the answer that she knew Elizabeth would give.

"Yes, I'll be right there," she said as she slowly started climbing up the stairs.

Chapter Forty-Five

Cate
Los Angeles, California
Summer 1953

That moment of sharing our oddly similar dreams had changed our lives in some strange way. We no longer felt saddened by the sale of the shop, or by the closing down of the mine, or even by the fact that we were now sharing quarters with Hector's family. We saw it all as a means to an end, and we both finally had some unexplainable faith that the end we sought included two shoeless little girls. I realize how odd that sounds, but it was all the catalyst we needed to keep moving forward.

It did, indeed, take quite a few months for the shop to sell and for Tony to tie up loose ends down in Mexico. By Christmas of 1953 we were officially free of both. We didn't end up being underwater on either one, as we had expected, but we certainly weren't walking away whistling to the bank either. Tony went straight to working laboriously for Hector, and I found myself working for him myself, doing the bookkeeping while Julia was still struggling a bit with her memory. After all the fuss and travel and business of the past few years, it was a relief to get back to simple things like a good day's work, dinner with your family, and walks on the beach on the weekends. Not much exciting happened, and for once that was okay with us. We knew we had more adventures ahead and that it was alright just to lay low for a while.

And lay low we did, at least for a few months. It was work, dinner, play with our goddaughters, and sneaking out for a few date nights by ourselves. In fact, I can honestly say that the most exciting thing that happened to us was that we got to attend a couple of Los Angeles Rams football games at the Memorial Coliseum. Once was against the Chicago Bears in late October 1953, and the other time against Green Bay in December. We missed the Lions game, which was fine by me because anything to do with Detroit was just still a bit of a sore subject. Tickets were expensive and we'd gotten to go for free, which was why it was so exciting. They were courtesy of another one of Tony's old friends, of course. So besides getting to see some live football action we just took the time we were given to relax a bit and stretch our legs. Something deep down—call it faith, even—told us we'd need to be well rested for the next chapter that was coming.

I need to back up for a moment, because just before the excitement of our football games I received some bad news from back home. I got a phone call in the middle of August from my mother, who was terribly upset. So much so that I had a hard time understanding who had died and had thought for a moment that it was my pop.

"Catherine, it's Mom." She was crying from the get-go and my heart caught in my throat. The next few sentences were rushed and garbled, mixed with salty tears and fear. I couldn't understand a word she was saying. I tried to calm her, but she just kept crying. It was like the dam she'd built up all over all of the past years with her non-emotion had burst and she couldn't stop it.

I finally shouted into the phone, "MOM! Stop it! I can't understand you." I got her attention as her sobbing stopped. I had also caught the attention of my whole household. All eyes were on me, including Josefina's and Carisa's. The girls had started to cry, probably because I rarely, if ever, raised my voice, and it had scared them.

"I'm sorry, so sorry, Catherine. If I had known earlier we could have helped her. Or at least tried…"

"Mom, who is it that died? Grandma? Granny? Who?" I didn't think she'd be that upset over either of my grandmothers. They both had lived a long and healthy life and it was no secret they were both fairly close to the end of their days, and my mom had seemed to be at peace with that idea when we had seen her last.

She sniffled, and I could picture her reaching for a tissue. "No, no. It's your sister."

Which sister? I had several, and I found myself just praying it wasn't Lina, the only one that I was still relatively close to. "Who, Mom?"

"Lillie. She's gone, Catherine. Untreated diabetes, they say. Shut down her kidneys." I could hear anger rising in my mother's voice, and then she confirmed it with her next statement, "Her goddamn husband, Clay, I swear that man all but dug her grave. They say he refused to let her get help. That he had the money, but he wouldn't pay for her medical care. Well, now he's paid with her life."

I didn't know what to say, really. Lillie was my older sister, and we had enough years between us that we hadn't been close. I think I was but a new teen when she married her husband and moved on. "Oh, Mom, I'm so sorry. I just don't know what to say…" My mind was trying to recall what I could about Lillie's life because we really didn't keep in touch much, she and I. We might as well have lived on different planets. I loved my sister because she was my sister, but I was just realizing how little I really knew her.

"All those kids of hers. Just ain't right, Catherine." My mom was enraged, and I could hear her breathing heavily, like she was trying to control herself so she wouldn't scream about it.

"Aren't most of them grown, Mom?" I remember she'd had quite a few running around when I'd last visited Kentucky so many years ago with Jack, but I seemed to recall she'd had few more since then. I later learned she'd lost a few as well, and that meant my sister and I shared a similar heartache. We both knew what it was to grieve for children.

"Most, yes, two are in the army and her eldest son lives across town working a dairy farm. But she's still got four at home. Two older, two younger. Which I guess means they can care for themselves, but kids still need a mama, Catherine. It just ain't right."

It was funny to hear my mom say those words because she hadn't ever been much of a mother to me. I wasn't bitter, though, and I could see she saw things differently now. "Mama, I don't think I can come out. I just don't have the money right now for train tickets. I'm sorry, I just don't…" She cut me off.

"No, Catherine, it's fine. It's not why I called. I just wanted you to know, is all, and, well, to see if you might be able to pitch in something towards funeral costs. Any amount will help. Otherwise her husband might well dig a hole himself in back of the house and pound in a wooden cross. She needs a proper service. She deserves it, really, she helped so many people over the years."

I guess I really didn't know my sister at all. I'd been happiest with picturing her out on some farm with a bunch of kids and a lonely life. It had been easier that way and made her less human, and made me less guilty for not having been more involved. And then I realized I wasn't even sure of her kids' names, and I felt incredibly ashamed.

"Of course, Mama, that I can do. She deserves that for sure, you're right. We can send a little something." I felt like a horrid person standing there with no emotion. My sister, my flesh, my history, had just passed away, and I felt so far removed from it that I couldn't even cry. I just wanted to get off the phone, and so I apologized again and told my mom I loved her and that we would wire some money her way so that she could bury yet another child. My heart was heavy, but perhaps not for the right reasons. There were, again, children who needed a mother, and there again I was denied motherhood. It was a cycle I feared I would repeat and repeat my entire life and never break.

But the strangest thing happened after I hung up the phone. I stepped out on the patio to catch my breath and think more about my sister for a moment, and a small bird came and landed beside me on the small beverage table in between the two patio chairs. As I looked closer I laughed, because it was a female cardinal, a red bird, as we used to call them. They weren't uncommon in the Los Angeles area, but were far more common in Kentucky. I'd grown up seeing them nearly daily, even through the winter, and realized I hadn't really seen even one my entire time in California, though I knew they were there. But here this little gal was, all brown feathers and her little streak of red, and all I could think was "Little Red." It was like the bird had whispered it on the wind and it had found my ear, and I started to laugh. It was what my sister Lillie had nicknamed me when I was small, because I too am quite small, and I also have a dazzling head of unruly red hair that I've given up trying to hide from.

Then I said it out loud. "Little Red, indeed, Lillie. I love you too." And then I laughed how she used to laugh, whole-heartedly, with a big wide grin. And I realized I still knew my sister: perhaps not her circumstances in the end, but I knew her heart, and I remembered what a kind soul she was. Then I gave the little bird a small shove off of the table, and I let my sister soar, high above whatever pain she had endured, free from her human cage for the very first time. I watched until I could see her no longer, and by then I couldn't help but think to myself that anything is possible when a red bird flies.

Chapter Forty-Six

Cate
Los Angeles, California
October 1953

They buried my sister, Lillie, a week later at Green Lawn Cemetery, and she was laid to rest next to the two sons she'd lost. As was customary then, they took pictures of her in her casket, looking peaceful and at rest, but it struck me really how old she looked for only being forty-four. I came to learn that her life had been anything but peaceful in her last years. My mother sent the photos with a thank you card for helping with the funeral costs and a note telling me how surprising the turnout was for her service. Apparently my sister, the farmer's wife, had made a big impact on our small hometown, and a lot of people had loved her. It was curious to me that it seemed so many folks had cared, yet no one had done anything to try and help her; but I soon learned the reason had a lot to do with the tall, lanky gentleman in the group photos in front of her grave site: her husband, Clay.

There were many familiar faces in that picture. My mom, my pop, and Clay to start. Then there was also my niece, Diana, who was by now an early teen, looking spotless and beautiful in her freshly pressed shin-length silk church dress and hat. But my sister Vera, Diana's mother, was not there. Then there were five others, who I could only assume were some of Lillie's children. The girls in the picture troubled me. I flipped the photo over and on the back it listed the names. Mom, Pop, Diana, Clay, Ben, Nola, Ada, Grace, and Sarah. I lingered over the last two names and ran my finger across them. Grace and Sarah, Sarah and Grace. I flipped the photo back over and looked at it again. The little ones had to be Grace and Sarah because I'd heard the names Nola and Ada before, and I wondered which one was which.

They were beautiful girls, with closely cropped hair and small eyes that were squinting because of the hot August sun. They both wore simple sundresses, and I imagine my mom had probably bought them because the smallest girl's dress was a tad too short and my mom had likely guessed on her size. They both wore white sandals and, as expected, had on long, sad faces. The older of the two, who I later learned was Lillie's eight-year-old daughter, named Grace, looked a little lost and stood off by herself a bit while Sarah, Lillie's four year old, stood clinging to her sister Nola. I know it sounds incredibly silly, but they haunted me, and all I could do was look at their feet. They couldn't be the girls in our dreams; they both obviously had shoes on and looked fairly well taken care of. I wondered, though, if that had always been the case.

I called my mom to thank her for the pictures and the note and just couldn't help myself but to ask about the girls. "Mom, how are Lillie's children?" I was hesitant and didn't want to sound pushy or nosy, but even I could hear the nervousness in my voice.

My mom didn't pick up on it, though. "Oh, fine," she said. "Well, as well as you'd expect, of course. Her three oldest were in a bit of shock for a while, and apparently had no idea she'd been sent to the hospital to die, thanks to their father. Connie and Joe, well, neither knew nothing about it until it was too late. They are both off in the service, you know. "

"Yes, I remember that. I think Joseph is in Korea, if I'm not mistaken, and Connie on the east coast somewhere. She's married now, with a little one of her own." I'd done a little digging on Lillie's family over the last few weeks, mostly out of curiosity, but also because I couldn't get my sister out of my head. "But I meant more the younger girls. How are they?"

"Well, Nola and Ada, aren't so young anymore, but I suppose you could tell that from the picture I sent you. Probably a good thing too, because without them I'm not sure Clay could manage on his own. I don't think he knows or cares much about raising children. He left that up to Lillie most of the time, I think."

"Yes, but how long will they stick around to help, mom? I mean, Nola will soon be old enough to marry if she wants, and Ada isn't but a couple years behind. I imagine they'll be wanting to start their own families soon and not raise little sisters. Besides that, until then, who's looking out for them? He's obviously not going to. "

My mom got really quiet on the other end of the phone, and I cleared my throat just to prompt some sort of response. "Mom? Are you there?"

"We can't take them in, Catherine, if that's what you're asking." It wasn't at all what I was asking actually, but I didn't correct her. "Diana's been a real blessing and we've enjoyed raising her very much, but I think our time raising little ones is coming to an end once she's all grown."

"No, Mom, you've done enough raising of grandkids, I didn't mean that, I…" She interrupted me and said something to me sternly that put all of my supposing to rest.

"Besides, Catherine. Clay would never allow it." She took a deep breath and then told me about the man who had all but killed my sister. The story she told made my toenails curl and my heart beat quickly with anger. While I realized my sister Lille wasn't perfect and had certainly made some mistakes along the way, I also saw how she had gotten stuck there and felt she had to stay.

I'll be honest that my first response was pure wonderment as to why she didn't leave him. I would have if I were her, or so I assured myself. Then again, the only reason I got out of that kind of life was because I was given an opportunity that was never presented to my sister. I realized that Lillie's life could well have been my life had I stayed in Franklin—or chosen differently along the way. The comprehension of that fact made the large gap that existed between Lillie and me close just a little bit more. In many ways Clay had had her imprisoned, in a much worse manner than my aunt had done to me, and I wondered if Lillie ever actually saw it that way.

While I too had felt interned up at my aunt's home, I realized now that I at least had options, and that I wasn't actually a prisoner. Towards the end Lillie probably actually was, and her options were limited at best; and then became almost nonexistent the longer her disease progressed. With my parents and my other siblings gone from the area, she'd probably felt she'd had nowhere to turn. Even if she could have left he would never have allowed her to take his children, and she knew he would probably have hunted her down and eventually found her. I wondered again how she'd dealt with it all of those years, knowing that, short of leaving her children behind or Clay dying or going to jail, there was nowhere to go but right where she was. Knowing my sister, she just tried to make the best of it and move forward.

Even more so, I realized my sister probably did what she was well-known for as a child. She probably saw all his ugliness and tried to love him anyway. She used to call it 'really seeing people.' It really was such

360

a sweet and noble trait she had. To me, though, with folks like Clay, it's akin to watching a fist come at you in a boxing ring and not moving out of the way because you don't want to offend your opponent. It was such a great and kind gift Lillie had in her ability to really humanize everyone in some manner. Yet, in the end, it was what ultimately killed her.

I know my mom's story was meant to warn me about messing with Clay's life and his kin, and it did in some ways, but in others it just confirmed to me that none of the girls should be in his care in any way, shape, or form.

My mom ended her story by saying, "So you see, Catherine, Clay's so stubborn that even if it was easier for him he wouldn't freely give them up. They are his helpers now, his workers on the farm, and I wouldn't be surprised if he pulls Grace from school soon and gives her a job to do. He'll never let them go, and certainly not to our family. They belong to him."

I was without words, and I felt like someone had just laid heavy weights around both of my shoulders. I mumbled a hasty goodbye to my mom and told her I'd call soon and to let me know if I could help in any way, but I knew that for her, the subject was a dead one. Lillie had died, and her husband had the kids. End of story.

Tony came home that evening to find me hiding in our bedroom. I hadn't bothered to do much the whole day and wasn't feeling terribly sociable. I just felt so sad because I knew logically that my mom was right, but something in my gut just felt off about the whole thing. I relayed the story my mom had told me to Tony, and when I was done he just sat beside me quietly. He reached over and moved a large red curl off of my forehead and smoothed it back into the rest of my hair, but as usual it fell back in its original place just over my brow. My hair was as stubborn as I was sometimes.

"Cate, love, I don't know what to say. I know they are your family, but we can't go hoping that every motherless child is meant to be ours." His face was soft, and though his words seemed harsh, they were laced with love.

"I know that, Tony." I pushed the curl back out of my eye, and it lazily crept back down by the time I put my hand back in my lap.

He looked me in the eye and asked, "Do you?" The longer he looked at me the more I felt closer to breaking down, but somehow I couldn't look away. I think I needed to let it go. For Lillie, for her children, and for myself; who, it seemed, would remain childless for now. I started to cry, but then I caught myself because something caught my eye. Another cardinal had landed on the windowsill just past Tony, and I stopped and stared at it.

"Cate?" Tony was trying to get my attention, but I was trying to listen. That bird had something to say.

"Tony, that bird..." He turned around and looked behind him, and as he did the little gal flew off out of sight. "I've seen that bird before."

"There's lots of cardinals here, Cate." Tony looked at me quizzically. I know he was beginning to worry about me. "I see them all the time, love."

"Funny, I haven't, and I've seen that particular one twice in the last few weeks. She has a small dot of red on her left wing."

"Cate, are you okay? You seem spooked by birds and so thrown off by your sister's death. I thought you said you weren't close."

"We weren't. She was so much older than I am." I got up and went over to the dresser where I'd put the pictures away. I slowly opened the drawer and again saw the faces that had imprinted themselves on my mind. I turned around and handed the group photo to Tony.

He stared at it for a few minutes and then flipped it over like I had done, searching for more information. He finally looked up and said to me, "So that's her husband, huh?"

"Yes." I waited, not wanting to prompt him. I wanted him to come to his own conclusions.

"Grace and Sarah," he said softly.

"Yes." I paused and added, "Grace is the older one."

"Hmmm. They're beautiful." He looked up at me, and tears brimmed at his eyelashes. "But they aren't ours, Cate... are they?"

"I don't know, Tony. But every time I look at that picture, something moves in me, like a pregnant woman who first feels her child quicken."

Was it real, or just my imagination?

"Hmmmm," was all he could say, and then finally he handed me back the photo and said, "I guess time will tell, Cate. But for now, we have to let it go."

"Yes, I know." Because I understood what both he and my mom were trying to say. But every night at bedtime, I couldn't help but to wish both girls a silent good night and then tuck the picture into my nightstand and turn out the lamp with a smile. And I often dreamed of tiny bare feet and soft Kentucky dirt in between itty-bitty toes.

I never saw the bird again, though I looked every time I stepped outside. Finally, I just came to the conclusion that she had given me her message already and wouldn't be coming back. Some days I felt content knowing that something big was going to happen for Tony and me soon, and I had that odd feeling still that it had something to do with my nieces, though no one from back home had given me any sort of indication that that was true. Some days I just felt like I must be a little crazy. Seeing birds with cryptic chirps and feeling an almost electric sense of change in the air. Regardless, that became my new reality for the next few months; and while I was smart enough to keep my thoughts to myself, I know Tony sensed a shift. I think part of him thought I was coming unglued a little bit too, but he had the heart and good sense not to say anything. I guess he figured that after all I'd been through I was allowed to fall apart a little bit, and he knew me well enough to know I wouldn't stay there long.

As it turned out, I didn't have to wonder long if I was crazy. It was a Tuesday night like any other Tuesday night. Julia and I had made beef stew, and she had baked up some of her famous homemade bread. It was early January, and the holidays had passed without much of a fuss. I couldn't believe that it was 1954 already and that Josefina was about to turn five in March. I was starting to understand it when folks say things like "children grow up so fast." It was like we'd all blink and the girls would grow another inch.

So that particular Tuesday night I was setting the table and thinking about how fast life was passing, and then something happened that changed our lives forever. Just as people say that children grow up so fast, they also say how one moment in time can change the whole course of your life's journey. I assume folks are referring to freak things like car accidents, or the birth of a baby, or the winning of a large hand in a high-stakes poker game. For Tony and me, our world was rocked by something far less radical, yet nonetheless monumental.

The phone rang.

Chapter Forty-Seven

Cate
Franklin, Kentucky
Thursday, February 11, 1954

I wondered if her feet felt funny in her new shoes. Like they were a foreign appendage, or an unwanted house guest. I imagine that the sole felt incredibly hard under her small foot as I watched her widen and curl her stubby toes so she could maintain her balance. The black-and-white leather probably felt constricting, and I knew it rubbed her heel uncomfortably as I'd seen the small blisters starting to form when she'd taken them off the night before. I smiled as I watched her walk back and forth on the linoleum of the bus depot. The clip-clop of the heavy rubber sole was an unfamiliar sound to her, and I wondered if the echo sometimes gave her the feeling that someone was following her. Clip, clop, clippity, clop—and she'd occasionally turn around to look at the no one that was there. I'm sure it was a far cry from the feel of the earth beneath her feet. I had scrubbed away the dirt in between and underneath her toes some days ago and had trimmed her tiny nails straight and clean.

Although she didn't seem terribly sure of her new footwear, she did seem to like the ruffled socks, even though her hard-earned callouses caught on the fabric and pulled every now and then. They were stark white and ever so elegant, even in her plain saddle shoes. It was the first feminine fabric that had graced her skin in all her five years, and the cotton and lace looked nice around her ankles. She told me later that she had seen other girls in town sporting the same fine stockings and shoes and had often wondered what it would feel like. Now that she knew, I wondered if she wished she could feel the gravel again and the tiny pebbles that were probably as soft as feathers to her beneath her step. The shoes seemed to make her feel unbalanced and awkward, as if at any moment a strong breeze might knock her off her feet. I wondered if she minded. I wondered a lot of things.

No doubt about one thing, though, she sure did like those socks, along with the pale yellow dress I had purchased for her for the trip. It was simple enough, lacking any frill or lace, but it was new and clean, and for her that was ample reason to adore it. I think she mostly loved that she was the first to wear it, straight from the clothing rack at the store. I knew that feeling. Being the youngest in my family had meant many a hand-me-down and very few non-essentials. I was sure that the dress felt almost as foreign to her as her shoes, but probably only because the fabric lacked the soft feel of cloth that had been washed many, many times. It was, again, a feeling I remembered well from my own childhood. The dress was rigid and held its shape without trying, and she appeared to find great joy in the swish, swish sound that it made when she walked.

I watched her again on the bus a few hours later as she swung her little legs rhythmically, one at a time—left, right, left, right, like a clock pendulum, steady and even. Occasionally her foot caught on the seat in front of her with a loud *thump* which captured not only the attention of the seat's grumpy occupant, but also garnered a disapproving gaze from her sister. In contrast to Sarah's playful oscillations, her older sister, Grace, sat silently with her hands folded gently in her lap as though we were in a church. It was as if she'd attended church her whole life, though she hadn't, and this was yet one more sermon to endure. I wondered what Grace was thinking, and whether she perhaps feared what retribution she'd meet if she fell out of line. I was sure she'd likely seen a good amount of punishments doled out at her house for the smallest of infractions. She finally laid a tender hand on her younger sister's leg and gazed down at her lovingly. "Enough, Sarah," Grace said quietly.

The pendulum legs stopped. "Will it be long, Grace?" I found it funny that Sarah didn't ask me, the adult; but then, I suppose she really didn't know me.

"Yes, it will be very long, I think." She snuck a peek at me to see if she was correct, and I answered her with a small smile and slight nod. "Try to find something to keep busy."

I saw Sarah look around and her eyes fell on my bag that I had tucked under my seat. "You want to see the books I bought? I can read one to you, if you like," I said cautiously. I felt so unsure of myself and how they'd receive me, but Sarah and Grace both looked at me with eyes as large as saucers. "Well, good Lord, girls! Hasn't anyone ever read you a book?" I asked them, but I already knew the answer.

"My mother used to, but it's been a long time," whispered Grace in a barely audible voice.

In the end their mother hadn't been able to see well enough to read a label, much less a book. And while Sarah had been too young to be schooled, Grace had been pulled out so many times to work the farm that she was dreadfully far behind in most subjects. It was something I knew I'd need to tackle quickly to get her caught up, and I had my work cut out for me for sure. Besides the fact that neither girl could read, most books cost twenty-five cents or more in town and were a luxury the girls rarely knew. I know I hadn't had many books as a child except for what was given me by the schoolhouse or what I borrowed from friends. Twenty-five cents was two loaves of bread or a gallon of gasoline, and unless you could burn it for fuel or eat it, it didn't get bought. I knew the world I was taking them from. I'd grown up much the same.

"Well, then, ladies. No time like the present to introduce you to the amazing world of literature," I said with my best bravado. I wanted them excited about it from the get go. I wanted to give them the world right away, but somehow starting with one book seemed like a better first step off of the farm. I sensed small steps were the way to go.

I pulled out a book, and the spine shone crisp and golden, stiff with its newness. While I unraveled a tale, the bus flew down the highway, heading west. Like its namesake, the blue and silver bus was so fast the Greyhound logo looked poised to win his race. Old Silversides was indeed holding his own amongst the rough terrain of the gravel road. I had wanted to purchase tickets for the train, but the bus fare out to Kentucky had already made the purse strings tighter than I'd hoped. Tony had also said it might be good to take our time getting to California, to give them a little time to adjust to leaving everything they knew.

Tony. It had been so many weeks since I'd seen him, and I desperately missed his kind eyes and gentle hands, but mostly I missed his laughter and reassuring way. He hadn't hesitated a bit when we'd gotten the phone call from Elizabeth that had changed everything. I wished he'd been able to come with me to Kentucky, but someone had to stay with the new shop. The moment we had learned that we had a chance, no matter how small, at getting custody of the girls, he had flown into frantic action. He said it was now or never to open his own shop again, and he went about making that happen like the house was on fire and only his swift action could save it. I knew it was a matter of pride and that, if he was going to be a father, he was going to support his children on his own and not under his brother Hector's care. Moon Bolt Products was born in the course of just weeks, and it ended up supporting us nicely for years to come.

Since our new company was just getting off the ground, there was no way we could both go. Besides that, I think he was afraid that if the judge saw the color of his skin, he might rethink his position about whether or not we were a proper home. Tony had said to me that if people were that discriminatory in Los Angeles, just imagine how they were in Kentucky, and I could only pray he was wrong. In fact, I placed my bets on the opposite being true, because I just couldn't stand to think otherwise. I phoned Tony as often as I could while I was gone and tried to keep him abreast of the new developments as they had happened, but it wasn't the same as having him by my side.

One phone call in particular had been difficult to place to him. I'd been in Franklin for almost a week and felt like I hadn't made any progress. I actually felt physically ill, and I sat for twenty minutes at my friend Beverly's kitchen table staring at the telephone, trying to will myself to call Tony. There it lay, that telephone, all shiny and new, haunting me with its voluptuously curved earpiece and beautifully rounded base. The rotary dial mocked me with its precision tick, tick, tick. Time to make the call, it seemed to say. Time is running out. Time. I ran my hand over the receiver repeatedly as if it would give me the strength I needed to tell Tony what was so very heavy on my mind.

As I sat there staring at the phone, my mind ran away in about a million different directions, and I kept replaying the last few days over and over again like a record that had gotten stuck on a certain part of a track. I was staying with this old friend of mine from childhood because she had offered when I called her to say I was heading her way and had asked her if she knew the best place to stay. Though I hadn't seen her in years, I accepted her sweet offer because she was so kind and lived in town and I wouldn't be requiring a car to get the things done that I needed. Besides that, I was sure I was going to need a little bit of emotional support, and Bev had always been good at that when we were younger.

I was thinking about how it was strange to be back in Franklin. The chill was colder than I'd remembered. California had softened me to the harsh weather of northeastern winters. I shivered constantly, though I'd be willing to bet most of it was nerves. Bev's house was just blocks from the courthouse, which lay in the middle of the town square. It was just blocks away from where I had turned in my application for custody earlier that week, on the first of February, just a couple of days after my arrival. Just blocks away from the clerk, an older woman named Mrs. Hodges, who had looked me up and down haughtily and said to me in a condescending tone, "Hmm. So you're Lillie's sister from California, eh?"

"Yes, Ma'am," I had replied, trying hard to be as polite as possible. I remembered her from when I was younger, but she apparently did not remember me. How she knew Lillie, I wasn't sure.

"Right sad to hear about Lillie," she said as she looked over my paperwork. When her eyes got down to the part that I assume was about my past and current marriages, her eyebrows arched upwards and she cleared her throat rather loudly.

"Yes, it is sad." I didn't want to talk too much because I was so nervous and I didn't want to take any chances at blowing this. I just needed these people to see me like Lillie would have, just me and not what was on that paper.

"Well," she said as she removed her glasses and rubbed underneath her eyes. Apparently being a county courthouse clerk was exhausting work, and she was hell-bent on letting me know she wasn't happy about an out-of-towner coming in to take away a few of their own. "It may be a while before you can get a session with the judge."

"Oh." I felt crushed. The state's Child Services knew of my intent, but without the document that said I had custody, they had to proceed with moving the girls up north to the orphanage in Louisville soon. I didn't want them in Clay's care any longer than they had to be, but I definitely didn't want them in an orphanage where Lord knows what might happen. Besides, once they were in the state's care, it would be a huge fight to get them out.

I also knew Nola and Ada were doing their best to protect them until I could get them, but even they couldn't tame the force that was Clay forever, and I'm sure they were taking the brunt of his anger about it all. I still hadn't figured out how to help them yet either, which was a weight heavy on my heart. The state official told me they were too old to take custody of and that both of them were adamant that they weren't going to willingly leave with me. I'm sure it was a mixture of fear and some strange sense of family loyalty that was holding them there. Clay might have been a bastard of a father, but he was the only thing they had ever really known. That alone held some mystical power over the two older girls. Or so I imagined.

"Can I ask how long it might take?" I asked cautiously, but I really didn't have much time. I also couldn't be pushy, so it was a fine line, and I knew I was at her mercy.

"Well, Mrs.—" she put her glasses back on and looked down at my name and then back up at me. "—Otera, is it?" I nodded, and she continued. "I don't know. His docket is terribly full. Lots of drunk and disorderly this week, winter makes folks go a little stir crazy round here. Bar fights and whatnot. County jail's just around the corner, and I hear it's bursting at the seams. Cases got to be heard, you know."

"I understand." I was searching for the right words and the right balance to let her know I needed her help. "Mrs. Hodges, I know you don't remember me because I left here some time ago, and I know I must seem like an out-of-towner to you poking my nose in business that isn't mine. And I know that Lillie and I weren't close, and that it's quite obvious you were fond of my sister..."

I paused, and her face softened as she nodded. "Yes, yes I was. She was a kind person, with a big heart."

"Yes, I hear she was." I swallowed hard and looked her in the eye, praying hard again that she would see me and see past what she'd just read on the paper before her. I gathered my strength and continued. "But Lillie wanted this. In fact, it was her gift to me, really, in the end."

"Oh? How so?" She knitted her brow, and I knew by the look on her face that she was getting there.

"I can't have children, Mrs. Hodges. Have tried for years, really, and can't—and well, those sophisticated folks in Los Angeles don't think that letting biracial couples adopt is a good idea. And like I said, my sister wanted this for her girls, and somehow, even as she lay dying, she made it happen. I came here hoping that the kind people of Franklin were a tad more forgiving than the agencies in L.A.. I know what I look like on that paper, Mrs. Hodges. Divorced once, and married again to a dark-skinned man. I know, but can you look at just me? These girls need me. And my husband and I—well, we need them too."

She stared at me for a long moment, not saying anything, and then shifted uncomfortably in her chair as she averted her eyes from mine. I could see tiny tears form at the corners of her eyes and wet her lashes as she avoided looking at me again. "Well," she finally said, "For Lillie, then, I'll see what I can do."

"Really?" I tried to suppress my excitement, but I couldn't help myself. She had seen me, I know she had, and whether or not she approved I had become more than a name on a paper with a questionable past. My trip out had been worth it for that moment alone, but I hoped it was just the tip of the iceberg.

"I said I'd try. You staying near here?" she asked without looking at me.

"Yes, with Beverly Jones, a few blocks away." I smiled kindly at her, but she still wouldn't meet my eyes.

"Alright then, I'll call you if I get an open slot in the judge's schedule."

I was beaming as I thanked her and she was half-smiling, half-scowling at me as she shooed me out the door and told me not to go too far.

Chapter Forty-Eight

Cate
Franklin, Kentucky
Friday, February 5, 1954

Days had passed, and Mrs. Hodges had not called. I knew she said it might take awhile, but she also said she would try; and with each ticking hour my faith in her faltered. By the fifth day, I was fighting hard against feeling defeated. It took all I had not to march myself over to Clay's and just ask the girls to come along with me. It was another reason I was glad I didn't have a car. That's when Bev found me, staring at the phone, like it could be my salvation or the death of me.

"Whatcha doing, Sugar?" Beverly asked. She'd startled me, and I jumped a bit.

"I need to tell Tony. I need to tell him I think we've lost them. It's bound to be too late." I said. I felt a mile away, floating above it all somehow.

"Ah, Catherine, Cate. Don't give up hope just yet. I remember my mama used to tell me, 'Abstain from many things, girls, but never from having hope. Most times it's all we got.' I've never known my mama to be wrong! You never know what that judge might say. Besides, I hear he's mighty kindhearted towards the ladies."

"Ya, but does he consider a once-divorced, twice-married thirty-five-year-old woman a lady? He might have a problem with that. Well, that and the color of Tony's skin. So ridiculous," I said, sagging into the chair in heap. It made my heart rate increase just thinking about it.

"Well shoot, Cath... Cate! What's with the dark cloud hanging on 'ya head? I reckon he may well see a woman willing to save some children from a monster, that's what I reckon," Beverly said as she placed a sympathetic hand on my shoulder. Bev was naturally an optimist, and I was glad I was staying with her. I responded in turn by placing my hand over Beverly's with a tender pat.

"Oh, Lord, Bev, how I hope you're right. What on earth do I say to Tony? All this trouble and the state may get them anyway on account of how I lived my life, even though I've never done anything wrong! Doesn't seem fair. Those sweet girls haven't done anything wrong either but be born to the wrong father." I closed my eyes and rubbed the bridge of my nose between my thumb and forefinger.

"Cate, you're right. You ain't never done nothing wrong indeed! You simply stood up for yourself and fell in love with an amazing man. Surely, surely, the law will see that. And you just tell Tony the truth now. Ain't do nobody any good to be keeping secrets."

"You're right. I know you're right, but still..." I sighed heavily, thinking about all that possibly lay ahead, and suddenly I was exhausted. "I just feel so bad that I can't do anything about Ada or Nola. Seems like they are in more danger right now than the little ones even, and still they won't leave him."

Beverly snickered. "Well, don't be so sure about that, friend..."

I was puzzled. "What do you mean, Bev?"

She smiled widely, showing me a few gaps in her mouth where some teeth used to be. She was always an attractive girl, and even with the missing teeth she still had a certain beauty about her. "Hmmm. Well, it was supposed to be a surprise, but seeing as how you're so down and all, I guess you could use a little pick-me-up."

"Do tell, please. I haven't gotten much energy left in me for surprises tonight." I half had a headache, and I just wanted to avoid the whole scene with Tony on the phone and go on to bed.

"Okay, Okay." She sat down across from me at the table and crossed her arms in front of her and leaned in on them on the table towards me like the whole town would overhear if she wasn't careful. "Well, I've been asking around town, to see if I could find either girl any work. I was thinking it might help them to get out from under Clay's thumb. Unfortunately, not many folks took too kindly to it, mostly out of fear of Clay, I think. They all know who he is and don't want no part of that mess. But this morning, Billy Roark, you know, the owner of the general store, he done told me he'd offered Ada a job last time she'd come into town for some items. She apparently turned him down."

I sighed sadly. "She did? Did he say why?"

"Well yes, that's the surprise!" She paused for effect, and then continued when she realized just how tired I was. "Anyway, she told him thank you, but that she wouldn't be living in Franklin for much longer."

My eyebrows shot up. Was it possible I was getting all of them to come with me instead of just the younger two? I suddenly felt relief that they'd be safe, and then hugely overwhelmed. "Oh. Did she say where she was going? And Nola? Did she say anything about her sister?"

"Yup. That's the best part. Apparently, Nola's found herself a husband-to-be, and he's not originally from here. He was extra help with the harvest in the fall, and apparently took a liking to Nola. Supposed to be a real nice boy, if not a little homely looking. Ada said that Nola would be telling their daddy that Nola was getting hitched and would be taking her with her when she left. She said they'd be telling him the minute that the state or you came and got the girls."

"Oh my gosh. Oh my gosh, Bev! That's wonderful! Where are they moving to exactly?" Questions reeled in my head, and it was more than I could have hoped for. Then fear struck me and reality set in. "Wait, he'll never let them leave. They're just teenagers. Clay would rather die first, I'm sure, because he'd be left alone."

"That's the beauty of it. It's foolproof! Nola's seventeen and old enough to marry in Kentucky without the need of parental consent, and Ada is old enough to leave home legally if she wants to. Besides that, Ada sort of let slip that Nola was likely expecting a baby come late summer." She was grinning wildly. "Isn't that exciting?"

My face had fallen, and had stayed there despite Bev's enthusiasm. "Doesn't matter, Bev. He'll kill them first. Clay will kill them before he lets them walk off of that farm like that with another man. He will, I swear it."

"Not if they leave with Nola's soon-to-be-husband in tow." She grinned at me sheepishly now, and I waited for the bombshell that Bev seemed to be holding. "Apparently, Nola's soon-to-be-husband, Howard, hails from Tennessee, and is a rather large guy, around six foot four and close to three hundred pounds or something like that. That's according to Miss Callie down at the salon..."

I looked at her as if to say *really*, and my eyebrow raised on its own as I couldn't help but interrupt her. "Really, Bev? Gossip? That's what you're passing along to me?"

"Girlfriend, you've been gone too long. Gossip around here is as good as reading the newspaper, and oftentimes more accurate anyway! Now you're messing up the best part, dang it, so shush!" She smiled at me and leaned in even more, lowering her voice as if Clay might hear her from his farmstead miles away. "Now this Howard guy has four older brothers, and rumor has it they're a big backwoods hunting family. You know what that means, right?"

I was starting to get the picture, and I couldn't help the little smile that was starting to play on my lips. "Um, Nola and Ada will be eating lots of deer meat next winter in Tennessee?"

She laughed at my attempted humor, and then said, "Maybe! Maybe. But no, Cate, picture this. Five strapping Tennessee brothers, lots and lots of hunting rifles, and a man named Howard coming to Clay's door to collect his pregnant bride and her little sister to take them back home across the state line. Lord, I'd pay a mighty penny to be a fly on that wall!"

She started laughing softly, but it quickly grew into an uproar of glorious proportions as I joined in. We laughed until our sides ached and tears hit the table cloth. When it almost died down to a chuckle, one of us would picture Clay standing there all alone. A grown man with nothing left but an empty house and perhaps some soggy britches from wetting himself out of fright on his own front lawn, and we'd start laughing all over again.

I don't think I'd ever laughed so hard in all my life, and it felt good to let it go. The only thing that finally sobered me up was a very solemn but happy thought.

"You know, Bev, that actually isn't even the best part of your story, though it was pretty darn good. The best part is...well, the best part is that Clay won't ever be touching any of those girls ever again."

Chapter Forty-Nine

Cate
Topeka, Kansas
Thursday, February 11, 1954

Sarah was a big-boned little girl, broad at the shoulders and thick at the ankle. She was a product of many generations of sturdy, hardworking women like my mama and grandmothers. Her feet were wide and flat, with stubby toes that would have provided the perfect platform to carry an ample load, if she'd only had that mass to bear. Instead, her ribs stuck out painfully, and her knees were knobby and lacked substance. It made me cringe to think about how much her belly must have ached sometimes. Her legs and arms had been made thin by lack of food on her plate for months, which was, I'm sure, a sharp contrast to the liberal platefuls her father had eaten in front of her.

It was late on the first day of our travels, and the girls and I settled into a large overstuffed booth at a scheduled stop in Topeka, Kansas. The Greyhound Post House didn't look like much of a restaurant from the outside as it was boxy, with large windows lining three sides, and lacked much in the way of architectural interest. But it may as well been a four-star establishment as far as Sarah and Grace were concerned. I found great joy in watching their reactions. They seemed fascinated by the light and clean atmosphere, and it seemed Sarah could hardly contain her excitement. I watched her tiny eyes dart everywhere, taking it all in, and she bounced ever so slightly on her the tips of her toes. She had surely never dined in a restaurant before, and for her I'm sure the experience rivaled that of an amusement park, or meeting the governor. The large menu was graced by items like steak and chops, breaded veal cutlets, and grilled king salmon with lemon wedges.

The waitress was prompt and cheerful and reminded me of a greeter at a town carnival. She was trying hard to please, and very proud to be carrying on the Post House tradition. She was also obviously oblivious to the fact that she was working at a pit stop diner in the middle of nowhere.

"Afternoon, ladies! What will we be having to drink here?" she piped, a little too loudly.

"I'll have cup of coffee please, black." I said. "Girls?"

Silence filled the little booth. Sarah looked at Grace and Grace looked at Sarah. They both looked like they knew what they wanted, but were afraid to say. I raised my eyebrows at them, prompting an answer.

"Soda pop, please," said Grace softly while staring at the table top.

"Me too, me too!" yelled Sarah so loudly that she turned the heads of the few other customers sitting nearby. A small laugh escaped my lips.

"A little quieter now, child! Good Lord!" I suppressed a smile and turned to the waitress. "Two cherry colas for the young ladies, please. I do believe my girls are thirsty!"

My girls. Had I said that out loud? Sarah grinned widely and snuck a peek at Grace, who suppressed a small smile of her own. The sound of it rolled around in my ears and on my tongue until it was as delicious as I remembered my first soda had been all those years ago at Roark's store with my pop and the sassy salesman. Bubbly and cool, sweet and refreshing, and most definitely surprising.

The soda came quickly and was as cold as the Kentucky winter days that we had just left behind. Resisting the urge to suck it down in one big gulp, the girls sipped it slowly. The fizz apparently felt funny on Sarah's tongue, because she started to giggle a little, and then wiggle a little, until in the course of a minute, she was filled with a laughter so hearty even I couldn't contain it.

"Now Sarah!" I started to say, but my eye caught the ear-to-ear grin on Grace's face, and I stopped mid-sentence. Laughter now rang out from my mouth, loud and clear, crisp and warm like the apple pie on the restaurant counter. It filled the booth and demanded attention like a Baptist choir, and startled the waitress so much that she knocked over my coffee. A moment of silence followed as the hot brown liquid spread across the table and threatened my blue dress.

"Oh, my goodness! I am so..." the waitress started to say. But I interrupted her with my laughter as it rang out again, and it was followed by Sarah's shriek of surprise and another fit of giggles, and finally by Grace's silent laughter, which she hid in her throat.

"It's okay, really," I managed in between howls. "No one ever got anywhere crying over a bit of spilled coffee!" Somehow, just then, I realized that all of those sad years waiting for these children had been a lot like the spilled coffee, and it wasn't worth crying over it for one more second.

After the coffee and the tears from laughter-filled eyes had all been wiped away, I said simply, "Alright, girls, we really ought to at least attempt to behave ourselves."

"Yes, Ma'am," the girls mumbled with straws fixed in between their teeth while the tiny bubbles filled their mouths like little sips of joy.

"Well then, what would you like to order for lunch?" The frazzled waitress was back, a weary smile pasted on her face while she tried hard not to appear thrown off by the outburst from her customers and the spilled coffee. Sarah and Grace ordered the deluxe hamburger. A quarter pound of choice meat topped with tomatoes, pickles, ketchup, and relish. I ordered the fried egg sandwich and a cup of split pea soup, at which Sarah wrinkled her nose, making me laugh again.

"I don't much like them peas whole, so I don't suppose splittin' em into a soup is gonna make 'em a whole lot better!" said Sarah.

"Well, it's a good thing you didn't order it then, isn't it?" I said, suppressing another grin. This child had come with spirit that, Lord knows, should been wrung out of her years ago, given her circumstances. The innocence of the young and all that, I suppose. I knew it would be her saving grace.

Our lunch came without the dramatics of our prior drink service. The girls stared at their plates in wonderment. I realized it was probably twice, if not three times, the portion size they were accustomed to. Sarah immediately went to work on her french fries, which I tried to remind her were just a side to her main meal. I hadn't touched my food; I was having too much fun watching the girls, and looked on with wonder as Sarah first took notice of her hamburger. She studied it at first with as much interest as a biologist hovering over a well-grown petri dish, and then promptly flung open the bun. She picked the beef patty up carefully with her thumb and pointer finger and placed it ever so gently to the side of her plate on the table.

"What on earth are you doing, Sarah?" I asked, staring at the round piece of beef sitting on the table cloth, discarded sadly like a used tissue. Sarah just looked at me and then at Grace. This spurred me to look at Grace, who herself was prodding the burger with one finger as if it would come alive on her plate at any moment.

"Sarah? Grace? What is it, girls? Don't you like hamburgers? I mean, you ordered them. You must like them," I was at a loss. Maybe raising these kids was going to be way more complicated than I had anticipated.

"Rosey from the farm next'a us was always yappin' about the hamburgers she'd get in town when she'd go and see her uncle. She said they was just delicious and so juicy they'd melt in your mouth the minute they'd touched your lips. But she never said they was so much meat," Grace said, eyebrows furrowed in a state of confusion. It was the most Grace had ever spoken, and I found it funny that it was hamburger she had chosen to speak up about.

I looked at Sarah, who by this time had slapped the two buns back together and was happily eating her bread, ketchup, relish, and pickle sandwich.

"Sarah, stop. Now wait one minute, girls. You mean to tell me you never had a hamburger before? Ever? Not even once?"

"No, Ma'am," said Grace as blush found her small cheeks. "Meat costs a penny much, and papa always ate whatever we might'a had. He was the one workin' the farm and all. We was just his soul-sucking brood." I knew she was just repeating words she heard her father say.

I felt my eyebrows raise and a flush hit my face as I took pause. "I tell you what girls. Just this once, give it a go. Your little bones could use the fat."

Sarah had been happy with the deflated version of her sandwich, but I could tell she didn't want to upset me. She slowly slid the patty back on the bun and put her hamburger deluxe right again. Sarah and the burger made quick friends, and soon she and Grace were licking the remnants of ketchup off their skinny little fingers. I was just so happy to see them eat that I didn't have the heart to scold them for lapping up the sauces like puppies. I just gave them a good once-over with a napkin when they were done and called it a day. Tony had been right; we would need to ease into our new lives, and it looked like today it would start with some wet roadside diner napkins in the bathroom sink.

After our spirited lunch and a brief stretch of our legs, the bus took off again. The flat terrain that had hosted the Post House became smaller and smaller in the back window of the coach. A few miles stretched into many, and just as the sun went down we passed Abilene. That's when Sarah began to whimper. Quietly at first, and then much more obviously. I felt a small panic rise up from my gut and lodge itself in my throat. I had feared this, the tears and the grief.

"Sarah, what is it, girl?" I asked as I leaned over towards her.

"I don't feel so well," she whispered, looking up at me with sunken eyes brimming with tears.

"What doesn't feel well?" I asked. *Oh God, here we go.*

"My tummy... it's... it's angry at me," Sarah said as she wrapped her arms around her tiny waist and pulled her knees towards her navel.

"Oh. Your tummy?" I felt better instantly as my knotted-up insides released with a sense of deliverance. A tummy ache I could handle.

"Yes my tummy is mad about the hamburger, Aunt Catherine. It doesn't like it. It's pretty mad at me, I think. Real mad." A tiny tear let go and ran down her face, landing on her new dress.

I hadn't thought about how the richness of the meat and the sweetness of the soda would set with an undersized tummy whose dinner fare mostly consisted of cornbread and sugar water. I quickly fumbled through my large purse and found a small bag that would make do, and placed it under Sarah's chin just in time to catch her masticated and half-digested burger.

"I don't think I like hamburgers much, Aunt Catherine," she said when she was done being sick.

"No, Sarah, I guess you don't. You know what darling? I don't think they like you much either. But I sure do..." She gave me a small smile, and I pulled my daughter in close as I completed my first motherly act with a ton of pride. As disgusting as that moment sounds, it was also quite a beautiful one for me. I knew then that I could do this, that I was born to do this, really. These two girls were the reason I had been born the way I had, unable to bear children. I was born to mother them. As I tucked a blanket over Grace and pulled Sarah's body closer to my chest, I had never felt more at peace than I did at that moment.

Chapter Fifty

Elizabeth
Franklin, Kentucky
Town Square
February 9, 1954

Many months had passed since Lillie had died on that warm August evening, but to Elizabeth it might as well have been years. She felt older and wiser, as though something in her soul had awoken from a dark winter slumber. Elizabeth pulled her winter coat a little tighter around her shoulders and hugged herself for warmth. She'd misjudged how cool the morning was going to be, and she wished she'd layered up a bit more than she had. All the signs of the season were there. February, more than any other month, had always made her wish for spring. She could picture the square in April as the leaves were starting to grow; as the grass was becoming just a tad greener than it had been weeks before; as the tips of the tulips in the flower beds were starting to poke through the soil. She could picture it, and in so many ways today felt like spring. The air certainly smelled of new beginnings, and somehow she knew that warmer days were ahead for all of them.

Her back began to ache from sitting so long on the wooden bench that lay on the edge of the square for, but she refused to leave until she knew. Mrs. Hodges, the clerk, was a family friend of Elizabeth's, and had been kind enough to quietly let her know that a date and time had been set; and Elizabeth wasn't leaving the bench until she knew the outcome of the proceedings going on behind the closed wooden doors of the courthouse. As she rubbed her hands together and occasionally blew warm air on them to soften the chill she felt in her fingertips, she thought she couldn't stand many more minutes of the cold.

As she waited, she thought back to all the moments that had brought her to be sitting and waiting on the cold hard bench. Naturally her first thoughts ran to Lillie and her last day with her. Lillie had left her a note, the same note that Elizabeth held tightly in her hand today to reassure herself that she'd done the right thing. That she was doing for Lillie what Lillie could not do for herself. That she would fulfill her friend's last request and somehow finally tip the balance of justice and grace in Lillie's favor.

Lillie's funeral had been riddled with paradox for Elizabeth. It had been a beautiful service, given at the Stevenson Methodist Church off of Highway 621, just a few miles down the road from Lillie's house. Reverend Thrasher conducted the final rites, and Brother Ditmore gave a heartfelt eulogy that had been written by Lillie's horrified and sorrowful parents. If only they'd known, it had said, if only they could do it all again. They were parents who were deep in mourning. Neither the pastor nor Brother Ditmore knew Lillie from church, and yet they, too, genuinely mourned her.

Elizabeth sat in the third row and had been so absorbed in her grief and in her shock at finally laying eyes on Lillie's kin that she hadn't noticed how full the little church had gotten. She hadn't noticed that there was standing-room only or that she knew many of the folks attending. Just before the service started she turned around, and the amount of people she saw took her breath away. Elizabeth felt incredibly puzzled and confused. How had a quiet sharecropper's wife drawn such a crowd? They came because they all had known her as a neighbor and a friend. Lillie had been kind, truly kind, and her very simple life mantra of really trying to see folks had not gone unnoticed by the people around her in her small town. There was chatter in the weeks to come that it was one of the largest funeral processions that Franklin had ever seen. Having witnessed it herself, Elizabeth was sure it was likely true. It had made Elizabeth realize how much most people just wanted to been seen, and how important it had been to Lillie to have Elizabeth really see her.

Until her funeral, Elizabeth hadn't been sure she would be able to do what Lillie had asked her. Until her funeral, Elizabeth had convinced herself she'd crossed that patient-nurse boundary and needed to take a step back and see Lillie for what she was, a patient who'd died. And yet, though she rarely did, Elizabeth attended the service anyway and went on to the cemetery to watch as they lowered Lillie's casket into the ground. While she watched the casket sink lower and lower, she also watched Clay.

The more she watched Clay and the way his children seemed to cower away from him whenever he neared them and the way his face seemed to be set with cement in a permanent scowl even at his wife's funeral, she knew she had to make it right for Lillie. She had to help put her soul at ease if she could, because she knew otherwise Lillie would linger and watch and never rest. And after watching and listening to all the folks who'd come to mourn Lillie Woodard because she was a loving neighbor, a caring friend, a warm-hearted person, and someone who just made you feel good about yourself no matter who you were, Elizabeth knew she'd earned her rest. She knew Lillie finally deserved some peace. Elizabeth knew in her heart that she was the only person left who could make that happen.

So, after many months of vigilance and what some might say was absolute spying, Elizabeth's choices had brought her to that bench in front of the courthouse on that chilly winter morning. Her life had changed so much since she'd left Lillie's funeral some six months before. Elizabeth had quickly seen that there was no way she was going to settle for the man who had been arduously pursuing her favor. He was a man enthralled with winning, and earning, and had only seen Elizabeth as the ultimate prize to be won. Elizabeth understood very quickly that he didn't really see her and that he never would. She knew deep down she couldn't live like that; that, even if he were a nice enough man, it would still be a prison of sorts, in a small way like the one Lillie had endured. The invisible wife was not who she wanted to be.

She'd also seen how her father, in all his goodness, had never really seen her either. He'd been so enveloped in his own grief over her mother through the years that he just couldn't. He'd only been able to see her as a stand-in mom—a housekeeper, and a caregiver to her siblings. When Elizabeth told him she'd made the decision to not marry her suitor but instead wanted to move down to Nashville to branch out on her own and expand her nursing knowledge, he'd just blinked rapidly, holding back tears, and stared at her. And she'd thought to herself that for the first time her father had actually seen her for someone other than all those roles. He'd seen his beautiful and grown-up daughter who was loving and giving and kind, and he'd smiled a small smile and pulled her into a warm embrace. Then, ever so softly, he'd whispered in her ear while holding her close, "My blessing, Elizabeth, my blessing. You'd have made your mama proud."

Her mind wandered over all those things and all of the changes she'd made in her life as she watched the minutes tick by on the large clock that graced the front of the tower on the courthouse. Her eyes scanned the intricate brickwork that made up the bulk of the eighteenth-century building, and she studied the four grand Romanesque-style limestone columns that upheld the simple portico over the white wooden front doors. And she wondered how many other people had waited outside while the county judge determined the course of someone's life.

She recalled how hard it had been to do what she'd done, and not just the leaving of the tiny Franklin hospital, or the packing, or the setting up of her new homestead in the heart of Nashville just over the Kentucky-Tennessee border. But all the months of investigation and talking with folks around town to try to get information that might help her to help Lillie's mission. Some days she felt as though she'd traded in her nursing cap for a gumshoe-style hat. She'd certainly been able to quickly confirm that all the stories about Clay had been true, for anyone who knew him had the same reaction when they heard Elizabeth speak his name. First their faces would fall, followed by a furrowing of the eyebrows, and finish off by whoever it was she was talking to saying something to the effect of, "Well, now, it isn't quite my business to say, but...." Story after story had strengthened Elizabeth's resolve, and finally, after months of carefully probing the folks around to town so as not to alert Clay, she'd bravely and boldly gone to Clay's stomping grounds and cautiously approached Clay's closest neighbor.

She pulled up in front of the two-story blue-and-white house and sat in the car, trying to calm her breathing. She already felt the flush of adrenaline from the danger of what she was doing, about what it might mean for her if she was caught, and she was trying to steel herself for what she might see or hear. From all her inquiries in town she'd learned that the people who inhabited the little house just a few acres from Clay and Lillie's little shack were an older couple, who were fairly kind, and had often been very concerned over the years about the welfare of Lillie and her children. But they'd been stopped by the code of farmers. Mind your business and let others mind theirs.

As she sat in front of the Bloodsworth's home she watched as first one stray dog, and then another, and then another, popped out of the woodwork. They looked well-fed and fairly well cared for, so Elizabeth assumed they belonged to Karl and Ellen Bloodsworth, but it didn't do much to calm her nerves as they, one by one, began to sniff and circle her car. After the sixth large dog joined the crew in letting Elizabeth know she wasn't exactly welcome, panic started to set in. She couldn't breathe, and she couldn't even move the car forward because obviously the sound of the running engine did nothing to strike fear into them and make them move. They were used to farming equipment that was much larger and made much more noise than her little Chevy sedan was able to produce, and she didn't want to honk the horn for fear that she'd alert Clay to her being so close to his property. Not that he'd know who she was, but she knew what he was capable of, and it wasn't a chance she was willing to take.

She glanced around the landscape to see how she could get out of the situation without being bitten or mauled by the pack of dogs. The house was on her right, and on the left hand side of the little dirt road was a large, rickety barn the color of rust with a large patch of trees and a small pond in front of it.

Elizabeth imagined how Lillie's kids probably had taken a dunk or two in that pond over the years to cool off in the sticky Kentucky summers, or had used homemade fishing poles to catch the small fish that inhabited it to fry up for Sunday dinner. She pictured Connie, and Ben, and Joe playing barefoot in the grass just up and over the small hill that separated the Bloodsworths' farmland from the Adams'. She pictured Ada, Nola, and Lillie's two youngest petting and playing fetch with the mangy mutts that were surrounding her now. She leaned forward towards the steering wheel to get a better look around the corner, and that's when she saw it. That's when she found her courage.

Just to the right, behind the small knoll, was Lillie's old house, one story and boxy. Elizabeth could just make out two windows in the front that flanked the doorway. It was all white, though for all the dirt and dust that had settled over the years it was actually more a beige mishmash of colors. Elizabeth's breath stopped and then caught in her throat as she watched two small little girls, hair cropped up to their ears and feet as bare as the day they were born, running around without coats in the crisp December air. That was all it took. That one glance and Elizabeth opened her car door with such authority that the dogs backed off. One came close enough to sniff at her shoes, but decided she was harmless enough and let her pass. She climbed the steps to the front door of the Bloodsworths' and gently knocked on the door.

When Ellen Bloodsworth answered, she look frail and tired, as though she'd just had a good cry. Elizabeth quickly learned that her husband of over forty years, Karl, had just recently passed, and she was alone for the first time in her life. Elizabeth expressed her condolences, and though the timing seem awkward she went ahead with what she'd planned to say. She explained about Lillie and what she'd heard about Clay, and told Ellen what concerns Lillie had expressed about the children she was leaving in Clay's care. She talked and talked without stopping for fear the old woman would slam the door in her face. She felt Lillie on her shoulder, egging her on to get it out, to tell her tale and just push forward. When she was finally finished with what she had to say, Mrs. Bloodsworth just stood there, staring at her with steely eyes and furrowed brows. Elizabeth thought she'd never seen anyone look so furious in all her life, but what came out of Ellen Bloodsworth's mouth next shocked her.

"You know, I loved my husband. He was a good and decent man. He never done did me wrong. We raised us some good children, too. Raised 'em up right. To treat others right."

"I'm sure you did, I..." Elizabeth wasn't sure where this was going.

Mrs. Bloodsworth put her hand up to stop Elizabeth and interrupted. "You done said your piece, Missy. Now it's my turn. So I loved my husband, very much. And I mostly think he made the right choices in life, that he treated people fairly. And he thought mostly of taking care of our own. And he rightly did that well too. But I think he done made a bad choice when it come to staying outta our neighbor's business just this once. 'Cause even though they's just sharecroppers to our neighbors the Adams, Lillie was one of our own. She was my friend, though I didn't see that for a long time. She was a friend to me even when I wasn't to her. And we knew she was struggling. Now, we didn't knows she was so sick, but we knew something wasn't right, and we knew that husband of hers wasn't doing right by her. And I'm right sad that we didn't help her. That she's gone and left them kids with him 'cause no one helped her. I'm right sad." Mrs. Bloodsworth paused, thinking of her next words carefully. "I done be watching them kids. Especially since my Karl's been gone, 'cause most days I got nothing to do but stare outta my window. I done watch them, and they ain't right."

"You mean something's wrong with them? Like they're bad kids?"

"Oh, Lord, no. They's good kids. Real sweet, despite their daddy. But they's neglected, see. Ain't nobody watching them two little ones. Nobody at all. The two older ones try—Nola and Ada, that is—but they's got their hands full, and something ain't right with that Ada since her mama gone. She done turned sullen and won't look you in the eye no more. Them kids ain't got no shoes, no coats. They ain't being fed right. Somethin' ain't right."

"No, it's not right." Elizabeth didn't know what to say as she swallowed back her nerves. Her worst fears were confirmed, and now she had to convince Mrs. Bloodsworth to finally do the right thing. The two women stood looking at each other, waiting for the other one to make the first move.

"Well, see, now that my Karl's gone, I'd like to help." Mrs. Bloodsworth shifted uncomfortably inside the threshold of her doorway, still not inviting Elizabeth in just yet. "But I'm just not sure that I can help. Not sure what I can do about it now…"

Elizabeth knew she had to show her Lillie's note, though until this point she'd shown no one. She reached in her pocket and pulled out the well-worn folded paper that had her name, Elizabeth, scrawled on top of it.

"What's this?" Mrs. Bloodsworth looked at the paper. "We a little old for passing notes…"

"Just read it," Elizabeth interrupted. "It's from Lillie. She gave it to me right before she passed. Just read it." Elizabeth stood there nervously watching the old lady fumble with unfolding the paper that she herself had unfolded and folded many times. As she stood watching, she could picture Lillie's written words as if they she were reading them again for the first time. She knew, as Mrs. Bloodsworth's face went slack and her color drained and her hand found its way to her mouth in shock, she knew everything was about to change.

Four lines. That's all she'd written. Four little lines.

> He's been touching my girls, mostly my Ada.
> I got two more little girls, they's next I sure.
> Please get them out. Please help 'em.
> Little Red will take 'em. Find her.

Mrs. Bloodsworth didn't say a word at first. She just stood there staring at Lillie's words, and then slowly opened the door and waved for Elizabeth to enter. Once Elizabeth was inside and the door was closed behind her, she asked, with a face full of sorrow, "What can I do? We got to get them out."

Mrs. Bloodsworth became an integral part of saving all of the girls. Elizabeth had already contacted the state before she'd gone to see her, and they'd said she'd need some proof. They'd need someone who knew Clay to come forward and report what they saw. The state agency needed a firsthand witness, and Elizabeth found one in Mrs. Bloodsworth.

Mrs. Bloodsworth made up for all the years she'd turned a blind eye to Lillie's pain and suffering in the name of minding one's business, and she herself called the state on the very day that Elizabeth came to see her. She watched out her window as a very tall gentleman and a squatty woman arrived on Clay's front porch eight days later wanting to poke around, and wanting some answers from Clay. She watched as Clay raged at the two state employees from Children's Services, his face full of red and his hands balled up at his side, only making his case worse for himself. She'd met the gentleman and the lady in town the day before and given her written statement and also given the names of a few others who might be willing to talk to them. They'd spent the rest of the day collecting statements and hearing stories. They'd even interviewed Elizabeth over the phone, and Elizabeth had provided them the information that she had gathered over the previous four months.

When Elizabeth had asked the lady from the state what would become of the girls once all the process was complete, she'd been told that if no kin came forward to claim them then they'd be shipped up to Louisville. St. Joseph's Children's Home was willing to take them in while they were placed on the list for adoption. That's when Elizabeth had decided to make the call herself. First she called Josie. She'd seen her at Lillie's funeral and had known right away who she was from Lillie's description of her. Her number wasn't hard to track down. She gasped when Elizabeth told her that Lillie had told her to find Little Red and then had quickly agreed that yes, indeed, that was a fantastic idea. Josie hadn't kept in touch with her over the years, being that Little Red was almost ten years younger than she and Lillie had been.

"She ran with a different crowd. She makes sense, she makes so much sense for this. Lillie got it right," was all Josie could manage before she gave Elizabeth Lillie's folks' number.

Lillie's parents were living up in Michigan at the time, and were raising their granddaughter, Diana, because Lillie's sister Vera couldn't take care of her. They were older and already raising another child, and they were very keen on seeing who else could take them. The very first name that Mattie Garrett, Lillie's mama, said before Elizabeth even had a chance to ask was her daughter, Catherine. Catherine was Lillie's little sister, the one she called Little Red, and Mrs. Garrett gave Elizabeth her number. Elizabeth had held the phone with shaky hands while she dialed the Southern California–based number and listened nervously to the ringing on the line. When Catherine answered with a cheery hello, Elizabeth smiled, and knew she'd done it. She'd done what Lillie had ask her to do all those many months ago.

Chapter Fifty-One

Cate
Thursday, February 11, 1953

I drifted off to sleep as the bus rolled closer and closer to California. As I slept, the events of the last three days played back in bits and pieces, and when I awoke I felt like I had re-lived them all over again. Mrs. Hodges finally did call on the morning of the eighth day. The calendar read Monday, February 8, 1954, and it was very late. She had awoken me from a restless sleep where I'd dreamed of chasing something I never could quite catch, like trying to hold a bubble in your fist.

"Catherine Otera?" I knew who it was on the line before Mrs. Hodges even said her name.

"Yes, this is she." I held my breath. This was it, I just knew, and I felt like if I took a breath it would blow the bubble just out of my reach.

"This is Mrs. Hodges dear, from the courthouse." Now I was a dear, that had to be a good sign. "Listen, I've been trying very hard to get you in, and I have an opening at eight o'clock tomorrow morning. If you can't make that time I'm just not sure that it'll be this week. We're pretty backlogged."

"No. I mean, yes! Yes, of course I will be there. Of course." I was still waking up, and it was hard to think straight. I let out my breath, and so far the bubble hadn't popped. "What should I bring? I mean, what do I need to do?"

"Just bring yourself, Catherine, and tell your story as best you can. The judge is a reasonable man, and I will try real hard to bend his ear a little about your case before he sees you if I can catch him before he enters the courtroom."

I was stunned into silence and couldn't believe how this previously unhelpful woman was now being so helpful. I finally said, "Thank you, Mrs. Hodges, Lillie would appreciate this."

She cleared her throat and said something I didn't at all expect. "I didn't do this for Lillie. I did it for you, and for those girls who will hopefully soon be your daughters. They need a strong woman like you to raise them, and they'll be lucky to have you." I heard a bit of a tear catch in her throat, and then she hurried off the line, mumbling about how she had to get going and get ready for bed. I stood frozen to the spot, holding a dead line.

Beverly came into the room slowly, moving as though she had cement blocks on her feet and yawning as widely as an open barn door. She scratched her tousled hair and looked at me funny. She pulled her robe around her more tightly as the winter chill in the house hit her.

"Why you holding the phone like that? It's late, Cate. Besides, it ain't gonna make it ring no faster, you know." She shuffled past me, and I broke out of my trance and returned the hand piece to the receiver.

"Tomorrow, Bev. My time before the judge is tomorrow." I looked up at the clock and nearly fell over. "Oh my goodness! It's in less than nine hours!"

"Catherine! That's amazing! We best try to get some sleep, though. I suppose we can't be looking all ragged and tired and trying to convince that judge."

"I know. But I just can't believe, I mean, I'm not sure I can sleep! And I have to call Tony and, oh my gosh, is this real?" My thoughts were a jumbled mess, and all I could think was there wasn't possibly a way for me to get rest tonight, though in the same thought I knew I needed to. After a frantic call to California and a hot cup of tea and honey in an attempt to relax myself, I finally drifted off on the couch at around three in the morning. It was a restless, dreamless sleep, the kind where it feels as if you were awake the whole time, even though you know you weren't. Right around 6:30 a.m. I was quickly awoken by a clamoring in the kitchen.

Bev had woken up before me and just flown into action. She got a pot of coffee started while I practically ran for the bathroom and quickly turned on the shower. I didn't even wait for the water to warm before I tucked myself in behind the curtain. I think I needed the shock of the cold water to wake me out of my surprise and nervousness. My heart was pounding in my throat, and as I pulled on my shower cap, carefully tucking my red curls underneath, I couldn't help but wonder if this was how pregnant mothers felt when they went into labor. I felt completely unprepared, terrified, and was trying hard to breathe away a sheer panic. I already had my court clothes picked out, and I had laid them out days ago because I wanted to be ready when the time came—but I'd had no idea that I would have such a short time to pull myself together and be presentable for what might be the biggest moment of my life.

I managed to get myself together rather quickly, and even got a cup of coffee and a slice of toast in me before I left for the courthouse. I was so fast that I got there at thirty minutes to eight o'clock and found myself waiting outside because the doors were still locked. I wasn't sure Mrs. Hodges was even there, and besides a few early morning risers who were opening the stores and one young woman sitting on a bench on the square near the courthouse, I was essentially alone. I knew I was the first case of the day and wondered if she was perhaps the second. I tried to keep my mind busy as I waited, and I fixated on the architecture of the old building itself to distract me.

Like many of the other older buildings in Franklin that were built in the late nineteenth century, the all-brick courthouse mimicked a late Victorian-style structure. It was a little bit boxy with a few beautiful details that broke up an otherwise simple design. It boasted four large white columns that were intricately detailed near the top and held up a small portico overhead.

I'd passed this old building for years as a girl and had never noticed how the first and second stories were delineated by a string course of what I assume was limestone, given that this area of Kentucky was well known for being rich with it. Come to think of it, I supposed the columns and sills were as well. Built in 1882, it had long and strong history as a fixture in the heart of town.

My eyes roved upwards towards the sky, and I caught sight of the large white clock tower topped off by a rather simple weather vane. The clock read 7:35, and I realized I'd only killed about five minutes by taking in the architecture of the building that would forever be a part of my life's story.

I kept looking through the glass-paned doors, trying to see if there was any sort of activity yet, although I wasn't quite sure what I would do about it if I saw someone inside anyway. I could see from the rounded windows above the double doors that there was a light on, but I assumed it was continually so and that the lobby rarely saw complete darkness.

I sighed, realizing that I would just have to wait out the next half hour or so. Even though I was outside and the temperature was barely thirty-five, I felt warm, bordering on sweaty. I'm not sure I had ever been that nervous in my whole life. This was so different from the other times we had applied for children. This time it felt like we had everything to lose.

I finally just settled on looking up at the naked trees, which were mostly large maples, and I couldn't help but think how beautiful they were with all of their secrets revealed for the world to see. It reminded me that it's easy to put on your best bravado in the spring, when the sun is out and we feel good and everything in us is blooming just like the leaves on the trees; and it's even easier in the summer when the world is full of fun and love, and the trees are so covered in leaves you'd be hard-pressed to believe that there were any gnarled and tangled branches underneath them. But in the winter, on days like today, where even the trees had nowhere to hide from the bitter cold of truth, it becomes a bit harder to be strong.

But then, I thought, the trees make no excuses for who they are, or how they grow their roots. They don't say sorry for the ways in which their branches turn and snake together, forming a labyrinth that only they can appreciate and understand. The trees had adapted, unapologetically, and had learned to bend and move with the wind. They gracefully and beautifully shed themselves frequently of the past and started over.

I realized that I myself wasn't much different than the large trees that surrounded me, with one exception. I didn't have to stand still and take what the wind and the elements had to offer. I could choose to move if I didn't like the way the wind blew, and I could change my step to find the best footing to tackle the wind gusts. And I realized that this was exactly what I had done.

I had come to Kentucky sadly afraid of my past, and fearful that it would affect my future; but, as I sat on that bench looking at the trees, I knew that wasn't who I was. I too would be unapologetic for the complexity of my branches, and I too would make no excuses for who I was. These realizations strengthened and calmed me and helped me center my thoughts. Tony and I would be great parents for these two little girls, and I would say as much to anyone who had ears if it meant getting the documents signed.

As it turned out, though, rather unexpectedly, I didn't have to put up much of a fight. With ten minutes to go, a small figure rounded the corner of Cedar and Main and slowly came into focus. I thought it was a woman at first by the small stature, but then I recognized the unusual gait of the man who was heading in my direction.

I hadn't seen him in years, but then again, I hadn't been back to Franklin in quite a long time. As he came closer and closer, I was absolutely sure it was him. He was looking down at the sidewalk as he walked, a habit I'm sure he'd formed out of a safety precaution, as his step had never been the same since his childhood bout of polio. He was dressed to the nines in a single-breasted charcoal gray suit and matching narrow-brimmed fedora hat. He wore a large overcoat that looked as though it might swallow him and his fancy suit in one loud gulp. His cufflinks caught a bit of the early morning sunlight and glimmered a little as he walked, and I thought he looked dazzling.

As he approached, I struggled with what to say to him. It had been so long, and I wasn't sure if he'd remember me.

"Harry? Harry James?" I asked politely, trying not to startle him.

He looked up at me and was a little taken aback at being approached on the street. I realized he had been so intent on walking carefully in the icy cold that he hadn't really noticed me sitting there.

"Yes, I'm Harry James. I'm sorry, Ma'am, and you are?" He squinted at me, and I thought how he must usually wear glasses and just hadn't put them on yet.

"Catherine Otera. Oh, but formerly Catherine Garrett. I think we went to school together. Of course, that was a long time ago. I wouldn't expect you'd remember." I felt a little foolish, because if he didn't remember me I wasn't sure what to say. I hoped he'd at least say a polite *oh yes* and a *how do you do* even if he didn't have a clue who I was.

He stepped a bit closer and stared at me like he really wanted to remember but just couldn't place me. He looked at me so long that it made me a tad uncomfortable. I nervously pushed a big red curl out of my eye in much the same way that Tony often did on my behalf, and that's when I saw a light bulb go off in Harry James' eyes.

"Catherine! Of course. Your hair, how could I forget? Didn't your sisters have a nickname for you or something. Something to do with your hair, I think?" He looked amused, as if I'd told him a familiar joke, and it set me at ease.

I laughed a little and said, "Yes. Amazing memory. They called me Little Red,. well until I got big enough to make it clear that I didn't much care for the name." We both laughed then, realizing I'd never really gotten all that big—thus the Little part of the nickname.

"Well then, how are you? What brings you back to these parts?" He looked at me quizzically, as if he were trying to calculate exactly how long it had been since he'd seen me.

"Well, it's a long story. I'm here to see the judge about a custody case." I smiled, trying to convey that I didn't want to divulge much more and hoping he didn't press me further.

"The judge, eh?" He had a strange look on his face that was a cross between amusement and surprise.

"Yes. Do you know him?" I'd take any bit of information I could get that would give me an advantage. If he was conservative I'd need to adjust my story a bit.

"Catherine, why don't you come with me and we can chat in private a bit. Catch up and what not." He gestured towards the front door of the courthouse, and I could only assume he worked there since the doors were locked and he was inviting me in. A clerk, perhaps, or court reporter?

"Oh, that would be lovely, Harry, really, but I have an eight o'clock appointment time, and I don't think the judge will take kindly to my being late."

He gave me a half smile, and then things got very interesting very fast. "Catherine, I am the judge."

"What?" I didn't know what to say. "That's amazing! When did you become a lawyer, Harry? I mean, Mr. James. I mean… oh gosh, now I don't know what to call you!" We both laughed, and then he quickly schooled me on the ways of the Simpson County justice system.

"Well now, you don't need to be a lawyer to be a judge in this town. My father was a judge, and now I am too. Nothing to it, really. Mostly a lot of small disputes and some domestic-type things. A few brawls here and there, you know, mostly where folks need to sleep it off around the corner at the county jail and then come see me in the morning for fines and such. Sometimes we have a bit bigger cases, but not too often."

"Oh. I'm not sure what to say!" I had expected to stand before an old man and plead my case. I had picked out my most conservative of dresses, a muted blue, and pinned on my best hat. I even wore my mother's old brooch for good luck, something I never did. I had picked out my best silk hose and had polished my shoes until they reflected every bit of light around. I had turned this moment over and over again in my head, and it had looked nothing like this.

"Well, it's freezing out here. Let's go into my office and I'll see what I can do for you." I nodded slowly and cautiously as he led the way up the few steps and held open the heavy white door so we could enter the courthouse lobby. I followed him through several doors, passing a very confused looking Mrs. Hodges who was setting up for the day, and finally found myself sitting across from him at his desk. It turned out that he knew well of Clay and had seen him in the courtroom when Ada had been hit by a bus some years back and Clay had sued. He also just knew Clay from around town, and apparently Harry James knew just what sort of man he was.

I quickly told Judge James my story and I held my head high while I did so because I decided I wasn't going to hide from the truth, nor be ashamed of who I had been. Tony never saw me that way, and I refused to let me see myself that way either. Then I told him Lillie's story, and made sure to include the bit about the note that Elizabeth had received. I told him everything I knew as openly and honestly as I could, and then I left it up to him to decide. I'd put my best foot forward, as Tony might say, and it was out of my hands. Harry sat quietly, listening to me in a way that told me he was good at listening and also slow to come to conclusions. After a few silent moments where he lightly drummed his fingers on the desktop, he finally looked me in the eye and spoke.

"Well, I'll make the papers, then." He looked at me as if that was that.

"Papers?" I wanted to be clear about what we were talking about.

"Papers, Catherine. For full custody. For both girls, Grace and Sarah, to both you and your husband Antonio. I can't rightly do much to help Nola and Ada—they are of an age where they can choose to stay or not—but we can help the younger girls. I suppose, too, that you'll need permission to take them out of state, given where you live." He paused and then added, "That is what you wanted, right?"

"You have no idea..." He looked at me funny, and then I was quick to add, "Yes, that's exactly what I wanted." I felt my fist close gently and decisively around the elusive bubble.

He folded his hands in his lap and sat back in his chair. "Well, just give it until the afternoon, and you can come back and pick up the documents. I can get a policeman to collect the girls tomorrow, as I'm sure Clay will put up some sort of a ruckus and you don't need to be a part of that mess. I'd make plans, though, to scoot out of town as soon as possible, given his propensity for violence when he's crossed." He raised his eyebrows, throwing the ball back into my court. "Sound okay?"

I was too stunned to move. Paralyzed was a better word. Could it really be that easy? After all my years of struggle it came down to a couple of simple words like *Sound okay?* It took me the better part of a minute to find my voice again.

I finally got out the quiet response, "Yes, more than okay..."

I started to thank him profusely, but I think he sensed my extreme gratitude and felt uncomfortable with it, so he interrupted me and said, "Well, then. All done. So nice to see you again, but I best be getting to the next case. I do believe Mrs. Hodges will have my hide if I fall behind on my docket." He gestured at the clock on the wall and smiled at me, offering me a handshake which I took stiffly, still too shocked to say much. He led me to the front door and reminded me to stop by for the papers some time after the lunch hour, and that Mrs. Hodges would work out the rest of the details.

With his last words to me of good luck and safe travels, I quickly found myself outside again at the bottom of the porch stairs, looking back up at the same trees I had just been contemplating minutes before. Somehow they looked different, stronger for sure, and even more beautiful than before. Like they'd just weathered the storm of a lifetime and now all there was left to do was bloom.

As I carefully descended the stairs, all that there was left for me to do was to smile. And as I felt it on my lips I knew that it was a smile as bright as the sun that was beginning to peek through the clouds; as genuine as the maple trees on the Franklin town square in the middle of winter; as cheerful as the wise and steady red birds flying freely overhead; as wide as the distance between Kentucky and California; and as deep as the love I felt for my family, which I knew in my heart was finally complete.

The day after Easter morning was April 19, 1954, and it was the day that I got the finalized papers in the mail telling me that the girls were officially ours; but by then we already knew that.

Chapter Fifty-Two

Elizabeth
Franklin, Kentucky Courthouse
Tuesday, February 9, 1954

Just a month after Elizabeth's call to Cate, she found herself sitting impatiently in the cold outside on the courthouse bench. Minutes felt like hours, but finally Elizabeth saw Cate, the petite redhead known to Lillie as Little Red, walk out of the doors of the courthouse wearing an enormous smile. Elizabeth felt Lillie's soul lift up and ride on into the breeze, and it was all the answer that she needed. She stood up and quietly walked away from the courthouse towards her car, and her small smile grew into a ridiculously huge grin. Suddenly she didn't feel the slightest bit cold anymore.

As Elizabeth walked away from Cate, the courthouse, and Franklin, she swore that the winter wind had an ever so subtle hint of cornbread and tobacco, and that she could hear the repetitious *chirp chirp* of a red bird somewhere off in the distance.

Epilogue

Just a week after Cate was awarded custody of the girls and took them to their new home in southern California, Ada and Nola broke free too. The scene played out fairly close to the one that Beverly had predicted, with Howard and two of his older brothers coming to collect Nola. Rumor has it that Clay didn't much mind that Nola was leaving, but he started to loudly protest when Ada crossed the lawn with her sister towards the waiting car. He stood there with his face the color of a ruby, his hands clenched, and his body posed in what looked to be a fighting stance. Angry words were flying over the girls' heads until Howard stepped forcefully in front of the girls, blocking them from Clay's view, and casually cradled his hunting rifle in his arms. He said only a few words to Clay, and they were something to the effect of "Do we have a problem, Mr. Woodard? 'Cause I sure would hate to have to explain to the sheriff how yous come charging towards us and hows I didn't have no choice but to fire this here gun at 'ya."

It was enough to stop Clay in his tracks as he stood just a few feet away from the porch of his suddenly very empty house. Being Clay, he wasn't prone to backing down so easily, and he started to protest, saying, "Now you look here, boy..."

Howard didn't let him finish. He interrupted him mid-sentence and loudly said, "Mr. Woodard. I think it's only fair you know that I been a hunter my whole life, and ain't never missed a target, sir. So I ask you again, we got us a problem here, or are we good to go?"

Clay was fit to be tied, and after many moments of attempting to stare down Howard, it became apparent that he was much too shaken to move even so much as a foot. So, he waved them off, in much the same manner as he had Lillie on the day he'd dropped her off at the hospital. He muttered something to the effect of how they were two worthless leeches and he didn't have no use for them anymore anyhow. To which Howard responded, "No, I don't suppose you do," and started walked towards the car with his eye on his target the whole time.

Nola went on to marry Howard and have many children of her own.

She raised them in much the same way she had been raised, on a farm with very little in the way of resources. However, her home had a lot of laughter and a lot of love, and never once did her husband touch her in anger. To her, that was more valuable than all the money in the world. She ended up living long into her eighties.

Clay eventually moved out of the Franklin area and went on to marry again. He eventually had more children. Only God and Clay know how those relationships unfolded, because he never spoke to his other children again. He lived well into his eighties, still as mean as ever, and still a broken soul.

Ada had it little rougher, though, and the scars that Clay had left on her ran deeper than anyone might have suspected. She stayed with Nola and Howard for some time, but eventually married young and moved into town. She bore two sons, both of whom she lost early in life, and the grief of it all ended her very short marriage. She was said to have lived alone after that. She was a bit of a lost soul, with hollow eyes and a shy smile that hid more horrors than she could ever speak of. Ada was strikingly beautiful even as she grew older, even more so than ever on the day that she passed away quietly at the age of 39. Some say it was a breast cancer that had ravaged her body, but Nola knew it was more likely a cancer named Clay that had fractured her essence at a young age and grown slowly into her bones over the years. Nola found comfort in picturing Ada flying wildly above it all with her mama Lillie at her side, both finally free of his grasp, with their wings spread wide.

Acknowledgments

First and foremost I would like to thank my incredible husband Mike. He gave me nothing but love and support from the first word of this book to the very last period. When I said I needed to do this project, he graciously encouraged me to go for it. When I needed time to write without distraction, he selflessly indulged me. He never once faltered in his belief in me and for that and many other reasons, he will always have my heart. To my children Corinna, Matthew, and Corbin, who are my inspiration and motivation in all things, and you have my utmost gratitude. You three make me a better person every day, and there are no words to describe how much I truly love you.

To my mom, Liz Caccamise, my late father, Don Caccamise, and my siblings, Jennifer Bay and Michael Caccamise, you all are my rock and my foundation and you have never wavered. Mom and Dad, I sure hope I make you as proud of me as I am of both of you—that's all I've really ever wanted. Dad, even though you are no longer here, somehow, every time I need you, you find a way to say "hi" and to remind me that you never really left. Our roots run deep and strong in love, and you all prove it every day. A huge thanks to my younger brother Mike for his amazing work on the cover photo. It's absolutely stunning!

A particularly loud thank you to Isabel Caccamise, my very gracious aunt. This project is as much yours as it is mine. The information, photos, help, encouragement, and guidance that you provided during this journey were absolutely invaluable and deeply character building for me. I will forever be grateful. I'd also like to thank Lula Graziano, Tina McKelvie, my mom Liz, and Jim Stahl for sharing your stories and allowing me to use them. There would be no book without you all. To the late Bill Hanley, thank you for your amazing kindness to a stranger. You will always be a part of my story. To the kind folks at the Simpson County Historical Society for your generosity and patience with an outsider, thank you. Franklin, Kentucky is an amazingly quaint and beautiful town chock full of incredible American history, and you all preserve its charming stories so well.

A gigantic thanks to Leah Andrews, Melissa Yubeta, Rachel Zohn, Stephanie Scott, Isabel Caccamise, Deborah Igou, and my mom for taking the time to ready my early editions and provide critical feedback. You helped make this story so much richer and deeper, and I am ever so grateful. To Kitt Gryskiewicz, you had very little to do with the writing of this book and yet everything to do with my ability to write it. Love, just love. Thank you also to Kerianne Newland for your generous heart and willingness to share your work.

To all of my friends and family who are too numerous to list here, you all have been my cheerleaders and champions and I thank you from the bottom of my heart for your belief in me and in my work. I had some doubts along the way, but you all never did, and I am beyond appreciative for your enthusiastic support. I am so blessed in so many ways, and I don't take any of you for granted. You all know who you are...

To my editor, Remy Benoit, my gratefulness for your gentle editing and your keen eyes is beyond measure. You have made this story so much better than I ever hoped it could be, and your cohorts Sarah Rodriguez and Paul Rodriguez at Front Porch Publishing have done an incredible job turning it into a real book. Remy, there are no coincidences in life, and you were placed in my path for a reason. I feel very blessed and honored that you took on my book and had such faith in me every step of the way. You're an incredible woman and the work you do with and for veterans is priceless, I hope you know that. Thank you really isn't enough...

About the author

Karen Evancic is a full time mommy to three beautiful children, a part time registered nurse in obstetrics, and a proud Air Force wife. She is also a veteran and grew up in a military family. Though she is currently residing in Olympia, Washington, Evancic calls Arizona home. Always an avid reader with an adventurous mind, she took up writing as a hobby and fell in love with the creative process. She was inspired to write this particular novel by her Grandmother, whose bold strength was influential in her upbringing. She also enjoys spending time with her family, travel, running, and the arts. *When A Red Bird Flies* is Evancic's first novel.